# THE HABIT OF ART

# THE HABIT OF ART

BEST STORIES
FROM THE
INDIANA UNIVERSITY
FICTION WORKSHOP

EDITED BY **TONY ARDIZZONE**

*Indiana University Press*
BLOOMINGTON AND INDIANAPOLIS

This book is a publication of

*Indiana University Press*
601 North Morton Street
Bloomington, IN 47404-3797 USA

http://iupress.indiana.edu

*Telephone orders*  800-842-6796
*Fax orders*  812-855-7931
*Orders by e-mail*  iuporder@indiana.edu

© 2005 by Indiana University Press

The paper used in this publication meets the minimum
requirements of American National Standard for Information Sciences—Permanence of Paper for Printed Library
Materials, ANSI Z39.48-1984.

MANUFACTURED IN THE UNITED STATES OF AMERICA

**Library of Congress Cataloging-in-Publication Data**

The habit of art : best stories from the Indiana University
fiction workshop / edited by Tony Ardizzone.
p. cm.
Stories by graduates over the past twenty-five years
of the Graduate Creative Writing Program at
Indiana University in Bloomington.
ISBN 0-253-34666-5 (cloth : alk. paper) —
ISBN 0-253-21807-1 (pbk. : alk. paper)
1. Short stories, American. 2. American fiction—
20th century. 3. American fiction—21st century.
4. United States—Social life and customs—Fiction.
I. Ardizzone, Tony. II. Indiana University, Bloomington.
Creative Writing Program.
PS648.S5H33 2005
813'.01089772—dc22                    2005011543
1  2  3  4  5  10  09  08  07  06  05

# CONTENTS

# EDITOR'S ACKNOWLEDGMENT

Publication of this anthology has been made possible
by the generous support of the Creative Writing Program
and the Department of English at Indiana University,
the College Arts and Humanities Institute, and the
Office of the Vice President for Research.
The editor has declined all payment and royalties.

# INTRODUCTION

Like an audience at a magic show, as the lights fall dark and then illuminate the magician's appearance on the stage, devoted readers of fiction await the next new work, hoping to be shown something they've never seen. All that either artist asks of the audience is that they pay reasonable attention to what is unveiled and that they come to the performance with an open mind and a willingness to suspend their disbelief. "Literature is news that stays news," Ezra Pound pointed out in his 1936 book *ABC of Reading*, and by this the modernist master meant not that literature should adopt the limited techniques of reportage but that the very best writing conveys something intrinsically vital and engaging to the reader. The energy and freshness achieved by such work has the capacity to stick in the reader's mind in much the same way that the surprise and thrill of the expert magician's trick can be recalled long after the show is over.

Magic and art. How all of us long for both, but how few of us can truly define either term other than to say that we know it when we see it? "The scientist has the habit of science; the artist, the habit of art," Flannery O'Connor proffered in "The Nature and Aim of Fiction," an essay made up of some of the public lectures O'Connor gave audiences during the 1960s about writers and the creative writing process. Frustrated with audiences who, in their attempts to understand and learn the art of fiction, would ask her whether it was better to compose with a number 2 pencil or a fountain pen or typewriter, or whether while writing they should sip coffee or tea, or work in the morning or afternoon or late at night, O'Connor responded by observing that the serious writer wasn't so much interested in external habits as he or she was in an internal process, or "habit of art," a term she learned from the Neo-Thomist philosopher Jacques Maritain. To O'Connor's way of thinking, the habit of art was not simply an external process—something as pedestrian as a daily routine or a writing schedule—but, more essentially, something internal, "a certain quality or virtue of the mind." O'Connor explained, "Art is the habit of the artist, and habits have to be rooted deep in the whole personality. They have to be cultivated like any other habit, over a period of time, by experience; and teaching any kind of writing is largely a matter of helping the student develop the habit of art." This quality or virtue, when combined with the writer's talent, is capable of heightening writing to a point that nears perfection.

This seems to me to be the highest aspiration of any graduate creative writing program: to instill in each of the writers who pass through the program a lifetime habit of art. The evidence of that success is the anthology of short stories you now hold in your hands, stories penned by graduates over the past twenty-five years of the graduate creative writing program at Indiana University in Bloomington.

A brief history. The study of creative writing on Indiana University's Bloomington campus began in the early 1940s, when a host of highly distinguished, internationally known writers—the beloved poet Robert Frost, who was awarded the Pulitzer Prize in Poetry in both 1937 and 1943; Indiana native Marguerite Young, remembered most for her exquisite novels, *Angel in the Forest* and *Miss MacIntosh, My Darling*; Robert P. T. Coffin, recipient of the 1936 Pulitzer Prize for Poetry; poet, novelist and critic Robert Penn Warren, who would later receive three Pulitzer Prizes; and the enormously influential critic and poet John Crowe Ransom, among others—were teaching courses to anyone interested in poetry and fiction. A few years later short-story writer Peter Taylor developed within the department of English a Master of Arts in Creative Writing program, making Indiana University one of the first North American universities to offer the graduate degree. The first writer to graduate from the program was poet and novelist David Wagoner. In 1980 Indiana University expanded its graduate writing program and began accepting students working toward the terminal Master of Fine Arts degree.

This anthology marks the twenty-fifth anniversary of Indiana University's Master of Fine Arts in Creative Writing program, now considered among the nation's best. The work included in these pages comes from twenty-one writers who have graduated from our writing program over the past twenty-five years. Since our program began, our students have come from all parts of the U.S. and Canada as well as Central America, the Caribbean, Europe, Africa, Australia, and Indonesia.

It is hoped that the anthology marking and celebrating that anniversary will appeal widely to readers of contemporary fiction. Indeed, nearly all of these stories collected here have been previously published, appearing in a range of magazines from small yet highly selective literary journals to more widely distributed venues such as *The New Yorker*. Several stories have received additional national awards and citations, among them inclusion in *The Best American Short Stories*, *The Pushcart Prize: Best of the Small Presses*, *Scribner's Best of the Fiction Workshops*, and *The Year's Best: New Stories from the South*.

In addition, instructors of creative writing courses may find this text a useful teaching tool and of significant interest to students in creative writing courses. The stories selected come from a variety of narrative perspectives, including works written by first-, second-, and third-person narrators, with a wide range of exploration within each of these narrative positions. Student readers will find some stories more traditional while others are more experimental and genre-bending. The collection also displays a wide range of styles, settings, and themes as well as a highly diverse array of characters. This last point mirrors one of the distinguishing characteristics of the graduate creative writing program at Indiana University: more than a third of both our faculty and our graduate students are writers of color, making Indiana University the most successfully diversified graduate creative writing program in the country.

It's said that when Harry Houdini, after an hour-long struggle, finally slipped loose from the handcuffs especially made for him by a London newspaper challenging his skills and brashness, some in the audience were so amazed they rioted. In truth Houdini staged the entire event, crafting the handcuffs himself (and in the process becoming thoroughly familiar with how they worked) and then giving them to a confederate at the newspaper who only pretended to challenge him.

Sit back and observe how these twenty-one writers slip free of the cuffs they've fashioned for themselves. Prepare to be delighted by engaging character and language, taut lines of conflict, and deft turns of plot.

Tony Ardizzone

# THE HABIT OF ART

# BOCCE

RENÉE MANFREDI

"Jesus Christ is a blood clot in my leg," Ellen says. "Right here in my calf, the size of a quarter." She puts her foot up on the bench where her mother, Nina, is sitting in front of the mirror applying makeup. "Do you want to see it?"

"Not now," Nina says, shadowing her eyelids with purple.

Ellen sighs loudly. She is ten, an ordinary little girl whose imagination sometimes intersects inconveniently with truth; all of her imaginary friends die tragic deaths and she grieves for them as though they were real.

Ellen sits on the floor beside Nina. Her mother is pretty today. She is wearing earrings and perfume, which she almost never does.

"Mama—"

"How many times do I have to ask you not to call me 'Mama'? It's infantile.

Ellen pauses. "Mother, my carnation didn't come today."

"It didn't? Maybe your father has finally had enough of spoiling you rotten."

Teresa of Ávila, "The Little Flower," is Ellen's favorite saint. Teresa levitated off the bed in her love of God and had visions like those Ellen herself has had: Michael the archangel has appeared to

[1]

Ellen in dreams, called to her from the top of a white staircase. Until recently, Ellen would shake her head no when Michael held his arms open to her. But one night he sang so sweetly that she walked half-way up, he halfway down. Ellen sat in his white lap and he rocked her and looked at her with his great violet eyes that never blinked and told her that heaven was perfect but lonely. When he touched her, Ellen felt as though all the light in the world was inside of her, and when she awoke the next morning the sunlight seemed dim and she felt a heavy ache in her leg that beat like a heart.

Ellen's father, Sam, indulges her: every Saturday he has a white carnation delivered to the house for Ellen to wear as a corsage. All the nonsense about saints and angels is perfectly harmless, he said to Nina, and if a flower every week keeps her out of trouble and happy he'd gladly have them flown in from Brazil if necessary. "There are ten-year-old junkies," he reasoned to Nina. "There are ten-year-old children who hate their parents and run away and become prostitutes. Besides, it could be worse. She might be interested in Saint Francis and then she'd be asking for little peeps."

Ellen links her arm through Nina's. "Mother, last week in Sunday school Mrs. Del'Assandro said that when God is mad he puts out a contract on our lives. Jesus is the hit man. If a blood clot moves to your heart it can kill you."

"Mrs. Del'Assandro most certainly did not say that." Nina takes the bottle of perfume that Ellen is holding, says, "Clean your fingernails, Ellen, then go tell your father to come up and get dressed."

"Where are you going? Am I going?"

"No." Nina sprays a cotton ball with perfume and tucks it in her bra.

"Where are you going?"

"Just to the club for dinner and dancing."

"Then why can't I come?"

"No children tonight. Please go tell your father to come upstairs and get dressed."

Sometimes Ellen doesn't love her mother.

Ellen finds her father on the phone in his study. The room is cool, dark, though it is May and still afternoon. But her father is rich enough to have anything, even the night when he wants it and autumn air in spring. She sits on the desk in front of him, wraps the phone cord around her neck. "I am being hung in a public square! I am being persecuted for my belief in God!"

Sam swats her away, holds up a cautionary finger. She wanders about the room, picking up this and that, then shuts herself in the adjoining bathroom. She has been in here only a few times. The sunken tub is rimmed with candles. On the floor is a pile of tangled clothes. Some of Nina's makeup is scattered on the vanity. Ellen spritzes herself with perfume, dabs a little red on her lips. She lifts her long black hair off her neck the way she imagines a man might and pretends the shiver at the nape is from a kiss so soft it is like a quiet she can feel. Something is different inside her; this whole day she has been restless, has felt something that is part like hunger, part thirst, and part like waiting for Christmas. She turns from the mirror when she hears in the tone of Sam's voice that he is nearing the end of his phone call. One of Nina's bras is hanging on the back of the door. Ellen holds it up to her chest, stands on the edge of the tub so she can see this part of herself reflected. The cups are as puckered and wrinkled as Grandma Chiradelli's mouth. If she ever has breasts this big, Ellen thinks, she will have them cut off; otherwise she wouldn't be able to sleep on her stomach. She puts the bra on her head, hooks the shoulder straps over her ears, and fastens the hooks under her chin. This is how they look on Venus. All of the women on Venus have breasts on their head and are bald. All of the men are tall.

"Come out here, Elena," Sam calls to her now. She yanks the bra off her head and opens the door.

"How many times do I have to tell you not to come in here without knocking?"

"Mama sent me down to hurry you," Ellen says, and sits on his desk.

"Hurry me for what, pet?"

"Dinner and dancing at the club."

"Dancing? What dancing?"

She shrugs. "Mama says I can't go."

"Of course you can go. Are those your glad rags?" he says, looking down at her jeans and T-shirt.

She laughs. "I'll go and change."

"In a minute," Sam says. "Sit here with Papa for a while." He draws her onto his lap and she leans back against him.

"Papa, my carnation didn't come today."

"I know, angel. Papa is fighting with the florist."

Sam strokes her hair, says, *"Bella. Bella,* Elena."

*"Ti amo,* Papa."

"How much?" Sam whispers. "How much do you love me?"

Ellen answers out of ritual: "To the moon and back and twice around the world."

"For how long?"

"Forever and a single day."

It is nearing dusk when they get to the club, a sprawling, white-columned structure that the Pittsburgh Italian Sons and Daughters of America bought from Allegheny township five years ago to use as a meeting place and family center. Sam, the vice-president of the ISDA since it was his money that imported the black-and-white marble and chandeliers from Sicily, named it the May Club in honor of the spring birthdays of his wife and daughter. It has the requisite swimming pools, banquet rooms, gymnasiums, and aerobics classes.

In the dining room, Sam, Nina, and Ellen are given their usual window table overlooking the bocce courts. Ellen likes to watch the players. Already the men are in their summer suits and fedoras. Ellen knows little of the game except that the brightly colored balls have to come close to the small white ball without touching it, and that, like church, the players must wear suits and ties.

"Stop. Stop that," Nina says, and puts a hand on Ellen's leg to still its swinging. "What's this?" She touches a bulge in Ellen's knee sock. Ellen pulls out a stack of religious tracts that she has taken from St. Anthony's, pamphlets with such titles as "The Road to Salvation," and "The Rewards of Piety." She carries them with her always to leave in public places. There are four ladies' rooms in the club. Ellen has spent a good part of every dinner here visiting each of them twice: once to leave the tracts, and a second to see how many had been taken. She is sure Saint Teresa would have done the same.

"Haven't I told you about taking these things?" Nina says.

She has brought too many tonight; usually she carries just enough to lie smoothly inside her sock.

"Mrs. Del'Assandro told me I could have them. She says we should carry God wherever we go. Mrs. Del'Assandro says all God's angels would sleep next to me if they could."

"Mrs. Del'Assandro is a disturbed, unhappy woman." Nina holds out her hand for the tracts.

Ellen shakes her head, holds tight to them through her sock. "These keep the blood clot in one place."

"You make me tired, Ellen," Nina says.

"Everything makes you tired, Mama."

"Please," Sam says, "let's have a nice meal tonight. Everybody pleasant and polite. If anybody is tempted to speak unkind words, chew ice cubes instead."

Ellen stuffs her mouth with three and crunches loudly.

Nina turns to Ellen, her face red. "Go. Go amuse yourself then if I'm so unbearable."

Ellen begins her usual tour of the restaurant, sitting down with strangers who most of the time neither welcome nor acknowledge her. Only once or twice has anybody complained and so Sam indulges her in this, too. The times he'd restrained her ended with Ellen ruining her mother's appetite to get back at him. Ellen frightens him a little. No one else can make him feel as she does. He spanked her once and promised himself and Nina never again. Ellen was four, too young to remember. She had done some small thing and when his threats had no effect, he swatted her. But the harder he hit her the more resolute she became in her refusal to cry. He had felt something beyond fury; it was as though she were mocking the impotence of his rage. It had ended with Ellen locking herself in the bathroom and Nina coming home to find Sam screaming crazy, threatening things about what he was going to do to Ellen when she came out: Abandon her in a large, strange city where no one would ever find her. Nina had intervened and the next day Sam bought Ellen a pony. Thankfully, Ellen seems to remember nothing of this.

Ellen likes the darkness of the restaurant, the way the corners are so dim that unless she walks right up to the table the people are just shadows. She goes to the farthest corner where the aunts Anna, Lena, and Lucia usually are, the old, black-dressed women who do embroidery and talk of recipes and sorrow. And here they are tonight. Ellen sneaks up, crawls under their table and pretends she is Anne Frank, hiding from men who want to kill her. The veins in the old women's legs are maps for secret buried treasures. She sighs, draws her knees up. There is a nice breeze brushing across her cotton panties. All of the aunts wear the same thick black shoes with Catholic polish: shiny, but not glossy enough to reflect up when Sister Mary Margaret did a line check. Ellen knows which pair of shoes are Anna's: Anna always has her stockings rolled down around her ankles like sausages. Ellen loves Anna. After her papa and Grandma Chiradelli, she loves Anna best in the world. When Anna discovers Ellen under the table, her hands will reach for her, welcoming, as though it has been a thousand years since Anna last saw her, and she will fold Ellen against her and her skin and clothes will smell like rubbing alcohol and lavender and grass. Anna is the only one who doesn't laugh or roll her eyes when Ellen discloses her dreams of angels, and it is to Anna alone that Ellen has confessed her desire of becoming a nun or a saint.

There is dancing going on upstairs; Ellen hears the music of a tarantella, the stomping of feet.

"Wedding," one of the aunts says. "Sal Benedetti and Rosa, the last of Vito's daughters, God bless her." The other two murmur agreement and Ellen hears them put their forks down in order to cross themselves.

"Which one is Rosa?" Lucia says.

"The ugly one," Lena, the mean aunt, says. She once told Ellen she would go to hell for wearing so much jewelry and that in hell her necklaces and bracelets would turn into snakes.

"Lena, so what ugly? What's the difference when the lights are out?" Lucia says. "Rosa is a work of God but not his masterpiece."

"I had the most beautiful gown for my wedding night," Anna says.

"I also," Lena says. "The chair looked very nice in it. All that needlework my mother did on it, and for what? They all want you naked."

The aunts chuckle.

Ellen searches through her stack of pamphlets until she comes to the one with "La Pietà" on the front. She folds it into a tiny square and slips it beneath Anna's shoelaces. Anna will find it there later when she is undressing and say a prayer for her dead and for Ellen.

"I feel a little mouse at my feet," Anna says, and lifts the edge of the tablecloth to look at Ellen. Lena and Lucia peer down after her.

"*Buona sera*, Anna."

"Look at the way she lies," Lena says. "*Puttana*. Good girls don't lie in public with their legs spread like crickets."

"I'm not a good girl. I'm spirited and tiring."

"*Sì, pieno dello spirito, e una valle delle lacrime*," Lena says.

"No speaka, *non capisco*," Ellen says, and covers her ears, but she gets it anyway. *Spirited and tearful. A valley of tears.*

"Hopeless," Lena says, and continues eating.

"And how is the future little novitiate?" Anna says, and hugs Ellen tight against her. "My, but it's good to see you."

Ellen whispers to Anna: "Something bad is going to happen to me, Anna. There is a blood clot in my leg from God. It might kill me. The next time you see me I might be dead."

"Why would God put a blood clot in your leg, dear?"

"He's mad at me."

"For what reason?" Anna says.

"He thinks I love Michael more than Him."

"Michael," Anna says dreamily.

Sometimes Anna drifts away when Ellen is speaking to her. Sometimes, Ellen thinks, Anna's head is stuffed with wet cinnamon as hard as stone; words can't get past it. Grandma Chiradelli sometimes plays a game with Ellen to help her sleep: she makes Ellen imagine that her head is filled with sand or sea water or flour and then she says one word over and over until it makes changing patterns like a kaleidoscope: *Bella. Serenissima. Desolato.*

"Anna," Ellen whispers. "Help me, Anna. I don't feel good. I don't feel right."

"Papa seems to be searching for you, Love," Lucia says.

Ellen looks up and sees Sam walking among the tables looking right and left. He might never find her. If she stays very still she is a shadow. She and the aunts are as invisible as dreams.

Ellen goes up to him and he tells her it's time to eat.

Oh how Ellen hates peas! There are fifty-six of them. She arranges them into a circle in her flattened mashed potatoes. Now they are pills, like the pink ones her mother takes from a blue plastic case each morning. Ellen swallows them whole, one at a time, with a sip of water. When they're all gone, she will be fifty-six days older. Inside each pea is a princess.

A man outside on the bocce lawn is smiling at her. Ellen has seen him several times before and he has never ignored or given her mean looks. He is one of the players and though a little old—forty, Ellen guesses—he is very handsome. His eyes and hair are dark and he is tall. She watches. When it is his turn he throws the ball too hard and it knocks against the little white one. He looks over at Ellen again, smiling, and she dimples back.

"Who got married anyway?" Sam says, looking at two men in tuxedos who have drifted outside to watch the bocce games.

"Vito Del Greco's daughter, Rosa, and Sal Benedetti," Nina says.

"Del Greco . . . with the six daughters?"

"That's right," Nina says. "They sit two rows ahead of us in church."

"Which one is Rosa?"

"The ugly one," Ellen says.

"Oh, yes," Sam says.

"Vito's wife is in my aerobics class. She said if we happened to be at the club tonight to stop in at the reception for a drink," Nina says.

"You said Mrs. Del Greco was a bitch," Ellen says.

Nina looks over at Ellen. "I most definitely did not say that."

"You said it last Saturday at the mall. You told Mrs. Genovese that Mrs. Del Greco was a ball-breaking bitch."

"I'd like to stop in and say hello," Nina says.

"No," Sam says.

"Why not?"

"Because I am fighting with Del Greco's pansy cousin, the florist."

"I insist," Nina says.

Ellen slips away while her parents argue. She makes her rounds in the ladies' rooms on the first floor and basement. She puts five or six tracts on the back of each toilet, a stack on the vanity, and slips one beneath each carefully folded towel. But she still has so many, even after leaving double her usual amount.

She pauses at the men's bathroom. Saint Teresa would probably do it. She puts her ear to the door and steals in when she doesn't hear anything. She stops and stares at the urinals. Planters, she guesses, except that there isn't any dirt inside. Artwork: standing back she sees that they are long faces, the jaws dropped down in shock, the mouth with a little pool of water inside. They are her parishioners, lined up and waiting. She moistens the edge of the pamphlets in the mouths, sticks one to each forehead. She is a priest. It is Ash Wednesday.

Nina and Sam are still at their coffee when Ellen returns. And the bocce players have come in. They are at a corner table opposite the aunts. The player who noticed Ellen earlier is looking at her and smiling. She saunters over.

There are seven players including the smiling one, who is the only one paying her any attention; the others are discussing something intently in Italian. She slides into the booth next to the one who smiles, sits as close to him as she dares. He asks her name.

Usually she invents a name for herself when strangers ask, but there is something about this man that makes her give her real name, as though she believes he will know if she is lying. She says, "Elena Serafina Capalbo Chiradelli."

"Those are a lot of names."

"Papa says I'll grow into them. My confirmation name is going to be Teresa. Then I'll have five names. When I get married I'll have six and if I get married twice I'll have seven then when I die I'll need a big headstone."

"Very true," the man says.

Ellen searches his salad for olives.

"Is that your papa over there?"

Ellen looks up and sees Sam motioning for her. "No. I never saw him before in my life."

Sam walks over. "Come, Ellen. It's time for us to go."

"Home?"

"Upstairs to visit the wedding celebration, then home."

"No."

"Come, Ellen, don't make Papa angry."

"No."

"Just for half an hour. Be an angel." Sam reaches for her hand.

"No! No!"

"Have some work to do on this one, yes?" the man says. "Why not leave her here with me while you go upstairs? I'll be more than pleased to watch over her. We'll be here for hours yet."

Sam looks at Ellen. She smiles at him coyly, cuts her eyes around slowly and glances up at him. This is—was—Nina's expression, something he hasn't seen for at least ten years. Where did Ellen see it?

"You bought your Saab from us," the man says.

Sam looks from Ellen to the stranger. "What?"

"Your car. You bought it from us last year."

"Are you one of the Falconi brothers?"

The man nods.

"I'm afraid I don't remember you."

"Well, there are eight of us."

"Which are you?"

"Carlo."

"Carlo Falconi," Sam says, trying to stir his memory. "Well, it's a great car. Has never given me a minute's trouble, unlike certain little creatures." He winks at Ellen and she smiles so sweetly that it makes him heartsick. Sam turns to Nina, who has appeared by his side. "Carlo Falconi," he says, but she is already moving away and heading toward the stairs. "Okay, then, I'll be back in half an hour or so. Be sweet, Elena."

"Always, Papa."

Ellen takes ice cubes from a water glass and rubs them over her eyelids. "Ice reduces swelling. I have hemorrhoids."

"You're a strange little bird," he says, and laughs.

Ellen draws up and spreads her knees, revealing her panties. From the dark corner across the room Ellen thinks she sees Lena's eyes flashing red and angry, Anna shaking her head, making the sign of the cross.

"What do you have there?" the man who calls himself Falconi says, pointing at her sock. She gives him the tracts. His eyes are so dark that when she looks in them she sees herself.

"'The Road to Salvation,'" he says and laughs. "But where do the wicked go after death?"

"To hell!"

"And what is hell?"

"The absence of God and an everlasting pit of fire." Ellen has been trained in all the correct responses.

"And how does one avoid the torments of this pit?"

"By not dying."

"Ha! Pretty good," he says, and slips the tracts into his pocket.

"You can't keep those!"

He smiles at her. His teeth are very white. "Says who?"

"Says me. Gimme," she says, holding out her hand.

But now the men at the table are quarreling about something and Falconi looks away from her. They are speaking argument Italian, something she has heard between her grandparents; it's like ordinary talk, as far as Ellen understands, but words mean more because you repeat everything twice in a shout and point at people while you say them. She sighs, drapes her legs over one of Falconi's and lies back. He glances down at her, rubs his hand over her calf. But there is a terrible tenderness there and she jerks her leg away, puts her crossed feet up on the table.

There is a pause in the conversation. "My God, whose *enfant terrible?*" somebody says.

Falconi looks down at her with his great black eyes, says, "Just a little elf that wandered my way."

If she listens closely enough, Ellen can hear the aunts talking in the opposite corner. Their voices are like the cool side of a pillow. She stares up at the ceiling. And here are the aunts now, swinging on the chandelier, back and forth, back and forth, arcing out wide and high and fast so that their hair and skirts blow back. Anna, her favorite, straddles the center chain, her legs straight out in front of her, Lena and Lucia hold onto the sides. They drop notes rolled in olives into the salads, contradict everything the men say as they swing over the table. Now the aunts and the men are singing a little rhyme Grandma Chiradelli made up.

(The men): *The moon is made of Swiss.*

(The aunts): *It's made of fontinella.*

(Men): *The angels waltz in heaven.*

(Aunts): *They dance a tarantella.*

Falconi pushes Ellen's legs away and slides out of the booth.

"Hey. Where are you going?" She follows him down a hallway where a yellow light from the lamps on the dark red walls gives everything a shadow. This is the corridor that leads to the conference rooms. She rarely visits the bathrooms on this side because people in the restaurant don't use them; she left a stack of pamphlets in the ladies' room once, and when she checked back two weeks later they were all still there.

Falconi is sitting on a bench around the corner, smoking a cigarette.

"Are you trailing me, Love?"

"My booklets. I want my booklets back now."

He flicks his ash into a potted palm and pats the bench beside him. "*Bella,*" he says. "You are a beautiful young lady. Sit here with me for a while and I will give them back."

"Do you promise?"

He nods. "Come closer. Sit close to me as you were doing out there."

She hesitates, then does so.

"Give me a kiss and I'll give you your booklets back."

"You said I only had to sit here."

He laughs. "If you give me a kiss, I will give you five dollars."

"On the lips?"

"Right here," he says, touching his cheek.

Ellen kisses him and holds out her hand. He gives her the bill and she puts it in her sock. She lets him touch her hair, her arms, her waist, and now inside her panties. This feels good.

Then it feels better.

Any place he touches becomes warm, tingly. She feels as relaxed as nighttime in her grandparents' house. Feels like she does when she is spending a weekend with them and falls asleep on purpose in the living room so somebody will have to carry her upstairs.

Then it feels like she is floating and she always hears Grandma Chiradelli's heavy step and voice behind her directing the invisible arms that bear her to the bedroom with the dark furniture and cool air that smells like cooking and leather and laundry soap.

She is as calm as that now. The man's hands make her feel so good that she thinks there must be a little piece of God in them. Her skin is like breath on a cold window: thin and warm and shifting. She is in the center of a circle that swirls blue then white then blue again, and it feels like he is making the colors inside her out of her own heartbeats: bubbles rising up white through black and his hand rubbing them into blue.

I am dying, Ellen thinks, because when there is no place inside her that doesn't feel good, the circle begins to break from the center out, like flowers dropping all their petals at once. Anna's face appears smiling before her, her head covered with a mantilla. Her lips move without sound: *Michael.*

But then it stops and her skin fits tight to her again.

"Elena, Elena, you make me so sad," Falconi whispers. He turns her face up to his. "I want to tell you something you won't understand now, but I want you to remember. More than anything in life I want to be a father. But my wife can't have children. This is the closest I will ever come to witnessing the birth of anything."

He stands, walks around the corner to the men's room. Ellen follows him in, right into the stall. He looks surprised, then says, "Oh, I suppose you want your booklets back."

She shakes her head. "I want more."

He laughs. "Go find Mama, little girl."

Ellen wraps her arms around his waist. "I think I love you."

He looks down at her and is silent for a few minutes. "You are not afraid of me?"

"No," Ellen says.

But this time it doesn't feel good; everything about him seems suddenly too big, too heavy. She feels as though she is being made to swim too fast, that his arms, tight around her, are holding her underwater so she can't breathe.

"You're hurting me," Ellen says.

"Look up. Look up at the light."

She does so. Years from now it will be this light that she remembers in detail, a dingy yellow bulb through an opaque frosted cover around the edges of which are moths in various stages of decay, and it will seem to belong more to seedy urban hallways than it does here.

Her heart is racing. With one hand Falconi pins her arms behind her back, the other hand is down there, pulling at her underpants.

She hears silver clinking, and for a moment thinks he is counting his change, but it is his belt buckle being unfastened, the snap and zipper being undone.

"Don't be afraid," he says. There is a sharp, unexpected pain that is as bad as someone tearing off her fingernails. She screams for Anna and he puts his hand over her mouth. She is a face on a chimney in a picture where you circle what doesn't belong. Nobody will find her for years and years. Her eyes and mouth are bricks that can't blink or speak. She might be here forever, staring at a light in the distance waiting for someone to look up and notice her.

But now she sees the faces of the aunts hovering around the light and knows from their expressions that she is not going to die: they don't look surprised or frightened. Anna's face is ordinary and tired, like after Saturday cleaning.

His body is still against her now. Ellen sits on the floor and cries. The blood clot, instead of moving to her heart, is moving out of her.

"Elena," he says. "Elena, I want to tell you something." He pulls her to her feet. "I have never done this before. I have never hurt a child before. Do you believe me?"

She doesn't respond.

"I didn't mean to do this. I took advantage of you. I want you to say you can forgive me. Not now, perhaps, but someday."

She shakes her head. "I'm telling Papa. I am going to tell my papa."

He squeezes her face in his hand. "You musn't. This has to be our secret."

"No," Ellen says.

"Sadly, if you tell your papa, I will kill him. I will shoot him tonight under a bridge. Do you want that? Do you want your papa to die because of you?"

Ellen can't speak, is mute while he washes her face, combs her hair. "Your booklets," Falconi says, and puts them in her hand. "I want you to think of what happened as a game. Like bocce with our own rules. I know it doesn't seem so now, but in the long run that's all the importance it will have."

She stands by the sink a long time after he leaves. She is cold, feels as though she is dreaming and has to imagine her legs before they will work. She looks down at the tracts. Some angels look more real than others, some have wings that look stiff, plastic. It must be that some angels are not angels at all, but ordinary men who bought their wings at Sears. God can't notice everything. Maybe some things are too tiny for Him to see. Maybe He made children small because He doesn't like them. From heaven, she must look no bigger than an eyelash.

She puts the tracts in the garbage. What she wants more than anything in the world right now is a purple crayon so that she could write her name on every smooth surface she passes.

Anna is gone, the bocce players are gone, the tables all have new faces. Upstairs, the wedding guests are in a tarantella circle. Ellen weaves in and out of legs, bodies, trying to catch her father as he dances by.

Papa papa papa. But her voice can't reach him any more than her hands can. Somebody steps on her feet. She sees Nina with her arm around Mr. Del Greco, and here is ugly Rosa with a big nose and a smile and too many teeth.

Then the music stops and Ellen feels hands reaching around her, a warm palm on her clammy forehead. She turns. Sam is smiling down at her and he seems to Ellen both too near and too far: as though his hand on her head weighs a thousand pounds but that if she called his name forever he wouldn't hear.

"You look worried," Sam says. "Did you have trouble finding us?"

She shakes her head.

"Did you see the bride? Too soon it will be your turn."

"Papa," Ellen starts.

"Yes? Why do you look like that?"

Ellen begins to cry.

"Elena, you're breaking my heart. Tell me."

"I can't," she says.

"Why? Has there ever been anything you couldn't tell me?" Sam strokes her hair and an image of herself with Nina's bra on her head—it seems so long ago now—flashes in her mind.

"You won't love me anymore if I tell you."

"That could never happen. Not in a million years."

"You will die if I tell you."

"I'll take my chances."

Ellen glances around. Any one of these men might be a spy. "I know something," Ellen says.

"What do you know?"

"God never wanted any children."

"How do you know that?"

"He killed His son. Jesus Christ is dead."

"Yes, but now He's in heaven," Sam says.

"He's in the men's room. He bled to death."

"Elena, Elena. Come now, dance with me like we always do," Sam says, and lifts her so her feet are on top of his. But even Sam's slow steps are painfully too wide. She feels a dragging pressure in

[17]

her lower belly, her own blood stinging against the places where her skin is raw. Tonight before she goes to bed she will stuff her panties behind the water heater in the basement.

The band is playing a slow song and people hold each other close. Ellen sees Nina dance by with Mr. Del Greco, who is saying something to her that makes her smile.

"I have good news," Sam says. "I have settled with the florist and your carnations will start coming again."

"No," Ellen says, looking up at the musicians on the stage.

"No?" Sam says.

"Those things," she says, pointing. "I want those things that man has by the drum."

"Cymbals? What do you want with cymbals?"

Ellen looks at him. "I have to whisper it."

Sam bends down.

"I want cymbals in case I get lost. I could just stand still and crash them and you will always be able to find me."

"Elena, all you have to do is call for me and I'll find you."

"But what if I have lost my voice, too?"

Sam draws her closer and Ellen concentrates on the warm pressure of his hand, his feet beneath hers moving slowly to the music. It is this image of herself she is already beginning to remember, the firm steps that lead her around and around through the confused crowd as though to tell her: Here is where you are. Here is where you find yourself.

# SIX WAYS TO JUMP OFF A BRIDGE

BRIAN LEUNG

Understand Blue Falls, how it got its name, how in dry years, in autumn, water slips over a flat edge, sheer and perfect, a wide liquid sheet reflecting a clear day—blue as an unraveling bolt of satin. But most years are not dry and most days are not completely blue. Not this morning, certainly, as Parker Cheung leans on the railing of the deck behind his home where he sees the falls and the observation bridge bisecting the line of water. Today is misty and the falls are loud, full after three days of rain. And there are people on the bridge. Parker counts four, one of them the sheriff, Katie Buckle. Someone's gone and jumped again, he says to himself. He takes a last drink of tea and walks inside, shaking his head.

Parker considers his dark living room, the *National Geographics* and *Reader's Digests* stacked everywhere, the mugs with their various levels of evaporating green tea. The answering machine in the corner blinks a single unchecked message. It could be his daughter, Susan, but he's afraid it won't be and so he's left it alone all morning trying not to think about it. Parker looks outside at the bridge, searching for the sheriff again. She'll be around soon to ask what he knows.

BRIAN LEUNG

At first he doesn't see her, but then she's back on the bridge, a brown-and-khaki thickness with a heavy walk. Maybe I've still got time, he thinks, turning to straighten the room, something he's still not used to even though it's been two years since his wife died. This was her part of their marriage, running the house, raising their daughter. He took care of the egg ranch, *Cheungs' Eggs "Something to Crow About!"* But now that his wife is gone, he's shut down the business, and he hasn't spoken to his daughter in nine years. But there is the message on the machine that came while he was showering and it could be Susan. She might have remembered today would have been her mother's sixtieth birthday.

Parker starts by collecting the dirty cups, setting them in the already-full sink. He turns on the tap and hot water sputters out. The kitchen smells like fish, more so than usual, and he remembers last night's meal. He lifts the lid off a cast-iron pot, the head of a small red snapper offering a milky stare, a xylophone of bones strung behind. He throws the fish out the kitchen window and watches for a moment as three cats that he insists are not his fight over the carcass. Beyond them is the bridge from a slightly different angle. Everyone has left except the sheriff. She is facing away, toward the falls, resting both hands on the railing. That's not the side people usually jump from, Parker thinks. It's too close to the falls. The water isn't shallow enough for death and no one jumps off Blue Falls Bridge just to get seriously injured.

The first one to go over was Jason Glass. He was sixteen. Parker saw it, too. It was in the evening, he remembers, after dinner. They had steamed salmon dumplings and bok choy. He was full and walked out on the deck while his wife and daughter cleared the table. The night was cool and it now seems an important detail to him that it rained the next morning and didn't stop for three days. It was dusk and the bridge looked like something etched, a sequence of thick black lines. He saw someone pacing, not someone, actually, just a form moving back and forth. Finally the figure stopped, and a voice cracked through the twilight air, the form bolting across the bridge. It was running, yelling "I'm Superman!" as it pushed off the rail.

Parker shuts off the water until there is just a small whining stream for rinsing. He starts with the silverware because that's how his wife had always done it. The water is warm and the wetness makes his hands look almost young. He thinks again of the Glass boy. He has never forgotten the sound of Jason's body hitting the rocks, the solitary thump, barely a sound at all. Now, remembering, it is not important to him that he ran inside and startled Annie and Susan, could hardly produce words, nor that somehow he called the sheriff. It is the sound of Jason's body meeting ground, how his life ended as a whisper, in a riverbed, the almost powdery tenor of it as if the world couldn't care if he was a boy or a sack of flour. A reporter for the *Northwest Trader* asked him to describe what it was like to see the young man end his life. Parker watched the reporter's hand scribbling notes on a small pad. How could he describe a person's life dissolving into night air, the shocking lack of reverberation? He was quiet for a moment and the reporter stopped writing, his pencil a fraction of an inch from the paper. Finally, Parker spoke. "It's like reading a sentence and arriving at a comma with nothing after it."

Later, it turned out that Susan knew Jason. She was a year behind him in high school. In the four days before his funeral, she didn't go to class, she stayed home, took meals in her room where she and her mother talked for hours. Once, Parker heard her crying alone. He stopped and knocked on her door but she didn't answer. "I just want you to know," he said, speaking into the wood frame, "there was nothing you could do. They're saying it was drugs. He was causing his parents a lot of trouble." She began crying louder and he put his hand on the doorknob but did not go in. Instead, he waited for his wife to get home.

Now, he has a message on the machine. There's no reason to think it's Susan except that it's his wife's birthday and no one ever calls. And why would she want to talk now after all these years? Parker isn't even sure of what he should say. There are ideas, forms of apology that sift through his mind nearly every day, but they all seem as vague as the reasons he and Susan stopped speaking in the first place.

As Parker washes the dishes, he keeps his eye on the sheriff. He watches her pace slowly as if she's trying to figure something out. But, as far as he's concerned, there's nothing to figure out. They should just tear down the bridge. Aren't six jumpers enough? Building it had seemed like a good idea at the time, but now. . . . Parker remembers when it first went up, and before that too, when the Chamber of Commerce held a meeting in the VFW hall, well before Seattle had its Space Needle. There wasn't any reason to come to Washington then, unless you liked lumber, or perhaps cared to see the Columbia covered by a flotilla of logs. He remembers how Joe and Ruth Kent took a summer road trip in their Thunderbird and came back with pictures of gigantic concrete cows, the names of cities painted on their sides, invariably followed by a slogan beginning with "World's greatest" or "World's largest." Either that, or it was the home of something or the birthplace of someone. He recalls the Chamber president passing around postcards and salt and pepper shakers the Kents bought, all of them bearing the name of a town. There was a picture of a huge ear of corn weighing down a pickup truck. From Las Vegas, they brought back a pair of plastic slot machine shakers. They said Blue Falls needed an identity, a reason to come and spend money.

Parker feels the edge of a chipped cup and, for a moment, considers throwing it away, about as long, he thinks, as it took to decide on building the bridge. Parker remembers that was a dry year and everyone had fresh in their minds how simple and beautiful the falls were, how glassy and reflective. Everyone thought people would certainly drive to see them. Mildred Thomas was even smart enough to recommend they hire a photographer to take pictures before the bridge went up because that would be better for postcards. By then, Parker had only owned the egg ranch a few years, bought with money he inherited from his father, a purchase he knew he would never have approved of. His father never wanted Parker to do any manual labor.

With the last of the inheritance, Parker put up most of the money for the bridge and he remembers how everyone started calling him by his first name, or tried to. That was when he still wanted people to use his Chinese name, Pak. Only Annie called him Pak, and even she preferred her American name over Ling. He remembers she wanted the bridge too, even proposed to the Chamber that they write Pat Boone to see if he would dedicate the bridge when it was done. Her accent was still so thick then he had to translate what she wanted.

We were all a mess, Parker thinks, searching the dishwater for any stray silverware, almost laughing. Pat Boone never wrote back, and Parker's wife stopped playing his records. Worse, though, after all the money invested in postcards and plaques made from diagonally-cut pine limbs, no one could ever say for sure if even one extra person had come into town because of the bridge, though Parker did report he spotted a family on it one summer a couple years after it opened. For about a week the people of Blue Falls allowed themselves to feel vindicated.

Now, forty years later, just as many people know it as Jumper's Bridge. Parker watches the sheriff tap her hand on the railing. It won't be long before she's knocking on his door.

The deeply stained bottom of one of the cups Parker has already washed gives him an excuse to turn his attention away from the window. He looks at the age spots on back of one of his hands. Old, he thinks, returning his attention to the cup. He considers what he remembers about last night so he'll have it all straight for the sheriff, though he's sure there was nothing out of the ordinary. He wonders who jumped this time, what was the reason. Sometimes, you have connections with these people. Like Jason Glass. It wasn't until years later, months after Susan moved to Los Angeles for college, that Annie turned to him in bed one night, shook her head and told him the truth. It had come out of nowhere. "Remember

Jason Glass?" Her hair was still long and black then, just starting to show a few strands of white.

Parker nodded, a bit startled. He was halfway into a textbook on light therapy and he set it on his lap. "Of course, the one Susan knew."

"She his girlfriend. They fight over his drugs."

He didn't know what to think. "Why didn't one of you say something?" He looked at his wife. "I could have talked to her."

She sat up in bed, her face tightening. "No. You wouldn't. You always too busy with the egg ranch. That your problem. Always your problem."

His wife stayed mad at him for days, which seemed unreasonable to him. Susan had gotten over Jason, hadn't she? After the funeral she started working a few hours a week at the egg ranch as a candler. That first week, he'd asked her as she inspected the back-lit eggs running by on a conveyer belt. "Are you okay?"

Susan did not look up from the eggs. "Fine, Pop."

"Good." Parker walked away. Now he thinks he should have said more. But she did seem fine, busy, occupied at least. And hadn't they later chosen a good career for Susan when she went away to study engineering? She'd even met a nice Chinese boy. At that point, at least, everything seemed okay. What more could they have done for her?

As he dries his hands, there's a knock at the door and he knows it's Katie. Parker goes to open it and catches a glimpse of himself in the dusty hallway mirror. He's still in his terrycloth robe, the sleeves rolled up for the dishes. The thin rim of his white hair bristles out all over.

He greets Katie with a calm smile.

"There's been another one, Parker."

He nods but does not invite her in. "I saw you over there." He and Katie go back a long way. When she was sixteen, working at the egg ranch was her first job. Parker made her an egg candler too, but she complained after only a day about the boredom so he moved her to the chicken houses, gave her a boy's job to teach her a lesson. By the end of the summer, she'd become his best worker. It wasn't long before he had her supervising other employees, including Susan. Even though she's in her forties now, thicker, her blonde hair cropped long ago, it is not hard for him to believe this woman with the gun at her side is the same Katie.

"See anything?"

"Not this time," Parker says, looking beyond her to see what she's staring at. The ranch is wet and shiny, the spring weeds in his wife's old hyacinth bed bent from early morning rain. "I really should get out here and do some yard work," he says, but there's no conviction in it. There would never have been flowers at all if not for Annie. He remembers how mad she was one year when she asked him to bring home lavender hyacinth bulbs, not the packaged kind, the bulk, so he could pick out good ones. The next year the whole bed came up white, though he swore he double-checked the bin label. Of course, he hadn't. It never mattered to him.

Katie shakes her head and scuffs a boot into the dark, wet ground. "Your cats are looking a bit scruffy."

"I don't claim them. They claim me."

"Not very smart cats," Katie says, turning around.

"Doesn't seem right the way the place is all closed down."

"A man can't work all his life."

Katie smiles and takes off her plastic covered hat. "You? Work?"

Stifling a smile and crossing his arms, Parker leans against the door frame. "As I remember, I spent most of my time picking up after *you*."

"Listen, you old coot. Gonna invite me in or not?"

Parker finally smiles and gestures her inside. "I suppose you're operating on that permanent warrant you keep telling me about."

She sits on the couch, lays her felt hat on a stack of *National Geographics*. "Jesus. So this is where the old growth forests are ending up."

"Got 'em at Henderson's yard sale. I like to read."

"I remember. But your taste used to run a little more sophisticated. And Jesus. Do you read with night-vision goggles?" She leans over and switches on a lamp.

Parker sits in his recliner, the arms so worn the wood frame shows in places. "Donated my books to the library." He sees the answering machine, the red light blinking over Katie's shoulder. "I can open the curtains."

As he gets up, Katie says, "I've seen enough of the bridge, thank you."

It *is* dark in here, Parker thinks, turning on a reading light. It casts Katie's face in a dim yellow, accentuating the wrinkles around her eyes. He measures her expression. She's not smiling anymore. "Was it bad?"

"It's always bad. But this time the body floated downstream and some kids found it." She pauses and leans forward. "Anything unusual at all last night? No lights? Voices?"

He had gone to bed early, had lain awake a long time thinking about Annie, about the next day being her birthday, and he was a bit ashamed he remembered the occasion now that she was gone. When she was alive, their daughter had to remind him almost every year. He recalls being awake long enough to watch the moonlight shift across the room, long enough to notice the clouds roll in. He'd fallen asleep to the sound of rain. "Nothing," he says, glancing again at the answering machine.

"This guy didn't leave a car or a bike or anything. He went out of his way to get to the bridge. We're just trying to make sure he jumped on his own."

"Maybe he isn't a jumper at all," Parker says. "Just some unlucky guy who fell in."

Katie has already started shaking her head. "I'd like to think that too, but he's pretty bashed up and we can see where he hit. Head first. Left half his skull behind."

"Local?"

"No I.D. But he was wearing a hunting vest and work boots, so he's from not too far."

"I don't understand how they get so crazy." Ed Cane had gone over something like this, Parker remembers. Got fired from his job as a welder at the Bonneville dam three weeks after his wife and kids moved away to Idaho. He just drove out to the bridge, weighed down his pink slip and divorce papers under a rock, and jumped.

It was summer and hot and everything smelled like burnt pine. Parker had gone out for firecrackers for the Fourth of July picnic. When he came home, Annie rushed out to the truck to tell him. One of the workers saw Ed jump. Said he stood on the rail, shrugged and dove straight as a pencil.

Katie checks her watch. "You got any coffee, Parker?"

"Just instant." Parker begins to get up but Katie stops him.

"I'll hunt around for it," she says.

He listens as Katie fills the kettle with water, opens the cupboards and drawers, looks for coffee, sugar, and a spoon. He could easily tell her where to look, but he likes the sound of someone else in the kitchen. Annie had always risen a half-hour before him and he sometimes stayed in bed just to listen. Even when Susan was born, he didn't mind the sound of her crying late at night. It was what made the house alive, these sounds coming from upstairs or somewhere down the hall, the comfort of hearing his daughter brushing her hair, the repetitive wisp of it, and the early clack of pans and breakfast dishes, how he could tell just by sound, before he left their room, whether they were having eggs or pancakes, sausage or bacon.

Even in those later years before Susan left for college, when they rarely spoke, Parker could listen to the house and somehow that was enough. How many times had he come inside from work and heard Susan playing too-loud music in her room and said nothing? Now he's beginning to believe that was a mistake, to be the father without a voice. Today, the answering machine blinks silently in front of him while Katie rummages around the kitchen and Parker is still looking for words. If it's Susan, he hopes she's left a number. Twice he's hired people to find her in Los Angeles.

Parker waits until he thinks Katie is done. "Find everything?"

"Just fine," she says from the kitchen. "Maybe they just need a little hope, Parker."

"That's not it. Hope means you know you're missing something." It's more about understanding the lack of something than the possibility. After Annie started sleeping in Susan's old bedroom, he believed for a long time she would think better of it and return. But she stayed there, died in that room, too, during her sleep.

Katie sits again, holding her coffee with two hands. "In a way, Parker, I think you're worse off than the rest of us. You've actually seen it happen. The Glass boy before I was sheriff and the Silva girl."

"That was awful," Parker says. Of all of them, Rebecca Silva's death bothered him and Annie most. She was just twenty-three, the same age as Susan. The jump first looked like an accident, but later, her parents found a note. Her father was a Baptist minister in Tacoma. The newspaper photo pictured her as fair-skinned, with red hair and a wide smile that showed only upper teeth. The story reported she was three months pregnant. Parker saw her sitting on the rail. She was wearing a white sweater and jeans. It was late afternoon in autumn. The falls were beautiful, and though he was concerned at first he thought she looked relaxed because she was swinging her feet staring at the water. Suddenly, she leaned backward and was gone. "Annie was upset for a long time over that one," Parker says. "She wanted us to move after it happened."

"I remember. She went around trying to get people to tear down the bridge, too."

Parker looks at Katie, surprised. "I didn't know that."

"Oh sure. After the Silva girl, Annie tried to convince anyone who'd listen that we should wrap some explosives around the braces and blow it up."

[28]

"She had a point." Parker wonders, though, if it was really the bridge she was concerned with. When the Silva girl jumped, Annie was already upset because things were going badly with Susan. She had quit school. There had been a letter, a note really. Parker even recalls the color of the ink, a thick green that soaked into the open spaces in her handwriting. It said *Dear Mom, I'm leaving school. I can't be an engineer. All I've learned is how nothing lasts.* The next day, Rebecca Silva jumped, and Annie was on the phone with Susan, crying, making plans to fly to Los Angeles.

Katie sets down her coffee and walks to the long curtains covering the sliding glass doors. She pulls the cord and they shimmy open, gray light wedging in with each pull. She steps outside onto the deck. Mist has settled among the tops of the pines. It makes Parker think of altitude, as if they are much higher than they are, as if his house is on some elevated precipice.

Parker walks outside, tying his robe tightly around his waist as Katie lights a cigarette. The falls are percussive and the sun, a disk beyond the clouds, silvers the bridge. "Sometimes it can be beautiful."

"That's the bitch of it. It's not the bridge." Katie crushes out her barely smoked cigarette. "It's just where they decide to stop being alone. That jump begins a long time before they make it out here."

"I can't figure why they don't snap out of it when they look down at the rocks." As Parker says this, he remembers that Jason Glass had gone over in the night and Sarah went backward. They didn't see where they were falling. What does that feel like, he wonders, the few seconds of going somewhere else before meeting the ground? And what if there is even one synapse of regret, a spark of mistake?

"You need anything else?" Parker says, the urge to check the message growing stronger.

"Guess not," Katie says. "I actually thought we could do it over the phone this time, but you didn't pick up."

"You called?"

"This morning. I left a message." Katie points inside. "See, it's blinking."

Parker hesitates. "I know," he says finally. "I thought it might be Susan. I was waiting until you left."

"Oh, I'm sorry, Parker. You two still haven't spoken?"

"She doesn't want to talk to me," Parker says. He catches the sharpness in his voice and takes a slow breath.

"Jesus. You can't let that crap go on forever."

"I don't even know where she is. The last time I spoke to her she told me not to call."

"All I know is that I've got Jacob off to college and Jamie still at home, and I couldn't live without either of them." Katie smiles and pokes Parker in the side. "Their father's a different story."

Parker does not smile back. He wants to tell Katie how the silence is his fault, how when Susan dropped out of school he would not speak to her. Annie wanted the two of them to go to Los Angeles together to bring Susan back, or at least make sure she was okay, but he refused to indulge her throwing her life away, refused to leave the egg ranch unattended. And he never spoke to Susan; kept a vague tab on her through his wife, but didn't even know her phone number. When Annie returned from L.A., she moved into the other bedroom where she'd stayed for all those years. And when she died, he couldn't reach Susan, couldn't find her listed under the name of Cheung, not under any of the Cheungs he called. There had been the funeral, the white roses over the mahogany casket, everyone from town. He had hoped that somehow Susan would have found out, that his wife had made some plan. But no, there was that whole quiet service without her in the little wooden church he helped paint every five or six years. "That's why I don't sell the place," he tells Katie. "That's why I bought an answering machine."

But Katie is quiet for a few moments. "I'm just small potatoes, but I could call L.A. again for you."

"I don't think so. You already did what you could." Parker's voice is suddenly soft and resigned. "It's my mess."

Katie offers an understanding nod. "So, what am I going to do about all *this* mess? It's only every few years, but they may as well've jumped in the same week." The two of them stand silently for a moment. "Well," Katie says, pulling up on her belt, "I should get going. If you think of anything, I know you have the number."

Parker walks her through the house. He stands on the front steps as she opens her car door. "Maybe this was the last one," he says.

"I'd like to think so," Katie says. "But there's more than six ways to jump off a bridge."

Parker listens to the snap of wet gravel as she pulls away. Then it is quiet except for a few sparrows quarreling in the trees. He looks at the three large chicken houses, still and long as docked ships. The old delivery truck with faded lettering and flat tires sits near the fence, two seasons of unpruned blackberry vines already overtaking the front bumper. It is all so different now, so hushed, no gurgle of chickens working through the tin buildings, no one walking around with cardboard flats or running one of the egg collectors, no one at all. Parker stopped that just after Annie died, laid off people he'd known longer than his own daughter.

He sits in his recliner and focuses on the answering machine's small red light. He watches until it begins to move in tiny circles. This is what it comes to, he thinks. It's not at all how he imagined this stage of his life when he first came to the United States with Annie and they started the business.

Parker takes a quieting breath and swivels around to face the open glass doors and looks out at the bridge. He closes his eyes but it is still there, only in his mind it is even clearer and the sound of Blue Falls becomes the sound of rain, becomes something even softer, the sound of a body dropping through the air. It is like some improvisation of wind. And there is Susan's face, tenuous as a thread of silk beaded with water, glistening, drops falling and again the sound of rain, something more, pushing off, letting go. Parker thinks that this is the sound of decision, what it's like to hear someone jump when not a word is spoken. It is not an act of abandonment. That happened long ago and it was mutual, and no one listened anyway. No one notices unless we've made it all the way down, he thinks. No one hears until we are completely quiet.

Now Annie is gone and unless Susan calls, she's gone too. All that ignored intuition, Parker thinks, those families of the people who jumped missed it completely, all that pointing to the spot on the rail where they jumped. They got it all wrong because it happened well before that. When it comes to the final moment, it's already too late. It started for Ed Cane when his family moved to Idaho, Parker thinks, and when Jason Glass didn't get relief from twenty bucks worth of plastic bag slapped in his palm. It started when Rebecca understood a fetus would be a punishment for the rest of her life. These are the irrevocable moments when we can't see we're already in mid-air, when we push our daughter so far away she is lost to us, and then our wife goes too and we are alone. Parker imagines a blue descent, mistakes peeling off his shoulders, and finally, in one simple trajectory, the lightness he'd sought after all that awkward navigation, the relief that surprises even him. I've wondered all along, he thinks, and suddenly I know that this is what it feels like when you're falling.

# SURROGATES

RACHEL HALL

There are times when history blows past, leaves you straggling and flustered, blinking as if you have grit in your eyes. So it was for me in Geneseo, New York, in 1959. Around me the other faculty wives had exchanged their sweater sets and circle skirts for maternity smocks and dresses—tent-like numbers with patch pockets and darts at the bust. Impossible that one could envy those dresses, but these wives were awfully pleased with themselves. One saw it in the way they lowered themselves gracelessly into couches and stayed there all evening discussing morning sickness or comparing cravings. Around them, cigarette smoke wafted (nearly everyone smoked in those days, even pregnant wives) and drinks were refilled. Imagine the fizz of tonic over ice, the reassuring glug-glug of gin or vodka as it is poured, the lime wedge twisted in the nimble fingers of the host. Drinking, too, is what one did; it wasn't yet pinned to sadness, its excess didn't point to some lack or need as it does today.

That year, the college was building a new dorm for the increasing number of married students, the wives filling the secretarial positions on campus while the husbands pursued degrees. From our house on Kimberly Street, I could hear the grinding and clanking of

the construction. I threw on a Pendleton shirt of Howard's and began the walk to campus. We'd had an exceptionally dry summer,
and I noticed that the leaves turned silvery before turning butter-
scotch or red or plum. I kicked the piles of fallen leaves as I walked,
the whoosh of it vaguely satisfying.

There was a word for my condition that I tried not to think of,
but that day, passing the fields in which only the dried husks of corn
remained, it was hard to avoid the word, a word rather like the sound
the wind made lifting and shuffling the brown leaves from the dying
stalks—barren, barren, barren. Surely there is a kinder way of saying
such things now, but no matter. I don't believe there is any era that
embraces the childless woman.

Howard and I might have become like the dry childless couples
in British novels, our bodies thinning and narrowing until we were
more like brother and sister than a married couple. "Take up a hobby
together," my doctor had said, himself a father of five. Our evenings
could be spent in heady discussion of the birds spotted during long
walks in nearby Letchworth Park or in debate about the exact acid-
ity of the soil required to achieve long-blooming roses. Perhaps Dr.
Stone imagined that the roses, named no less—Carlotta Pink, Isabel,
Gertrude's Glory—could be our surrogates.

To be honest, I did join the garden club, but the meetings were
as bad as the cocktail parties; the folding chairs in the basement of
St. Michael's creaked beneath the bulk of the pregnant wives or worse,
babies too young to be left at home slept in their arms, or toddlers
gummed Zwieback by their feet. I couldn't concentrate on conversa-
tions about mulching or tulip beds. And who ended up weeding
those beds? Not the pregnant wives, with their swelling ankles and
nausea, not the young mothers with naptime to consider.

As I neared the center of the village, I saw a couple approaching me on the sidewalk. In a town this size, the spotting of a new
face was remarkable, and here before me were two new faces—not
students, of whom there were many each fall. The woman was tall

and thin with pale eyes set close together. Her long, wavy hair was so blond, it looked white—the color of the fluff in milkweed pods. The man was tall and thin too. His hair was a darker blond and long by Geneseo standards, covering his ears and curling up at the neck of his shirt. Together they looked like a pair of Afghan dogs—elegant, leggy and slightly disdainful. (Dog breeding was another hobby suggested, rather insensitively I'd thought, by my doctor.) I have so many other memories of Nick and Tory, but this one remains the clearest: these two beautiful strangers against the backdrop of the gray western New York sky, the leaves golden beneath their feet.

I slowed to say hello. Perhaps this was the new art professor I'd heard about. He had missed the college's opening activities because of a fellowship he'd had in Italy. No one had mentioned a wife, however.

"I'm Joyce Markham," I said. "You must be the new professor in the art department."

"Yes," the man said, "and you?"

The way he said this was both ironic and expectant, and the words felt tinged with possibility, as if I might be something other than I appeared—a frustrated faculty wife in faded dungarees and her husband's old wool shirt.

"My husband," I stammered. "He's at the college—in geology." And at that moment, I saw an image of Howard bent over a microscope, utterly focused on the trilobite before him. Someone could easily sneak up on him, I thought, knock him flat.

The man nodded. "I'm Nick Swander. And this is Victoria."

"Tory, please," she said. "It's easier." She smiled at me.

"Are you settling in all right? Finding everything?"

"There isn't much to find, is there?" Nick said.

"I suppose not," I agreed. "Well, if you need anything, we live right over there." I gestured back up the hill. "35 Kimberly."

"Right," Nick said, nodding.

"Nice to meet you, Joyce," Tory said.

I resumed my walk, but couldn't help seeing my destination as Nick and Tory would—a pathetic small-town diversion. And yet, I didn't know what else to do. I'd finished the laundry and my baking. I'd vacuumed yesterday and it was too early to prepare dinner. I had signed on as a faculty wife when I married Howard and had thought myself lucky. I envisioned a life of baking lemon bars for receptions, attending performances of the college's orchestra, and raising precocious children. I was finding, however, I had time on my hands. The other wives were busier, raising children or reading books from the public library in preparation for childrearing. Do I make them seem single-minded? Simple? They weren't without intelligence or talents: Jeanette Larson had been a dancer before her marriage; Sallie Reynolds was so witty she could make me laugh until I cried; Anne Niehus had been valedictorian at Smith. It was only that their lives were progressing as expected, so they weren't moved, as I was, to consider the narrowness of this path.

What to do? Howard, I knew, was lecturing to his intro class. Sometimes I'd attend his classes, sneaking in when the lights were out and Howard was illuminated by the overhead projector. I loved the careful way he spoke, pausing for emphasis and to allow students ample time to record his words. In the back row of such a classroom at the University of Illinois, I'd fallen in love with Howard as he described the process of fossilization. His obvious passion stirred me, a farm girl from Dekalb accustomed to looking to the ground in terms of what it would yield—corn, soy, winter wheat—and not for the clues it might offer of the past. But today I didn't want to listen to Howard. He'd left this morning annoyed with my request that he come home after his class; I had taken my temperature that morning and knew I was ovulating. Whatever else I was, I was determined.

Nick's voice and manner had something British to it, I thought—or perhaps that was just affectation. As I neared the construction site, I wondered if Nick and Tory had children. There was a joke among the young faculty, something about the water here and automatic pregnancy. I could even imagine the leggy blond children Nick and Tory might have, could imagine Tory behind a stroller. It is possible to feel, as I did then, bereft, even though the thing one wants has never been hers. *Just one child,* I pleaded at night while Howard slept or pretended to sleep beside me. *I could be happy with one.*

At the construction site, men in hard hats were smoking cigarettes. A yellow digger gnawed at the slick soil. The noise was fierce, echoing off the walls of nearby buildings, rattling windows. I saw my neighbor, Anne Neihus and her son, Jamie. She waved to me from across the muddy pit. I waved back at Anne but was saddened to see that she and I were wearing nearly identical clothing. The only difference was the bolder plaid of her shirt. I was glad the Swanders weren't here to note this, or to see how hungrily I embraced Jamie, once he spotted me and raced around the site to say hello.

"That's a digger," he said, pointing and speaking loudly to be heard over the motor. "They don't have a cherry picker here or a steamroller. I like steamrollers the best."

"Pipe down, Jamie," Anne said. She placed her hands on his shoulders. "He loves trucks," she said, shrugging.

From my kitchen window, I'd seen Jamie in their backyard, pushing trucks back and forth across their patio. "Yes, and he knows so much about them," I said.

"We're heading to the café for cocoa, if you want to join us."

"I'll walk that way with you," I said, "but I've got to get back to the house." We moved towards Main Street, Jamie running ahead, then turning around to wait for us to catch up. The blue pom-pom on the top of his hat bobbled as he ran.

Anne was not the only faculty wife who invited me out or along with her children, and she wasn't the only one I refused. I sensed pity in their invitations, the awareness that they had what I wanted. This inequity sat between us, solid and impenetrable. Later, much later, I had friends who spoke of the loneliness of motherhood, and I understood only then that Anne and the others had probably been desperate for adult conversation. At the time, though, my grief prevented me from seeing others' unhappiness. Even in the months to come, when I was happier than I'd been in years, I still didn't observe the sadness all around me, the grainy sediment of it settling before my eyes.

We passed the flowerbeds where the black-eyed Susans were nearly finished. The mums were blooming—yellow and burgundy and lavender—the last hurrah before the long gray winter.

"Look," Anne said, "isn't that Howard?" She pointed past the fountain to where Howard stood, ready to cross Main Street.

"He must have decided to come home for lunch," I said, noting with pleasure Howard's dark hair, his strong shoulders beneath his tweed jacket. "Nice to see you, Anne," I said, "and you too, sweetie." I bent and kissed the silky spill of bangs on Jamie's forehead.

"See you tomorrow at the Larsons'?"

"Oh, I'd almost forgotten. Yes, see you there." I dashed off to catch up with Howard, thinking as I ran about the contents of our icebox. What would I feed him?

We had chosen our house instead of all the others the realtor had shown us, because of its large picture windows that faced the back of our treed lot. Both the living room and the bedroom had these windows. We could keep the curtains open, and have privacy and a view. I imagine that the trees were a riot of color by then, that Howard and I stood a moment before the window in our bedroom; perhaps we even felt hopeful, moved by the beauty just outside our window. Behind us was the queen-sized bed we'd bought together after our marriage, though the salesperson had recommended two twins with matching quilted headboards.

"Shall we?" Howard said, taking my hand and leading me there.

It would be easier to recall this past, the hurt I caused, if I could say that Howard and I were incompatible in the bedroom. If he were selfish, say, or unimaginative or clumsy, but he wasn't, and we weren't. There was always a certain point in our lovemaking where I forgot about trying to conceive, forgot about everything, really, and felt only a warm silkiness. But afterwards, the quiet of the house would return, its stubborn hollowness, and I would remember.

"I need to get back to the lab," Howard said, sitting up and reaching to the bedside table for his glasses.

"Already?" I said. "It's not even one."

"I've got some grading to do too."

"Can't you do it here?"

"Joyce."

I knew I should stop, knew Howard's contract was up for renewal this year, that he was worried because his research was going slower than he'd hoped, but the afternoon and evening stretching out before me made me panicky and grasping. "I won't bother you—I promise."

"Joyce, you've got to stop this," he said, as he might to a recalcitrant student.

I rolled over. In a moment, I heard the shower turn on. Outside our window, the tiny, yellow leaflets of the honey locust tree were dropping like tears.

The Larsons lived on the other side of campus, in a rambling older house. During the Depression it had been split into multiple apartments, improbably-shaped, with narrow, windowless hallways. The Larsons were in the process of tearing down all the dividers, refinishing woodwork and disassembling the cramped galley kitchens on each floor.

As we pulled up, I saw a car in the driveway I didn't recognize. The Niehuses weren't here yet, though we'd seen Frank ushering in their babysitter before we left.

"I don't see how they can bear the constant mess of this old place," Howard said.

"Jeanette told me Norm likes to work with his hands," I said, remembering the cupboards from the original kitchen that he'd salvaged from the barn and sanded and refinished.

"Norm should spend more time on his research."

Like Howard, I preferred our tidy new ranch to the Larsons' house with its ornate moldings and nooks—what a pain to dust all that, I'd thought when we first saw their home. But something about Howard's voice surprised me—it was churlish, tight. He thought everyone should spend time as he did, I understood. Had he always been this way and I hadn't noticed because of the way my ambitions overlapped with his, required his to sustain my own? And what part of his bitterness was due to my failure? I took his hand as we stepped over the granite threshold of the Larsons' entryway.

What can I say of those dinner parties? The wives spent days preparing, consulting cookbooks and magazines like *Better Homes and Gardens* or *Ladies Circle*. We tried out recipes on our husbands, watched as they ate crab dip or chicken a la king on toast points or individually molded tomato aspic. For the guests, the good china was brought out, the tablecloths and napkins fresh from the ironing board. This was my life, and still it felt like we were pretending to be adults, like these were parts we'd agreed to act out in some interminable play.

My costume that night was a sleeveless black cocktail dress that nipped in at my waist and flared out over my hips. It came to my knees and I wore black heels, which I hoped would make my legs look longer. Jeanette was wearing a dress too, but hers had a matching cardigan. I'd forgotten how drafty their house was—I'd be shivering all night.

"Come in, come in," Norm said. "Let me get you a drink. Give Jeanette your jacket and wrap—and follow me."

I could hear them in the hallway and Howard's answer: "Scotch."

"Pretty dress," Jeanette said. "You've got the figure for it."

"Thanks," I said. "Can I help with anything?" The countertop beneath the refinished cupboards was lined with salad plates.

"Go on out, I'll be there in a sec—just need to make radish roses."

In the back parlor, I found Howard sipping his drink next to the Swanders. Nick wasn't drinking, but Tory had a glass of wine.

"So, we meet again," Nick said.

"You know each other?" Howard said.

"We met walking the other day," I said.

"I was just telling Nick that you were an appreciator of art, and not a bad artist yourself." Howard put his arm around me.

"Do you paint?" Nick asked.

Tory smoothed her hair back from her eyes and watched me.

"No," I said. "I used to draw."

"She won the student contest back at U of I," Howard said.

"Joyce, the usual?" Norm said.

"Thank you." I accepted a glass of sherry.

"OK, everyone all set? Sure I can't tempt you, Nick?"

Nick shook his head.

"Then I'm ready for the tour I promised you." Norm led the Swanders up the creaking servants' stairway.

I rolled my eyes at Howard, and he smiled at me. The Neihuses and the Warrens arrived then, and Jeanette brought out what she called "the nibbles."

Perhaps every dinner party is an experiment worthy of a lab report. Think of the variables: the guests (both known and unknown), the weather and season, world events and the way they impinge on the moods of those gathered. All have potential to alter the evening. Perhaps we all hoped the Swanders' presence at the long walnut table would affect some kind of change, if only new topics to discuss, new stories to hear and retell to others not invited this time. But the Swanders were quiet, listening, it appeared, but only speaking when directly addressed—about their house, Nick's painting, their travels. It turned out that Tory was a painter, too.

The talk was mostly of college politics, the appointment of a new vice president for academics. The wives listened, their hands in their laps. When Jeanette began to clear the salad plates, Anne and I leapt up to help.

"Delicious," we murmured to Jeanette. "Can I get the recipe from you?"

Later the talk turned to the school board, to funding for a playground in the park that had once been the train depot, a particularly strict teacher at the middle school. The wives were animated now, gesturing with their hands, the candlelight glinting off their wedding rings.

"We absolutely must have that playground," Anne said.

I twisted the thick linen napkin in my lap. I was waiting, but for what? From across the table, I noticed Nick looking at me, his mouth in a crooked, ironic smile. I flushed and looked away. And then, from the other end of the table, I heard Tory say, "No, Nick and I don't want children."

I never thought that what I perceived as my lack might make me attractive or appealing, but it did to Nick and Tory. "They're always talking about little Susie or Billie," Tory said. "It's all apron strings or bib strings with them," Nick said.

"That sounds like a country-western song," I offered from the back of their Rambler. We were driving to some land near Conesus Lake that Nick wanted to paint. I should've defended the other wives, or at least pointed out how they'd been groomed for this role, taught to believe (as I had) that there was no greater calling. But when Nick and Tory laughed, I joined them.

We'd been taking outings like this one for several weeks, ever since the Larsons' dinner party. Today our destination was a spot across the winding road from the lake. We parked and crossed into the high weeds and grasses—thistles and yellow puffs of ragweed, and something viney with thorns that caught on my shirt. The sun was warm on my back as we started out, but as we walked the wind picked up, hurling the clouds over the sun.

"This is interesting light," Tory said. "So dramatic, don't you think?"

It was striking, both dark and bright by turns.

"I think I felt a rain drop," Nick said.

As I looked up, I saw lightning.

By the time we made it back down the hill, we were soaked. The heater in the Rambler blew only tepid air on us. The rain was coming down so loudly we couldn't hear each other speak. Nick drove straight to their house, which I'd never seen before. We ran in, covering our heads with our arms. Inside, Tory made tea. Nick brought me a sweater to replace my wet clothes. "We don't have any pants small enough for you," he said, "but if you take those off, I'll hang them by the heater to dry. Here's a blanket."

I expected him to leave, but he stood there, waiting for my jeans. My childlessness may have set me apart from the others, but I wasn't certain about my status; I wasn't about to let my modesty diminish me in Nick's eyes.

"Lovely," he said, when I was standing there in only his scratchy wool sweater. "I'd like to paint you."

"Me too," Tory said. On a lacquered tray, she had a teapot and three cups without handles. She was wearing a peacock blue robe and wool socks. She smiled at me and at Nick and set the tray down by the couch. "Nick, what do you think about a fire?" Tory said. "The logs under the awning should be dry."

"Wonderful," he said.

Nick's sweater smelled peppery, which is what he smelled of, I realized. Outside their windows the rain didn't let up.

"It looks like it's never going to end," I said, but I didn't really mind. I didn't think of the pot roast I'd planned to make or of the whites I had soaking in bleach or even Howard who, if he came home, would be relieved to have more time to work. All of that felt very far away, as if from another life. Tory's tea smelled of cloves and cinnamon, and it tasted delicious. Wrapped in the quilt, with Tory curled next to me and the fire blazing, I was utterly content. Nick had taken his tea and gone off to his studio. I could hear him opening and shutting cupboards.

We talked, that day, about the things women talk about when

they are alone together, when they have come to see that they share a way of looking at the world that is both critical and amused. Tory hadn't asked me about my drawing again since the first night we spoke of it, as if understanding I would make light of it too. Instead I told Tory how I'd met Howard, making it seem as if our courtship raised eyebrows, but really there had been nothing improper about it; Harold had waited until he turned in the final grades before asking me to dinner.

"How did you meet Nick?" I asked.

"Art school," Tory said. "A story not so unlike your own, only in this case I was the teacher."

"Oh," I said. And then because I didn't know what else to say: "But you don't teach now."

"No, and I don't miss it at all. Nick is really better at it than I was, more of a performer that way."

"You have more time for your painting, too, I suppose."

"Yes," Tory said, drawing her blanket tighter around us both.

Once walking past the dorms at Geneseo, I'd felt a sharp kick of nostalgia for my old dorm: the blue bolster bed, the radiators that clicked and groaned, the peeling paint on the shower room ceiling. But it wasn't those things that I yearned for really; it was the sense I'd had then that I was on my way somewhere. I missed that anticipation and striving. Now in Tory and Nick's living room, covered in their clothes and blankets, I was aware that I was feeling again that anticipation, and if not a striving exactly, then an adventurousness, something bucking, rearing up inside me.

At what point did it seem perfectly natural to take Tory's hair—her glorious hair!—in my hands, to smooth it as if she were a beloved child? And when did Nick join us, guiding us down to the blankets he'd placed before the fireplace? I could blame the long hike or my sleepiness, the sedative quality of the tea, even my vanity which had been polished by the prospect of being painted. But what I felt at the time was that all the pieces of me were gathered together, snapped into place.

I began coming to Nick and Tory's as soon as my housework was done—and I was finding it possible to do less of it with no objections from Howard, who had never cared much about the gleaming furniture, the spotless kitchen. Or Tory and Nick would come get me in the Rambler and we'd drive into the small neighboring towns and villages, and out into the wide-open countryside, which reminded me in a comforting way of Illinois. We'd stop sometimes in impossibly cheesy highway hotels—the Ho-hum Resort, the Last Stop—the tiny cabins a reproach we acknowledged with laughter. Other days we were chaste, our drives taking us to Rochester to the galleries there or the bookstores. On days when Nick taught, Tory painted, and so I stayed away, prepared Howard's favorite meals, listened as he talked of his work and didn't complain when he went back to campus for a review session or to continue his work in his lab.

"That Swander sure has a following," he said one night.

"The students like him?" I was afraid my voice would betray me.

"They seem to—I have yet to see him alone," Howard said.

"How's your lab assistant?" I asked, standing to clear the plates. I needed to move, to put things in order.

"Fine." Howard looked at me over his coffee cup. "Why do you ask?"

"Weren't you concerned with his methods?"

"That was last semester, Joyce."

"Sorry," I said. "Shall we take a walk?" It had snowed while we ate, and a thick dusting of snow now covered the ground. More was falling—fat, lazy flakes, and I wanted the chill against my face. I didn't expect Howard to agree to join me, but he did.

Outside, he took my gloved hand and we walked down our street, the parallel indentations our steps made quickly filling with fresh snow. It was beautiful and calm—almost dizzyingly so. In the far-off distance I could hear the purr of snowplows moving along the curves of Route 5.

We turned onto Oak Street, started down the hill to campus. We passed the houses of Howard's colleagues, the snow blanketing their gardens and roofs and walkways. It was too early for Christmas lights, but in the next few weeks ladders would be dragged out of garages and sheds so they could be hung. Lights were on inside the houses and we could see families at their tables. In the morning the children would build snowmen and snow forts; they'd lie down in the snow and flap their arms and legs to make snow angels, while their mothers watched from inside. It didn't pain me to think of this, I realized. I thought about mentioning this to Howard, but how would I explain this freedom from my old yearning?

Instead, I scooped up a ball of snow and threw it at the lamp-post, a yard away. Howard smiled at me as it missed, bent and made his own.

"Like this," he said, throwing. His snowball hit the post and burst.

I tried again and my snowball hit just below his.

"That's my girl," he said.

We were turning onto Second Street when I saw the Rambler inching toward us. It slid, veered toward the sidewalk and then straightened.

"Not a good night for driving," Howard said.

I realized he didn't recognize the car as Nick and Tory's. It passed us, the windows frosted, so neither driver nor passenger was plainly visible.

"I've been thinking we should get a dog," Howard said.

I watched the Rambler take the hill, slipping only a little before disappearing over it.

"Jack's springer just had a litter. What do you think?"

"But you don't like dogs."

"I thought you might like a pup," Howard said, "for company."

"I don't know," I said, "All that mess to clean up." But what I was thinking was, *too much time, time I could spend elsewhere.*

"Just wondering," Howard said.

"Thanks." I felt woozy with guilt, and had to lean against the lamppost for a moment.

When Howard and I returned from the Midwest after the holidays, I resumed my trysts with Nick and Tory, regaling them with our droll adventures in the heartland. All that winter we talked by their fireplace, curled together in their bed, the curtains drawn against the sunny cold. Or we sipped tea in those handleless cups bought, I learned, in San Francisco's Chinatown. After Nick purchased a space heater for the studio, I modeled for him or for Tory or both. Sometimes I watched as they drew each other, while I curled in the loveseat, naked under the thick blanket.

It has been my experience both before and after my time with Nick and Tory, that people become someone different during sex—shyer or bolder, retreating to someplace faraway, shutting their eyes, their sounds private and foreign. But with Tory and Nick, it wasn't like this. Nick might stop moving above me to make a crack about the college president or Tory, practically asleep in my arms, smelling of me and of Nick and her own clove smell, would mention a position she wanted to paint me in, or her craving for mango chutney. Did I mention that we laughed and laughed? We did, it's true, though I can no longer recall about what.

Perhaps when I wasn't with them, it was different, though at the time I didn't like to think about it. I didn't understand the way a couple might need a third person, not so much for sexual variety, but for the audience she would provide, a flattering and receptive one; one that would remind them of their talent and desirability, their well-suitedness for each other.


I was surprised when Tory called me on a Wednesday morning in early March, since this was a time she usually painted.

"Can I come get you?" she asked. "I need to talk."

As I was waiting for her outside, Ann waved and poked her head out her front door. "What have you been up to, Stranger?" she asked.

"Let's talk soon," I said. "Here's my ride." I waved to Ann as Tory pulled in.

"Can you please drive?" Tory said. "All this open countryside unnerves me." She looked pale in her dark coat.

"Sure, where are we going?"

"Anywhere," she said. "Let's just go."

We left town, passed the horse farms and the cornfields, where a few brownish stalks swayed in the wind.

"What is it?" I asked.

"It's really awful, Joyce," she said, raking her hair back with her fingers.

"What?"

"I'm pregnant—and already sick as a dog. Do you have to drive so fast?"

"Pregnant?" I braked, and grit and gravel pinged the underside of the car.

"Yes, pregnant of all things."

"What does Nick think?"

"Oh, Nick!" she said. "He's a child himself."

I'd never heard her complain about Nick before, but then he'd always been with us or close by.

"At first he talked about the lack of paintings of pregnant women. He's considering a series, but I can already feel he's losing interest."

"In painting?"

"No. Never that."

We were nearing Mt. Morris. "Which way?" I said.

"Keep going." She gestured ahead. "Listen, Joyce, you should know, Nick's been seeing a student."

I shouldn't have been surprised, but the information made me slam on the brakes and pull over onto the gravely side of the road. I put my head down on the steering wheel.

"I know," Tory said, "I know." And then: "I'll need your help."

As she spoke she grew calm. She was so sure of the plan that I was convinced everything would be OK, that things would continue as before. In the days before we left for Canada, while Tory found a doctor willing to perform the procedure and made hotel reservations, I began to notice how hard she worked tending to Nick. There were always delicious smells emanating from the kitchen—soups and stews made with exotic spices—even though Tory was too nauseated to eat them herself. She answered all the phone calls, preserved his quiet while he painted, never spoke of her own work when he was struggling. And how had I never noticed the dark side of Nick's humor? The way it wove together cruelty and wit with a grim determination? These observations registered only briefly at the time. Later, though, they would come back to me and I would see how sad they were, how desperately sad.

I'd told Howard that I was going with Tory to an opening in Toronto and he accepted this without question. The day I left, he slipped a folded fifty-dollar bill into my coat pocket. Of the drive to Toronto, I remember little except that we listened to the radio when we could pick up a station; otherwise we were quiet. Perhaps there was still snow in the fields on either side of the road. Likely it was cold and gray as it often is that time of year.

In Toronto, I dropped off Tory at the doctor's, watched her pass through the foyer and out of my sight. The doctor's office was adjacent to his house, but he was a legitimate doctor with a sign out front. Later, Tory told me the waiting room had the same awful chairs all doctors' waiting rooms have, the same thumbed-through magazines.

After leaving Tory at the doctor, I was to go to our hotel room to wait for her call. She insisted that she wanted to do this alone. I was trying not to think about the procedure Tory was enduring, the possibilities it blotted out, and I thought walking might help me. I parked the car around the block.

The neighborhood had seen grander days, but it had a shabby cleanliness as if the residents were trying hard with what they had. The streets were swept clean of debris. Faded awnings jutted out from storefronts—a dry-cleaner, an Italian bakery, a grocery store with canned goods stacked to its high tin ceiling. The sidewalks were crowded with people—women in saris with red dots on their smooth foreheads, bearded old men in black except for the fringe of their prayer shawls, Slavic-looking women in heels, sheer kerchiefs on their heads. The trees lining the street were beginning to bud and I could imagine them in a month, full of waxy, bright leaves, the branches forming a canopy over this street, a street where one could start anew as if the past were a country far away.

The college's records show that Nick resigned his position the following year, that Howard was tenured and promoted with full department approval, that he went on to become department chair for a record thirteen years. Naturally the records say nothing of Tory or how she packed up and went to California six months after her abortion. Nothing is mentioned of Nick's marriage to a student from Albany, though perhaps there is an angry letter from her father filed somewhere. In the years that followed, there were many such letters from parents dismayed by their children's long hair and clothing, their radical political views, their disrespect for authority.

There is nothing at all in the college records about the wife of Howard Markham, or the way she left him after filling their freezer with individually packed meals, and cleaning their house from top to bottom. Nor is there any mention that on the day she left Geneseo for good, the forsythia by her kitchen window was too bright to look at without crying. There is nothing—not a photograph or a painting or a letter—but her own memory, growing faulty with time, to prove that any of this ever happened.

The Geneseo garden club minutes list a Joyce Markham as absent all that spring and summer, before her duties were reassigned and her name disappears entirely.

# IN THE DOORWAY OF RHEE'S JAZZ JOINT

D. WINSTON BROWN

## 1

In walked Russell.

A man in the doorway of a bar—in the doorway of Rhee's Jazz Joint—is no longer a man, he is a piece of an atmosphere and its history, engulfed within a tiny, tight, brass and whiskey and wood universe of played and unplayed notes, existing both behind and ahead of time.

Rhee's was comfortable, and they knew his drink. That's what Russell Claypool liked most.

Letohatchee Davenport took down a glass from behind the bar. She dropped in a couple of ice cubes, poured in some Scotch, and set the drink on the counter.

"L.C. been in?" Russell picked up the glass of Johnny Walker Red from the counter.

"I haven't seen him," she said.

"What about Dillard or Lester?"

"No, Russell." Letohatchee waved her hand. "Look around. There's only two people here. And no, none of them are here, not Dillard Cleckler, not sorry-ass Lester Sheets, not L.C. Scooba, and not Maxine Kirk."

They stared at each other. Russell watched closely the face he had seen for most of his fifty-six years. Letohatchee and Russell had long since established their eternal feud which dated back to when Letohatchee had first moved to Birmingham with her grandparents when she was six. Russell still wore a scar on his left cheek bone where Letohatchee cut him with the top of a can of Pet Milk because he told her that children whose parents die can't have children.

Letohatchee owned Rhee's. Close to twenty years ago she had won it playing poker from a hustler named Reese Alexander, who had hustled it from Lester Sheets shooting craps behind the dumpster in the alley. When Lester wouldn't take it back because he felt too dumb for losing it, Russell convinced Letohatchee to hire someone to run it for her. For the last two years, since retiring from her day job, Letohatchee ran Rhee's herself with a firm smile that made it a sin not to order less than three drinks. In that year, there had only been two shootings at Rhee's, one inside—people had stepped over the corpse on their way out—and one outside. Last night.

Russell and his friends had been gathering there most Mondays, Wednesdays, and Saturdays since before Letohatchee owned it.

"You holding back, ain't you." Russell held his glass up between them.

"You'll be here all night," Letohatchee said.

Russell sipped from the glass while he looked around the room. He didn't know the few people in there. His watch read six. They were late, he thought. He and his friends usually gathered there around five-thirty.

"Lettie, you think they heard?" Russell said, turning back to the bar.

"Of course they heard," she said. She kept cutting limes.

"Maybe they didn't," Russell said. "They would have been here. They wouldn't have been late, not if they'd heard."

"They'll be here, Russ." Letohatchee freshened his drink. "What'cha want to hear?"

"You know that boy's blood still on the ground?"

"Maybe I'll play one of the young cats," Letohatchee said. "How about some Joshua Redman?"

"Children," Russell said, "little children walking right through it, like it's not even there."

"Better yet, I think I'll play some Cannonball."

"And they're stepping right under the police tape like it's a game."

"Or maybe Mingus." Letohatchee had turned to the stereo.

"I bet people don't even know his name. I had to think twice myself, and I've known the boy all my life. It hadn't even been twenty-four hours, and I bet they already forgot his name."

"I got it," Letohatchee said. "We need some blues. That's what we need to hear. Some good ol' slap yo' daddy down-home stanky blues. How about—"

"You remember his name, Lettie? What was that boy's name?"

"Zakie Salem." Letohatchee turned back to Russell, the bar between them. "Zakie Salem. And it's still *that boy's* name. He's not dead, Russell. He's not dead, so quit speaking about him in the past tense. You act like only you know the boy. He's been coming in and out of here with those petitions and making speeches and asking for votes for years. Now have a drink and listen to some Howlin' Wolf while I finish getting ready for tonight. You know when Arthur Salem plays we get some young people in here."

"I just wanted to know if you remembered what his name was—is." Russell leaned over the bar on his elbows. He wanted to ask why the boy's father was still playing tonight, his boy being shot and all last night. "Can I have a little more Scotch," he said instead, and then, as if he were a child begging for more, "pleeeese."

## 2

In walked L.C.

L.C. Scooba had deadstill eyes set deep in a face controlled by carved cracks that ran along his cheeks and splayed outward from the corners of his eyes, the severity of which resembled—in his leathered face—a weathered and crumbling tombstone full of sharp fissures. He drank only beer. Miller Lite.

"Over here, L.C." Russell had staked out their table. Rhee's was box-shaped, and Russell and his friends always sat at a table against the wall nearest the bar, so they could watch people from a distance, and as they came in the door.

L.C. grabbed the chilled glass of Miller Lite, then sat down with Russell. Both of them angled where they could see the entire room. Howlin' Wolf seeped down out of the speakers mounted in the ceiling's corners.

"You late," Russell said.

"Last I heard, you ain't give birth to none of my children." L.C. peered over a pair of black half-frames.

"You hear about Zakie Salem?" Russell asked.

"Two bullet wounds. One in the thigh, went straight through, and one in the abdomen. Lost a lot of blood, but he'll be alright."

"I can't believe I forgot your wife's a nurse," Russell said. "I must be losing my mind."

L.C. looked at the door.

So did Russell. A tall young man with a woman in a red business suit entered. Her skirt was short, halfway up her thigh. She's young, Russell said to himself. He watched the couple sit next to the spherical stage at the other end of the room.

"When was the last time you saw that boy?" Russell turned back to L.C.

"Don't know. But he's been calling me at my office for weeks," L.C. answered.

"What did he want?"

"Money, I suppose," L.C. said. "I hear he's trying to run for city council again."

"He's been calling me too," Russell said, "to come talk about Dynamite Hill to those kids he teaches. What he needs to do is teach them how to talk so when they go to college on a sports scholarship, they won't sound stupid on the interviews, embarrassing everybody." Russell removed the stirrer from his drink. "I remember when that boy was still a little boy, around ten or so. Now *he* was bad. One day that little Zakie ran right into my car. I was on my way to work and that boy runs slap into the passenger door on that blue Ford I used to have. I was at that red light by the school's run-down basketball court when I see a bag come flying over the fence and little Zakie right behind. He still knee-high to a grasshopper. He picks up that bag and runs straight at my car, but looking back the whole time to make sure no one's following him. Then *bam*. He thumps right into the door. I know he's cutting class, but I ask where he's rushing off to, anyway. He looks square into my eyes, just like Rev. Hazzard does sometimes, looks square at me, and says, 'I'm going home, Mr. Claypool, to turn my roast or it'll burn.' All I could do was laugh. That afternoon—I couldn't turn him in after hearing his little excuse—I wound up telling him about Dynamite Hill, about how white folks bombed all those houses around Center Street." Russell fingered the sweat on his glass. "You know, I haven't talked about it since."

Russell finished his drink.

"Yeah, I remember all that bombing crap too," L.C. said. Then, "You talk to his daddy yet?"

## 3

In walked Dillard.

Dillard Cleckler, III, co-owner of Dillard's Soul Food Emporium, I and II, always seemed to enjoy crowds, even small ones like what was gathering slowly in Rhee's. Talking to people, whether they listened or not. About anything, though his most consistent topic was food. Dillard was a thin man with thin arms usually engaged in some sort of odd gesticulation, as if not having food in front of him to prepare left him in a quandary about what to do with his arms. It seemed he could seldom decide.

"L.C.," Dillard said, approaching the table, "Russell. What are you guys drinking?" He waved his hand at Letohatchee until she came to the table. "Give my friends here another whatever, Lettie." He passed his hand at the glasses on the table. "Give me a Hennessy, please."

"Where's Maxi?" Russell knew Maxine wouldn't be too far from her husband. She managed the Emporium II, and Dillard's drinking. Russell had known Maxine since high school when their parents had set them up on their only date, which amounted to rolling around in an old Plymouth Satellite while drinking three entire fifths of Thunderbird with grape Kool-Aid mixed in. She was the only one who hadn't thrown up that night.

"She's closing up Soul Food Emporium II." With each syllable Dillard swung his arms like an orchestra conductor. He had become prone to do the sweeping movements since going to the symphony last month. His arms would swing like sleeved broomsticks. "Is that Lil' Dime over there? That fool owes me money."

Russell watched Dillard swerve through the crowded chairs and tables.

L.C. rose also, going the other way, toward the back of the club where the restrooms were. He couldn't lick an ice cube without having to pee ten minutes later, Russell thought.

People had begun to fill the vacant chairs at the tables nearest the stage, and there were a few more people at the bar. But it was no longer Russell's crowd. His friends were either too busy dying, or staying at home praying to keep from dying. The older his friends got, the easier they seemed to find religion. This crowd was young. Rhee's had become a young joint on certain nights, especially when Arthur Salem's quartet played; it would be full of the kind of men— what they used to call *clean* or say were *sharp as a mosquito's peter* kind of men—that Russell could recall being at a previous time in his life, and there would be the kind of women that Russell could remem-

ber saying were *fine as cat hair*, the kind that could get his whole
check on payday, the kind he would fall in love with every Friday
night.

But it was the absence that moved through him like the slow
trickle of ice melting, a drip then another, cooling his lungs, cooling
his breath. The absence of that boy's clipboard stacked with petitions for better trash pick-up, better school lunch programs, better
policing; it seemed Zakie Salem never set foot to ground without his
clipboard. Mr. Claypool, he would say, I know you ain't down with
Islam, but this is for the neighborhood. I'm workin' with those brothers 'cause they doin' somethin' good. And Russell would say, Boy,
ain't nothing I hate more than youthful arrogance. You don't know
about this neighborhood's needs. I could tell you stories, boy. Then
Zakie would say, I know, like the one about Dynamite Hill. That's
what I want you to do, tell them. Then Russell would say, weary and
ready to end the conversation, Ain't nothing left to say Zakie. It's a
different time now. Then Zakie would be at another table, talking to
other people, but still glancing back at Russell. Sometimes, he'd stop
back by before he left.

In walked Maxine,
straight to the bar. A word with Letohatchee. A shot of whiskey. A Vodka Cranberry. She surveyed the people. Maxine Kirk—
she had refused to be called Cleckler despite marrying Dillard—had
the kind of face that could control her feelings no matter the intensity. She walked with her shoulders high and her chin higher. Her
body was fleshy in a way that Russell liked to call *down-home*.

"How you doing, Maxi?" Russell stood when she reached the
table.

"Zakie Salem's father was in my place tonight," she said.

"Arthur?" Russell said. "How is he?"

"He was soppin' up mashed potatoes and gravy like he had a
tapeworm," she said in an exaggerated tone, then, "How do you
think he's doing? The man's son was just shot. Jesus Christ. How is

he doing," she repeated sarcastically. "What kind of question is that? How is he *supposed* to be doing a day after his son gets shot? The man's son stomach splayed out like a bucket of chitlins, and he's too stupid, scared, or stubborn to set foot in a hospital, and you ask how the man—"

"Cool down, Maxi," Russell said. "Just cool down."

Duke Ellington's big band played low from the speakers. The quiet chatter of conversation had risen, spread throughout the club. Three guys were halfheartedly setting up instruments on the stage.

"I know the man is hurting. I feel for him," Russell said. "I just wondered how he was coping. That's all."

"He asked about you, Russ."

"Me? Why?"

"Don't know," Maxine said.

"You didn't ask?"

"What'd I say, Russ. Jesus Christ." Maxine sipped the cranberry-colored drink. "Just cool down," she said. "Cool down." She said down like dowwwwwwwwn.

Russell popped a piece of peppermint into his mouth, scanned the people.

"Did you ever help him out?" Russell asked.

"Help who?" said Maxine.

"Zakie," Russell said. "With any of the thousand projects he's always working on."

"Now, Russell," Maxine said, "you know I don't support those Muslim niggers. If they can't eat my pork ribs, I damn sure ain't eating no damn bean pies. Besides, Dillard and I give money every month to the church."

"You haven't been to church since King was shot," Russell said.

"You only go on communion Sunday to get free wine," Maxine said.

Russell paused, then said, "You know they only serve that sorry grape juice now. I got Welch's at home. But at least I go, sometimes."

## 4

In walked Kufere,

barreling straight toward the bar, a hovering shaved head on a thick neck spearing through the people crowded near the door. He was tall. He was taller than Zakie, his older brother. Kufere Salem's name was the only surviving evidence of his parents' involvement in the sixties Civil Rights struggle and the Black Power Movement. That and a picture of him when he was seven with an afro that could soak up the Atlantic doing his best black-gloved impersonation of Tommy Smith at the '68 Olympics in Mexico City.

Russell could tell he was upset. Even as a kid, Kufere had never been able to keep his emotions below his face. He must be close to twenty-five or thirty, Russell thought. Kufere bent his mass across the bar to talk to Letohatchee, who nodded her head from side to side, shrugged her shoulders, nodded her head again, then turned toward Russell's table. Kufere turned also.

"Isn't that one of those Salem boys," L.C. said

Russell hadn't noticed L.C. return. Maxine craned her neck to see behind her.

"That's the youngest one," Maxine said. "Koofoo, or kookoofer, something like that. He comes in the Emporium sometimes. Gets nothing but vegetables."

During the time it took Kufere to walk the thirty or so feet to their table, Russell fought with himself, the way he had when he first heard Kufere's brother had been shot.

Though sitting, Russell felt he was eye to eye, eye to eye with Kufere *but he saw Zakie*, even though the two brothers only somewhat favored each other. The wide chin, the naked eyes, those were the same. But it was last Thursday, again, and Zakie was speaking. Russell saying yes to make the boy shut up, yes, he'll meet him Friday night even though he won't and he knows it because he's playing poker with some Masons out in Bessemer. That boy is pushy and Russell doesn't like to be pushed anymore; he likes to exist in the simplicity of watching the young people in Rhee's, their half-smiles and crossed thighs still naturally tight, watching smoke blown up and out the corners of dark lips, and the Johnny Walker Red Letohatchee knows to put on the bar when he enters; he likes to listen to Arthur Salem's weekend sax make a young couple sometimes lean in close over their drinks, or cheek to cheek bellyrub a little bit on the dance floor. But not to talk of the distance he came through to enjoy those things, the distance he survived. Zakie was saying other things now, almost forgotten things, and Russell was thinking things now; Zakie said them now the same way he'd said them then, last Thursday, when Russell said yes though he felt, he knew, that *no*, was the only answer. He could hear Zakie speaking from a murky distance as he watched the tight set of Kufere's approaching jaw.

"How's your brother doing?" Maxine asked when Kufere was next to her.

"Ms. Kirk." He said this without looking away from Russell's stare. Then, "Where were you, Mr. Claypool? Were you drunk? Were you trying to fuck some woman half your age?"

"Look here, boy," Russell said. "I was—"

"No. *You* look here. And listen close. I don't like you, and I don't care about all this crap you supposedly went through in the sixties." He leaned onto the table. "All my brother wanted to do was talk to you. He waited outside this damn club until one in the morning. Three hours he waited on you. You're no better than the white folks that screwed up your mind. At least they used to give Zakie donations when he was willing to go over the mountain begging. All you do is sit in this bar and drink. I can't remember a time when I *didn't* think you were a drunk. That's all I remember about you." His voice was competing now with the music and the chatter.

"That was the hospital calling." Letohatchee was standing behind Kufere, a hand on his shoulder. "Your sister says you better get back to the hospital. Zakie's condition is worse."

Kufere didn't move, but Russell could see the minute changes in his face. Worry worked between the web of redness into the granite eyes. Russell had nothing to say to the boy. While Kufere had spoken, Russell had gathered words for the boy, but now, they were like grains of salt dissolving on his tongue. He watched Kufere straighten. In the moment before Kufere turned to leave, Russell thought he saw in Kufere's face something alongside the anger and worry. Disappointment. Kind of an instinctual disappointment, Russell thought, like when he sometimes got upset something had changed, even though he couldn't remember what life had been like before. There was a sudden lightness in Russell's stomach, a quick sting of weakness in his knees, as if he were being urged to some act.

"I tell you one thing." Dillard plopped down into the empty seat. "That koofoon boy is right about one thing. White folks. That boy's brother got shot because white folk don't like black folk that won't pray to *their* God. You know that Koofoofoon, or whatever his name is, don't believe in God. He believes in Allah. What kind of shit is that. Allah."

"That's his brother that hangs with the Muslims," L.C. said. "That was Kufere in here. He's the one that played football at Auburn."

Dillard glanced toward the door as if Kufere were still there.

"I know that boy, too," Dillard said. "He got run away from Auburn for screwing some pink toes. See, it's just like I was saying before. White folk. They'll let a nigger come pull a plow, but when he starts getting too many pieces of white p—"

"Jesus Christ, Dillard. Don't you ever shut up?" Maxine said. She asked Letohatchee for another drink.

"Sure," Letohatchee said, "I'll put it on Russell's tab. And by the way, I made that up about the hospital calling. I didn't want that boy to bust up my bar in the process of busting up Russell's head."

Dillard looked around for a couple of seconds, then, "You know those Muslims want their own city. They want Africa."

"It's people like you, Dillard," L.C. said, "stupid people like

[61]

you that call Africa a city that made someone have to create *Sesame Street*. I think you got your mama's ignorance. Your mama so dumb, she thought a quarterback was a refund."

"Yo' mama so stupid, when it came time to name you she couldn't remember more than two letters at a time, so she just gave you them two initials. She couldn't even think of a name for you. Just LC. Here's a dollar, go buy yourself a vowel so you can turn those initials into a name." Dillard glared at L.C. "Anyway, I know Africa's not a city. I meant they'll name it Africa. Can you imagine living in Africa, South Dakota? White folk would freak." Dillard leaned forward, laughing.

"You two are too old to be playing silly games," Maxine said.

"You know what," L.C. said, "children these days are crazy. I never would have done anything like Kuferee did tonight. Not at twenty, thirty, forty, or fifty, not ever. And you can't say anything to them. They don't listen to anything." He finished his Miller Lite. "I think that's because they don't know *anything* and think they know *everything*. Dillard's right about one thing. They spend so much time learning how to kiss white folk's ass they don't learn how to treat grown folk with respect. I could tell them a few things about this world."

Russell knew his friends were trying hard to make him forget about Kufere, but the glacial trickle was still making him shiver inside. His legs stiffened. He needed to stretch them. "I'm going to the bar," he said. "Anybody need anything?" He felt heavy when he stood, like someone large was riding piggyback on him. Dillard placed an order for another Hennessy. Maxine rolled her eyes at her husband. L.C. said bring him another Miller Lite while he went to the bathroom. Then Maxine started humming along with the Thelonious Monk tune plinking smooth out of the speakers.

As Russell walked to the bar, he recognized the tune but couldn't remember the name. But Monk's piano Russell knew anywhere. The notes dropped odd around him, odd dropping odd and between the dropping the notes bent time like a minor chord mirage hovering in front of Russell, odd notes like the trinkle tinkle of dropping spoons into metal tins, or rainwater tap tap tapping ploptapping on corrugated tin roofs, bing bang, the trinkle and tinkle and plop and tap dropped odd like odd wasn't odd. Not odd at all.

Like an uglybeauty.

I'm having an epistrophy, Russell said to himself, and smirked, half-heartedly.

## 5

In walked Arthur.

Arthur Henry Salem wore a stress on his face that made it look like he was reading intensely at all times, even when there was no book in front of his searching eyes. When he laid his hands on the bar, his fingers stretched long and sleek like thin hazelnut-colored skis, but with thick knots at the knuckles. A thin man, Arthur Salem had about as much presence in his clothes as driftwood buried in shallow sand. But Russell knew without looking who was standing next to him.

"What'cha need, Art?" Letohatchee said.

"Bourbon and water."

"What kind of bourbon you working on tonight?"

"Basil Hayden," Arthur Salem said, "and forget about the water. Just ice. One cube."

Russell waited until after Arthur Salem sipped his bourbon.

"Arthur, your boy was in here earlier, looking for you," Russell said.

"I know," Arthur Salem said. "He wants me to go to the hospital, but I don't go in them places anymore. Haven't been in one since sixty-nine when those crackers strung my brother to that tree out in Leeds and chopped his dick off."

The story was familiar to Russell, and avoidable. At least talking about it was avoidable. It was hard to control what swam through his mind while sleep, the distorted images of corpses and bodies beaten up, sometimes beyond recognition. Violence was what he dreamed, what he once lived in the shadow of, but no longer discussed. To talk about it was to make it real, and Russell refused.

"I don't guess you're playing tonight?" Russell said, even though he had already noticed Arthur Salem's saxophone, which Arthur never let get more than an arm's length away, was not with him.

"My own boy is in the hospital and all I do is call to check on him."

"You know he was supposed to meet me here last night?" Russell said.

"I was here last night," Arthur Salem said, "I heard the two shots." He sipped his bourbon, let its warmth settle in his mouth before he swallowed. "I just thought it was another nigger dead. Just another nigger shot dead. One less nigger to try and steal my horn when I'm leaving a club late."

"I didn't show up here last night," Russell said. "I knew I wouldn't."

"You know he doesn't like being in here when I'm playing. My own son. I've tried to teach him about jazz, but he won't listen. Always talking about Islam. Allah." Arthur turned to Russell. "He don't understand, Russell."

The thought had been there. On Russell's tongue. *We don't understand,* three words sitting like three grains of salt on his tongue, the words dissolving into the moistness of his tongue and mouth, unspoken. Russell had felt them there while Arthur Salem had talked, and when the feeling left, Arthur Salem had told Russell that Zakie shouldn't have been waiting outside in the first place, that Zakie was the one to blame, that Russell had always been like an uncle to both Zakie and Kufere, that Russell had done all that could be expected.

Russell, watching his friend speak, probed his eyes for what never appeared. Belief.

Arthur Salem finished his drink then drifted out through the chattering people until he reached the doorway. Russell watched him crack the door and stop. Arthur looked back for a second into

Rhee's. Through the sliver of an opening a blade of pale light sliced softly across Arthur Salem's face so that an eye and below was the pale lifeless color of the lamp on the wall outside the door; the other half of his face was still in the dim and warm light of the bar. Then he left, and when the door shut, it cut off the outer glow seeping in. Russell thought of a vault door lumbering to closed, but he heard no deep thud of closure, no heavy thud of closure.

The song changed.

Another Monk tune.

In his chest, as he breathed in then out, Russell could still feel the cold trickle crawl slow along his lungs, small icy rivulets that made him shiver under his skin as if he were breathing deeply the frigid air in a closed freezer; then the shiver stopped—it just stopped —and he sensed as if he, Russell Claypool, had just walked in.

# RAMONE

JUDY TROY

At the beginning of August, a week after my fourteenth birthday, my stepfather, McKinley, my mother, and I left Houston for Ramone, Texas. McKinley's dying father was our reason for going. He was eighty-three years old and sick with lung cancer and had only a few months left to live, and McKinley wanted us to care for him. He said that he and my mother could get jobs in Lubbock.

We left on a humid Friday morning before the sun came up. In the pale sky we could see Venus and a half moon. McKinley turned on the inside light to show me how Texas took up five pages in the road atlas. "We're driving six hundred miles without crossing a state line, Roberta," he said.

I was in the back seat, and my mother was driving. She was afraid that McKinley, talking about his father, or his sister, who also lived in Ramone, would start to cry. He hadn't been home in nine years—he'd been in the Army, and had married the wrong person before he married my mother—and he was an emotional person, just as my real father had been. My father, who my mother never talked about except sometimes after church, had died of a heart attack five years before.

The sun came up, and as we left refineries and oil wells behind we came upon empty flat fields, nowhere towns, and more historical markers than probably exist in any normal-sized state.

"Let's stop," McKinley said, each time we passed one. My mother stopped twice; each time, the marker was for a man who'd come from Alabama and tried to grow cotton.

"Isn't this interesting?" McKinley said to us.

"To be truthful, no," my mother said.

"I'd rather just get there," I said. "The sooner you start a new life the sooner it becomes an old life."

"What's your hurry to make it old?" McKinley asked.

"I don't know," I said. But I felt my heart speed up, which told me that the answer had to do with being afraid. My father had told me once that I was hooked up inside to a kind of lie detector.

"I like the travelling part," my mother said. "I'd just as soon never get anywhere."

"That's weird," I said.

"It's not," my mother said.

"You two argue because you're so much alike," McKinley told us.

It took us all day to get there, even though we'd left so early—loading the car and U-Haul the night before, in darkness, because my mother was worried that we'd be robbed by somebody watching. The only person I saw was Roy Lee Hollis, standing under a stairway at our apartment complex, trying to apologize. He was my best friend—the only person I'd bothered to tell I would miss—and he had refused to kiss me. He proved for me something that my mother had always said—that it was foolish to like a boy more than he liked you. But it made moving away easier. I'd be in a tiny town in West Texas with a dying person I'd never met, but at least I would never again have to see Roy Lee Hollis.

I didn't expect him to show up at the last minute. I hardly let him speak. I walked away—in the stiff-legged way I'd seen high-heeled women in soap operas do—just as McKinley came down the stairs with a suitcase. "Why wouldn't you say goodbye to that boy?" he asked me later.

That question and Roy Lee's sad expression were on my mind as we drove into Ramone. The sky was darkening over a one-block street of one-story buildings. At the end of the block the pavement ended and the street became dirt. That's where our neighborhood began.

McKinley drove past three shabby houses, raising behind us a storm of dust, then stopped in front of a two-story, caved-in, paint-peeling dump.

"Jesus Christ," he said. He didn't move to get out. My mother put her hand over her mouth.

The door opened, and an ancient, smaller, yellow version of McKinley stepped onto the broken porch. He slowly lifted one hand in a wave.

"I guess that's Grandpa," I said.

My mother laughed.

"That's not funny," McKinley said to us.

McKinley's father had emphysema and liver disease in addition to cancer; he'd been sent home from the hospital to die.

"At least they came straight out and told him," my mother said later that night. "At least they didn't sugarcoat it."

"You wouldn't want any sympathy creeping in," McKinley said.

It was after ten. McKinley's father, Emerson, had gone to bed, and we'd investigated the house and the neighborhood and walked the short distance into town. We'd had dinner at Luigi's Lone Star Pizza, which was a convenience store and gas station as well as a restaurant. Now we were settled outside, in back, on the weedy lawn. We couldn't see each other in the hot darkness. Behind us in an empty field cicadas were buzzing. My mother and I were too depressed to talk, but for some reason, sick as Emerson was, McKinley had gotten happier being around his father. McKinley said he hoped his daddy would live long enough to see the house repaired.

"Repaired by who?" my mother said meanly. It was doubly mean, because both my mother and McKinley had been construction workers before they married. It was how they'd met.

"I know you're disappointed," he said, "but sniping at me won't make it better."

"What will, then?" she asked.

"Cheering up. Seeing the good things. Finding a little brightness in the dark corners."

My mother scratched her leg. "I'll tell you what's in this corner," she said. "Chiggers." She stood up and walked off toward the house. Overhead you couldn't see a single star.

"I think we'll end up liking it here," McKinley said.

I slept in a tiny room upstairs. McKinley and my mother were next door, in the double bed McKinley's father had been born in. Sometime in the night I heard McKinley cry out in his sleep.

"It's no wonder you're having a nightmare," I heard my mother say.

I fell back to sleep and dreamed that my father wasn't dead but only in a room that I couldn't find the door to. Then I dreamed that Roy Lee chose me as his partner in biology class but couldn't remember my name.

McKinley woke me at seven.

"Your Aunt Mavis Jean used to sleep in that bed," he told me. "Wait till you meet her."

"She's not my aunt," I said.

"I forget that," McKinley said. "It seems to me you've always been mine."

"I've never been yours," I told him.

"Don't you get tired of being so tough?" he asked me.

Then he disappeared. A moment later I heard him downstairs, saying to Emerson, "Just hold on to me, Pop. I won't let you go."

Across the narrow hall, in the bathroom, I could hear my mother trying to get clean water out of the bathtub faucet. I'd tried the night before.

"I think it's sewage," I shouted through the wall.

"Goddam shit," my mother said. It was such a shock to hear her say those words that I went in and looked at her sitting on the floor in McKinley's boxer shorts and undershirt.

"Why are you wearing that?" I asked.

"Why shouldn't I wear it?"

"Well, it's not exactly attractive."

"Pardon me," my mother said. "Let me get on a negligee."

"Don't do it for my sake. I'm not married to you."

"So those are the words you choose to start the day with," she said. "Fine."

We stared at each other stubbornly. As usual, I looked away first.

When my mother and I came downstairs, McKinley said, "Daddy was just asking about you two."

It was hard to tell if that was true. Emerson was partly deaf and looked confused. McKinley had fed him and got him into a lopsided chair on the broken porch. McKinley sat down next to him. I thought that the two of them, side by side, were like a before-and-after "Don't Smoke" advertisement.

"Hello," Emerson said.

"Hi," I said.

"Step out here into the yard," McKinley said.

My mother and I went to stand in the dandelion grass. Last night's clouds had blown off; the sky was bluer and wider than it had ever seemed in Houston. Wind was moving through the branches of the cottonwood trees and rippling the wheat field across the road.

"I told you it was pretty, didn't I?" McKinley said.

"Where did you get that thing on your head?" my mother asked. He was wearing a cowboy hat.

"Hello!" Emerson said again. He needed to shout.

"Hello!" I shouted back.

"I knew you two would have a lot to talk about!" McKinley said.

I was afraid he'd gone crazy. But he hadn't. He was just happy and sad at the same time.

A few minutes later, McKinley's sister, Mavis Jean, drove up with her husband in a boat-size Chevy. They were both large people. Mavis Jean was as tall as McKinley but not as skinny, and had reddish hair like his. She walked right over and hugged me; my mother moved herself out of range. Mavis Jean's husband was big and bald, and a tobacco chewer. I thought he might not know how to talk until I heard him say "Thank you" very quietly, in the dilapidated kitchen, when Mavis handed him a doughnut. She'd brought two boxes of them, plus a thermos of coffee. She'd brought orange juice for me.

"I have pictures of the both of you in my living room," she said, beaming down at my mother and me, where we stood side by side in front of the rusty refrigerator. "You're already family."

"Neither one of us takes a good picture," my mother said.

At the cluttered table, Mavis's husband and McKinley were writing up a list of tools and supplies they'd need to fix the house. After they left to get them, Mavis sat down with us and showed us Emerson's pills—which ones he needed to take when.

"He gets the pain pills whenever he wants them," she said. "Sometimes I give him one just when he looks real bad." Her eyes got wet, and she let tears run down her face. "I've seen Daddy almost every day for the past thirty years," she said. "It's like seeing the sun. You don't expect it to disappear."

My mother looked out the window. She tapped her nails on the table. "Is there a Presbyterian church around here?" she asked.

"The minister's already got your name," Mavis Jean said. "McKinley said you were religious."

"I don't like that word," my mother said. "I prefer 'churchgoing.'"

"I don't go myself," Mavis told her. "Maybe I should. But I feel I have God in my heart."

When my mother didn't respond, Mavis said gently, "Not everybody makes it personal like I do."

In the afternoon, my mother and I shopped for supper groceries at the convenience store. The temperature was up to a hundred and six degrees, we heard on the radio, and on top of that there was a drought. We were both having trouble with our hair, which turned limp with no humidity.

"We look like dogs," my mother said as we got out of the car. "If we're lucky they'll put us in the pound."

Inside, she got a cold, quart-size beer and drank most of it as we walked around the store. On the way home, she pulled the car over and stepped out into an overgrown field and threw up.

"Don't mention that when we get home," she warned me.

"Why would I?"

We didn't talk after that, not even when we pulled up to the house and saw Mavis Jean in the yard, swinging a rug beater at the moldy gray living-room carpet she'd hung from a tree.

McKinley, on the porch, was carefully holding up a stained pea-colored plate. "Mama's china," he said reverently to my mother.

Inside, Emerson, positioned next to the window air conditioner, was wheezing out some sort of song.

Just then my mother snapped. "Get the groceries in, Roberta!" she yelled at me.

She tore at the loose, rotten upholstery on the couch and the chair; ripped up a corner of the kitchen linoleum, which had half risen and curled; yanked down the bathroom wallpaper, which had a kind of yellow dampness seeping through.

We all got out of her way, including Emerson: Mavis Jean's husband came in and lifted up him and his chair and deposited them both in the back bedroom.

McKinley stood in the doorway and watched. He'd never seen my mother exercised like that, although I'd told him once how right after my father's funeral she went into their bedroom and boxed up all his things. "Helen, let that go for now," my grandmother had said. She and I had stood in the doorway—just as McKinley was now—watching my mother sort through mismatched socks. She'd wanted to pair them up, even though she was putting his clothes in boxes to give to the charity-drive ladies at our church.

It was almost dark by the time my mother stopped. We had all—except for Emerson—tried to stay on the outskirts but still help.

"Just think of us as worker bees," Mavis Jean had said light-heartedly to my mother, when Mavis got in her way for a second. My mother had been holding a putty knife, though, and for a moment none of us were sure what she might do next.

Finally, she collapsed on the front porch, where she'd been prying up boards. Her sweaty hair was sticking to the back of her neck. Her sleeveless shirt was so wet you could tell where her bra was held together with pins.

"Honey, you need some new underwear," Mavis Jean said quietly.

We had supper in the cramped kitchen and then sat in the cool dimness of the living room. I fell asleep and dreamed again about Roy Lee—he was kissing and touching me—and I woke afraid that I'd been making noises. But the noises I'd heard must have been Emerson's breathing. He'd seemed all right earlier, although he hadn't eaten any dinner. "Sometimes the only food you want is sweets," I'd told him—that was how my father used to tempt me to eat when I was sick. But Emerson hadn't wanted so much as a cookie.

"Daddy?" Mavis Jean said. "What's wrong? What do you need?" She was sitting close to him, holding a pair of his trousers in her lap; she was sewing up a ripped hem.

He opened his mouth to speak but all he did was take in air. McKinley got up and went to his side; my mother went into the kitchen and came back with a glass of water. We all, except my mother, crowded around him, watching his chest rise and fall, and the look in his eye, and the way his hands were clutching the arms of his chair.

"Give him some room!" my mother shouted in a high-pitched voice.

Mavis Jean was taking his pulse, her head bent down, her eyes on her watch. Her husband put his hand on her shoulder. McKinley was all but holding his daddy in his arms. I stood right next to McKinley, leaning against him even, although I hadn't meant to. I heard him tell his father he loved him.

Then it was over. Emerson's breathing grew regular; he looked less scared; and he didn't die—not for another six months, and it was in his bed, during the night, while he was asleep.

It was an hour before we trusted that he was O.K. During that time only my mother left the house; she went out to the porch and sat on the steps.

"Come help me get coffee and cake," Mavis Jean said to me.

I followed her into the kitchen, and when she picked up the coffeepot I saw that her hands were shaking.

"I can do that," I said.

She went over to the sloping counter under the window, looking off into the dark back yard. Then she turned around and looked at me.

"What was it like," she asked softly, "having your daddy die?"

"I only know what it was like afterward," I told her. "I wasn't there when it happened."

"Oh, no," she said. "You didn't get to say goodbye."

She came close and pushed back my straggly hair, and I saw that her own hair was more gray than red. I'd forgotten that she was older than McKinley.

"'Cross at the light, Roberta,'" I said. "That was the last thing he said to me."

"That has some sweetness in it," she said. "Sweetness and good advice."

In the living room, Mavis Jean set the coffeepot down and put a blanket over Emerson's shoulders.

"You don't need a chill on top of everything else," she told him.

"It's ninety-seven degrees outside," my mother said, her voice still strange. She stood in the doorway, ignoring that she was letting in hot air and letting out cool.

"He seems most comfortable at a hundred and two," Mavis Jean said.

"Close the door, honey," McKinley said to my mother. "Come sit here by me."

My mother went outside instead. She left the door open, and her work boots were noisy on the broken boards and the cracked sidewalk. After a few minutes McKinley went out after her. Through the window I could see them standing in the road, my mother facing the empty field on the other side, and suddenly I knew how afraid she was—not of Emerson's dying but of how it made her feel, to feel too much. It was like loving a boy more than he loved you, I thought; you couldn't help it, and you couldn't stop it, and you made him love you in your dreams.

They stayed outside a long time. I sat down finally and ate a piece of cake, watching the way Mavis Jean double-rolled the hem of the pants leg before she sewed it.

Behind her, Emerson was eyeing me. He leaned forward to speak.

"Does that little girl belong to me?" he asked Mavis Jean.

She told him yes.

# WHO'S YOUR DADDY?

BOB BLEDSOE

Louis liked the paddle more than the man who swung it. He re-spected the instruction, the ritual, the organization of his thoughts when the paddle struck its target. He enjoyed the stinging clarity, the expedient way the paddle transmitted its message. "You're a bad boy, aren't you? You're Daddy's little pig," the man with the paddle said, but Louis—jeans around his ankles—was mute with pain. "Tell Daddy you're sorry. Tell Daddy you'll be good from now on."

Daddy didn't seem to mind Louis's silence. He raised the paddle higher, brought it down with a judicious slap. At the end of the session, he took Louis in his arms, cradled him like a small child. "Daddy doesn't like to spank you," he whispered into Louis's ear, and Louis smelled peanut butter. "Why do you have to be such a bad boy?"

Louis squirmed away and put on his underwear. "Can I write you a check this time?" he asked. "I didn't stop at the ATM."

"The agreement was cash. This isn't Nordstrom's."

"A check's all I've got."

Louis pulled on his jeans, the brush of denim against his un-derpants like a metal rake across sunburn. He would feel the sore-ness for days, heat like chili fire on the tongue. "And since I'm the one paying," he said as he wrote the check standing up, "would you mind not eating right before I come over?"

Louis's mother didn't recognize Armando anymore. Louis and Armando had been together a year and a half, and after the first family dinner, Natasha didn't acknowledge Armando at all. Alzheimer's brought her prejudices to the surface. She had terrible things to say about the gardener, the letter carrier; even her neighbors Dr. and Mrs. Matsuda, Louis's beloved childhood dentist and his nice wife, were reduced to stereotypes. "They keep bringing me vegetables," Natasha said about the zucchini and tomatoes from the Matsudas' garden. "And you know how the Asians are about their vegetables."

"Mother, what do you mean? They've always shared their vegetables with us, and we've always enjoyed them," Louis said.

"Oh, never mind," she said. "You have no idea."

At the onset of her Alzheimer's, before she'd been diagnosed, she'd asked Louis when he thought he might meet the right girl and settle down.

"Mother," Louis said, "I'm thirty-five years old. I'm with Armando. The 'right girl' is just *not* going to happen."

"But you never know. Your own father was older than you are now when he and I got married. Maybe you're just a late bloomer."

"Mother, I'm gay. I've known I was gay since I was fourteen, and you've known it just as long. I don't understand why you're bringing this up now." Louis had grown up with his mother's mood swings and bad behavior—long periods of sulking and miserable silence that he attributed to disappointment over her failed career—but this was something else. Alzheimer's peeled back layers, revealed a woman he never knew; this peek into her psyche made him long for the silent treatment.

Now Natasha mistook Louis for her own dead brother; Louis couldn't remember the last time she called him by his own name. "Ian, Ian, come over here. Put on that Cole Porter record we like so much." Louis had researched the disease, been counseled not to argue. He fought the urge to draw his mother back: "I'm not Uncle Ian. It's me, Louis." Instead, he improvised, distracted his mother as he would a young child, played along with whatever whimsical misapprehension occupied her at the time.

Natasha had begun singing everywhere—in the yard, at the mall; the world was now her concert hall. She'd once had a beautiful voice, and in her twenties and early thirties had tried to get an acting career off the ground. Alzheimer's had limited her musical repertoire—she sang the same few songs over and over—and changed her delicate soprano to a bird's screech, high and shrill. At the supermarket, she was gloriously, magisterially oblivious to the people who stared at her from a hill of lettuce in the produce aisle or through a fogged door in frozen foods as she shrieked, "Tomato, tomahto, potato, potahto, let's call the whole thing off."

Louis read the personal ads at the back of West Hollywood's alternative newspaper. He fantasized about the men who advertised for romance and sexual services; above all, the spanking ad bore an erotic charge that he couldn't deny. *Bareass spankings for disobedient boys. In or out. Call Daddy.* Each time he saw it, and it ran week after week, his heart pounded, his focus narrowed to the throb of an erection.

"Louis is a tattler," his third-grade teacher told his parents during a discussion about his otherwise good behavior. When they returned home from the parent-teacher conference, which Natasha had insisted her husband attend, he snaked his belt out of its loops on the walk from the driveway into the house.

As Natasha's disease stripped her mind of its utility and made her more dependent on Louis, he called the telephone number from the spanking ad and listened to Daddy's recorded greeting. He called a dozen times, in a masturbatory haze, before he left his cell phone number. He was dizzy with the fantasy of discipline, of this man taking control.

"You called about my ad," Daddy said when he returned the call. "What'd you do to deserve a spanking?"

"I, well, I'm . . . ," Louis stammered.

"What is it, boy? Cat got your tongue?"

"I've never done this before."

"A virgin. My favorite. Tell Daddy why you need your ass paddled, and maybe we can do business."

"Can I tell you in person?"

"That's what Daddy likes to hear."

Louis was a small man: at five feet six inches, he weighed one hundred twenty pounds. His red hair and apple blossom skin made him look like the kid in second grade sitting out recess with an asthma inhaler. "Stay away from the bigger boys," his mother insisted, even when he was in high school. Louis once heard her use the word diminutive when talking about him on the telephone. Sports were out of the question, so Louis involved himself at school in other ways, learned to compensate: he was a charmer and an overachiever. He was Homecoming King and valedictorian of his high-school class.

He got the lead in the drama club's production of *Oklahoma!* He was so nervous during the first performance that he barely got the words out; his one extravagant arm gesture knocked his cowboy hat not only off his head but off the stage. Louis had used the marching-band trick of stretching a section of pantyhose over his head to keep his hairline clean. Without the hat, the dangling flap of pantyhose resembled loose flesh, and Louis looked like he'd been scalped. He stood silent until the director ran onstage and slapped another hat on his head.

When he saw his mother and father after the show, embarrassment stretched their faces into distorted smiles. His father said nothing. Natasha gave Louis a silent opera clap of her hands and whispered, "Good show, honey. Good show." Louis understood that his only future in show business would be behind the scenes.

While Natasha didn't have the emotional wherewithal to comfort her son, she had a mother's instinct to indulge; in the days following the play, she put her credit card to work—with her husband's approval, for they were a family who threw money at emotional difficulty—so that Louis's spirits were lifted just above despair. He had his father's disappointment, his mother's languid care, and a fabulous wardrobe.

For the last ten years Louis had navigated the treacherous road of the Hollywood film industry from entry-level production assistant (a low-paying job he took because his family money afforded him the luxury) to assistant film editor. He used skills perfected in high school—gossip, networking, self-promotion—and the movie industry bowed to him. He was about to start a new job working on a big-budget romantic comedy as first editor with his own assistants and a credit line on the film. It was a big deal. He'd worked hard, played the game: going to a movie with Louis meant staying until the final credit while theater employees waited in the aisles with brooms and plastic bags. The credits were a *Who's Who* of Louis's employment history, a way of keeping track of his colleagues and monitoring his competition. His calculations rolled along with the credits—Director: potential employer; Producer: ass-kisser; Editor: nice guy; Screenwriter: insane.

On one of their first dates, Armando tried to stick it out, made it through the cast credits, but lost interest during the endless list of the film's production crew. "I'll get the car and wait for you out front," Armando said.

"Sit with me," Louis whispered. "It'll only be a few more minutes."

"I want to move my legs."

Louis and Armando met making a soda commercial. Armando was an extra, Louis an assistant editor. Louis was on the set at the end of a long shoot to take the day's film to the lab. The director barked an order at Louis, and Armando rolled his eyes in a way that only Louis could see.

On his way out, Armando slipped Louis his telephone number.

Armando was the most breathtaking man Louis had ever seen. He was tall, slim, and muscular: his body was as hard and beautiful as polished river rocks. Sex with him was as satisfying as licking those rocks. In bed, Armando held the unresponsive pose of a statue; he was there to be admired, and that worked for both of them for the first few months. Then it was a torture of instruction for Louis, who had to ask Armando to kiss him back.

"Baby, I need you to touch me, too. I can't do all the work."

Armando arranged himself on the bed as though it were a photo shoot, hands cupped behind his head, abs flexed to highlight every striation of muscle.

"I get off on you enjoying my body," Armando said.

"And I do. But can you see how that might not be *totally* satisfying for me?" Louis said.

Armando shrugged. He was twenty-three to Louis's thirty-four, and the age difference gilded his confidence. Armando was gay royalty; men's desire exalted him, made a prince out of a son of East Los Angeles Mexican immigrants. Armando ruled with a smile.

"When you don't kiss me back, it makes me feel," Louis tried to explain, "like a daddy."

"Come on. You're not that much older than me. I mean, you aren't actually old enough to be my *father*," Armando said.

"That's not what I meant."

After six months of this, the sex didn't improve, but the relationship didn't end. They were in love, said so to each other, kept saying so until they could not believe the alternative. It was like surviving a terrible accident: Louis felt like he should be dead, that all the elements added up to a kind of end, but he and Armando went about their lives, and the relationship chugged along, balanced by equal parts denial, need, and a meticulous silence about their sex life. Louis's desperation to make the relationship work blinded him, moved him past awkwardness and humiliation into a faux-European arrangement, *un mariage blanc*; to say they had a "Don't Ask, Don't Tell" policy about what went on outside of their relationship would have been to exaggerate their level of communication.

Armando was an actor and a model and a personal trainer at a fancy health club in Hollywood. He trained celebrity clients, taught spin classes, and appeared on the covers of several men's fitness magazines. A college anatomy textbook featured Armando's legs. None of which added up to a stable living wage; Louis asked him to move in four months after they met. He kept Armando in Gucci loafers and took him on a vacation to the Virgin Islands.

A few months into their relationship, Louis and Armando drove to Newport Beach for dinner with Natasha. "You're tall, queeny, and brown. My mother is going to hate you," Louis said in the car.

"She'll adore me. Mothers always adore me," Armando said. "And I'm not queeny, you little bitch."

"You just wait. I'm only trying to prepare you."

"But I'm exactly the kind of boy to take home," Armando said. "She'll compare me to your other nasty boyfriends, and it'll be a done deal. She *has* met other boyfriends, hasn't she?"

"I didn't always give her details. She assumed what she assumed."

"What if I were some hot Latina hoochie mama?"

"She'd see female, and that would be enough. Her prejudice isn't all that refined when it comes to me."

"So the gay thing trumps the brown thing?"

"Something like that."

On the freeway home, stuck in midnight traffic, Armando said, "You know, as a good Mexican boy, it breaks my heart to say it, but your mother is a fucking nightmare."

"I told you," Louis said, and looked from side to side. Traffic was at a standstill. People sat in their cars staring straight ahead, as if at a drive-in theater.

"Yeah, but everyone always says their mother is a nightmare, and they never actually turn out to *be* a nightmare. She hates me. This has never happened."

"I told you she was going to hate you. She hates everyone."

"What's wrong with her?"

"She has problems."

"Do I ever have to see her again?"

"If you're lucky, she'll invite you over for Easter, and you can pray the rosary together."


Louis had worked out a system of care for Natasha that involved neighbors and friends and a part-time home health nurse, but it was no longer enough; his stubborn mother, who often refused help, was a danger to herself. Louis moved her into a nursing care facility, sold the house, and left himself a weekend to clear everything out. Louis wanted Armando's help, and dangled Disneyland as a lure. He figured they would work all day Friday, go to Disneyland on Saturday, and finish up on Sunday. Even with all he had to do, he would sacrifice a day. Louis couldn't bear an entire weekend alone in his abandoned family home with his mother's friends picking over the remnants of his childhood, realtors opening closets and kitchen cabinets.

"I've got to choose the things I want to keep," Louis told Armando. "Then I'll decide what to give away, what to donate."

"What about that chaise longue in the guest room?" Armando asked.

"You want it?"

"If you're just going to get rid of it, I'll take it," Armando said.

"Sure. I told my mother's friends they could have whatever I don't keep."

"What about the rest?"

"Goodwill."

"Isn't there some way to sell all that stuff?"

"I can't deal with it," Louis said. "I'm going to take what I want and get rid of the rest."

"So why exactly do you need me?"

"I need help lifting some furniture. Rolling up rugs. It'll be fun—we'll work one day and go to Disneyland the next."

"You know I've never felt comfortable at her house."

"Neither have I. But this time she won't be there."

Louis moved his mother to the nursing home in Santa Monica by himself. He borrowed a friend's truck, loaded the few personal items that would fit in her small room: a charcoal sketch of Natasha drawn by her brother, Ian, several family photographs in silver frames, a crystal vase, a Turkish rug, her favorite chair. The packing had confused and upset Natasha, so Louis turned it into a game. He directed his mother as though she were an actress again, gave her motivation for the scene: "Mother, pretend you're going on a trip and you have to pack clothes. What will you take? Pick your very favorite things." She stalled and paced. When Louis pulled a few items from her closet, mostly casual clothes, a pair of khaki pants and a blue button-down shirt, she pushed past him and took out a dazzling St. John's suit with beaded cuffs and collar; a beautiful Hermès scarf in vivid pink, green, and turquoise, showing all the seasons; a pair of navy blue Chanel slingbacks; a pair of pink silk trousers with a matching cashmere sweater set.

"We'll need to dress for dinner, Ian. I want to look presentable."

She didn't pack any undergarments, so Louis became intimate with the private world of his mother's underwear drawers. When he held up a bra, she looked away, walked out of the room. He selected bras from the front of the drawer, reasoning that those in back were there because she no longer wore them. He selected pant-ies for his mother, a dozen white pairs he dropped into the suitcase as though they were hot coals. At the back of one drawer, wrapped in faded tissue paper, was a silk crêpe de Chine nightgown that must have been fifty years old; there were holes in the delicate embroidered trim.

On the way to the nursing home, Louis played Cole Porter and urged his mother to sing along. He engaged her in small talk, treated her like an elderly stranger, worried that she'd open the door on the freeway. They talked about the weather.

"Will we get rain?" Natasha asked.

"It never rains in Southern California," Louis said, recalling a line from a song he and his mother sang along to on the car radio when he was a boy. The reference didn't register.

Louis convinced her that they were going on a long trip, but she thought the luggage was excessive. "When we went on the trip to Europe, Ian, we took one small bag each. Here you've got boxes and boxes and suitcases of things."

"This is a much longer trip," Louis said.

"But why are we bringing pictures? And furniture?"

"We want to be comfortable."

"Well, then, Ian, what about the phonograph?"

"It's in there," Louis said, another in a long series of lies and deflections that spilled forth without hesitation.

Louis spent the day with Natasha unpacking and organizing. When it came time to leave, he saw his mother alone in her tiny room, her possessions melting into the bland institutional décor. Natasha was captivated by the staff's constant professional intrusions and forced pleasantries—condescending behavior that would have infuriated her before Alzheimer's. Louis excused himself, walked down the hallway and into one of the public restrooms. He locked himself in a stall and cried for twenty minutes, then returned to say goodbye.

"You can call me anytime," Louis said.

"Good show, honey. That's lovely."

Louis sped out of the nursing-home parking lot, and later that night knocked on Daddy's door for the first time. He held a sheet of paper with directions that he'd ripped out of his day planner. It was nine o'clock. He'd drunk four martinis.

"You Louis?" Daddy asked after he opened the door. He was taller and more than a few years older than Louis expected.

"Yes."

"Yes what?"

Louis looked at him like a child stumped at a spelling bee.

"Yes, *sir*," Daddy said.

"Yes, sir."

"That's right. Now get in here, boy," Daddy said. He led Louis down a dark hallway to a room with a box spring and a mattress covered with a faded Scotch plaid sheet. There was a pegboard rack screwed into the wall, with dozens of metal hooks from which Daddy's play toys hung: heavyweight ping-pong paddles with holes drilled in the center, an assortment of leather whips, riding crops, handcuffs, chains, padlocks, rope, fly swatters, a calfskin flogger, feather dusters, a rainbow of colored handkerchiefs, and leather belts with big brass and silver buckles. Daddy grabbed a cop's billy club and slapped his left palm with it, a scene Louis would have edited right out of a film.

"Sit down on the bed," Daddy instructed. "Take off your shoes, leave your socks on."

"Shouldn't we—"

"Just do what I tell you."

"Okay."

"Okay?"

"I mean, yes, sir," Louis said.

Daddy had a big, solid gut, a silver brush-cut, a goatee, and a black tattoo of a tarantula crawling down his left bicep. His demeanor suggested a retired army general gone to seed. He instructed Louis to pull his pants down and lie on the bed. When Louis got his pants down around his knees, he took an awkward step and stumbled.

"Get your pants all the way down, boy. I want you on the bed with your ass up in the air," Daddy said.

"What about my underwear?"

"Keep your underwear on, pussy boy, and stop asking questions."

Louis knelt at the foot of the bed. "Like this?"

"Get up there, goddamn it," Daddy said, and moved toward him with his hand raised. "Quit fucking around."

Louis dropped, face-first, onto the mattress. He lifted himself up using his forearms, his butt in the air, the weight of his body resting on his elbows. He held this position until his arms got sore, then let his chest down, his right cheek flat against the bed.

Daddy sat on the edge of the bed and rubbed Louis's ass through his underwear as he might rub a dog's belly.

When Louis left, his ass was speckled with red dots, which turned into a net of bruised skin like purple cellulite.

Louis managed his pain. He did everything cautiously. The simple brush of fabric caused a burning sensation so intense he broke into a sweat. Sitting down was a challenge; bending his legs stretched the sensitive skin tight before searing it against the softest surface. On the drive to work a few days after the first paddling, Louis pulled off the freeway, stopped at a convenience store, and chewed a mouthful of ibuprofen on the way back to his car. At night, he took another handful of ibuprofen and two sleeping pills and slept on his stomach.

He hid his ass from Armando, maneuvered his body in awkward ways. He showered facing the clear glass door and twisted to reach the shampoo behind him. He wrapped a towel around his waist even though they both walked around nude all the time. When he undressed, he did it quickly, furtively, ass out of sight and eyes on Armando, as though to control the direction of his gaze. Armando never took his eyes off the television.

Louis visited Daddy once a week. When his ass was too sore, Daddy would discipline him in other ways, with handcuffs and leather restraints. He paddled the backs of his legs. He shackled him to metal hooks screwed into the wall. He used nipple clamps.

Without the martinis, Louis saw Daddy more clearly. He saw his name—Ralph Mercer—on a phone bill on the kitchen counter; the Confederate flag hanging above the bed; the gray hair on Daddy's shoulders. The sheets smelled dusty, like the sweat of strange men. The photo album of Daddy's other "boys" included pictures of a man with welts so red and swollen they might have required an emergency-room visit.

Daddy poured Grape-Nuts and two-percent milk into a wide pasta bowl and set it down. He returned with Louis on a leash—on his hands and knees—and made him eat the cereal from the bowl on the linoleum floor. Louis crunched the hard Grape-Nuts, worried about breaking a tooth.

"Good doggy," Daddy said. "That's a good boy."

Louis looked up from his Grape-Nuts and started to say something, but Daddy cut him off. "Finish your dinner, boy," Daddy said. "You've got work to do."

"But I—"

"Eat," Daddy said, and pushed Louis's face into the bowl.

"I'm lactose intolerant," Louis gasped, milk all over his face.

"Oh, hell," Daddy said, and jerked the leash, dragging Louis out of the kitchen.

Louis pushed his luck at home. He talked to Armando as he took off his underwear, angled himself so Armando—if he were at all curious—could see the bruises and welts on his ass and the backs of his legs, the lash marks below his shoulder blades. Louis winced when he sat down, when a tight shirt grazed his sensitive nipples. None of this inspired so much as a questioning glance from Armando.

"Are we still going to the concert this weekend?" Louis said, underwear around his ankles, daring Armando to look.

"It's up to you. Tickets are expensive," Armando said, hypnotized by the television.

"Do you want to go?" Louis asked, trying to engage him in conversation.

"I could take it or leave it."

"So that's a no?" Louis said, and walked over to the bed.

Armando gave him a quick glance. "I guess."

"Well, then, no." Louis walked out of the room naked, his backside fully exposed.

Armando didn't say a word.

By the time Louis and Armando got to Fantasyland, the day had gone wrong. Armando's cell phone rang, and he held up the screen to show Louis the famous name on the caller ID. It was a hot young actor beefing up for an action-adventure movie. Louis rolled his eyes and simulated masturbation. Armando stepped away to take the call.

Louis waited on a bench near a doorway where larger-than-life characters were leaving the park after a tour of prancing, waving, and posing for pictures. Snow White, a couple of Dwarves, and Mickey and Minnie waved goodbye at an exit painted to resemble an enchanted forest.

A little girl rushed toward Beauty and the Beast, and Beauty said, "Excuse us, honey, excuse us, don't run in front of the Beast," but the girl didn't stop. Then in an octave just above the Beast's cartoon growl, Beauty—her face a mask of concentration and annoyance—snapped, "For fuck's sake, kid, get out of the way."

The little girl stopped as though shot, dropped her cotton candy, and ran crying back to her family. Beauty and the Beast left without a goodbye.

When Armando returned from his call, Louis was transfixed.

"You just missed it," Louis said. "Beauty just screamed at that little girl." He turned Armando around by the shoulders so they could both look at the little five-year-old, who was still crying and pointing to the exit. "Beauty and the Beast were just here, and Beauty—"

"You mean Belle? Beauty's name in the movie is Belle," Armando said.

"Whatever. Beauty's a bitch."

"You can say that again," Armando said, and batted his eyelashes. "Come on. Let's go."

"This is Disneyland. It's not supposed to be like this," Louis said as Goofy and Donald worked their way to the exit. The little girl, fully recovered, ran behind Goofy and threw her cotton candy tube at his back.

"Tough crowd," Armando said. "Look at the kid's mother. Someone should tell her she *does not* need that hot dog and extra large soda."

"What do you care what other people eat?" Louis said.

"It's the principle of the thing. Your body's a temple."

"You mean *your* body is a temple. The rest of us just walk around in our bodies and eat when we're hungry."

"Yeah. And look at the results," Armando said, and motioned toward a Mickey Mouse T-shirt stretched tight across a man's big belly.

"I came here for you, thinking I had to entertain you to get your help with my mother's house."

"I don't know how you could ask me to go to that woman's house after the way she treated me."

"*That woman* is sitting in a nursing home, and she doesn't even know her name," Louis said.

Armando walked over to a vendor across from the bench where they were arguing. He returned with two ice cream bars. Without saying anything, he handed one to Louis. They tore open the paper, bit into a frozen layer of chocolate, and watched two white swans paddling in the moat surrounding Sleeping Beauty's castle.

"We have to talk," Louis said. "About us." They walked away from the castle, toward Main Street. Louis hurled his ice cream at one of the swans, which flapped away with a splash.

"I have to use the bathroom," Armando said.

"I'll go with you."

While Armando stood at the urinal, Louis washed his hands. Then he approached the urinal next to Armando, dropped his pants, let his belt buckle hit the tile floor, and stood like a boy peeing into an adult toilet for the first time, butt and legs exposed.

Armando noticed. "What are you doing?" he said. "And what's wrong with your ass? And legs?"

Louis said nothing.

"Someone's going to walk in. Pull your pants up."

Louis didn't comply, didn't turn to see Armando's expression, but stared at the tiled wall, the chrome plumbing and flush handle.

"I'll wait outside," Armando said. "What's wrong with you?"

After Armando left, Louis pulled his pants up, terrified that a Cub Scout troop in matching Donald Duck T-shirts would walk in and be traumatized for life. He passed a man and two young boys on his way out.

Armando looked at Louis as though he'd just watched him strangle one of those boys in a dark corner of the restroom.

"Louis," he said. "Who did that to you?"

"Some guy."

"Some guy? On purpose?"

"Yes."

"Why would you let someone beat on you like that?"

"To feel something," Louis said.

"Why?" Armando reached for Louis, who backed away.

"I want you to leave," Louis said. "Take your car and go home. I'll finish up at my mother's house."

"Louis, I don't understand what's happening."

"I can't explain it to you. Not here, not now."

There was no line when Louis approached the Disneyland Railroad. He sat in the seat with the best view. As the whistle blew and the train lurched ahead, Louis saw Armando on the platform behind the wrought-iron fence. Armando raised his right hand and waved. Louis faced forward, fixed his eyes on Tomorrowland, and took out his cell phone.

Daddy answered on the first ring. "Yep."

"It's Louis. I'm wondering if I might be able to come over twice this week. I was thinking Tuesday."

"You were, were you? How about you speak to me with a little more respect."

"Yes, sir. May I come over on Tuesday, sir?"

"That's better. But Tuesday won't work. Wednesday night. Nine-thirty."

"Yes, sir."

"What's that music in the background, boy?"

"I'm at Disneyland."

"Jesus. Of course you are."

Louis arrived at Daddy's twenty-five minutes early, and knew better than to knock. He waited in the rental car with the engine running, the green digital clock glowing. He had worked alone at his mother's for four days, hadn't shaved, hadn't returned any of Armando's calls. He walked from room to emptying room, discovered dust and spider webs in what had once been his mother's immaculate home.

Dr. and Mrs. Matsuda, people he'd known his whole life, stopped by.

"Louis, how are you?" Mrs. Matsuda asked.

"Well," Louis said, and swept his arm into the house. "The place is a mess, but I'm getting there."

"You're a good son," Dr. Matsuda said.

Louis invited them in, and they stood facing each other in the dismantled living room.

"I'm still sorry I sawed down your jade tree when I was a kid," Louis told them.

"Oh, why bring that up now? I haven't thought about it in years," Mrs. Matsuda said, in a way that indicated to Louis it was, in fact, the first thing she thought when she saw him.

"I still feel so bad about that," Louis said.

"Forget it," Dr. Matsuda said.

"We're sure going to miss your mother," Mrs. Matsuda said.

Louis had asked them over to visit, to give them something, some memento, and in the end Mrs. Matsuda carried out an orchid in a beautiful rattan pot. Dr. Matsuda shook Louis's hand. "If there is anything we can do, please call," he said.

Other people stopped by, got information about the nursing home, made promises to visit, then left with books, clothing, furniture, kitchen utensils. Goodwill showed up and cleared the place out, took the last bed. Louis had assembled his own stockpile, cordoned it off, and slept beside it, like a sentinel, on the plush carpet of the living room. His back ached from the floor, but he would not leave the house until everything was finished.

"What's with the extra visit?" Daddy asked. "You been extra bad?"

Louis sat down on the bed and curled up on his side with his knees to his chest. If he'd had the nerve, he would have put his thumb in his mouth.

Daddy took a black leather belt from the rack and whipped the mattress just inches from Louis's ass. "What's wrong with you, boy? Tell Daddy all about it," he said.

"My life is fading, it's fading away."

"What?"

"Everything just fades and drifts and goes away. I can't . . . "

"You can't what?" Daddy said, grabbed Louis from behind, and pulled him up. Louis felt the scratch of Daddy's goatee on his neck. He twisted his body around so they were face-to-face, and kissed Daddy on the mouth.

"No, boy. No kissing allowed."

Louis buried his face in Daddy's neck and kissed him, breathing hard and desperate.

"Cut it out," Daddy said, and held Louis so tight he couldn't move.

"But I want—"

"I know what you want," Daddy said, and pushed Louis away. "Now get your clothes off."

Louis lay on his back. He didn't tell Daddy about his mother, and he didn't tell Daddy about Armando. He loosened his jeans, and arched his back to slide them off. He took off his shirt, and as he reached for his underwear, Daddy said, "Underwear on."

"But—" Louis said.

"I'll tell you when to take them off. You're not in charge here."

Louis lay still on the bed, and waited for his next instruction.

# MOUTHFUL OF SORROW

DANA JOHNSON

Why don't you come and sit with me for a spell, keep me company? That's right. Right c'here on the porch with me. It's evenings like this I get to thinking bout things. When the heat start to break and the sky get that gray-blue in it, touching the tops of the trees out yonder. Best time of day in the summertime. I like to just sit back, listen to them bad children playing, cussing, and carrying on over in the holler. There they go, too. Hear how they voices carry? That echo almost picking at you, the sound of it making you sad and happy at the same time.

Now ain't that something you remember me! You wasn't nothing but a little bitty thing last time you come round from California. You grown and look just like your mama. You her picture! You ain't got no babies, is you? Good. That's all right. Ain't no need of you rushing it, hear? You ain't but what? Seventeen? Take all the time you need, honey. Sit right c'here with me and pass some time.

Bout this time I start looking for the little spirits. That's what the lightning bugs look like early nighttime. What you say? Fireflies? They was always lightning bugs to us when we was coming up. At the start of night they come out drifting and floating and blinking such a little bit at first you ain't even sure you seen em, like something you caught out the corner of your eye. Put me in mind of little ghosts. Little ghosts just trying to find they way.

But listen at me just running my mouth. Honey, you ain't got to sit up on this porch with this old lady if you don't want to. I ain't even that old, but you wouldn't know that, with this ragged house-coat I'm wearing, house shoes, hair all over my head. I'm telling you the truth, seem like I woke up old one day.

You know where them kids is playing, down in the holler? Used to be a little joint down there called Lonnie's. Everybody'd be down to Lonnie's on a Saturday night. Get all dressed up, even though the place wasn't nothing but a shack, really. If you was looking for somebody Saturday night, you knew where they'd be at.

Now hand me my spit can. Look at you, handing it to me with your little finger all turned up like you giving me my slop jar. I used to do the same thing with Mama, my nose all wrinkled up, talking bout *I ain't never gone dip snuff.* And here I am. Don't talk bout what you ain't never going to do. You make a liar out of yourself every time.

One of the meanest tricks of life is not knowing what's gone be the last time you do something or see somebody. You be talking bout "See you tomorrow" and the next thing you know, they be dead or gone. That ain't right. Might be the Lord's doing, but I don't got to like everything he do.

What's on my mind when I'm telling you this is my best friend, Addie. You talk bout being close. Honey, let me tell you, we was tight. You hardly saw one of us without the other right up under her. People always used to pick at us and ask which one of us was the man, trying to be funny, you know, because we was always to-gether. But back then, I didn't b'lieve I loved her like that. Shoot, I had me a man, had Mosely. I loved her like she was my sister, cept maybe a little bit more. Wasn't nothing we wouldn't do for each other. Seem like whatever one of us needed, the other had it to give, before you know what it was you wanted your own self! I knew her like you know how to walk. Course we sho could scrap from time to time, too. Used to fight each other like we was crazy, but bother one of us and you had both of us to try to whup.

Let me tell you what I'm talking bout. When Mama first started letting me go out, one of the Bradley boys, Bobby Jean, thought he was gone get something from me, and you know what I'm talking bout. I fought him on it. So he popped me, and I mean good. Had my eye all black and swole up. Mama said I must of acted like I had the same thing on my mind that he did, else he wouldn't of tried nothing. But Addie! We caught up with Bobby Jean one night down at Lonnie's. She called his name out real nice and soft, and when he turned around she kicked him in his information. That boy fell to his knees, squeezing out tears, while I kicked him in his behind. And never did a thing to us. Not a thing. Come to me a week later, talking bout he was sorry!

But when me and Addie fought each other!

You prolly too young to remember Mr. Burl Spicer, lived up the road a piece in that shack on the edge of the creek. He dead now. When my daddy passed, he and Mama started helping each other out. He used to bring Mama well water, and for that she'd cook him up fried chicken every Sunday and have me run it to him. He was just as nice as he could be. One Sunday he come around the road when me and Addie was playing patty-cake. We was bout nine years old at the time, singing our little rhymes and cuttin' up, not paying Mr. Burl no mind, till we saw the kitty cat, all gray and fluffy, tucked in the bib pocket of his overalls.

"Oohh look, a kitty!" Addie said, and started petting it and kissing it on the nose and carrying on like she ain't never seen no cat before.

"I brung it for Sticks," he said, grinning at me. That's what he used to call me to pick at me. "I told you, soon as they was old enough, I'd brang you one."

"Thank you, sir," I said, and took the cat. I never really did like cats. I didn't think Mr. Burl was going to give me one. Shoot, when I saw them kitty cats and was talking to Mr. Burl about them things,

I was just talking, really. To me, cats is uppity, act like they don't want to be round you, don't want you giving them love and attention. I ain't got no use for all that.

Well, Mama must of heard us talking to Mr. Burl cause she come out on the porch with his chicken and set it down on the railing. "Spicer," she said to him, "long as you knowed me you know I hate cats, so what you mean giving that chile a cat!" She put her hands on her hips, cutting out any kind of talk about it.

The sun itself just about broke out on Addie's face. "Give it to me." She grabbed it from me. "My mama likes cats and she ain't gone mind."

Well, I jerked it back from her. She was just acting all silly over that damn cat, excuse my mouth. "He didn't give it to you," I hollered. "He give it to me!"

Addie looked at me like I'd lost my mind and grabbed that poor kitty cat back and, honey, we just went at it, pulling and pushing and the cat scratching us both up, then Mr. Burl trying to get in on it to break us up. It was a mess, I'm telling you the truth. I had Addie good by the hair when she broke from me.

"You make me sick!" she said, and threw that poor little kitty cat across the road. It knocked over Mr. Burl's chicken plate that was setting on the porch railing before it hit the wall of my house and slid down the wall, dead. The chicken plate was making that wobbly sound, you know how plates and things do, wobbling faster and faster till they stop and then you don't hear nothing.

"Cain't nobody have it now," Addie said. "How you like that?"

Well, that shocked everybody, even Mama, who'd seen and done some things in her life, let me tell you. I just kept staring at the cat on the porch. It looked all fake like one of them animals you win at the fair.

Mama said to Addie, "I think you best go home, Miss Raleigh."

"Yessum," Addie said, and started down the road, like all Mama had said was have a good time at the picture show.

Mr. Burl and Mama give each other the eyebrows, and then

Mr. Burl dusted off his chicken, said God made dirt and dirt don't hurt, thanked Mama, and went on about his business. Mama stared down the road after Addie, wiped her face with the rag she'd tucked in her chest, and then told me to bury the cat out behind the house here. Next day, me and Addie got together like usual, jumping rope and whatnot, and we never said another word about the kitty cat.

That's the kind of fight we had, fights that never made no kind of sense. And most of the time, Addie come out on top, but one time she made me so mad, I had to tell her like it T-I-*is*. That girl was wrong like two left shoes and she knowed it.

To this day I cain't see no baldheaded man and not think of Lucien Smith. *Honey*. You talking bout *fine*. He wasn't nothing but a boy, round seventeen like me and Addie, but I'm telling you the *truth* he was bout the blackest man you ever did see, and back then, wasn't no saying it loud you was black and proud. Most of the girls in our class was running after David Spears, with the yellow skin and gray eyes, hair all sandy and wavy. But to tell you the truth, David Spears wasn't all that fine. Might of been closer to white than the rest of us, but that's all he had going for him. Lucien, though, honey. His skin was just as smooooth. Kept his head clean, cause he say he didn't want to worry about no hair. And folks teased him, too, cause that wasn't the style—less you was an old man! Called him Skeeball, Shinehead. Just did him wrong. And here I was, I loved me some Lucien Smith. Addie knowed it, too.

Anyway, Lucien heard tell what I thought of him, and he finally come round to asking me to the show one day when me and Addie was walking home from school. Course I said yes before the chile could even get the words out, but I was scared to go with him alone, so I ast if Addie could come on along with us. Lucien didn't look happy about that, but he said he didn't mind.

Well. That Saturday roll around and Addie'd told me she was gone meet us at the thee-ater. We waited and waited till we couldn't wait no more, we was gone have to go up to the balcony and get our seats before it got too full. Black folks could only sit up in the balcony, and if those seats got full, you was out of luck cause they wasn't gone let no black folks sit down there with no white people. But just as we fixing to go on up and get us some seats, who coming up the street dressed like she was a ten-cent ho from the big city? And don't ast me where she got them clothes, cause I don't know. But they was tight, and they was loud, and Addie's lips was painted on looked like permanent! You talking about red!

She walked up to me and Lucien with her hips swinging like she knocked down walls on either side, all breathless, talking bout "Sorry I'm late."

"Late!" I say. "What in the world you got on!"

"What?" Addie say, like she was all surprised. Like she don't know what I'm talking bout. She turned to Lucien then, and looked at him a little too long for my taste. He was looking back, too!

How she gone make me feel like I'm wearing a potato sack from Mama's kitchen on my first date with the man I thought I'd die from wanting so bad?!

"Oooh. You heifa!" I said, and just commenced to snatching at anything I could get my hands on. Honey, folks gathered. Finally Lucien broke us up, and neither one of us ventually ended up with him. He started going with some little mousy thing later, and that ain't last but a minute.

Mama got after me when I got home later, cause word travel fast. Say she better not hear of me acting common like that again, fighting in the streets over some man. "We may be on the poor side, Maybonne, but we know how to act like we got some sense. Womens fighting over a man is just as trifling as can be. You don't let no man come between you and your friends. Not no good friends. You hear?"

Sho nuff, me and Addie was thick as thieves not two days later.

You know, you can reach the point of hating a person as much as you love em. Hate em for making you lose yourself in em cause you want to be just like em and have everything they got. I had that kind of love for Addie, and Addie had that kind of love for Fella, thought he hung the moon.

Wouldn't of been that bad for me if Addie had loved somebody worth all she was giving him. I wasn't the only one heard about Fella carrying on with some girl over in Nashville, and before that, somebody else. Seem like as long as I been knowing Fella—and he sho was fine, ain't no need of me lying bout that—he was always sticking his business in some women when he already had one woman or another to tend to. I guess cause he was so hard to hold down, Addie's way of thinking was that he was that much finer the prize. She had him, didn't she? And she thought since she had him he wouldn't step out on her cause she wasn't like them other girls. She was special. She was, too, but that man wouldn't of knowed special if it walked up to him, handed that fool one of them business cards, and introduced itself!

Well, nobody told Addie about Fella carrying on, least of all me. That chile saw what she wanted to see and I'd a rather had somebody cut my heart out than to hurt Addie. You know what I said bout one of us always giving what the other one needed? Well, she needed not to know bout Fella.

My last night down to Lonnie's, me and Mosely hadn't been too long through the door when Addie snuck up behind me and smacked me on my behind. Lonnie's was always dark and smoky, but I could see her little pixie face grinning at me. Still can sometimes.

"Maybonne, girl, I got something to tell you." She grabbed my hand and drug me through the café to the bathroom. Right there, her grabbing my hand and leading me is just as clear. B. B. King was singing "Every Day I Have the Blues" from the jukebox, and Squeak was getting his tail whupped at dominoes by John Lee like he always did. Folks was drinking and dancing and having a good time mostly cause Lonnie kept pouring em drinks. And I stole one quick glance at Mosely and Fella up at the bar. Fella was looking me dead in my eye. He was stroking his shiny mustache and grinning, them white white teeth against his black skin. He winked at me with one of his great big eyes the color of a caramel apple, before Addie jerked me into the bathroom.

"Girl," I said, "what you mean just a pulling me all through the café? Shoot. Stretched my sweater all out of shape." I was trying to fix myself up and wasn't paying her no mind.

"I'm gone have Fella's baby, May," she said, looking all bashful and proud. "Folks say he going to take me with him to California."

Thoughts was coming in my head and leaving before I had a chance to make anything of em. Couldn't even open my mouth. Me and Addie come up together from babies and I never thought bout a time when we wouldn't be together.

Addie stared at me, her mouth real tight like she was about to get mad. She said, "What? Ain't you happy for me? You hear what I say? Fella taking me out of this piss-pot town!"

Wasn't no way in the world I could have been happy for that girl cause I was selfish and thinking about myself. I started crying like a baby. "You cain't go!"

Addie stepped up to me and wrapped her arms around me. We was a funny picture to folks coming into the bathroom, tall and skinny as I was with Addie not even coming up to my chest, trying to comfort me.

"Ain't you even happy bout my baby?" she ast with a little smile. When I didn't give her no answer she pulled a cigarette out of her purse, lit it, and put it in my mouth. She untied the scarf round her neck and used it to wipe my eyes and my cheeks. That scarf was her favorite one, too. Let me see, bright blue with red specks in it. When she was done, she tied it back round her neck, smeared makeup on it and all.

Addie looked down at my shoes and said, "I see you wearing them old run-over loafers. Ain't even got no pennies in em."

"Forget you, heifa," I said to her. "What you posed to be in them muddy white pumps back up here in these sticks, Doris Day or somebody?" I took a long drag on the Pall Mall she give me and blowed it out right slow. We both was laughing. Then I stopped cause I remembered. I went from sad to mad then, hating Fella for taking my friend away, thinking bout how Addie was giving me up for him. He wasn't even worth the spit in my mouth.

"That man," I said. I put my cigarette out in the sink and leaned up against it. "That man ain't all you think he is, girl." I couldn't look her in the eyes. I was looking at them green walls, the paint all chipped and peeling, the lightbulb hanging from the ceiling. Moths was throwing themselves at it. There was another girl in there with us, in the stall across from the sink, but I didn't care. I knowed with them words that I had done got it started. You couldn't start no mess with Addie and not finish it.

She crossed her arms and shifted her weight on her right hip, her head all tilted, squinting at me. "Ain't all I think he is? What you talking bout?"

"Throwing your life away for that dog."

"Dog!" Addie took a couple steps toward me. I stepped back.

"Listen, I know you better than I know my own self. You starting all kinds of mess cause you jealous of Fella. I love you, but this shit I ain't going to let you do."

I said, "You know me. Then you know I ain't lying when I say Fella be with some other woman when he ain't with you."

Addie pressed both her hands on her belly like she was trying to hold it down. Her eyes got all small and right, like she was trying to see something she couldn't. Then she said, real low, "You a evil cow. I don't b'lieve nothing you telling me."

That girl in the stall, Georgia Shields, come out finally. She said to Addie, "You the last to know, girl," and got out of there quick and in a hurry! All the good times and music coming from outside the bathroom poured in and then shut off when the door closed. Addie was still holding herself and looking past me. I wanted to tell her that me and Georgia was lying.

"Addie," I said, and went to her but she snatched her arm from me. I was scared cause I'd never seen Addie all broke down like that. She was looking how other people looked when she got done with them. "Add." I tried to touch her again, but she wouldn't let me. "We—I don't know what I'm talking bout. Them's just rumors. Folks talking bout what they don't know."

Addie quit looking past me and watched me try to act like everything was light, like I ain't brought no heaviness tween us. I pushed my sweater sleeves over my elbow, crossed my arms, and pulled some kind of tight smile across my face.

"Maybonne." Addie called my name out funny like. "Maybonne, Maybonne. I cain't collect what make me the maddest. That you knowed about Fella and ain't told me nothing, or that you telling me bout it at all. . . . Unh." She kept on watching me and I was looking everywhere but where I should of been. In her eyes. "Hm," she say. "I b'lieve what make me the maddest is you telling me now. For yourself. All these years I ain't figured you to be this selfish and evil. Hm," she say again, deciding something, seem like. She straightened herself out, stood as tall as her little short self could, and left me by myself in the bathroom.

I wasn't in there but a second or two after she left cause it gave me a funny feeling, something that went all over me. So I just ran out the bathroom, out Lonnie's, out to the road. Mosely come out after me, asking what was wrong. I hollered at him to leave me alone and ran through the woods. I know every bit of McEwen, every tree, so I didn't have no trouble getting home, though it was black as could be. When I got home, Mama ast me why I'd turned up so early and I told her I was tired. It was a lie and the truth at the same time.

I tried sleeping, tried listening to the radio, but it didn't do no good.

I was still up when Mosely come knocking at the door bout one o'clock in the morning. Had his hat in his hand, looking right strange, not saying a word. He was standing here on this very porch. I say to him, "Addie OK?" thinking that she love that fool Fella so much she might try to hurt herself. But I shoulda knowed better than that. Mosely opened the screen door and come on in. Told me to sit down.

"Baby," he said, "Addie. Addie stabbed Fella down at the café. He tried to get away from her, but she wouldn't let him. Got him twicet. He dead, Maybonne."

Might be hard for you to understand, but I got mad at Mosely then. He was standing there, in my mama's house, talking crazy, telling me Addie'd killed somebody. "You a lie, Mosely!" I hollered and slapped him in the face. He let me do it. Never even tried to stop me.

Mosely sat next to me on the couch and hugged me. He was quiet for a piece before he said, "It's the truth cause I was there. Wisht I wasn't though. Wisht I wasn't."

And that's all that come from Mosey's mouth bout that night. He wouldn't tell me no more cause he knew it'd hurt me. We just sat there staring out the screen door till Mama told him he'd stayed long enough.

Well, you know it ventually got back to me what Mosey wouldn't tell before. Lots of folks was there and saw Fella's shocked look when Addie come up behind, called his name kind of sweet like, and put that knife in him when he turned around, grinning. He was grabbing his chest, eyes popping out of his head, stumbling through Lennie's doorway. She jumped on him and stabbed him one more time before folks got sense enough to take the knife from her. But Fella was already dead by the time her mama come and got her out of there.

I ast Mosey if Addie said anything when she was stabbing Fella. Felt like I had to know. Mosey said she just took off her scarf and give it to Sue Baby, this yellow, cross-eyes girl, kind of slow in the head, used to wear them rhinestone cat's-eye glasses all crooked on her face. She told her, "Wipe his face off." And that was it. By the time the police got there, wasn't hardly anybody in Lonnie's but Lonnie—and Fella.

Lonnie's closed down after that cause didn't nobody want to set foot in the place no more. The body was gone and blood had been all scrubbed up, but that thing that was still in the place, well, ain't no cleaning that up. It was haunted, sho nuff.

You can see near bout all of McEwen from this porch, that's how little it is. We ain't never had no murders before then nor since then—come close, though, with all these drunk fools and they shotguns. It ain't like over in Nashville, though, where they just killing each other over them drugs and carrying on.

When Addie killed Fella, her mama packed her up quick and in a hurry! She went to Missouri, and ain't never had to go to jail. Sounds funny, don't it? How you gone to kill a man and not spend a lick of time in jail for it? But that's all the law did. White folks round here then never cared if we killed each other. Just better have sense enough not to mess with 'em.

A little after all the trouble, I got the number to where Addie was living from her mama. Picked up the phone I don't know how many times, but couldn't never finish dialing them numbers. Before I knowed it, years went by, and then my mama died. At the funeral, I was watching the casket go down into the ground when something told me to look up, and there she was, Addie, standing off to the side and looking at me all calm, like she'd seen me yesterday instead of ten years ago. I'm telling you the truth, the sight of her scared me. My heart jumped into my throat and stayed there. After Mama was laid to rest and folks was leaving, petting on me and telling me they was sorry, Addie started walking towards me, and I started towards her. When we met, we didn't even hug, chile. I think about that. We was talking, but talking like you talk to somebody you don't know, bout the weather, or okra that's only fifty cents a pound down at Green's Market. Stuff that didn't matter. Then she said she had to go, but before she started off, told me to take care. Then, seem like she floated away, walking and walking till she got to the top of that green cemetery hill. *Take care.* Now you hardly got to think to tell somebody that. Anybody and everybody says that to folks.

I'm fixin to tell you something, girl. I hope you never know what it feels like to have that kind of conversation with somebody you knew better than yourself. I hope you don't never know what it is I'm talking bout.

I remember after Addie killed the cat that time. Mama said there was something that wasn't right about her. But you know what? That's everybody, including me and you. It's something that's not right with a lot of folks.

I miss Mosely a lot. He living in Chicago with a wife and kids that treat him right, like they got some kind of sense. Ain't had nobody worth a mention since him, really. He tried to stick with me after that night at Lonnie's, but was all the time talking bout how I'd done changed.

Didn't nobody ever say nothing to my face bout why Addie killed Fella. But folks talk, and I know that little so-and-so Georgia Shields had to go and tell it all bout what was said between me and Addie. Myself, I never told my own mama, not Mosely, not nobody. But the more I tried to get on with things and be happy with Mosely, the more I felt I was doing wrong and trying to get by with it. Felt like any day Mosely was liable to jump up and say, "Girl, what you think you selling me?"

I took to acting like I didn't care whether I had him or not, spending all the time by myself I could, barely speaking to Mosely when I did see him. He finally left me, and I was glad for him, honey. Glad for him.

When Mama died, she left me this house, and I ain't changed it a bit since. I been working down at Ben Franklin's at the cash register for twenty-five years and expect to be there twenty-five more, till they wheel me out in a chair or on a stretcher with a sheet up over my face, honey.

You ain't got to be looking at me like you all sorry, cause you don't know sorry. And I ain't lying when I say this is bout the happiest I'm gone get, sitting out on my porch dipping snuff and watching out over McEwen. Closest to peace I'm gone get.

What I keep looking at? Nothing, I guess. Just thought I saw something over your shoulder. Must be them fireflies, drifting, looking like ghosts. Just like I told you.

# THE PENANCE PRACTICUM

ERIN McGRAW

Father Dom was pleased with his reflection in the mirror. To the front of his cassock he had stapled a big dot cut out of white paper; below the cincture he had stapled two more. Tonight was the seminary's Halloween party. He was going as a domino.

He was ready to enjoy himself, although the party was one of the things that had turned iffy around St. Boniface. Some of the younger seminarians, shiny men of God who ran every five minutes to look something up in one of John Paul II's encyclicals, had raised objections: The proper end-of-October celebration for Catholics was the Feast of All Saints, not Halloween.

"We'll celebrate the All Saints Mass," Father Dom told the stern contingent who came to his office. "We always do. But the Halloween party is harmless. People like dressing up."

"The magisterium has not approved Halloween as a holiday for the faithful," said Sipley. His beefy face, above the Roman collar he'd worn every day since taking his first vows, was implacable. Two of the men behind him shook their heads. Father Petrus called this group Rome's hall monitors.

"It isn't forbidden," Father Dom said.

"We won't be attending," Sipley said.

"There'll be punch," Father Dom said wearily. He wouldn't miss them, but he hated to add mortar to the wall separating the men who fluently discussed the mystical gifts of the Holy Father from the rest of them, eating pizza and telling jokes down the hall. Father Dom had bought the pizza.

He smoothed one of his dots. He himself had been on the admissions committee the year Sipley applied. Even then the man was talking about Holy Mother Church, coming on like cutting-edge 1600s. Still, the committee had voted to admit him. The committee had voted to admit every applicant, all five who sought one of the thirty slots. St. Boniface's picking-and-choosing days were long gone. But every time Father Dom thought about a priesthood filled with Sipleys leaning over their pulpits and confidently instructing their congregations, his heart hurt. Father Dom had never felt as certain about anything as Sipley felt about everything.

Hearing voices in the hallway, he opened his door. Several men were heading toward the lounge, laughing, dressed for the party. McCarley wore a cardboard cone taped over his huge nose; he'd drawn lines of scurrying bugs around the end. "Anteater," he said cheerfully. Father Dom's spirits started to rise.

"I hope you have a good sacerdotal defense. You never know when the magisterium's going to be checking up."

"Anteaters are God's creatures. Nobody can challenge me. What about you?"

"I'm a domino. I intend to impart valuable lessons about tipping over."

Behind McCarley, Terley shook his blond hair out of his eyes and fiddled with one of his pencils. He had a dozen or so, sharpened and taped to his shirt as if they'd been shot into him. There was always at least one St. Sebastian. And beside the two men, to Father Dom's delight, walked Joe Halaczek, dressed in salmon-pink Bermuda shorts, a plaid shirt, dark socks and sandals. A cushion under his waistband gave him a burgher's paunch. "I give up," Father Dom said.

"The Race Is Not To The Swift. It's a concept costume," Joe said. Then his voice took on its usual marshy unease. "Is that all right?"

"It's perfect," Father Dom said, hoping the white leather belt came from the second-hand store and not Joe's closet. Someone must have helped him with this—the concept of a concept costume was beyond him. With his frightened hands and unsteady eyes, ordinary conversation was often beyond him. Father Dom could hardly bear to think about his arriving at a parish, this damaged lamb attempting to lead the obstreperous sheep. But right now it was a hoot to watch Joe stroll along, hands behind his back, imitating a confident man.

"We tried to get him to come as Joan of Arc, but nothing doing," said McCarley. Already his cardboard nose was starting to work loose.

"I was afraid someone would set me on fire."

"Only if you start hearing voices," Father Dom said, smiling when worried Joe glanced up.

Inside the lounge, festivities were puttering along. Four men shared the couch in front of the TV, talking and half watching an NFL round-up. Another group was playing darts. Everybody else was hovering over the snack table, from which the buffalo wings were cleared out. Most of one of the pizzas—cheese—was left.

"'The Assyrian swept down like a wolf on the fold,'" said Father Benni, the rector, nodding at the decimated food.

"At least they're not letting the pizza get cold. Where's your costume?"

"This is it. The Good Priest." He folded his long arms and assumed a benevolent expression, and Father Dom forbore from reminding him that generations of students, reacting to his firm command, had called him Sheriff. "Bing Crosby will play me in the movie. I don't know who's going to play you."

"Robert Redford." Father Dom reached over to the table and snagged a wing.

"What do you think, Joe?" Father Benni said. Joe's head snapped around when he heard the rector say his name. "Do you think Robert Redford could play Father Dom?"

"It wouldn't be easy. A man of Father Dom's experience," Joe said carefully.

Father Petrus, standing nearby, snorted. "Hey," Father Dom said.

The rector was still looking at Joe. "Have you asked Father yet? I think this would be a fine time."

It wasn't a fine time, whatever they were talking about—Father Dom both did and didn't want to know. Joe was braiding his fingers, looking at the carpet, and the color had dropped from his face. When Joe spoke, Father Dom had to lean close to hear. "Father Benni would like to observe our class tomorrow. I told him I'm not the one who makes the decisions."

"You are, actually. You can say if you'd rather not be watched," At this moment Father Dom would happily have strangled the smiling rector, who was of course within his rights.

"What's the point of the class, if you're not watched?" Joe said.

"The practicum is the best of all the seminary classes," Father Benni said. "Getting feedback is a real gift. You're able to see yourself as others see you. I miss that."

Joe's face was expressionless beside Father Benni's basking, nostalgic smile. Father Dom said, "We can give you a taste of the old medicine, Greg."

Father Benni said, "I was seminary champion in practicum. Everybody wanted to confess to me, because I gave the easiest penances."

"What made you change?" Father Dom said.

"I haven't changed," the rector said sunnily. "I'm a lamb. Isn't that right, Joe?"

Joe was studying his shoes. "When I first got here the fifth-year guys told me that you were easy." His mouth twitched. "They said you were easy, but to go to Father Dom if I had anything bad. He forgave everything."

"That's why we have him teach the practicum," Father Benni said equably. Glancing at Joe, he added, "It will go fine. You'll see." His voice was full of reassurance, but Joe's proto-smile had dissolved, and Father Dom guided the rector to the other side of the room.

"The practicum isn't Joe's best class," Father Dom said quietly. From the couch came a small whoop; the TV was showing a beer ad that everybody liked.

"I'm not sure Joe has a best class," Father Benni said. "His paper for Mission & Ministry was a page and a half. In homiletic practicum he fell apart completely—got up and just couldn't speak. He doesn't look like a man on his way to ordination. He looks like a man on his way to the electric chair."

"So what do you want?"

"To be reassured."

Father Dom studied Joe, standing in line for darts. He lingered at the side of the group, not the center, smiling at someone else's joke. But there was no rule that said the priest needed to be the life of the party. Plenty of parishioners would appreciate Joe's gentle manner, his ability to listen rather than talk. While Father Dom watched, Joe hitched up the cushion that held his shorts in place—his concept costume, worn in wistful good faith.

"No problem," Father Dom said.

Problem, all right. No course could be designed better than the penance practicum to showcase Joe's shortcomings. Every week, in front of the rest of the class, the students role-played priests hearing confession, with Father Dom as the penitent. He tried to keep things light, presenting goofy sins—once he'd played a woman having visions of the Blessed Virgin saying, "You must wear natural fabrics." Sometimes the hardest thing for the students was keeping a straight face.

After the simulation the other students provided feedback, pointing out where the role-playing priest had done well and where he showed room for improvement. The men were considerate with one another, but there were still so many ways to fall short—hints

[113]

gone unheard, hobbyhorses saddled up. In their responses the students revealed themselves, which was why Joe had been ducking the role-play all semester. Now Father Dom would have no choice but to call on him. He'd have to call on Sipley, too, who volunteered all the time.

Father Dom lay sleepless until three-thirty. Then, moving softly—the walls separating the priests' rooms were like cheesecloth—he turned on the light and started reviewing notes. His desk drawer was stuffed with class outlines, files he kept because he'd been trained to keep files, though he almost never returned to them. Now he was grateful. Surely these hundreds of pages held some forgotten scenario that would demonstrate Joe's particular gifts.

Working without method, Father Dom riffled through the syllabi, glancing now and then at a note he'd written. He searched for a confession that required from the priest more sympathy than guidance, some transgression that would turn Joe's shy heart into a bridge between the penitent and God. No splashy sins like murder or embezzlement. Nothing requiring close discernment or tiptoeing among competing ethical schemes. Nothing about girls, it went without saying. Simply the extension of forgiveness, which had always seemed to Father Dom so easy.

At one time that ease had worried him. He had yearned to be valorous, rich in the grace that comes from spiritual struggle. He had worked with burn victims, telling them how a turn in life's road, even a terrible one, could be the beginning of a happiness never guessed at. "How, exactly?" asked a sixteen-year-old girl, gesturing at a face that had become a cluster of shiny ridges when she stumbled into her parents' sizzling barbecue grill. Another patient, once a mother of three, had been folding laundry in her basement when the house caught fire. Of all her family, only she was still alive, and every day she cursed God with brilliant inventiveness, then yelled at Father Dom, "Are you going to forgive *that?*"

He did. The more he looked, the more he saw only God's

carelessness, work left undone when God got distracted, when God moved on to something else, when God went to get a cup of coffee and left Father Dom's mouth filled with inadequate words. Father Dom had been called, he knew, to be God's hands and voice in the world. He was just sorry that God couldn't find a better class of servant. Helplessly, he got the woman more ice chips and rested his hand tenderly on the side of her bed. Anybody could be forgiven for cursing in a world where somebody like Father Dom was left holding the bag for the Infinite.

He tried not to think about these things anymore. Seminarians of his generation had been taught that every priest was given his particular struggle of faith—the struggle, Father Dom's novice director had said often, that would last a lifetime. But Father Dom turned instead to the easier tasks of ministry, which were so plentiful—teaching, outreach. He could be a good priest without trying to solve the questions of suffering that even Augustine admitted were untraceable. He could help Joe.

He read until early gray light began to seep into the room and it was time to go to chapel. There he prayed his usual wordless prayer with more than common urgency, through breakfast, rising only when it was time to start class.

In the classroom students were seating themselves and pulling out their folders and books. Joe volunteered to fill the water pitchers. Then he volunteered to get cups. His face was the color of dust. He stopped beside Father Benni and murmured something; Father Dom watched the rector shake his head and gesture for Joe to sit down as Father Dom stood up. This week's assigned reading had centered on difficult confessions, surly or abusive penitents. It was important to have coping strategies, Father Dom said.

"You have to *listen*," said Hernandez, a thin-faced student with a smile like sunrise. "Don't just listen to what they're saying, but how they're saying it. People bring in their shame and guilt, so they're angry. If the only person nearby is the priest, they'll get mad at him."

"Have you ever had a penitent threaten you, Father?" Sipley asked Father Benni.

"I had someone pull a knife," the rector said. "He said he would cut out the screen between us to get to me."

"What did you do?"

"Gave him three Our Fathers and a Glory Be." Father Benni waited for the mild laughter to die down. "All you can do is be a priest. Of course, that's a lot."

Father Dom returned to the text, dragging out the discussion as far as he could, but after half an hour every syllable had been covered, and Sipley volunteered to do the first role-play, striding to the front of the room where two chairs stood, separated by a screen. The burly man kissed the stole lying on one chair, placed it around his neck and said, "Hello, my son," as if he'd been doing these things all his life.

Father Dom pulled out a dependable scenario: the teenage boy who liked to kill cats. Once he'd had a student sputter, "You did *what?*" But Sipley was smooth, listening through Father Dom's resentful confession—his mother, he said, had forced him to come—and then talking about the sanctity of God's creations. "We are called to be good stewards," he said. "Our job is to protect the defenseless."

In the discussion afterward, everyone praised Sipley's clarity. Joe said that he admired Sipley's calm demeanor. Hernandez suggested that Sipley might have spent a little more time exploring the reason the boy was tying firecrackers to cats' legs. Sipley nodded, taking notes.

An anxious silence took over the room when Father Dom asked for further comments; the air seemed to prickle. Joe was already trudging to the front of the room, where he hung the purple stole around his neck and sat down. "Okay," he whispered.

Reciting the opening prayer and adding that it had been six years since his last confession, Father Dom wondered if he looked as nervous as he felt. He hoped so. A good priest would try to put a parishioner at ease.

"What brings you here today?" Joe finally asked. His voice was faint. Sipley jotted a note.

"I didn't think I'd ever come to confession again. I don't really believe in this. But I just saw my doctor. He says I'm HIV-positive." Father Dom paused. "I'm twenty-six years old."

He had gone over Joe's transcripts. Part of the young man's fourth-year field education had been hospice work; he could draw on his experience with real patients, people he'd known and liked. But now, while Father Dom waited, Joe didn't say anything. "Are you there?" Father Dom said.

"Go on."

"Did you hear me? I'm twenty-six years old, and I'm HIV-positive. I just left the doctor. You're the first person I've told. I'm not sure I can tell anybody else." Father Dom left room for Joe to ask about his family, or to murmur that the church was a good place to come. "How could this happen to me?"

The silence stretched and thickened until Father Dom felt anger start to buckle his thoughts together. What was the matter with Joe? All he had to say was *Are you afraid?*, *Do you feel alone?*, *God is with you, even now. Especially now.* A kid who tied firecrackers to cats could figure out that much.

"The only place I could think to come was here," Father Dom said bitterly. "Don't ask me why. It's not like the church has ever helped before."

"Have you made plans for your death?" Joe said.

Air actually seemed to fly out of Father Dom's lungs. When he looked up, every one of the students was writing. Even Sipley looked stunned.

Joe was still talking, his voice like sand. "You need to study the teachings of the Holy Father, and then accord yourself with them. The Church is very clear about the sinfulness of homosexual behavior. You should have come here sooner."

"That's not good enough," Father Dom said. He'd never mentioned homosexuality. Twenty-six years old! Maybe that sounded

ERIN MCGRAW

old to this reedy voice behind the screen. "What am I supposed to do now? I need help."

"There are several hospices in the area."

"What is the *matter* with you?" Father Dom said. He stuck his face up close to the screen. "It is your job to care."

In the long silence, Father Dom imagined Joe standing at the top of the cliff. His hands were tucked safely up his priestly sleeves while Father Dom slipped off the edge.

"Peace be with you," Joe said.

Father Dom opened and then closed his mouth, unable to think of one more thing to say. The students were silent until Sipley, of all people, laughed. At that small, embarrassed noise the others laughed too, looking at their feet. Even Father Benni, whose lips had been tight, joined in. Only Father Dom remained silent. When Joe stood up, Father Dom saw the dark spots on the stole where the boy had sweated through it.

"I want to be a priest." Joe's voice was desperate.

"Why?" Father Dom said.

Father Benni called a faculty meeting that afternoon. "What are his strengths?" he said, palming back the thick hair he was normally vain about. He didn't have to explain what had happened in the practicum. Word was out before lunch.

"He pitches in," Father Petrus said. "He's not a shirker."

"Or a know-it-all," Father Wells said.

"There's a real sweetness there," said Father Radziewicz, who didn't generally talk in these meetings.

"I know we all like Joe," Father Benni said, "but this sounds like we're describing the president of the Altar Society. How would he do with a headstrong parishioner? With a parish council? Can he lead?"

"He hears a call," Father Dom muttered.

"Calls can be misheard," Father Benni said.

"You think he doesn't know that?" Father Dom stared at the whorls in the table's laminated surface. "He goes around listening all the time. Priesthood is the one thing he wants, and he's terrified that we're going to take it away from him."

"That's hardly our job. Still, when I compare him to some of the other men—" Father Benni shook his head.

"That's exactly why it's important for Joe to be here," Father Dom said. He wished he could curb the desperation rocketing through his voice. "He has his own gifts. The seminary isn't supposed to turn out identical priests, each one perfectly sure of himself, rolling off an assembly line with his collar in place and his opinions set for life." He stopped under the weight of the rector's sharp gaze, then added, "A little uncertainty isn't a bad thing."

"What I saw in your classroom was not enough uncertainty," Father Benni said. "If that had been a real confession, the poor man would have left the church and walked in front of a bus. Joe did everything but push him."

"Why don't we assign him a mentor?" said Father Radziewicz. "Someone he can talk to, who has better judgment."

Father Dom couldn't hold back his sigh. Was the mentor going to follow Joe to his parish and slip into the confessional with him? But Father Benni was steepling his fingers, pondering the suggestion, and Father Dom's imprudent heart lifted.

"Joe might improve if he's taken in hand by someone at his own level," the rector said. "He might be less defensive. Some of the men have volunteered to help."

"Greg, you're not thinking of assigning one of the students?" Father Dom said.

The rector nodded, apparently indifferent to the horror in Father Dom's voice. "It's win-win. A fine opportunity for growth on both sides. Besides, none of us wants to stay up as late as the students do."

Fathers Wells and Berton, those toadies, laughed. Father Dom said, "Students don't have the experience. They think they know more than they do. Joe needs trustworthy guidance."

"He's had the benefit of your guidance for four years," Father Benni said. "I'd say it's time for a new approach."

"Just not this one," Father Dom said. The priests laughed and pushed back their chairs. Dependable Dom, always good for a joke. He stayed at the table until he and the rector were alone in the room. "Nobody wants Joe to succeed more than I do," Father Dom said. "But it's going to take a miracle."

"Good. That's our turf."

"Right," Father Dom said bitterly. "I keep forgetting."

Father Benni chose Sipley to be Joe's mentor. And he chose Father Dom to oversee Sipley—to mentor the mentor. Father Dom was overscheduled with classes and field experience and his outreach program at the youth center, but he was glad for the assignment. Every night Sipley came to him to describe Joe's progress, and Father Dom imagined Joe as a fragile boat that he could still see in his spyglass.

"He's shy, is all. Once you get him in a situation where he's comfortable, he opens up." Sipley was sitting in Father Dom's office, cradling between his big hands the cup of coffee Father Dom had offered.

"Where is he comfortable?"

"You should have seen him in the soup kitchen. He was jawing with everybody who came through. 'Hey, how's it going, you want gravy with that?' And nobody gave him a hard time. I think they could see what he is." Sipley shifted his bulky thighs on the hard chair. "In his way, he really brings out the best in people."

"But can you imagine Joe setting up the soup kitchen and overseeing it? A priest needs to show initiative."

Sipley shifted again. Even in his discomfort he gave the impression of being fundamentally comfortable. "He's heard a call, Father. It isn't up to me to question that."

"It is up to the rector and me to question that." Looking at Sipley's polite, averted face, Father Dom added, "In the service of the church. Joe will be a representative of the Holy Father. And we're asking you to help us make sure he can be a good representative."

The speech had the desired effect: Sipley leaned forward and rested his elbows on his knees. When he spoke, his resonant voice was confiding. "Joe's never going to be a take-charge guy. He's all heart. But if he's working with somebody who can direct him, he'll give a hundred percent. He wants this so much."

Father Dom analyzed the young man's ruddy face and broad, chapped hands. Everything about him breathed with vibrancy. Had he ever wondered why quailing Joe could be drawn to the same priesthood Sipley was so confident about? Had he thought about the role of a man in society but not of it, safely shut away from human contact by vestments and a collar? Probably not. Sipley himself wanted to be a priest so he could tell people what to do.

"I can't believe there's no place for him," Sipley was saying.

"We're still looking," Father Dom said.

Sipley nodded. "If you don't mind my asking, Father—did you question my call, too?"

Startled, Father Dom said, "You don't present the same issues."

"But still."

Sipley's wide-set eyes were alit with new curiosity. This chance would not come again. "Of course we did," said Father Dom. "There's no such thing as an automatic priest."

"All my life people have told me I was born to be a priest. My mother, for one. Half the time it's a compliment."

"It's not something to be taken for granted."

"So I'm being tested? Is that why you asked me to help with Joe?"

"You're likely to pass," Father Dom said. "Don't lose any sleep over this." But he could see already, as Sipley stood and shook Father Dom's hand, how the young man's body was bright with new energy. Father Dom should have been grateful; his own weariness had increased a hundredfold.

In the days that followed, Father Dom expected Sipley to lay siege to Joe, intent on their mutual salvation. But Sipley was a better psychologist than Father Dom had given him credit for. He met Joe casually, in the halls or over coffee, and twice he reported to Father Dom that he hadn't spoken with Joe that day. "Figured he could use a vacation from me."

Father Dom was giving Joe a vacation, too. Aside from the weekly meetings of the practicum, he saw Joe only from a distance—in the library, the dining commons, on the walkway in front of the soccer field. When he believed himself unobserved, Joe took his place easily with the other men, and from time to time he tipped back his head in laughter. But as soon as he saw Father Dom, his gaze dropped again, and dread clung to his pale, chewed mouth. Father Dom understood that Joe had assigned him the role of the enemy, obstacle to Joe's happiness. The perception wasn't wrong, but still Father Dom felt stung.

Every day he defended Joe to one priest or another, pointing out how the young man was the first to help clear tables, the first to donate to clothing drives for countries rent by earthquakes. He heard the words' puniness as they rolled out of his mouth. Everyone in the seminary was waiting for Joe to prove himself with something more than a clothing drive. In these priest-starved days, when Father Radziewicz predicted that St. Boniface would have to start ordaining dogs, it was a special humiliation to be re-evaluated, and Father Dom knew that Joe felt persecuted.

So Father Dom was relieved when, after three weeks of mentoring, Sipley told him that he had a new idea about Joe, a breakthrough plan. "It's nothing that you'll object to. I've put in a few phone calls, and I'm waiting to hear."

"Give me a hint, in case the rector asks."

Sipley paused. "The battle is not to the strong."

"That's not going to be much help if he presses me for details."

"Joe just needs the right chance to shine." Sipley beamed. As always, he was confident in the goodness of his actions. But Father Dom wondered if the young man remembered the end of the passage he had quoted: "all are subject to time and mischance."

A week passed before Father Dom returned to his office and found a note tacked to the corkboard. *Could you join Joe and me in the dining room? We'd like to propose something.* Father Dom turned left, toward the cafeteria, worrying at a hangnail as he walked. *We.*

The dining room was empty except for the two men sitting by the window, whose heads swung up in unison at the creak of the swinging door. Sipley said, "Thank you for coming, Father."

Father Dom seated himself beside Joe. Since the young man was pretending he hadn't edged away from the table, Father Dom pretended he didn't notice.

"An opportunity has come up," Sipley said after Father Dom turned down coffee or iced tea. "I think it's too special to miss. One of the staff members at St. Thérèse House had to leave, and they need someone to step in right away. Joe and I could go together."

"Are you serious?" Father Dom said.

"It's a special opportunity." Joe's voice was dim. "Our men don't usually go there."

They sure didn't. St. Thérèse House was a two-story facility downtown for terminal children, youngsters dying from cancer or brain lesions or frenzied infections Father Dom had never heard of. Children went to St. Thérèse House when they couldn't survive another faltering transplant or more scorching chemotherapy. A hospice for six- and seven-year-olds, it drew patients from three states away. Doctors in the area were proud of the institution, which appalled Father Dom. Sweet Jesus, it was not to be proud of.

Although he had never been in it, he realized he could describe the place as if he'd lived there. For every child who died with a face filled with light, three others left this earth looking puzzled or disappointed or so crocked on morphine they couldn't feel the oils of the last rites being thumbed onto their foreheads. His stomach turned heavily.

"Their people are trained," Father Dom said.

"They're short-handed," Sipley said.

Joe studied his clear brown tea, and Father Dom automatically thought of Gethsemane. He wondered whether Joe was also thinking of that utter despair. In a brief burst of viciousness, Father Dom hoped he was, then was ashamed of himself. "When would it start?" Father Dom said.

"That depends on you," Sipley said. "There's only so far the staff can bend the rules. We can come, but a faculty member has to supervise."

Father Dom opened his mouth and shut it again. "I don't have medical training," he said.

"The staff will be keeping an eye on the patients," Sipley said. "They want someone to keep an eye on us. Since you've been working with Joe and me, I thought you should be the one. Of course, I could ask somebody else."

And somebody would agree. Priests always went: the jails, the hospitals, the shuttered, stinking houses. "Beats reality TV," Father Wells had said one day after a visit to the prison, his eyes blazing. He might very well go to St. Thérèse House and train his gaze on those withering children. His gaze would also land on Joe, helpless at the bedside.

"I'll go," Father Dom said, lifting his chin. "I'll *go*," he added, not that Sipley or Joe had asked a second time.

St. Thérèse House smelled like apples. Most of the children ate through feeding tubes, but one or two could manage soft foods, and every morning ferocious Sister Lupe, who looked thin even in sweat pants, made a fresh batch of applesauce. "At lunch you will feed them," she told Joe and Sipley. "Until then you will visit with the children who are alone." The two young men nodded, as did

Father Dom, standing a step behind them. Sister Lupe glanced at him with flat eyes, then led them down a corridor.

Bedrooms unfolded in wings from the central hall, and in either apple-smelling direction lay children, one to a room. The children were bald and gray faced, lying in what looked less like sleep than suspension. Parents, murmuring steadily, sat close beside the beds.

"How long do they stay here?" Sipley was asking.

"Two weeks, typically," Sister Lupe said. "The one you're going to see has been here almost three months, our longest ever. You're getting her because she already knows all of our jokes." Father Dom tried to imagine a joke coming out of Sister Lupe's lipless mouth.

"What does she have?" Sipley asked.

"Leukemia."

"Where are her parents?" Joe asked.

Sister Lupe's smile was vulpine. "Several agencies would like to know." She breezed into the girl's room, then looked back and gestured impatiently for Joe and Sipley to follow. "Look, Cindy. Father Sipley and Father Halaczek are here to see you. And Father Dominic." The girl smiled at them with half her mouth. Father Dom didn't know whether she had lost motor control on one side or she meant the expression to look ironic. "Hi."

Bruises ran in chains up her arms and ringing her neck, and around the bruises her skin was a dry non-color. Her skull made a hard dent in the pillow. Father Dom guessed she was twelve years old, but he could have been three years off in either direction.

"They're going to visit with you until lunch," Sister Lupe said.

"That's a long time," Cindy said.

"It's good for you to see new faces," the sister said, already on her way out of the room. "Enjoy yourselves, Fathers."

Cindy's expression was clearly long-suffering, and Father Dom revised his age estimate upward. "Are you here to talk to me about dying?" she said.

"Not if you don't want to," Sipley said. "What's on your mind?"

"No offense, but I'm scared of priests. It's not good news when you guys come around."

Joe reached behind his neck and unsnapped his collar. "I don't have to wear this. I haven't been ordained."

"You're in training?"

"I'm on probation. I messed up, and I'm being given one last chance."

"So you're here to show your stuff."

Joe nodded, and Cindy said to Father Dom, "What does he need to do?"

"Just be with you."

"Some test." She closed her eyes. Father Dom had stood beside hospital beds for twenty-five years; rarely had he seen a face so dwindled, her forehead collapsed as if someone had stuck a thumb into it. He flattened his wet palms against his thighs. Sipley and Joe were talking to her. He could slip out of the room and no one would notice.

"Well, do it," Cindy was saying to the young men, her eyes still closed. "I'm not going anywhere."

Joe said, "What do you want to talk about?"

"You talk. I'll listen."

Father Dom's stomach seemed to tip. Shamefully, he couldn't stop thinking that he was breathing the air that had passed through Cindy's diseased membranes. He pulled a tissue from the box on the ledge and held it before his face as if he were going to blow his nose.

Joe said, "Our Father."

"No," Cindy murmured. "I don't like that one. Do your own."

Joe smiled crookedly. "Please. That's the only good prayer I know."

Cindy didn't open her eyes. "Sister Lupe says the best prayers are one word. What's your word?"

"Please," Joe said promptly.

"Keep going."

The smell of apples billowed softly from the corridor. "Please. God," Joe said, the word like a cough. "You are in heaven. And your name is—praised." His white face was damp, and he stood at a tilt, as if every muscle in his body were locked. "I could use some help," he said to Father Dom.

"What do you want me to do?" Father Dom hadn't meant to sound savage, and he was embarrassed when Cindy looked at him with interest.

"Aren't you supposed to be telling me about heaven?" she said.

"Ask Father Halaczek. He knows," Father Dom said, a bit of malice to add to his lifetime sins of evasion and cowardice, sins he yearned for now as his eyes slid away from the girl's cheeks, molded to the bone. All a priest could do was plead for her release, and hope that pleading would do some good. Joe knew that lesson as well as Father Dom. Joe, who pleaded so much, knew it better.

The young man grasped the corner of Cindy's sheet, his hand tightening and releasing, his voice shaking. "Please. Your will is going to happen," he said, then broke down. Pressing his hands against his face, he stood beside the bed, his shoulders racked. "This is the worst thing that's ever happened to me," he said. "And it's going to get worse." He wheeled to face Father Dom, who had backed up until his shoulders touched the wall. The smell of apples rose around him, and his nausea was roiling like a sea. "Isn't it?" Joe said.

"Yes," said Father Dom.

"Are you going to stop my ordination?"

"No."

"Why not?"

Sipley said, "Fathers, we're here to pray for healing." He began to move his lips unself-consciously, a powerful man who could probably hold the seventy-pound girl in one hand. Here, Father Dom realized, was the test Sipley had set for himself: to halt death's advance, even though death was on the march. Death had already won. Father Dom wondered when Sipley was going to acknowledge that.

"Why not?" Joe repeated, louder.

"Who else would come here?" Father Dom said.

"I don't think you're supposed to say those things where I can hear them," Cindy said.

"Father Dominic is a special priest," Joe said. "You're lucky to even see him. Why don't you lead us in prayer, Father? We need guidance."

Joe probably didn't hear the rage that rang through his words. And Father Dom would forgive the boy—just as, when he looked at Cindy's shrunken, darkening body, he already forgave her parents for running away. In the end he forgave everybody, which was half the reason Joe would never forgive him.

Father Dom dampened his lips to say something unobjection-able about faith and perseverance. He breathed in the apple-drenched air. The instant he opened his mouth, he vomited where he stood. Sipley managed to get a basin under Father Dom's mouth for the last of it, but the room was full of the stink, and when he finished Father Dom could not lift his swimming eyes.

"Usually I'm the one who does that," Cindy said.

"I'm sorry," he murmured, afraid to say anything more. Sipley was probably warming up to quote St. Paul: the Spirit expresses itself in outcries that we ourselves do not understand. If Sipley said a word, Father Dom would retch again.

"Father," Joe said. "You should have told us you were ill." He pulled a chair beside Cindy's bed. She said, "Do you mind not talking?"

"I'll get you something to drink." His thin voice wavered. When Cindy shook her head, he said, "We have such a long day ahead. Let me get you something. Please."

# THREE PARTING SHOTS
# AND A FORECAST

CHRISTIE HODGEN

## JOHN WILKES BOOTH

### HIS PICTURE

A three-quarter shot, Booth leering just left of center, casual, as if turning toward someone who has called his name. No doubt a beautiful heiress, an adoring fan. He has a devil's ear, angled tight and sharp against his head, and his hair is brushed into nonchalant curls. Dark-eyed with eggshell skin, he wears a black moustache combed into a frown. At the time of the picture Booth is one of the most celebrated young actors in Washington City, and he dresses the part. He models a loose jacket, cut in the latest fashion, its collar and breast pocket trimmed with silk thread. The top button is fastened, and the rest of the jacket falls open in a triangle like a teepee. The pocket sprouts a starched handkerchief. His right hand, fat and smooth as a baby's, props a delicate bamboo walking stick. A small brass key dangles from his vest's middle button. (A remembrance? A safe-deposit box? The door to his room? No one is sure.) A gold ring wraps the little finger of his left hand, which grips the handle of something resembling a whip. He is a gentleman, a gentleman.

It is a good time for actors. The President himself attends the theater with some frequency. Theater-going is a pleasant diversion, and Lincoln's only opportunity to nap in peace. The President's box hovers twelve feet over stage left, and is about the size and shape of Lincoln's childhood log home. It seats four comfortably, five in a pinch. The President lounges in a distinctive rocking chair. It is one of Lincoln's favorite places, cozy and warm as a cradle.

Imagine, one evening, that Lincoln has trouble dozing off. A loony Hamlet trots underfoot. The actor's interpretation requires a certain amount of gymnastics. It is a promenade of leaping and screeching. "TO BE!" Booth booms, looks skyward, drops to one knee, rolls onto his back. "OR NOT TO BE!" He clutches the open neck of his shirt and howls. Booth turns a cartwheel and decides on the question. The crowd loves him. Perhaps they find his aerobics refreshing in such solemn times. What's a play these days anyway but a moment's distraction? Who wants to look death too plainly in the face?

The President decides to sleep out the rest of the performance, chin slumped on his chest. Just then, Booth steals a glance at the shadowed figure. Asleep! In the middle of his soliloquy! He stops for a moment, stumbles on the verse. Lincoln's legs are outstretched—propped on the banister—and the giant, scuffed soles of his shoes face the stage like twin hecklers. Imagine living under the reign of such an unmannered buffoon. Booth decides, then and there, to take some kind of action. Curiously, as the play wears on, Booth's performance improves. The audience remarks how distressed and convincing he is, as if he were really and truly at odds with an un-rightful king.

Lincoln wakes rested as the lights come up. It is his best sleep in weeks.

There is little rest for Booth after his plan begins to material-ize. During the first months of 1865, Booth dreams—nightly—his own set of tragedies. They take different forms. The worst of the lot occurs on stage. Just as he has the crowd in his grip, just as he works

Hamlet or Romeo or King Lear into the most innovative and tortured interpretation of the century, the crowd howls with laughter. The gas lights jet up, flickering blue and then white. He sees people twisting in their chairs, the men clutching their stomachs, the women covering their faces with gloved hands. Booth checks to see that his fly is buttoned. "What!" he demands, stomping a foot. "Blast!" Booth likes to curse in the manner of all true southern gentleman—forcefully, but with restraint. The audience can't seem to get ahold of itself. Booth storms toward the curtain, bats at it to split the seam so he can slip off stage. But the curtain is stitched together at its center, and only sways from the rafters like a bemused spirit. The theater takes on the look of a large carnivorous mouth, its domed ceiling like a palate. The wooden seats like false teeth, the audience rolling and flapping like a crazy tongue. They will swallow him. There is nothing to do but submit. Booth drops to one knee and makes the motions of a prayer—an act, but isn't everything.

Suddenly the audience calms. Booth hears his name announced from overhead, a high pitched and familiar voice, not quite human. "Booth," he hears again, and looks skyward. Lincoln stands in his elaborate box, tall as Goliath. He extends an arm toward the stage and turns his mouth into a wry smile.

*Young man, you remind me of a story*, starts Lincoln. Another one of his roguish yarns. A bawdy type of chatter, a rail-splitting, chain-gang story, a perverse parable. Lincoln continues: *One afternoon a fellow stopped by the office asking to be appointed minister abroad. Sensing my hesitation, the gentleman came down to a more modest proposal.* The audience snickers. Lincoln adjusts his atrocious hat. *After much of the same to and fro, the man asked to be appointed a tide-waiter.* The crowd crackles to life, even before the punch line. The old bag of wind is like a re-oiled machine. There's color in his cheeks, a twinkle in his eye. He strokes his beard and draws out the ending. *Now, let me see.* He smiles, rocks back on his heels. *Where was I?*

"The waiter, the waiter!" yells the crowd.

*Oh yes. When the man discovered he could not have that, he asked me for an old pair of trousers.* There's hooting and roaring from all corners of the room. Booth sits on the stage in a droopy pile, playing with his fingers. *My boy,* says Lincoln, *it is best to be humble. Especially when one is illegitimate.*

Booth flushes red. His worst secret revealed by his worst enemy. It is true. Booth is a bastard, the spawn of an unholy entanglement. By rank he is less noble than the bumpkin Lincoln, born in wedlock. Worse, Booth is not really a southerner, as he so often claims. Hailing from Maryland—the gutless, wavering Maryland. Booth feels as if his very face were a fiction, a cloth mask stretched over borrowed bones. He tugs at his hair to make sure it is fixed to his scalp, and it plucks out in lovely curls. He gasps. He goes to scream but his teeth fall out of their sockets, long and narrow with ghastly pointed roots. He wakes with a furious heart.

# LINCOLN

Lincoln's story is one perhaps best told by others, the ones left behind. Those things and people in Lincoln's employment during his final days. What remains is a curious testimony. Loosely stitched, and of course, unfinished.

### HIS PICTURE

Of the hundreds of images taken of Lincoln, one photograph is without question the most striking. One of a series of formal shots, taken the morning after Lee's surrender. He is seated in an ornate chair, its four legs formed from a series of polished wooden bulges, that in threes resemble the curves of a woman's body. His legs extend forward toward the camera, long and crooked like the branches of a thin tree. His polished dress shoes could hold a half-gallon of milk apiece and a little more. He rests his arms uncomfortably in his lap, thumb and forefinger of each hand pinched as if he were measuring salt or conducting music. He wears a wrinkled, silk-collared jacket, a white dress shirt that is loose in the chest, and a lopsided bow tie. His hair, reasonably smoothed, is recently thinned. His beard—grown as a disguise while he took the railroad to Washington for his first inauguration—has, in four year's time, grown thick and then thin again, patchy in the cheek. Perhaps Lincoln loses his hair from sheer exhaustion. The follicles quit their grip on the strands.

Lincoln eats a bird's diet and rarely sleeps. At times it seems impossible that he is alive. Lines mark his face cruelly—long and deep. His flesh is loose on the bone, and his eyes have ceased to hold color. They are now like the skin settled over warm milk. Translucent, tenuously draped over a weak surface, barely holding shape. On this day of victory he looks like someone who is disappointed with death. He looks like someone who has been kept waiting a long while.

### HIS DOORMAN

The doorman is one of four guards hired to protect the President during the last months of his life. The guards are chosen more for their size than know-how. There is no reason to trust any of them to act well in a bad situation.

One spring evening, well past midnight, one of the doorkeepers hears a close-by, double barrel gunshot. He wrings his hands under the dim light of the White House's front entrance. Who else but the President would draw fire in the darkest hour of morning? The doorkeeper looks up and down the avenue, searching for light in the shuttered windows of neighboring hotels. All is dark. There is no moon. Soon the doorman perceives the gathering, crooked rumble of hooves over cobblestone. He peers down the avenue and recognizes the President, dwarfing his full-grown horse. Lincoln is bareheaded and without a jacket. His white shirt flags in the wind. He struggles with the reins, half standing in the saddle and tugging back at the horse's long neck. Lincoln jolts to a halt and dismounts, breathing heavy.

"Riding alone again, sir," says the doorman.

"I can't seem to get to sleep." Lincoln hands over the reins and smooths the horse's mane.

"What happened to your hat?" The President is never outdoors without his trademark stovepipe.

Lincoln touches his hair absently. "I must have lost it." He nods goodnight and shuffles inside, stooped. He is small and weary looking, his hair blustered into haphazard curls.

The doorman ties the horse at the front gate and leaves his post. He is not one for standing still, even under orders. He treks up the road, heels clicking on the stone. He walks in the middle of the street, head down. The square stones are wet with spring, caked with mud, swelled and upturned in places where they've burst with cold. On instinct the doorkeeper turns down a narrow alley between two boarding houses. The muddy pass is lined with garbage. A loose rooster pokes around in the dirt, clucking idly, pecking at various smelly heaps. It is not uncommon for fowl to roam the streets, feeding themselves from discarded scraps. What is peculiar about this rooster is its shape, its walk. The doorkeeper watches its silhouette for some time. The rooster seems to struggle under the weight of its own gobbler, tipping forward and losing its footing. The doorkeeper inches closer. In better light he sees that the rooster beaks the President's hat, which dangles and dips in the mud. He stalks forward, crouching, hands outstretched. The rooster squawks and flaps its wings, attempts flight. But the stovepipe is too much to bear. The doorman stomps his feet and manages a low growl. The bird releases the hat with what appears to be a certain amount of grief, as if it were abandoning the body of a favorite child. The doorman scoops the collapsed hat and examines it in the dark. It is mud-covered, the black silk patched with stains, the brim trampled and bent. The top is tilted like a crumbling chimney.

Then he confirms his worst fear: The crown of the hat is pierced with a fat hole, the wound of serious ammunition. This marks the third known attempt on Lincoln's life, the closest shot yet. A bullet whisked through the hat's narrow cylinder, less than a foot from Lincoln's head. Still, until the very night of his death, Lincoln continues to ride alone at night, Paul Revere-ing around, announcing his sorrow at every door.

After Lincoln's death, the doorman cannot help himself. He tells the story to anyone who will listen. Each time it is different. Each time his own role improves. Sometimes there is no rooster, and the doorman finds the hat in a driveway. Sometimes the doorman is shot at by rebels trying to finish the job. It is always the same with the hat, though. Pierced through the crown. A miss so narrow and terrifying it defies explanation, no matter how many times he tries, no matter how fantastic the circumstances.

The doorkeeper never forgives himself. He rubs his fingers together absently, obsessively, for the rest of his life, imagining the silk hat against his skin, its thin, crumpled frame, its black band of mourning. He recalls the fabric torn in a rough circle, how the bullet left a star-shaped scar.

### HIS CHAIR

Lincoln is shot in a rocking chair. John Ford, the owner of the theater, brings the chair from his own residence when the President plans to be in attendance. Surely the President esteems the chair's construction, the ease it allows his legs. Or maybe he simply admires its beauty. It is a sleigh built for one. Cushioned in a rich red fabric, puckered with covered buttons, swollen at the neck with extra padding. The slender arms are carved from a dark wood. They run straight for the length of an average arm, then dip toward the floor and curl under themselves. The four legs are short and fat, perched on long, thin rockers. Today the chair would be placed in a nursery. It is small and delicate enough to raise suspicion. How could a man of any size—and a President at that—favor such a dainty throne? The top of the chair is marked with a biscuit-sized stain, seeped into the upholstery, thought by some to be Lincoln's blood.

In fact it is the mark of a popular gentleman's hair pomade. In terms of evidence, indications of the President's brief and tragic patronage, the chair offers nothing. No print, no stain.

From Booth's vantage, the chair poses a particular problem. High backed, it obscures most of Lincoln's head, leaving a narrow, crescent-shaped target. Booth slows his breathing and pulls a brass-handled gun from his vest. He aims deliberately, both arms extended, head cocked. On stage, the play continues with its comic twists. Booth's shot is not heard over the crowd's laughter. When a frenzied man leaps to the stage waving his pistol, the crowd believes it is part of the script. Some clap and chuckle, drowning out Booth's dramatic parting soliloquy, borrowed from Brutus: *Sic semper tyrannis!*

Meanwhile the rocking chair thrusts forward and washes back, allowing Lincoln's body to ease into the blow. Perhaps it spares him a certain amount of pain. Doctors stretch him across the floor, find the wound and work a clot from the back of his head, just above the left ear. Someone provides brandy. Someone parts his lips and eases in the fluid. False blood, false hope. Someone holds his hand the nine hours it takes him to die.

Later, someone washes the blood from his hair, loosens the dried stain with water, sets it running again. Later, someone places silver coins over his swollen eyes to weigh down the lids. And later, the chair retires to an ill-frequented museum. It creaks and sighs whenever it is cleaned.

## BOSTON CORBETT

### HIS PICTURE

Not an unattractive man. His long hair is parted down the center and pulled together at the nape of the neck. He wears ill-fitted Union blues, a fat stripe running along the vertical seam of his loose trousers. He sits at a round table reading an enormous Bible. He is clean-shaven. His boots are knee-high, made of black leather, and have probably trampled across acres of blood-soaked ground.

Before Boston Corbett shot John Wilkes Booth at close range with a Colt revolver, he was a sergeant in the Union army, and before that, a hatter in Boston, Massachusetts. One of twenty-six men hired to pursue Lincoln's killers, Corbett did not shoot Booth under orders, in self-defense, or any other set of condoned circumstances save this: God told him to. The mandate from Secretary of War Stanton was to round up Booth alive and squealing. What good was a public hanging of the conspirators without their gallant leader, the most famous actor in Washington City? At the very least, Booth would provide an afternoon's entertainment, his final speech choked out as his trim legs kicked uselessly over the platform. Instead, Stanton has to settle for a dead fugitive, shot in the neck by a mad hatter. As Secretary of War one learns to take what one can get.

It seems that Corbett was always waiting for this to happen— that he had spent his life in preparation for this one act, this favor to God. Even as he shaped hats in Boston he was practicing the gestures of precision, studying the relationship between his methodical labor and its eventual divine purpose. Just as Jesus spent a certain amount of time learning carpentry, Corbett apprenticed himself in a tidy shop, fixing practical hats to warm his neighbors' heads.

Hats are made by hand then, meticulously. It is rare for a gentleman to walk the streets with an uncovered head. Every respectable man owns at least two, one for dress and a second for weather. It is considered good form to touch the brim of one's hat upon passing an acquaintance, to remove the hat completely when bowing to a lady. In Washington City, the fancy top hat is in style. A black collapsible wool-felt blend with a grosgrain ribbon trim. The streets are teeming with them. A taller-than-average person can watch the hats from above, clogging the streets with black and brown and gray, bobbing to and fro like shifting silt, like fish bellying around on a lake's surface. Corbett is familiar with the President's unusual choice in head wear. The lonely, poor-selling stovepipe. Why an overly tall man wishes to accentuate the problem is his own business. Corbett makes a few hats on the chance that locals will want to imitate the Presidential fashion. He sells one to a traveling merchant, and the others sit on a shelf for most of Lincoln's administration.

In this part of the country the practical fur hat is still in style. Corbett works late in the shop washing the bloodied pelts of beavers and muskrats. He wets the fur in a basin of water, then soaps vigorously. The fur makes a munching noise against itself. Corbett runs the soap up his own arm, his hairless skin pink with foamed blood. When the pelt dries he applies mercury to separate the skin and fur. He rubs it into the roots with his fingers, and the poison seeps through his skin. He takes a moment to admire the cool liquid, how it skates across his palm and divides into an arrangement of spheres, like planets and their moons, a whole universe in silver reflecting the warm pink of his palm. He thinks of God's hand and his place in it. A small mirror.

The hair pulls from the skin and Corbett steams it onto sections of felt. His fingers are silver-tipped. When he licks them after a meal he sucks on the poisonous traces. It tastes like suffering. There are flecks of mercury in his blood, running slick through the veins like silver bullets, up to the brain. The mercury chimes in his head, God's voice. Corbett's hats become something of a legend in town. So precisely detailed, so finely stitched, so comforting and necessary. Tucked in the store window, such small and attractive wonders.

One summer Corbett works for a few weeks without hearing from God. His hats turn out mediocre, and he begins to worry that he has sinned in some way. He examines himself with unflinching scrutiny before settling on a minor transgression. Lately his thoughts have wandered some. He has begun making ladies' hats, harmless enough. But in the process he has on occasion imagined himself unfastening a lady's bonnet, soaping a woman's hair right there in

the shop, in his basin. He has even looked wantingly at the prostitutes across the street in their feathered caps.

Corbett crosses the dark room to examine an unfinished bonnet, sprawled across a work bench like a spider. The bonnet is light
in his hands, made of a fine off-white muslin, lace-edged with mother
of pearl buttons under the chin. He strokes the fabric with his fat,
red thumb. He circles the chin's button with a finger. *Women and
their articles*, he thinks, and rips the button loose. It pops on the
floor like a weak gunshot. The room seems to shrivel. Its blue walls
slant inward and the floor pushes up. It is always this way when
Corbett thinks of women—their stifling and irresistible bodies. His
breath comes quick, and suddenly the fumes clog his breathing.
There is only one solution.

Corbett castrates himself with a pair of scissors to avoid the
temptation of women. Only one of the sacrifices a true man of God
must be willing to make. For it is better for a man not to marry, lest
he be distracted from the Lord's work. Corbett sharpens the blades
on a rod to make the music of a ritual. Afterwards, he wraps himself
in the same manner used to diaper Jesus on the cross.

Corbett then eats a generous dinner and makes conversation
at the table. He uses the right fork at the right time and remembers
his prayers. He retires casually and takes a short stroll around the
neighborhood before deciding to visit the hospital.

He is now a passionless man, unsuited for war. And he joins
the Union Army, and re-enlists several times to preserve the sanctity
of the whole. And now, to ensure the final peace, he is sent after
Booth to end it all. In his own estimation, Corbett serves as the
final blow in the Civil War.

On April 26, 1865, Corbett and his company track Booth to a
tobacco farm in Northern Virginia. They have been twelve days on
the hunt. The Virginia spring is cold, the pale grass still scattered
loose over the frozen earth, crunching under their boots. It is a lot
like war. The men keep low as they file through rows of planted
greens and circle a large barn, weapons poised.

The barn is a limp wooden structure, warped in places and leaning to one side. Inside, Booth and his toady, David Herold, make assessments. A dozen blues at least, maybe two. Closing in on them. The commander orders an immediate surrender and Herold, tired from days of scavenging, knows it is over. He steps from the barn, arms raised. Booth remains, waiting for the soldiers to approach. He picks up an old scythe from the corner of the barn and leaps around, slicing through the air. He holds it like a woman and takes a final spin around the barn. So little room for Booth's beloved gymnastics. The floor of the barn is littered with scraps of old tobacco. One of Booth's favorite smells, warm and genteel. The fumes engulf him. The soldiers have lit the barn on fire, and the flames leap from the ground high and fat, smoking furiously. The tobacco curls under the heat, mulching the floor. There is a crackled roaring, and the air goes soft, rising in waves. Booth decides to make a run for it, and he stands for a moment, gets into character.

Outside, Corbett inches closer to the barn, crouching under the heat. Squinting, struggling for breath. It is something of a miracle that a man in this situation gets off a fatal round. Through a crack in the barn, two warped boards separated with a six-inch gap. Corbett raises the revolver. He aims through the traces of his own breath.

The bullet lodges in Booth's neck, severing the spinal cord. While the shot still sounds in the air, while the powder from Corbett's revolver lingers over the earth, several men race into the barn and drag Booth from the flames. One of the men swipes Booth's hat with a mind to sell it to the highest bidder. The other men take turns guarding the body. Booth remains conscious for a few hours but says little. It is not until his final moments that Booth asks the soldiers to hold up his paralyzed hands before his face, so he can admire them. The soldiers take turns puppeteering. Booth stares into his palms and utters the word *useless* on his next to last breath. These faces peering over him. He flutters his eyelids and practices his most disdainful expression. An act? It is hard for even Booth to say.

FORECAST

Boston Corbett is excused of all criminal charges in the shooting of John Wilkes Booth. He moves to Kansas, where he is less of a celebrity, and takes a job as doorkeeper for the State House of Representatives in Concordia. He tips his hat to the representatives on their way in and out of session. He stands with his hands clasped behind his back and guards the door while men of good faith discuss earthly situations. Corbett imagines God's house to look a little like this, a single room where one must answer to his sins, where one is considered for approval or disapproval. Where one is discussed in a reasonable manner and occasionally fought over, good against evil until someone wins out. Corbett keeps his post without incident until one afternoon when he overhears two representatives mocking the ceremonial opening prayer. He pulls a Derringer from his pocket and waves it around the room. He is seized and institutionalized before getting a shot off. Upon his release he tells a friend that he is headed for Mexico, and is never heard from again. Possibly he makes it all the way south, where he is recognized by no one. Where the hats are fat and wide and simple, made of cheerful straw. Possibly he dies happy.

Perhaps Booth suffers the worst fate of all. He simply dies. He leaves a legacy of a name and little more. The occasional footnote, the odd wax statue in roadside museums. Historically, Booth is cast as the rogue and Lincoln the gentleman. If anything, Booth only heightens Lincoln's fame.

Lincoln is the first President to be depicted on American currency. A bill and a coin, both in threat of extinction. Given the popularity of the one and the ten, who needs a five? Pennies are kept in children's banks, out of circulation. There is talk of abandoning the cent, rounding everything to the nearest nickel. But no one can bring himself to do it. The whole system breaks down, falls apart in the absence of its smallest denomination.

The money artists are flattering. Lincoln's features are softened on the currency, his hair brushed in place. The penny's face shows Lincoln in profile with a regular nose and a dainty ear. We have our way with him. His image becomes something else, someone else, minted a thousand times over, practically worthless.

Lincoln's truest image is the least known. Look close at the tail side of a new penny. Between the two middle columns of the Lincoln Memorial you can make out a miniature seated figure. It is barely perceptible when new, nothing more than a scratch, and the first thing to rub off with time. Scraped against the cashier's drawer and moistened with sweaty fingers. He is always sitting far off, waiting to escape, to slip between our fingers, to ride off unaccompanied and catch his death. Now it is hardly worth the trouble to fetch a penny off the ground.

# CASUALIDADES

CAROLYN ALESSIO

On the street near the bus stop a group of teenaged boys stood in a circle, sharpening their rusted machetes. Berta pulled her market bag closer as she walked toward the bus. The ladrones, the thieves, weren't likely to rob anyone until payday—two days off—but Berta moved with caution. Three rotting onions knocked together inside her bag, next to a vial of medicine. She always carried old onions with her medicine because the people in her village were nosey and if they tried to look into her bag they would smell the odor and stay away.

This morning she had taken off work to go to the hospital on the hill for a checkup. She had not had a seizure for two weeks, but the medicine gave her gas, a constant rumbling that pained and embarrassed her. A week ago she had stopped taking the full dosage.

The faded green bus started uphill, groaning and halting. Berta looked in vain for an empty seat. The bus driver shifted gears jerkily, and Berta nearly stumbled. As she reached for the bar above to steady herself, a woman in an embroidered smock pulled her basket of chicks onto her lap and gestured at the empty seat next to her. Berta smiled and sat down.

At the sewing cooperative where she worked, none of the

women wanted to sit by Berta anymore. Her seizures had increased in the past year, and the women had begun to treat Berta like someone they thought the priest should exorcise. She took to working alone, hunched over in a dim corner of the cinderblock building, but even that didn't work. Two weeks ago she had been cutting out striped jaspe fabric for a vest when the strange singing rose up inside her, the low song without words that always heralded her attacks. She tried to muffle the sounds, to quiet her trembling hands, but the rumbling notes escaped from her mouth and her fingers shook, releasing the scissors. They landed a foot away from her nearest coworker, Esperanza, but Esperanza screamed anyway. Later, when Berta opened her eyes, the women stood around her in a circle and the gringo boss told her that she needed medical attention.

A man sitting near the front of the bus stood up, pulled out a package of colored pencils, and began to call out their virtues. Berta shifted in her seat near the back, next to the woman with the basket of squirming, squeaking chicks. She wondered if they could smell her onions. The vendor walked down the aisle. In a clear plastic case he held a rainbow spread of pencils: red, light blue, green, yellow, and an orange that nearly matched the pair of vinyl shoes Berta wore, a purchase that had cost her nearly a month's wages. "Good prices, a bargain," the vendor said, strolling up and down the aisle. Neither Berta nor the woman next to her looked as he passed, but inside Berta's head she had begun to draw, starting with a red pencil for the clay along the road, then moving upward, shading in the sky as it looked at daybreak, a blue-gray haze that covered the mountains and the inactive volcanoes. This was her view from the roof of her mother's house as Berta fed the chickens and roosters in the early morning. The bus lurched and Berta felt a nip from a chick at her elbow.

The seizures always began with singing, a low thrumming that started below her breastbone and traveled upward, swirling in gritty circles around her throat and emerging from Berta's mouth in syllables that many villagers thought were too low for a woman. Sometimes they started at work, but mostly the attacks happened at home, the strange song catching her as she leaned over the pila to wash a glass sticky with rice drink, or tend the fire for tortillas that her mother had started but forgotten to watch.

Berta's house was made of cinderblock and sheets of thin wood that darkened in the rain and shuddered during the windy season. She was twenty-nine and lived with her mother. Every other woman of her age in the village had a man and children; some even had grandchildren. Berta babysat for her sisters' and neighbors' children, not minding even when they rubbed their grimy hands in her hair. Some of the other mothers were a bit uneasy about Berta babysitting, though; they worried about the evil eye she might carry, and asked Berta not to look into the children's eyes.

These days Berta rarely looked in the mirror. Mornings when she pulled her glossy long hair into a barrette, she remembered what her mother said once when Berta asked if she were pretty: "Mija, you have beautiful hair."

Gray letters arched over the steel gate, announcing "El Hospital Mental Público de Guatemala." Berta had disembarked from the bus a mile before and walked uphill, muddying her lovely shoes as she trudged past a long shallow garbage pit whose odors mixed with the day's heavy humidity and clung to her skin. She approached the guard, who slouched against the bumper of a military truck. He stood up, crushed out a cigarette, and asked for her identification.

Berta reached into her bag for her medical card, the one that her gringo boss had gotten for her when he drove her there for her first initial consultation. The guard glanced at the green cardboard pass, grunted, and motioned with his gun to the path beyond the gate.

The grounds were a maze of low, squat buildings connected by dilapidated paths. The grass looked tired, yellow-brown in patches. Berta stepped over snarls of dirt and roots.

A man with a ragged beard approached her, and began to ask for money in a high staccato voice. Berta shook her head no, but he persisted, calling her pretty, complimenting her hair. Berta's head hurt.

"Por favor," the man said to Berta, "just a few quetzales." Berta sucked in her breath. She thought of the few coins in her pockets, and wondered why her country's currency was named after the nearly extinct national bird. The man reached for her arm, with a grip that was surprisingly tight.

Berta remembered her father before he left the family, on nights when his boss hadn't paid the workers their due at the coffee plantation. Drunk, he raced around the house, ripping laundry off the line, sometimes throwing pots into the street.

"Listen," she hissed now, turning around. "No hablo espanol," she said, trying to sound nasal like the gringo boss at the sewing cooperative. "Speek Ing-lish."

The man loosened his grip, stood back and studied her. "Gringa?" he said, his heavy-lidded eyes widening.

"Sí." The laughter rose in her like odorless gas as she turned to look for the big building with the high padlocked gates.

The doctor didn't call her name during the first hour she waited, nor the second. When he finally got to her, Berta's back was stiff from leaning so long against the damp wall, and the doctor didn't even say her full name—Berta Francisca Torneo de Monterosso—but simply, Señorita Torneo. Her face burned as she got up to follow; everyone seemed to know just by looking at her that she was still Miss, Señorita.

A torn, faded curtain divided the examining room. Berta hesitated at the edge, noting the fabric's uneven cut, when the doctor waved her in.

The doctor spoke slowly and his lower lip was punctuated with dark indentations, like bruises on mangoes past their time. Berta wondered if he were nervous. He looked up from her file and said, "This is too early for your follow-up appointment."

Hands in her lap, Berta told him about the medicine's side effects. She tried to explain how she could not stand rumbling with gas out in public; making a rude sound at Mass just before the offertory, at work when she and the other women presented their wares to a traveling missionary group. Nearly whispering, she mentioned she had lowered her dosage, and suffered a flareup at work.

The doctor said, "Do you want the seizures to return?"

She shook her head. Outside an ice cream truck played a jangly, carnivalesque tune.

"Señorita," the doctor said. "I could switch you to another medicine but you'd have different problems. Sleep too much, thirsty all the time. With all epilepsy medications," he said, sweeping his long thin arm across the desk, "there are casualidades."

Chances of side effects. Berta looked down at her market bag and the odor of old onions rose to her eyes.

A woman with matted hair pushed into the examining room, yelling that she had lost her son, and pulling at the dirty rags wrapped around her wrists.

The doctor glanced at her. "Suleni," he said quietly, standing up. "They need you down at lunch."

The woman stared, pulled at her wrists. "My son is missing," she said. "He doesn't know I've moved."

The doctor went to her, placed his hands gently on her shoulders. "Let's find a nurse," he said, leading her toward the doorway.

A moment later he returned. He did not sit down, but reached for Berta's file from the desk. "Well," he said, turning back to Berta. "You will try the medicine a bit longer?"

She stared at the barred window for a moment, at the dingy walls. She imagined her shiny long hair matted, and putrid rags wound around her wrists. The doctor looked at her and she nodded.

Berta reached for her market bag and stood, moving toward the door. The doctor's voice stopped her: "Before you leave, let's see you take your noon-time dosage."

The pills left a bitter white paste on her tongue. Berta stopped on the street near the bus stop to splurge and buy a Coke, but even as she sucked the sweet soda through the straw in the plastic bag, she could not rinse the sourness from her mouth.

On the ride home she dozed a little, leaning up against the window that rattled and shook as the bus plodded forward. The metal clasp of her crooked barrette pushed into her scalp so finally she sat up. At one of the stops a group of schoolchildren in uniforms got on, waking Berta with their laughing and talking. Judging from their pressed uniforms she guessed they lived in the residential areas downtown. The children unwrapped bright red suckers and tamarind candies, and as they searched for seats some of them tossed the wrappers on the floor. Dry wind blew in from the windows and Berta remembered playing in the wind as a child, pretending as her skirt billowed out that she was a flower.

The bus pulled into the last leg of Berta's journey. One-room cinderblock houses and wooden shacks pressed up against the sides of the road, their doors only feet from the sewage ditch.

Berta straightened her blouse, and wondered if, when she returned to work, the other women would ask her where she had been. Maybe she could slip into the corner, and they would be too busy to notice as they stitched tiny brown-faced dolls onto barrettes to ship up north to the States.

A sharp pounding shook the bus as it pulled near the sewing cooperative. The bus slowed and everyone turned around to look. Two young men had climbed on the back, yelling and beating at the windows.

The stooped, gray-haired driver stopped the bus and stood up. He pulled a tiny knife from his pocket, stepped off the bus, and went around to the back. Berta heard shouts and curse words. Inside the bus she saw other passengers pulling their bags closer. She did not have to be told they had been stopped by ladrones.

Finally the driver returned to the front, but he was followed by a young man waving a machete. Berta recognized the tall ladrón with unusual green eyes.

"Don't worry yourselves," the bus driver called out to the passengers, but the ladrón stamped on the floor with a ragged boot and pushed him back to his seat.

Another young man with a machete entered from the side, also carrying the bus driver's tiny knife. A schoolchild began to cry.

"Pass up your money," the green-eyed ladrón called, slightly slurring his words. Everybody began to dig in their pockets and purses. Berta heard muttering. Payday at the factories and fincas was not for two more days—most villagers were down to bus fare and enough for bread and a few eggs. She thought the ladrones must be desperate, drunk or high on sniffing glue bought at the shoemaker's shop. Berta looked in her bag: two onions and a vial of medicine. She swept her hand beneath them, found a single quetzal note. She handed it to one of the ladrones as he passed down the aisle, scraping his machete along the floor. The bus driver slouched in his seat, holding his face in his hands.

Nobody had much more to offer than Berta: single quetzal notes were pressed into the ladrones' hands, some loose change. Even the schoolchildren with the nice uniforms only had enough for another bus fare or two: they had spent most of it on candy.

The ladrones counted the money at the front of the bus, cursing every time a handful of loose change appeared. Berta estimated that at most they would have enough for an evening or two of beer, the regular kind with the rooster's head on the label. They counted the money again, then the green-eyed one muttered something. They talked back and forth a little, conferring, and spitting in the aisle. Berta could not see the globules of spit, but she imagined them with white centers, like the albumin in the eggs she collected on her mother's roof.

Outside the bus, people from the neighborhood were beginning to gather. Berta thought she saw Esperanza from the cooperative, the woman she had scared with her scissors. She did not see
her mother or sisters. Nobody ever called the police in their village,
because the police were scared of the ladrones, too. It was hard to
enforce law in their village, and revenge only came rarely, usually in
the form of a midnight beating in the garbage dump.

The ladrones stared at them and paced, walking up and down
the aisles and panning the passengers with their too-wide pupils.
Finally the green-eyed ladrón turned to the passengers and said,
"Pass up your shoes."

Nobody spoke. Many of them had been robbed before, of bus
fare, jewelry and even food, but Berta had never heard of this. She
looked down at her own, orange vinyl shoes. Until she was twelve
she had gone barefoot, like most of the other young women in the
village. After that she had worn plastic beach thongs, the cheapest
kind at the market. But a month ago, she had treated herself to
these beautiful durable shoes, after finishing a shipment of thirty-
five purses, ten vests, and twenty-five barrettes. She still knew the
numbers. The ladrones began with the schoolchildren, urging them
to hurry as they passed up their dark-soled loafers. One child even
passed up his socks.

Berta looked around. The adults who hadn't worn shoes in
the first place looked the most frightened. One woman had pulled
several mangoes out of her bag as if to offer them in compensation.
The others with shoes were taking them off, slipping their feet from
plastic beach thongs, and unlacing boots in clumsy hurried movements. The muscular ladrón paced the aisles. His machete looked
like it had once been used on a plantation.

Berta removed her shoes, stroking the smooth orange vinyl.
The muscular ladrón hissed at everyone to hurry up. In the front of
the bus the green-eyed ladrón was piling shoes into the T-shirts he
and the other one had stripped off, makeshift knapsacks. Berta held
her shoes for a moment longer in her lap, cradling them, then she

slipped one into her bag. The other she slid beneath her shirt, hoping that in the commotion she wouldn't be noticed. The vinyl felt warm against her chest, and she crossed her arms to camouflage.

The bare-chested ladrones now had full knapsacks. Outside the bus more villagers lined up, talking and wringing their hands. Berta thought she saw the priest, a friend of her mother's. She hated her town, herself, for always backing away from danger.

Everybody on the bus had bare feet now. The shirtless ladrones walked along, grabbing some shoes and purses that had not been handed up. The green-eyed ladrón stopped at Berta's seat. "Pass it," he said, staring at the bag on her lap. "Señorita," he said, grabbing her wrist. "Pass it here."

"Only vegetables," she began, but he emptied it. Three mottled onions fell out and a medicine vial, then the thud of one orange shoe. The ladrón let the onions roll down the aisle in off-white rotations, but he stooped to pick up the shoe. Normally the drugs might have interested him, Berta thought, but now everybody was watching. He held the single shoe in his hand, gripping it by its muddy sole.

The other passengers turned around to stare at her, but Berta was used to this. She knew how to be a spectacle.

The shoe dangled in front of her head. "Your other shoe," the green-eyed ladrón said. His assistant walked toward them. "Hey, crazy lady," the muscular ladrón said, a glimmer of recognition crossing his broad face, "give us the shoe."

Berta shook her head. Inside her blouse, the vinyl felt cool against her clammy skin. "Now," the green-eyed ladrón said.

"It's mine," Berta said, clutching the shoe to her chest, then cradling it. "Mío."

The muscular ladrón moved forward, but the green-eyed ladrón waved him off. She could tell he thought he had a way with women. "Señorita," he said, in a voice that reminded her of her visit to the doctor, "your shoe, please."

Berta shook her head. He was so close she could smell the

perspiration on his chest. Only a few times before had she been this close to a man. The green-eyed ladrón reached for a lock of her hair, not pulling as hard as Berta expected.

The bus was quiet. The green-eyed ladrón worked a strand of her shiny hair in his fingers, then muttered something to the muscular ladrón behind him. The muscular ladrón laughed, and Berta spit in the green-eyed ladrón's face.

Now he yanked her by the hair, pulling her down the aisle to an empty seat at the front of the bus. He tugged so hard her barrette snapped open and the orange shoe fell out from under her shirt. The muscular ladrón lunged for it, but the green-eyed ladrón shoved Berta to the floor, a handful of her hair still caught in his fist. Her head smarted and her hands felt numb. Outside the bus people had begun to shout. Breathing hard, the green-eyed ladrón laid her hair out straight on the seat. As he positioned his machete to cut her hair, Berta opened her mouth and began to sing.

# SCARLET

MANDY SAYER

Scarlet was eleven years old when her mother moved them to a flat in Kings Cross and began dealing. Scarlet was small for her age; her skin was so white and translucent that one could see a delicate map of blue veins on her arms and legs. She had long red hair, which her mother brushed each day and plaited into a rope down Scarlet's back. One of her mother's friends called her a thoughtful girl. She read books borrowed from the Kings Cross library; she buttered her bread precisely, smoothing a square around the crust first, then filling in the rest; her friends at school marveled at the way in which she had embroidered a perfect S on her red velvet jacket.

After school, she often walked circles around the El Alamein Fountain, watching bare-legged women wearing too much make-up crawl into the backs of cars. There was a drunk who played an air guitar and sang songs she'd never heard before. Occasionally she'd catch him lowering his trousers and pissing into the shrubbery out-side the Fountain Café. Sometimes she'd stroll into the Gazebo Hotel, ride the lift up to the eighth floor and swim in the heated pool. One day, when an attendant questioned her, she named a room number and told him her parents were in the bar.

She was usually allowed to wander around the Cross on her

own, as long as she was home by dark. But lately she stayed in more often because she'd heard on the news that a man had raped a tourist in Kellet Lane. It was then reported that he'd cut off the woman's ponytail and taken it with him. Another attack had occurred on William Street; the woman beat him off before he'd had a chance to molest her, but he managed to snip off her hair and get away with her ponytail before the police arrived.

Scarlet's maternal grandfather was only forty-five. Like Scarlet, he had a slight build and thick red hair. His cheekbones were high and his eyes a bright green. Scarlet called him My Beautiful Boy. When she visited Grant, he let her paint lipstick and rouge on his face and play with his false eyelashes. Sometimes they'd dress up in his glittering gowns and sing songs from *The Wizard of Oz*. It was Grant who'd given Scarlet the red jacket. He'd made it on his foot-peddle Singer sewing machine from leftover material he'd used for a strapless evening dress.

Grant and Scarlet's mother didn't speak to each other any more; they'd had a fight over money. Grant had scored from her mother a few months ago, on spec, and he'd never paid her for it. They'd had such a blue that when he moved from his terrace on Glebe Point Road the month before, he never bothered to ring and tell them his new address.

"Promise me, you'll never touch this stuff," her mother often said as she weighed the white powder on electronic scales in the kitchen. Scarlet would make a face, shake her head, but the truth was she touched it often, when her mother was too ill. It wasn't so different from following the recipe for the carrot cakes she sometimes baked: she'd watched her mother long enough to know how much to mix in the spoon, where to tie the tourniquet, how to jack back the plunger to between .20 and .30 mils. She didn't mind doing it, as it always made her mother better. When the kid upstairs glanced at the detachable head left drying on the sink and asked what it was for, Scarlet blinked and calmly replied, "My mother's a diabetic."

Scarlet was curled up on the couch reading one of the Famous Five adventure stories when Grant finally called again. She hadn't heard from him in weeks. He said, "How's my beautiful girl?" like always, but his voice was thin and shaky. She replied, as usual, "Not as beautiful as you."

It was their ritual, and she thought it might cheer him up.

"Put Pat on, Letty," he said.

Scarlet glanced at her mother, who had nodded off in the bean-bag over an hour ago.

"She's not here," Scarlet lied. "She's up at the Soho."

Grant sighed into the mouthpiece. "You're there on your own?"

"I'm doing my homework."

There was a pause. It sounded as if Grant was lighting a cigarette. He exhaled and began coughing.

"What's wrong?" She began to wind the telephone cord around her wrist.

He coughed again and spat something out. "Letty, would you do your boy a favour?"

She glanced at her sleeping mother. "What?"

"I'm sick, see? I'm really crook."

Scarlet turned her back to her mother and listened to his instructions. She wrote down his new address in Darlinghurst on the back of an electricity bill. After she hung up, she pulled on her red velvet jacket with the white embroidered S on the front.

The basement they lived in was on Hughes Lane, which was mostly populated by garbage cans and stray cats. It was a wintry August day, and even at five o'clock the sun was beginning to set. Scarlet shivered and folded the collar of the jacket up around her neck. Grant had told her that she'd be fine as long as she stuck to the main street and followed it through the Cross and into Darlinghurst.

"Don't take any short cuts," he'd warned, almost out of breath. "And don't talk to any strangers."

"Everyone's strange around here," she'd joked, before hanging up.

She walked quickly up to Macleay Street and turned right, relieved to be on the main thoroughfare she knew so well. Thick black clouds were forming in the sky and she knew she'd have to hurry. She looked for the air guitarist, but he was nowhere in sight. The only person she recognised was the overweight woman who was banked up with plastic bags in the doorway of the closed real estate agency. She was spouting random numbers at everyone who passed by. "Four hundred and thirty one! Sixteen thousand and seventy-eight!" she caroled as Scarlet hurried past.

The plane trees that lined the street rustled in a sudden gust of wind. Scarlet crossed at the lights. It was happy hour in the Bourbon and Beefsteak and she could hear the band playing "Since I Fell for You." The black-suited bouncer, who was picking his teeth with a corner of a matchbox, winked at Scarlet and blew her a kiss. She nodded back and quickened her pace.

It was almost dark, but she could still see the rain clouds pressing down over the street. Electric neon pulsed across the footpath, bright pink outlines of naked women and signs flashing *Live Sex, Pussycat, Love Machine*.

One of the strip clubs had been renovated recently, so that coloured lights flashed through the floor of the perspex entrance and a video monitor just inside the doorway revealed hazy images of curvaceous women kissing one another. Scarlet knew they weren't lesbians, though. One of the women was a friend of her mother, and when she visited she sometimes brought her boyfriend along, a slim, older man who had three bluish tears tattooed below his right eye.

"Men get turned on by women having sex with each other," Grant had once explained to her. "Even if they're only faking it."

Scarlet had then asked if it was the same for women, if they liked watching men.

Grant thought for a moment. "Not really, no. Women are different. Though they like watching men when they're dressed up in drag. Most of my fans are girls."

She could smell stale urine as she passed the railway station. A white man lay in the entranceway, his limbs wrapped around a long didgeridoo, as if it were a lover. Scarlet had often seen him there, coaxing howls and moans from the hollow piece of wood for small change. One day she'd noticed he'd darkened his skin with make-up, and figured he was trying to pass as an Aborigine in order to increase his tips. Now he was asleep, a big wet patch rising through the crotch of his jeans.

"What's the S stand for?" asked a drunk outside the Capital Hotel. "Sexy?" He threw his cigarette down and shot her a lewd grin.

"Suck eggs," she replied, hurrying past him.

The large red-and-white Coca-Cola sign flashed a luminous neon aura across the intersection of the Cross. Cars crawled between traffic lights. Grant had told her not to stay on Darlinghurst Road because the lighting was bad, and because there was a weird gay scene happening on the strip outside the TAFE college.

"Cross over to the left-hand side of Victoria Street," he'd instructed.

"Just follow it down to Oxford. Don't take any short cuts. Stay away from the park."

She could hear his voice in her head as she rounded the fire station. Two firemen standing in the open doorway tipped their helmets to her. There were only a few people left outside the cafés, sitting on portable stools and sipping coffee. Parmalat was closing up, and so was the Coluzzi. The smell of garlic wafted out from one of the Italian restaurants. She remembered, from watching an old movie, that garlic kept vampires away. She'd never been this far into Darlinghurst on her own; she and her mother were still quite new to the area and there was enough activity each day in Kings Cross to keep her entertained.

A crowd was spilling out of the Green Park Hotel. Schooner glasses lined the steps. A uniformed policeman stood away from the crowd, sipping from a bottle of Strongbow. His hair was the colour of sand and he had a pale, heart-shaped face. Scarlet thought his uniform looked too big for him. Beneath her jacket, she hugged Grant's package close to her, drawing the folds tighter so that no one, least of all the policeman, could see what she was carrying.

She did not make eye contact with anyone outside the pub as she passed, though she heard a woman remarking on her pretty jacket. The wind gusted around the corner when she reached the hospital and she began to shiver. The next block loomed ahead, dark and empty. All she had to do was make it to Oxford Street. She had never been to Grant's new house, but she had the address in her pocket. And once she found it, everything would be all right. She would make Grant better, and then he would sit her by the fire and they'd eat raw chocolate cake mix and he'd let her stay the night.

She paused at the lights and fumbled about in her pocket for Grant's address: 4 Short Lane, she'd written. Down Oxford, left at Bourke, second on left.

Down Oxford, she thought. She glanced up at the intersection glowing at the end of the street. She wasn't sure if down meant turn left or turn right. People often said "down" when they meant "up" and "in" when they meant "out," and "over" instead of "across." Once she'd heard someone in Sydney say, "I'm going up to Canberra." And, "Chatswood's just over the bridge," as if you needed to scale the top of it in order to get to the northern suburbs.

Scarlet was just about to step off the curb when she heard footsteps behind her.

"What's a little girl like you doing out on her own at night?"

She turned and saw it was the policeman in the baggy uniform who'd been drinking at the pub.

"Visiting my grandfather," she said.

"At this hour?"

Scarlet hugged the package under her jacket. "He's sick."

"Don't you know it's not safe around here?"

"I'm taking him some medicine."

SCARLET

The policeman smiled gently. "Sorry. It's just that you, well . . . I've got a little girl about your age." He bowed over and touched her shoulder. "You looked a bit lost for a moment there."

"I'm supposed to go down Oxford Street." She nodded at the intersection. "Do I turn left or right?"

"What's the address?"

"Short Lane." She passed him the piece of paper.

He studied it for a moment and rubbed his chin. She noticed he had pale green eyes, like Grant's.

"Bourke Street's just behind Taylor Square," he said, passing back the note. "Just cut through the park here, walk up to Oxford Street and turn right."

"I'm not supposed to go into the park."

"That's right." He nodded. "It's dangerous." He smiled at her again. She noticed how white and shiny his teeth were. "But I could walk you through the park, you know. I could walk you all the way to your grandfather's house."

"That's OK," she said, gazing into his eyes. Her mother thought all coppers were pigs, but this one seemed to be all right.

"I'm paid to protect little girls like you," he said. "It's not far."

She ventured a smile back at him. "Do you think I need protecting?"

He hooked his thumbs through his belt loops and glanced about, as if he were scared of a lurking monster. "We could protect each other."

"Where's your gun?" she asked.

He touched the empty holster and grinned. "I don't need a gun. I've got you."

She laughed at that and shook her head.

"So what about it?" he said. "Should I walk you there?"

She blushed and looked down. Even his shoes seemed too big. She knew Grant would have a fit if she arrived at his place with a cop.

"No," she said. "I'll be fine."

[159]

He looked disappointed. But he stuck his hands in his pocket and pulled out four dollar coins.

"Here," he said, palming them into her hand. "Buy your grand-dad some flowers."

She gazed at the gleaming gold coins. At that moment a fat raindrop plopped onto her hand, then another. "Thanks," she said, pocketing them.

"So I turn right at the end of the street?" She stepped down off the curb.

He nodded. "And then Bourke Street will be on your left."

She hurried across the road, against the flashing DON'T WALK sign. The rain was growing heavier.

"Hey," he cried out after her. "What's the S stand for?"

"Sexy," she called back, and laughed.

It was night now. As she made her way up to Oxford Street, she thought she saw the policeman walking through the park, rounding the rotunda and disappearing beneath the trees. Part of her wished she'd gone with him, as their encounter had buoyed her spirits and, in spite of the rain, she no longer felt quite so scared.

She followed his instructions and turned right on Oxford, walking under the shop awnings. Two men were kissing in the doorway of a café. Chefs stood in the front windows of restaurants, barbecuing steaks and rings of calamari.

There was a fruit and vegetable cart on one corner of Taylor Square. The vendor stood beneath an umbrella and was hawking the last of his wilting roses. She stopped and pointed to a bunch of half-opened buds, the outer leaves of which were already beginning to darken into a deep magenta.

"Three dollar for you," he said, whisking them out of the big plastic bucket.

"Two," she replied.

The vendor looked at her doubtfully. "These fresh today."

Scarlet held out two of the dollar coins. "It's all I've got."

A couple of Asian tourists were standing beside Scarlet, each holding a pineapple. One was fumbling with his money pouch.

The vendor sighed and muttered something under his breath. He finally wrapped the roses in a small plastic bag and scooped the coins out of her hand. She bought a large Cherry Ripe with the remaining money, for she hadn't yet had her tea. She stood outside a dirty bookstore and ate it slowly, savouring each bite, for Grant sometimes forgot to shop, or wouldn't buy food because he was on a diet.

Scarlet washed her sticky hand in a puddle of rainwater. After walking a little way down Bourke Street, she paused and looked around. She finally found a narrow, unlit alleyway a block away. There was no street sign, but painted on the door of a house, in large white letters, was 1 Short Lane. She moved across to the other side of the alley, to the second house on the right. It was a drab brick terrace with barred windows. Only a faint light leaked out from behind the drawn blinds. Above the metal mail slot in the door was a tiny wooden 4.

She rapped on the door quickly. She waited for footsteps, but there was no sound at all. "Grant?" she called, knocking on the door again. She peeped through the mail slot, and could make out a hallway and coats hanging on a hat-stand.

"Come in," she heard him call. His voice was still croaky. "Door's open."

She turned the knob, but had to push hard before the door finally gave. Off the hallway was a small, dark parlour. She recognised Grant's furniture immediately: the old rocking chair, the tapestry ottoman, the Singer sewing machine. He'd had to sell a few pieces in the last year to pay his rent. The only light came from a small fire that burned in the tiled hearth.

She looked across to see him in the three-quarter iron bed, which stood in one corner. He lay beneath the thick patchwork quilt he'd sewn when he first got out of gaol. It was pulled up to his chin. She rushed over and kissed him on the cheek. He was wearing his blonde Farrah Fawcett wig and his face was all made—red lip-stick, eyelashes, mascara—as if he were about to do his show.

"Did you have any trouble finding it?" he croaked.

Scarlet had never seen him so strung out. "No," she replied, shivering. "But I got all wet."

An open doorway led to the kitchen. She entered it and put the package on the sink. "Where's the light switch?"

Grant didn't answer. She popped her head around the door-jamb.

"The globe's gone," he explained. "You can manage, can't you?"

She found a box of matches by the fireplace and lit the gas stove in the kitchen. It provided a little light.

"Take your clothes off," he said. "And dry them by the fire."

"OK." She walked back into the parlour and stood by the danc-ing flames. She took off her red jacket and hung it over the back of a chair.

"Take your frock off, too," he said. "You'll catch your death of cold."

She unbuttoned her tartan dress and slipped out of it. She placed it on the seat of the chair. She kicked off her wet black shoes and socks. She stood by the fire, wearing only a white singlet and underpants. Her skin was pale and gleaming in the half-light. She noticed Grant was staring at her.

"What are you looking at, Big Eyes?" she chided.

As she walked by his bed on her way back to the kitchen, his hand stole out from beneath the bedclothes. He touched her long braid and pulled on it. "Why don't you crawl under the covers with me and keep warm?"

She laughed again. "What have you been smoking, Grant?"

Scarlet pulled away and went back to the kitchen. She'd brought a syringe with her, just in case Grant didn't have one. It had been used before, but only by her mother, and Pat never shared needles with anyone. She picked up the detachable head, turned on the tap, and sucked up water into the syringe. She squirted the water out and repeated it a few times, trying to dislodge the dried blood caked around the bottom. Through the doorway she noticed Grant's bare feet sticking out from the quilt at the end of the bed. She searched around for a teaspoon, but couldn't find one. She crossed the kitchen and lit a match. Some clothes were thrown over a metal garbage can in the corner—a light blue shirt, dark trousers, both wet. A pair of black shoes poked out from beneath the china cabinet. There was a wet blue cap stuck underneath a chair.

She swallowed. The flame dwindled down and burned her fingers. She quickly opened a drawer and rummaged around until she found a teaspoon. After opening the small plastic bag, she tapped out some white powder—twice as much as usual—and mixed up.

"Come here under the covers," he called again. "And keep your poor grand-dad company."

"All right," she piped, trying to steady her voice. "Your medicine's almost ready."

Her mother had always told her to fill the cylinder to .60 mils so that there was enough room to jack back. But she'd seen some people use even more smack than that. Scarlet dipped the needle in the spoon and drew the plunger back to .90.

She popped her head around the doorjamb. His wig sat a little crookedly on his head.

"Why don't you take your underwear off, too?" he suggested. "It must be damp."

"I will if you don't look," she replied. "Let's play a game. Don't open your eyes until I tell you to."

He smiled. "You're a funny girl."

"You're a funny man."

He sighed and closed his eyes. He turned away and faced the wall.

"No peeping," she warned, turning back the quilt.

She slipped into the bed beside his naked body. His flesh was soft and warm. "Don't turn around yet," she said.

He whimpered softly.

She began to stroke his hair, his neck. "Not yet," she whispered, caressing his shoulder, the quivering Adam's apple. Her mother had directed her to the neck area once or twice, when they'd run out of veins on her arms and legs. But Pat had always told her to steer clear of the jugular. Scarlet recognised the long, ropy bulge instantly, knew it as well as the beauty spot on Grant's left cheek.

He was still whimpering when she raised the needle, aimed and plunged it in. He cried out and writhed for a moment, then rolled onto his stomach. He balled his fist and went to hit her, but his arm went limp and he moaned again. Scarlet crawled over him. The needle was still stuck in his neck like a dart in a board. She pulled back the plunger to .30, watching the blood flower into the plastic cylinder, then carefully pushed forward again, as she'd been taught.

He was still moaning, but he seemed unable to move. The blonde wig had fallen off and his sand-coloured hair was matted with sweat. She plucked the syringe from his neck, leapt from the bed, and pulled on the damp red velvet jacket. Suddenly he turned onto his side and vomited onto the pillow.

The fire had dwindled and she couldn't see very well. She crept through the dark house, opening doors—the bathroom off the kitchen, the cupboard beneath the stairs. She walked out to the tiny backyard, down toward the brick loo near the fence. It was there that she found him, pale and shivering, his make-up smudged, his mouth sealed with gaffer tape. He was tied to the cistern and his arms and legs were bound with nylon stockings.

"How's My Beautiful Boy?"

She leaned over and ripped the tape from his mouth quickly, as if it were a band-aid.

He sighed and shook his head. "Not as beautiful as you."

# WAYS TO KILL A SNAPPER

GREGORY MILLER

𝔤

The snapping turtle had spent the entire night chained to the birch tree near the old boathouse. There had been a question of its survival—this was, after all, northern Minnesota—but when morning arrived the boy found the seventy-eight-pound turtle alive and well, unaware that a pair of brightly colored moths had settled onto its shell, and that it was to be killed later that afternoon.

The boy found the afternoon came quickly.

"It's older than I am," the boy argued. "It's *prehistoric.*"

"They're bad for the lake," repeated his grandfather. The truck smelled like mints; his grandfather would shake three or four of them into his mouth at a time and then roll them around with his tongue, never biting. "They eat the eggs of fish," he continued, as he drove. "Northern, sun fish, walleyes. How would you like Lake Alice without northern?" The boy could hear the turtle slash at the sides of the pickup, claws grating against metal. In the distance, the Sheck's place came into view.

"But I caught it, not you. You didn't catch it."

"We're not going to argue," his grandfather said finally.

The boy had never met the Shecks in person, but he'd heard enough about them: how they barely supported themselves on the hard land, how they were missing toes and fingers, how their young daughter had once strayed into the deep woods and lost herself there for two days. To the boy, this harsh part of Minnesota was a place to *visit*, not live. It was his grandfather who owned the cabin, who related all the stories, who had a history with Mr. Sheck, but the family didn't listen to the grandfather anymore. He was like a radio playing in a dark corner. They'd had enough of him.

"How are they going to kill it?"

"I'm not sure," his grandfather replied. "We're only dropping it off. We'll leave that to him."

They pulled into the Shecks' place. It was a clapboard house, much more like a garage, really, with small open windows and large areas of gray rotten wood, places where the thin layer of blue paint had chipped and fallen away. Shingles were strewn haphazardly on the roof as if they'd been flung there from below. A picket fence wound around the yard, but the fence had fallen apart in several places, as if recently under siege, and husks of automobiles sat on the far side, idle. A rusted-out Chevy van, apparently the only running vehicle, was parked in the gravel driveway, above it hanging a twisted basketball hoop. They parked beside the van.

The boy's grandfather cut the motor and opened his door. The boy remained sitting there, listening to the turtle crawl around the back of the pickup. "Just going to wait here?" asked the grandfather.

The boy replied, "I'm coming," and opened his door and climbed out. He looked at the house and the sky above the house and thought it looked like rain. If it rained, all fishing would be off. He decided that if he caught another snapping turtle he would free it right away rather than make the same mistake twice. He should've freed the turtle, he thought, instead of hoping to keep it. He should've known better.

They were in the middle of the driveway when the torn screen door opened and Mr. Sheck came out. He held a rifle, and for a long moment the boy was afraid Mr. Sheck meant to shoot them as trespassers.

"George," declared Mr. Sheck, nodding and coming toward them. He wore dirt-stained overalls without an undershirt. A black bandanna was knotted in a tight skullcap around his head. His eyes were beady but bright, his face rough and red, cracked like pavement from the summers and winters of northern Minnesota. He looked at least as old and just as tall as the boy's grandfather, but in a fight the boy didn't have to wonder who would win. The Shecks had Ojibway in them. Maybe they've been here forever, the boy thought. Maybe they have arrowheads stacked up like pennies in their bedrooms.

"It's in the back of the truck," the grandfather said. There were no handshakes.

"I figured," Mr. Sheck said. "Didn't think you carried it in your lap." He looked down at the boy. "And who is this?"

"My grandson, Ricky."

"Well, let's see that turtle you caught, Ricky."

All three of them stepped to the back of the pickup. The boy climbed onto the bumper in order to get a better look, and immediately the turtle's head sucked inside, though not entirely. It couldn't quite fit its entire head inside the shell, as if it had long ago outgrown it. It hissed, its head accordioned in and surrounded by folds of thick flesh, and it seemed to dare them.

"You could stay for dinner," Mr. Sheck said.

"We've got a dock to take down tonight," the grandfather replied, which was a lie.

"Well, then," said Mr. Sheck, leaning his rifle against the side of the pickup. It was an old Remington. He walked around the truck and reached into the back without the slightest hesitation, seizing the turtle by its tail. With one hand, he lifted the seventy-eight pound turtle out of the truck and held it a safe distance from himself. Succumbing to gravity, the turtle's head dropped down from its shell, revealing its long and vulnerable neck, and it hissed louder now. It smelled musky, like the bottom of a rotten lake—like Lake Alice. Its shell was about the size of a man-hole cover. Keeping the turtle from his legs, Mr. Sheck said, "I'll need some help. Grab the rifle."

The grandfather replied, "What kind of help?"

The boy and his grandfather followed Mr. Sheck to his back-yard, which was small, devoid of any grass, with two more old trucks sitting beneath a wooden shed that looked about ready to collapse on their hoods. The boy watched the turtle. Every now and then, the turtle would swing its heavy head up to see if it could punish Mr. Sheck, but then drop it back down again wearily.

In front of the shed, Mr. Sheck flopped the turtle to the ground and the turtle grunted, feet churning into the red dirt, its tail, long and tapered, slashing behind it. Mr. Sheck put his bare foot on its shell and leaned down on the turtle with all his weight. "A real fighter."

"Yeah," replied the boy. Yesterday afternoon he thought he'd snagged the bottom of the dock itself and was about to cut the line of the bamboo pole when something had suddenly given, and, pull-ing with his entire strength, he'd watched the wide, horny shell rise to the surface and suspend there for a moment in the dark water. He screamed up to the cabin behind him and then the turtle came alive, fighting in awkward jerks and plunges, and his father came running down the dock with a net, thinking it was a big fish. "Just cut the line," his father said, when he saw the turtle, but the boy screamed "No!" and so his father dipped the net into the lake. The net wasn't large enough. "Don't lose it," the boy kept saying, as his father managed to somehow balance the turtle in the net, half-in and half-out, and then, clumsily, they ran it ashore together, with the turtle hissing and bleeding from its open mouth.

"Ever eat turtle?" Mr. Sheck asked the boy now, and the boy shook his head. Then Mr. Sheck started digging into the deep square pockets of his overalls. With his hand inside, his pockets bulged and it took a lot of searching before he eventually gave up.

"You're not going to *shoot* it?" the grandfather said suddenly.

Mr. Sheck looked at him.

The grandfather cleared his throat. "That's no way to kill a turtle. All you do is lop off its head with an axe. Just hold it against a tree—"

"There's plenty of ways to kill a snapper. Anyhow, my ax broke yesterday, chopping wood. Handle came off. So this is how we do it."

"Well, this isn't any way to kill a turtle," the grandfather said again, shifting on his feet.

Mr. Sheck, looking unconcerned, turned and glanced at the boy. "Here, hold him like this." The boy walked over to the snapping turtle and his small hands took the place of Mr. Sheck's larger ones. He squeezed the saw-toothed tail with his right hand and held tight to the shell with his left and felt the power of the turtle as it tried to pull away from him. The turtle was low to the ground, its shell cold now, bits and pieces of dried mud flaking in the boy's hand. The boy used everything he had to keep the turtle in place.

"I'll get the tongs," Mr. Sheck said. The boy wasn't sure why tongs were necessary, but kept pushing the turtle down to prevent it from getting away. It reminded him of Florida and riding the old blue tortoises, but this was different. The boy wasn't sure he wanted to see the shooting but at the same time felt entranced by the possibility of real violence. Mr. Sheck moved away and went through the back door of the house.

"I should've known to bring my ax," the grandfather said. They boy looked at his grandfather, who was looking away, behind the broken shed and old trucks. He still held the rifle and it looked somehow out of place in his hands.

A moment later the back door opened and Mr. Sheck came out with a large pair of metal tongs, the kind that hangs from a grill. "You want to shoot it or hold it?" he asked, walking toward them again.

"Neither," the grandfather replied.

"You shoot it, then. I'll do the harder part. Boy, let go now. Let's see what the devil does."

The boy rose from the turtle and hurried away from it, taking his place near his grandfather. Finding itself surrounded, the snapping turtle opened its hooked jaws and elevated itself by its hind legs, hissing louder now, its golden eyes bright and star-like. It didn't blink.

"Lookit that," Mr. Sheck said. Inside the turtle's mouth it was gummy and pink, the color of candy. The turtle tried to move with Mr. Sheck but Mr. Sheck was too quick for it; he circled it, and this time kneeled over the turtle and held it down with one knee and his left hand. With his other hand he opened and closed the metal tongs. The turtled lowered itself back to the ground and its head accordioned in once more, but the hissing never stopped.

"I left my glasses at the cabin," the grandfather said, feeling his face.

"You don't wear glasses," the boy said.

"A devil," Mr. Sheck said, looking down at the turtle.

"I don't want to shoot it," the grandfather said. "I'm against shooting it."

Mr. Sheck seemed not to hear. "When I pull its head out, shoot. I'll give you a square shot."

"I haven't shot a gun in years," the grandfather said. "I might shoot you in the hand."

But Mr. Sheck had already started to plunge the metal tongs into the recess where the turtle's head was. He wanted the turtle by the neck. The boy could see the tendons in Mr. Sheck's hands working, as well as the snout of the turtle as it tried to evade the tongs. A low mewl came from inside the turtle. "Come here," he said to it. "Come on out to James," he said, and it sounded like he was calling to a child.

The boy, captivated by the turtle, barely noticed the rifle rise to the side of him.

Mr. Sheck soon had it. He squeezed the tongs and pulled the turtle's head out, having caught it squarely by its neck, just behind its head. He stretched the turtle so that its neck was fully extended, affording the boy's grandfather a good look, and the turtle, understanding its sudden vulnerability, kicked and scratched at the red earth with a renewed intensity. Mr. Sheck had his hands full. He used his weight. The boy glanced at his grandfather, who was staring down the sight of the rifle, one concentrated eye a slit of green and gold.

The boy looked back at the turtle and closed his eyes.

"Shoot him now," Mr. Sheck said.

A moment passed. There was no report yet. The boy thought of opening his eyes.

"I don't have all day," Mr. Sheck said, his voice strained.

"I don't want to miss," the grandfather said.

"How can you? You're two feet away."

The gun went off, louder than the boy expected. When he opened his eyes he saw the turtle's legs were still kicking and now there was a small bead of dark blood welling up in the precise center of the turtle's head. The turtle shook its head, as if trying to dislodge the small bullet from its brain. The boy was horrified to see that it was still alive, Mr. Sheck straining to hold onto it.

"Again," he said.

"It's just nerves."

"Shoot it again."

The grandfather lifted the gun once more, and this time the gun went off without hesitation. This time the boy saw everything: how the turtle shuddered from the momentum of the shot, how Mr. Sheck let go of the turtle and then quickly grabbed onto it again, how a similar bead of blood appeared to the right of the other, and then melted together with the other, and now blood was winding down the side of the turtle's head, which seemed heavier, a burden. Its mouth opened. Mr. Sheck let go with the tongs and the turtle retreated once more into its shell, blood dripping from its nostrils.

"It can't still be alive," said the grandfather. The boy could smell the sour smoke from the gun. The turtle was crawling but getting nowhere. Mr. Sheck still had it with his knee.

"Tough son of a bitch," Mr. Sheck said, and laughed, and they all watched the turtle.

It was not long before blood pooled below the turtle, dark and thick, and the boy stared at it, not wanting to forget this picture. It was, after all, real blood.

Mr. Sheck finally let the turtle go and it began crawling. With its head still tucked in, it crawled forward a little ways, as if uncertain, and then stopped. The boy could hear a small clatter of pans from inside the house and also the muffled sound of a tractor somewhere. The three of them waited awhile around the turtle.

"OK," Mr. Sheck said, rising and depositing the tongs into his overalls pocket.

The grandfather handed Mr. Sheck back his rifle.

"Do you want the shell?" Mr. Sheck asked the boy. "I can have it for you by tonight. Cleaned, even."

"We don't need the shell," the grandfather answered, before the boy could say anything.

Mr. Sheck looked at the grandfather, then picked the dead turtle up and dropped it flat on its back. The boy stared at the bottom of the shell, something small and cross-shaped. He had never seen it before. "I guess I need my knife," Mr. Sheck said and started back to the house.

"We're going," the grandfather said.

"I'm going to make a lamp out of the shell," Mr. Sheck mentioned before disappearing into the house, the screen door slamming hard behind him.

The two of them walked around the house to where the pickup was parked. The boy watched his grandfather shake his head a little and put his hand on the hood of the truck. "That's no way to kill a turtle," he said. "All you need to do is lop off its head with an ax. He's a goddamn fool to shoot it like that."

"You shot it," the boy said, unable to resist.

They both got into the truck, where the grandfather started the engine and the boy took one last look at the Shecks' place. He was glad he would never have to live in such a place, eating someone else's turtle for dinner and trying to dribble a basketball on impossible gravel. The turtle was dead now, all seventy-eight pounds of it.

"I haven't shot a gun for years," the grandfather said, and made to look behind him. The boy glanced at him and then went back to looking out the window, trying to remember the sound the turtle had made scratching at the back of the pickup. He thought about the empty shell. He thought maybe the empty shell would've been something good to look at in the afternoons, after school was out. Something good to hold in his arms, something good to keep on his shelf, for memory's sake. He thought maybe he'd wanted it.

# SELLING THE APARTMENT

DANIT BROWN

Your parents' friends, when they hit sixty, will begin moving south in couples: one to North Carolina. Another to Florida. A third to Texas. At Rosh Hashanah you'll be down to ten. Hanukah eight. Purim four. Finally, one Passover, it will be just you and your parents. You will sit across from them in the dining room, eating *gefilte fish* by candlelight while your mother plugs speed dating at the local JCC: Everybody's doing it! It's easy! It's cheap! Then the phone will ring—it will be your mother's sister from Israel, calling to wish her a happy holiday, shouting over the din of crying babies and someone plinking the Four Questions on the piano—and your mother will look so sad you will fantasize about running away—spending holidays by yourself eating turkey and mashed potatoes at the Big Boy—running away (like a teenager!) even though you're thirty and have just finished paying off your student loans. Outside, it will be March and snowing and you will think, God, please, anywhere but here, anywhere but here, the next twenty years stretching in front of you flat and gray and silent—but how can you leave them—your parents—alone without friends? And there you'll be, watching your mother swallowing hard and trying to sound cheerful, and that's when it'll come to you. You have a perfectly good family, just not in the U.S.

When you talk to the Israeli *Shaliach*, you will find there is a category for people like you: *Returning Minor*. There are benefits as well: tax breaks, a free flight, graduate school, Hebrew lessons. Your parents, of course, will be supportive. They will notify the tenants living in your apartment that it's time to vacate. When your parents left Israel, they couldn't bear to sell the apartment, to admit they were leaving for good. Back then it was still wrong to leave—a kind of betrayal—and besides, they couldn't take money out of the country. Now they will tell you that they kept the apartment just in case, for this very reason, so you would have a place to go. In this respect, your parents are like all the other Israelis you meet in the States, forever going back just as soon as . . . and right after. . . .

So you will go back and sleep in the same room you slept in as a child. The view from your windows will be exactly the one you remember: a smokestack, a small airport, a traffic light. Behind them: the Mediterranean, a flat blue line, thick or thin depending on the time of day. The part you won't remember is the way the heat keeps you sweating, how bright and relentless the sun is, the way it bleaches colors and washes them out.

Of course, it won't work out. You'll spend holidays with your extended family—imagine! eight first cousins! forty-three second cousins!—but other days, they will be too married and pregnant and busy trying to keep up with inflation to see you. You will spend most of your time alone, or with other English speakers at work writing technical manuals; at restaurants, complaining about the service; in cabs, trying to convince the drivers to turn on the meter—just turn it on!—while they speed along, charging you four times the going rates. In your apartment, the roof will leak every time it rains and the man who will come to fix it will take one look at you and tell you that what you need is a European man, one with manners, and not the typical Israeli who—you'll soon discover—thinks what American women want is sex without commitment (90% of Americans end up leaving anyway) and finds the fact that you already own an

apartment as exotic as any of your American boyfriends ever found
the dark hairs on your arms. You will want to make a snappy come-
back, but your Hebrew will be too weak. Instead you will smile,
baring your teeth like a dog, even though you already know Israelis
don't smile at strangers.

There is more, all of it trivial, and you will be ashamed that the
things that wear you down aren't the ones you expect: not the heat,
nor the terror, nor the flying cockroaches. Instead, it will be the way
people will brush against you in the supermarket as if you're invisible, the way it's so easy to forget you're something more than a
body and an accent, that you at one time had friends who wanted
to be with you not just because there wasn't anyone else around.
You'll give it two years and switch jobs four times, and when the
third year rolls around you will start to fear that this new person
whose body you've been walking around in—teeth clenched, heart
pounding, shoulders hunched—is who you're really been all along,
that you'll forget ever having felt any other way. And you will give
up. Of course, your parents, tired of your 7 A.M. phone calls—who
else can afford the long distance or put up with your whining—will
be supportive and tell you to put the apartment up for sale—by then
the laws will have changed, and it will be possible to take the money
out—and come back. Come back.

When things don't work out, your parents will fly in to sign
the papers. It's their apartment, after all. Before they come, you will
find a real estate agent, a tanned man who dresses in linen. He will
place an advertisement in the newspaper:

In *Ramat Aviv*: 6th floor, 3 rooms, balcony, 92 m², spectacular
view.

You'll want to show it to someone, so you'll knock on the door
of the neighbor who still remembers you from when you were nine,
and who still remembers your father with hair and your mother
without glasses. From inside, you'll hear a shuffling and things falling on the floor. When he finally opens up, he'll be struggling with

his shirt buttons. His stomach, unleashed, will seem white and fleshy, enormous. Behind him, you'll catch a glimpse of his wife wrestling with a lacy black nightgown, blue cream on her face. You'll check your watch: 4 P.M. You'll secretly suspect they are nudists, but still, you will show him the paper, and the neighbor will look at the ad and say, "You miss them, huh, your parents?"

The apartment is the same age you are. Your parents moved in the year you were born. You'll worry about what they'll think when they see it—the paint swollen and peeling where the walls got wet, the rust on the refrigerator door (the salt in the air eats through everything), the hairline crack in the bathroom sink. You'll order a cleaning service and—when the man promises to take twenty years off the floor tiles—you'll agree to pay him an extra $200. After he leaves, two workers—a Nigerian and a Russian—will arrive. You'll trade jokes with the Nigerian (in English, of course!) and help him move furniture while the Russian scrubs the bathtub. They'll both work wearing nothing but shorts. Later, you will notice that every time the Russian man squats, his penis hangs out of his right leg opening. When he urinates, he'll leave the door open and stare right at you. You'll think about asking the Nigerian to do something, but how can you? The floor, when the Nigerian is done buffing it, will still look its age. Everything will still seem dirty, even though you know that it isn't. You'll spend the night cleaning the bathroom again. When you turn off the lights, you'll think you can see the places where the Russian's penis touched the porcelain shining yellow like glow-in-the-dark stars.

At the airport, you'll notice that your parents are white and fleshy too, and that they've already begun to shrink. Their ears, the tips of their noses, will seem too large for their faces. There will be three curly white hairs on your mother's chin. When she hugs you, she will feel less substantial than you remembered. After months of not being touched, the hug itself will make your hands tremble. Although you'll feel tired and haggard, your parents will say you look wonderful, very tanned. When they see the apartment, though, they will suck in air through their teeth. You'll know how it must look to them—how it looked to you when you first returned—small, dirty, old. "My God," your mother will say, but this won't be when she starts crying. That will be later, when she makes plans to meet your aunt over the phone. Your father will look at you grimly, then nod, as if he's just verified something. You will let them sleep in your bed—their bed—in your room, and you will sleep on the floor in their room. You'll realize that you can look into the kitchen window of the penthouse apartment that sprawls above you from where you are lying (your building is shaped like an X). You will watch the upstairs neighbor eat microwave popcorn from a bag and read the newspaper. You'll have ridden in the elevator with him a few times, but you won't know his name, only that he has lost a leg in a motorcycle accident. To avoid thinking about what might be scurrying across the floor, you'll concentrate on willing him to stand up and look out the window and down at you. He won't.

In the morning you'll discover that your parents have gone on strike. They will sit on the couch in the living room, their arms crossed over their chests, and wait for you to go to the mini-market next door for fresh rolls and chocolate milk in a baggie. When you return, they will move to the kitchen table, where they will sit listlessly, propping their heads up on their arms, waiting for you to make coffee and set out silverware. Your father won't close his mouth when he chews and will make a thick rumbling noise—mnnnnnh—when he drinks. He'll pant slightly after swallowing. His Adam's apple, once prominent, will be hidden in the folds of his neck. It'll be the first time you notice it's gone missing. You'll look down at your plate: what other parts of him are lost?

When you're done eating, they'll take turns in the bathroom while you wash the dishes and make their bed. When you shake them out, their sheets will smell sour. You will open the windows to air the room out. Across the way, in the apartment in the next building, you will see a woman feeding a parakeet. When the traffic light below you turns red, you'll believe you can make out a distant chirping.

At 10 A.M., the real estate agent will stop by with the buyers he's found: a man, a woman, a teenage daughter with a slicked-back ponytail. The woman's hair will be hennaed red, and next to your mother she will seem firm, fat and vigorous, ready to knock down the wall between the kitchen and the living room all by herself. She will tell your mother they plan to put in central air, replace the Formica, redo the bathroom in muted maroons. After a while, her words will blur and all you'll hear will be the ugly parts of Hebrew— the guttural CH sounds that remind you of phlegm, the R that you'll never be able to pronounce properly. When the real estate agent tells her the leaky walls can easily be fixed, both your parents will look down at the floor, silent and guilty, and you'll realize that this is your chance to halt the sale. You'll stare at the husband—a short man with a solid gut and hairs poking through his T-shirt— and imagine him on top of her, balancing belly to belly, legs and arms in the air, a naked, hairy, human propeller. In this apartment? Where you grew up? Impossible.

After they leave—the daughter smiling thinly at you, lips clenched around her braces—the real estate agent will wipe his palms on his pants. The wet marks will dry before he's through shaking your parents' hands. You'll have an urge to lock the door behind him.

"That's that," your father will say once the real-estate agent is gone. "Good riddance." He will pull out a camera and take pictures of all the wet spots on the walls, protecting himself against some future lawsuit. "Here's hoping for a drought."

You mother will say nothing and look at her hands. They'll be covered with liver spots and crisscrossed by veins. She'll sniff them cautiously. "I can smell his cologne."

The plan will be for your parents to drop you off at work—a tall building in Ramat Gan, next to the Diamond Exchange—and then drive up to Netanya to see your mother's sister. Instead, ten minutes after you arrive at your desk, your father will call you from the lobby downstairs: "I can't drive in this traffic. Take us home."

You'll explain the situation to your boss, a South African who lives in the West Bank. The bus he rides into work has steel mesh in its windows and dents from thrown stones. He is Orthodox and not frightened easily. When you gave him your notice, he said, "Yes, it's hard to live here without conviction." But you, you come from a family of atheists and leftists. In principle, you're against oppression and for a two-state solution. In reality, you have talked to exactly one Arab in your life: the fourteen-year-old boy who delivers your groceries, and who you tip generously as if that changes anything. In fact, it's only recently that you've learned to tell Arabs and Jews apart—they look so similar! What do you know about conviction, other than that you've got none?

About your parents, down in the lobby, your boss will say, "Do whatever you need to do." He's already managing without you. On his desk will be organizational charts on which your name has been crossed out. Downstairs, your father will have parked in the bus bay in front of your building. The incoming busses will be honking at your little Peugeot rental, the drivers yelling, "Move your car, *koos ochtok!*"

"Hurry up," your father will say, wringing his hands. "Get us out of here."

You will drive them up to Netanya, to your aunt's small house, and drop them off without going inside. Instead of returning to work, you'll decide to go visit the dogs that guard the airport. The airport, even though it's noisy, is the only reason you can see the Mediterranean from your apartment. You'll weave your way through rusted nails and broken bricks—construction waste from down the street—to the fence that blocks off the runway. Every few hundred yards there is a guard tower, and, in the nearest one, you'll be able to make out a soldier reading a book. When he hears your feet crunching in the sand, he'll look up at you and wave. The dogs are on the other side of the fence, chained to railings that are twenty yards long. They can run back and forth, their steel chains clanging behind them, but the railings are spaced out so that neighboring dogs can never quite reach each other. When it's hot—and it's always hot when you visit—most of the dogs will be sleeping in the shade of their doghouses. Only the one furthest left, a Doberman pincher who is missing an ear, will bother to bark at you. You used to imagine bringing them chewy toys and jerky treats, but when you finally did, the guard reached for his megaphone and yelled at you to stop: "Can't you see they're working?" The dogs depress you. Each time you visit them, you'll promise yourself it's the last. This time, it really will be.

All the first cousins—eight! not counting the children!—will gather at your aunt's for dinner. The women will each bring a casserole. You'll watch them slide easily in and out of the kind of small talk you never managed to master: reserve duty, daycare, politics. You'll catch yourself mimicking their facial expressions: shoulder shrugs, raised eyebrows, pursed lips, open palms facing up. All of them—you too—have the same wide mouth, the same nose, the same dimple in your left cheek. How can you leave these people who look like you?

Back at the apartment, you'll be brushing your teeth when you hear someone announce: "Citizens, step away from your windows!" The voice will be staticky, the wording oddly formal. Your parents will obey and retreat to the hallway, but not you—you'll go stand in the balcony and lean over the railing, and try to make out the police blockade and the small robot that blows up suspicious objects. Your skin will prickle, waiting for the blast. This will be the first time they've found something in your neighborhood. The silence around you will buzz with energy—all the traffic below will be stopped—and you'll imagine all your neighbors standing on their balconies, in the dark, waiting, just like you, on the balls of their feet, ready to leap back if necessary. Nothing. Nothing. Then, just as you begin to relax, a small explosion, like a car backfiring.

[181]

You'll sense you mother standing beside you. "Well," she'll say, "that's one thing you won't miss."

The breeze off the Mediterranean will be cool and salty. In the distance, you'll see the blinking lights of a small plane getting ready to land. You will realize these are the moments you like best—the ones when you're near danger but not in it. You'll remember the time one of your Israeli coworkers gave you and a couple others a ride home. He asked you about the move, whether it was difficult learning to live with the terror, and you said you didn't know enough people to worry. Later, after he dropped the others off, the coworker told you that the man in the backseat had lost both his parents, the woman next to him a boyfriend in Lebanon. Now, watching the police clear the barricades and pack up their gear, you'll note how lucky you are, leaving unscathed: lucky enough to avoid busy markets and crowded intersections, always arriving a day too early, or else a day too late.

Instead of sleeping, you will listen to your father pacing up and down the hallway as if he's never heard of jetlag. He'll keep stepping on a loose tile in rhythmic intervals: tap tap tap clack, tap tap tap clack. You'll consider leaving the buyers' teenage daughter a gift under the tile—something she could use, like a purple marker or glitter makeup, but worry she'd lose them, or worse, throw them out. A better plan: carving your name in the doorframe or the windowsill, something that can't be replaced the way this dour teenager with braces will be replacing you. The only thing that keeps you from doing it right then will be the sound of your father still pacing outside your room: tap tap tap clack, tap tap tap clack.

In the morning, after you're done feeding your parents and airing their room—the smell, if anything, is worse, not better—you'll start scratching the letters of your name into the frame of the west window with a screwdriver, in a place the teenage daughter will surely see when she watches the planes taking off. Before you have time to finish, the doorbell will ring. Your parents won't move—it's part of their strike—and when the doorbell rings again, you will tuck the screwdriver into the pocket of your shorts and let in the real estate agent and the mother who—if anything—will seem to take up even more space than she did yesterday. You and your parents will trail the woman as she walks in and out of each room, looking closely at the furniture you've bought with your Returning Minor discount.

"This wardrobe isn't real wood," she'll say. "These burners don't ignite automatically."

She'll sit in front of the piano—the piano that waited patiently for your return—the one the technician had taken four hours to get back in tune—and tap out *Doe, a deer.* You'll worry that she'll burst out singing, but she won't. Instead, she'll spin around on the rusty piano stool—again, the salt air—and say, "I'll give you one hundred shekels for the wardrobe. I don't want anything else."

When she leaves, the real estate agent will reveal that she is planning to install all new windows and replace all the doors. Your parents will nod and accept her offer, which is substantially less that the real estate agent's initial estimate, but still more than the apartment is worth.

"Don't forget," the real estate agent will say, "I get a percentage."

While they set up a time for the closing, you'll excuse yourself to pee. Washing your hands, you'll glance in the mirror and remember that you're actually closer to the mother's age than to the daughter's, that you already have gray hair and wrinkles and varicose veins of your own. Still, you'll think, there must be some way to leave a mark, some sort of signal that even this woman, with all her renovations, won't be able to erase until long after you've gone.

After the sun sets and the air cools a little, you will walk with your father to the Ramat Aviv mall. You will have to pause twice while your father wipes his forehead with a handkerchief and pretends he doesn't need to catch his breath. Inside, the stores' names are in English: Golf, Aldo's, McDonald's. Your father will sample the kosher Big Mac and say it's too salty. The French fries, though, still taste the same.

"This is hard on your mother," he'll tell you, as if you haven't figured this out. "It's like leaving Israel, all over again."

"What about you?"

"You know me." Your father will open another packet of ketchup. "It's your mother I worry about."

But he's wrong. You don't know him. You never paid attention. All you have are pictures of him in uniform, his hair cropped close to his head, or squinting into the sun, his arm casually draped around your mother's shoulders. Once you moved to the States, he started wearing shoes with socks instead of sandals and shaved off his sideburns. You'll know there has to be more, but what is it?

When it's time to head back home, even though it's only ten minutes by foot, your father will hail a cab. "I'm sixty-four," he'll remind you. "I'm tired of walking." When the driver refuses to turn on the meter, your father will shrug. "Look at that," he'll say in English. "He knows I'm American. It must be the clothes."

Back in the apartment, the two of you will find your mother making a list. "These are the things I want," she'll tell you, handing you the piece of paper. The list will include a vinyl tablecloth, a horsehair broom head and rags with which to wash the floor.

"You can't be serious," your father will say.

"But I am." Your mother will sigh. "I just want *something*."


When you're through packing up your desk at work—a hot pink plastic slinky; a picture of your dog, now long dead; three ballpoint pens with the company logo—you'll go home to discover the men who are supposed to cart away the piano (an Ecuadorian and a Thai) smoking in the lobby, listening impassively to your neighbor the nudist declaim the ills of foreign labor: "Look at this mirror, the way it hangs crooked! Look at the grout between the tiles, only two years old and flaking already!" When he sees you, he'll say, "These people all live together in camps, you know. Yell at one and you've yelled at them all." Then he'll ask, "Where are your parents? I keep knocking and knocking, and nobody opens."

Upstairs, your parents will be sitting at the kitchen table, arranging yesterday's crumbs into small piles. Your mother will accuse you: "There's no milk. Your father is starving." And you'll accuse her right back: "Why didn't you open the door?" Even though you're a family that never yells, you will feel a shout forming deep in your lungs and rising to the back of your throat. The only thing that will stop it is the Ecuadorian mover, who right then will announce in broken English that the piano doesn't fit in the elevator. You'll spend the next half hour on the phone reminding the man in charge that you did, in fact, tell him the elevator was too small, yelling at him instead of at your parents, who are now tracing the patterns on the tablecloth as if they've gone deaf. After a while, the owner will instruct the Ecuadorian and the Thai men to leave, and they will, not bothering to close the door behind them. After they go, you'll run downstairs and buy milk, run back upstairs and slam it down on the kitchen table.

"What's the matter with you?" you'll ask. "Why are you doing this to me?"

For a while, your parents won't say anything. Then your mother will say, "To you? To *you*?" And you'll know you've done something wrong—but what? What? What could you have done that's bad enough for *this*?

Later, the three of you will go out to dinner in Jaffa with your father's rich brother who likes to golf in Caesarea and go skiing in Switzerland. Your uncle will spend the evening grilling your father about money: "What are you getting for the apartment? How about that piano?" When your father finishes accounting for all of it, your uncle will proclaim: "You've been robbed!" To you he'll say, "Why didn't you call me, if you were so lonely?"

Outside the restaurant, the air will smell like rust and urine and, while your father and uncle say their goodbyes, you will watch a large rat who's missing a tail gnaw on what looks like a black piece of rubber.

"What is that?" you'll ask your mother.

She'll peer in the direction you're pointing, and even though she'll smile, you'll realize she can't see it. "I don't know," she'll say, "but wasn't the fish delicious?"

The three of you will climb slowly up the stairs that lead from the harbor to the old city. There will be a full moon, and the stone buildings around you will shimmer. Below you, you will see waves crashing white into the wall.

"Maybe we shouldn't sell," your mother will say. "We could find new tenants."

Your father will be the one who notices she's shivering, who pulls her close and wraps his arms around her: "The roof leaks. The paint is peeling."

"So let's sell it and buy a different place," your mother will say. "Maybe over in Kefar Saba. A nice house or something."

"We're not coming back. You know that."

"No," your mother will agree. "We're not. But what if we change our minds? We have family here."

"We have family there too."

"Who?" your mother will ask. "We have no one."

"We have a daughter," your father will remind her, winking, and your mother, startled, will look up at you, her *daughter*, almost thirty-four, older already than she was when she had you, and you'll find yourself thinking your uncle was right: she's been robbed. She's been robbed.

While your parents sign the papers in the presence of the real estate agent and a lawyer, you will pass the time riding the elevator up and down, up and down. Other neighbors—the nudist, the family from #9—will hop on and hop off, but you will stay in there and wait for the woman, the husband, and the dour teenage daughter to leave. Tomorrow, you will hold a moving sale. In two days, the packers will come. In three days, you'll follow. Seventy-two more hours, you'll think. You can get through this.

It's only when you're holding the elevator for the neighbor from the penthouse that a solution will come to you. You will ride up with him to 7, trying to work up the courage to ask, and then ride down to 6 and walk up the stairs. By then, he will have already gone inside, and you'll have to ring the bell.

"What is it?" he'll ask you. When you start stuttering, he'll say, "You can tell me in English."

"No," you'll say. "It's not that."

The apartment, behind him, will be dark, the furniture modern, with black metal frames, the shades closed against the afternoon sun. The neighbor will lean on one crutch, the left leg of his jeans neatly pinned up below the knee. He'll patiently listen to you tell him about the apartment, about leaving, about the teenage daughter and her thin-lipped smile. You'll follow him into the kitchen and wait while he looks for a screwdriver and a hammer. There will be a half empty bag of popcorn on the breakfast table.

"There you go," he'll say when he gives you the tools. His hands, you will notice, are large, with dark thin hairs on the knuckles. "Let me know when you're done."

You'll clear a space on the counter underneath the window and climb up. Form there, you'll be able to see down into your parents' old bedroom. Your sleeping bag, the pile of laundry in the corner—you need to do laundry—will look like shed skin left behind by some animal. The exterior of the building is a dusty beige stucco. To pound on it properly, you will need to stick your head, and your shoulders and arms, out the window. At first, the height will make you dizzy, but then you'll learn to avoid looking down at the parking lot. The bits of concrete you hammer loose will fall on the cars parked below, but will be too small to do any damage. Soon, you'll be sweating from the effort, and the neighbor, who will have showered by now and changed into sweats, will offer you a glass of water.

Although in your mind you imagined him to be about your age, now you'll see that he's actually much older. He is losing hair on the crown of his head. There are laugh lines carved around his mouth and eyes. You'll watch him watching you drink, but you won't know what to say to him. It'll be too late anyhow—your flight already booked, your books sorted into piles, your parents in the living room shaking hands with strangers—you'll be leaving, and he'll be staying. So what if he's missing a leg?

"Can I see it?" he'll ask you once you've finished, and together you will take the elevator down to 6 and find your parents slumped on the sofa in their standard positions, their copy of the contract on the coffee table, pinned down by empty cups and saucers. In your parents' old room, you and the neighbors will take turns standing by the window, admiring your handiwork: your initials, large and loopy, the date, the apartment number.

"If she turns out to be nice," the upstairs neighbor will say about the teenage daughter, "I'll tell her to look for it." When you shake hands goodbye, he'll say, "I'm sorry things didn't work out better," and you'll say, "I am too."

That night, while you listen to your father pacing, you'll wait for the lights to go on in the penthouse kitchen, for the upstairs neighbor to come to the window and wave. He won't, of course. This is your story, not his.

All the things you can't sell, your family—eight first cousins! forty-three second cousins!—will pick through, checking the non-stick cookware for scratches, the sofa for broken springs. In the early afternoon, you'll drive down to Jaffa and pay the State of Israel back for the Returning Minor discounts and tax breaks it gave you—you didn't stay long enough for the loans to be forgiven. Back in the apartment, the bed will be gone. In its place you'll find your parents sitting on folding chairs the nudist neighbor has lent them, your father reading the newspaper, your mother folding fifty shekel bills into complicated paper airplanes. The sour smell will seem sharper, like window cleaning fluid and sweat, but when you look around, all you'll see are discarded sheets, pillows, your parents' neatly packed suitcases.

"Where will we sleep?" your father will ask you, looking lost.

Emptied of furniture, the apartment, if anything, will seem smaller. You'll call up the Hilton and reserve a room for the night. Breakfast won't be included, but there will be cable TV. You will leave your parents in front of CNN, where the headlines will be about the peace process. The Israel you glimpse in this newscast—a yellow, dusty, third-world country where dirty children throw stones— will be nothing like the Israel you know.

After that there will be nothing let to do but haul the laundry off to the Laundromat, then sort it into the things you'll take with you and the things that you'll ship. The only other people there will be the American exchange students from Tel-Aviv University, chubby and tan, their toenails painted a metallic blue. While you fold, you'll listen to one of them complain about her boyfriend: "He was like, what do you think this is? America?"

Only when you get home and stack everything into piles will you realize all but two of the towels are missing. The wardrobe will be empty, the bathroom cabinets too. You'll stand in the middle of your bedroom, chewing the loose nail on your index finger, and wonder where they've disappeared.

For dinner, the three of you will go to a dairy restaurant where they make smoothies and pancakes larger than your head. For once, your parents will seem cheerful, admiring the photographs of cows in the middle of the desert that are hanging on the walls.

"Too bad we don't have more time," your mother will say. "We could have gone down to the Dead Sea."

You'll feel like throttling her, but she's your mother, and you won't. Still, you'll resent her for perking up as if all she'd needed was some time away from the apartment, some time away from you.

Later, you'll stop by their suite to use the bathroom, and that's when you'll notice that the smell has followed them here, and that now it's so strong you think you can taste it. You'll pull back the shower curtain, then check under the sink. And that's where you'll find them, the missing towels, all five of them, and you'll realize it's much worse than what you've imagined—the towels, balled up and wrinkled, are damp with what can only be urine.

You'll stay in the bathroom so long your father will knock on the door and ask if you're all right. You won't know what to do, so you'll lie: "Must be something I ate." You'll wash your face and your hands, but the smell, you'll imagine it clinging to your hair and your clothes like a crying baby you can never set down.

When you're finally ready to come out, you'll flush the toilet and blow your nose. Your parents will be sitting up in bed, watching the news, and in the blue light of the television they will seem fragile and younger than you've ever known them: your children. The air in the hotel room will feel stuffy and close, but there it will be, the rest of your life: you will ship off your belonging and go back to the States, and in years to come—and there will be many—when friends ask you what went wrong, why you left, what happened exactly, over there in Israel, you'll have nothing to say. From where you'll be standing—on the other side of the fence, the dog chain pulling you back, your parents almost within reach—the simple truth will be this: you just won't remember.

# RELEVANT GIRL

TENAYA DARLINGTON

Everything before this is irrelevant: one day Gum, a small-time lawyer, comes home from the office early, changes into his jeans, sets
off down the street with his hands in his pockets, and begins to
follow a woman. She is young, in her early twenties. He is in his
thirties, has been married for several years. The girl, in her own way,
is irrelevant. Who she is or what her name is, they're irrelevant
facts. Still, she is in every way relevant to all the successive events in
his life despite the fact that their interaction is minimal—lasts not
even ten seconds. She is attractive, from behind anyway, and has
long dark hair that waves down her back, shining like a pelt, almost
to the waist of her khaki pants. A black bag is strapped to her back,
and in one hand she carries both her umbrella and what looks like
a brown velvet suit coat, perhaps a man's, perhaps her own. Gum
does not know, though he is curious.

It is important to point out that Gum has not sought her out
in any way. He has not chosen to follow her over other women. He
does not even realize he is following her until he is. They seem to be
heading in the same direction, though he has no particular destination in mind. He has simply come home early from work and, finding

his wife to be out of the house, has gone out for a walk. He cannot remember the last time he just strolled. In fact, he cannot remember the last time he really indulged himself or took time to go off alone, unless he includes the occasional drink after work. He sometimes sits at the bar and shoots the breeze with the bartender over a Jack and Coke. Sometimes there is an old-timer slouched over an ashtray or another businessman with whom Gum talks. Then they joke around and exchange occasional glances with the waitresses.

When Gum thinks back on the girl he followed home on this particular day, he will wonder what made him continue down the walk after her in his crisp white sneakers. He will wonder what came over him. He will not be able to remember his thought process at all, and he will even question the reality of the situation, despite the fact that it will change him for good. He will, from time to time, see other women like her, women who resemble her from behind, and it will make him bend down and tie his shoe or dodge into a store for a gumball.

The woman does not remind him of his wife, whose name is Belle. The woman does not remind him of any of his clients or of any former girlfriends or even women he has thought about in secret. She is just a woman ambling down the street. She stops to check her bag for something. He stops to wind his watch. When she crosses the road, he keeps up his pace so that soon he is only feet away from her. He sees that she is carrying something square in her back pocket, perhaps a thin wad of bills, perhaps a love letter. He can see the edge of her neck where it meets the collar of her blouse. He can see a bracelet with blue stones around her left wrist. She is wearing sensible shoes, the kind in which one can easily run.

After a few minutes, he can tell that she senses him. She looks slightly to the side without turning all the way around to check his position in relation to her. She speeds up a little, then slows down to let him pass, but he does not. He is not doing anything out of the ordinary: he is walking down the street. They have just passed the grocery store where all the people with food stamps go. To his left is a row of four houses, all of them two stories with porches upon which there are swings and pots of bedraggled, brown leaves—the remnants of summer flowers. It is a neighborhood not much unlike the one where he and his wife live. It's broad daylight. Anyone looking out a window can see them. Cars pass in various colored blurs on a busy street ahead of them. It's four in the afternoon.

Perhaps he did not expect her to be so surprised, though he still cannot remember if she called out, if she gasped, if she yanked his hand away. He does not remember the minute before nor the minute after, though he remembers her face, her hair caught in the edge of her mouth. He remembers her moving quickly away, her gait unrhythmic and haphazard as she half walked, half ran to the house on the corner. She had gone up the steps and through the door. No, she had literally flown up those steps, casting only a quick glance his way through the shrubbery.

He had stood there, still hearing his own voice, though he could not recollect hers or recall now if she had even spoken. When he looked down, his hands were open to the air, as if holding something—the moment gone, yet heavy in its past existence.

At dinner, Gum tells his wife about a woman with long blond hair who came to see him about a case she was interested in taking to small claims court.

"I hope you didn't take it," his wife says, serving herself small potatoes. "The more of those little cases you take on, the more you get mired in minor scuffles."

Gum nods and nods. They've been through this before. He's had a rough start in Belchertown.

"This is a different sort of case," Gum says, and his wife can see that he is visibly shaken, so she listens with her special cheetah ears that are capable of hearing the most minute sounds.

Here's what happened: a woman, a young woman, a young attractive woman is minding her own business and walking down the street when a man begins to follow her.

"What does the man look like?" his wife breaks in, setting down both her fork and knife. "Maybe I've seen him. I was out all day."

Here's what he looks like: he has a crew cut or maybe it's just a very short cut. He's of medium build. Slightly muscular, not wiry. Definitely not wiry. He's wearing a dark shirt, jeans, sneakers.

"How old was he?" Mrs. Gum asks, chewing slowly, craning over her plate to catch every word.

"Thirties, mid-thirties, late thirties," says Gum, giving a shrug.

"That doesn't tell you anything at all," his wife says with concern, putting an index finger to her temple. "That could be anyone."

Gum nods and stirs his peas around on his plate. Then he continues, his voice low. His wife's neck stretches across the table like a giraffe's. Gum feels himself getting smaller, less articulate. How can he explain what really went on?

"He did that in broad daylight?" his wife asks, astonished. "What a strange thing to do."

Gum nods. Yes. It is very strange. He can still feel where he touched her. He is holding a spoon in that same hand. He has a dark napkin tucked down into his collar, covering his chest where he can still feel the indentation of her bag as he came up behind her.

After dinner, Gum and his wife watch television and drink port out of small, bulbous glasses on their new sofa. There is nothing on, nothing they like—which is almost nothing. His wife stands up, straightens her skirt, and says, "Why don't we watch a movie?" She holds up a black case, something she rented from the library. "As long as you don't mind watching *Barefoot in the Park* again," she says. His wife is a huge fan of Robert Redford, to the point that Gum sometimes gets jealous. In the scene where Redford runs around in the rain, feeling desperate and shattered, Gum's wife always cries into the arm of the sofa, ruining the upholstery with her mascara.

There will be no Redford and Fonda tonight. The tapes must have accidentally been switched, for what comes on is a documentary about the zebra. "In this case," his wife says, "we better pour ourselves more port." And she goes into the kitchen and returns with a tall glass.

Outside their tiny house the wind knocks the branches of the bushes against the windows, but Gum is immune. He is watching the zebras with fascination and awe. A baby zebra is being born. It stands almost instantly, bending then straightening its pool-cue legs. Now the crucial moment, says the narrator. The female zebra must circle her young so that she can memorize her mother's stripes. If the foal sees another pattern, even out of the corner of her eye—if another zebra comes up unexpectedly behind them, for instance— the foal will be lost. She will never be able to recognize her mother's pattern, and she will eventually get separated from the herd and die.

Gum sits entranced, his thumb pushing against his front teeth, a habit from childhood. Sight is a kind of memorization, he thinks. The eye spots something and holds on to the imprint somehow. A single vision can change the route of our existence, can help or hinder our survival in the world. There are some visual experiences that we forget right away, but others remain with us until death. Sights have shelf lives, Gum thinks. For instance, Gum cannot remember what he wore last Friday, yet he can remember perfectly every pair of pajamas he has ever owned, especially the ones he wore as a child. He can also remember all of his mother's different bathrobes: the silky pink one; the furry red one; the aqua blue one with the white zipper up the front; the quilted white one. And on and on. He thinks of his mother circling his bassinet in her different robes, his eyes fixed on her, memorizing just where the pockets were, the eyelet lace. Why do we remember the strange things we remember? What about the things we forget? Do we choose to forget them, or do they begin to decay on a shelf far back in one's mind, turning into a puddle?

Gum thinks about the girl he followed down the sidewalk. He can remember everything about her, at least almost everything. Parts of her have begun to fade, like her face. He does not remember the color of her eyes, for example—if her nose was large or small. What does she recall? What will she remember for the rest of her life? Will she be able to forget what happened on the walk? Will she choose to forget it or will it be forgotten for her? And if she remembers all through time, think of that! She will carry his face with her forever. The notion terrifies Gum. In the head of an unnamed, unknown woman, his visage might reappear numerous times in the course of her lifetime. Even as he grows old and she grows old, she will remember his face exactly as it was on October 21, 1996.

Gum turns to his wife. A herd of zebras is racing across her eyes.

"If a man came up to you," he says, swishing around a circle of port in the bottom of his glass, "and did what I described over dinner, would you ever forget it?"

His wife turns to him and blinks.

"What you described," she says, stopping for a gulp of port, "is something no woman could forget."

The credits roll until the screen goes fuzzy. Gum's wife has fallen asleep, her head on his thigh. She is probably drunkenly dreaming of zebras, their lines rippling and blurring. He lays a hand on her brown curls and finishes his drink, watching the fuzzy screen, which after a while begins to look like busy fabric. It moves so fast, it almost stands still. The mind plays tricks on you; the eye is rarely a lie detector.

The storm outside knocks over some lines, and the lights go out. Gum cannot see a thing. He lifts his wife's head, lays it back down on the couch, makes his way to the kitchen, pushes aside a chair, opens the far drawer, reaches in, feels the candles in with the knives, and lights one immediately with his Zippo. He stands there with the candle, looking at his path of travel through the living room and dining room and kitchen, unsure why he even bothered to find a light. He can remember where everything is in the dark. So he blows out the candle. Its burning smell lingers in the air for a second, then he sets the candle on the counter. He stands there in the dark, unable to see anything, and the event of the afternoon begins to replay itself in his mind, only backward.

The girl walks backward down some steps that lead away from a house. She walks hurriedly backward in her shoes, swinging her arms backward, her hair blowing forward in the breeze. She is visibly shaken, but backward. Likewise, he walks backward. They face each other, several feet apart. He says something, but backward so that it is nonsensical, and she gasps backward so that it sounds like a sigh. Her face breaks into a smile, which is a frown backward, and then his hands have grabbed her, they are reaching, they are just beginning to reach around and touch her, he has just begun to think about it, he is coming up behind her, he is walking home backward, he is taking his hands out of his pockets, taking his shoes off, taking his jeans off. He is standing in front of the mirror, not looking at himself.

Gum replays the scene over and over, forward and backward. He begins to see more and more of her face each time she spins around—that horrible, aghast look after being violated. He wants to take off his hands. He wants desperately to take off his hands, to run them through the dishwasher. The lights are still out. The tub is ice cold. He is thankful that he cannot see his face in the mirror, the same face that will come up behind her in her sleep, haunt her forever. *Had he thought, he never would have, no one wants to, no one means to, no one, certainly not him.* Here he is watching a zebra movie with his wife. Here he is squirting some Pert into his hand. Maybe the girl uses Pert. Everyone uses Pert. He's not that kind of man.

This goes on for days and weeks. The irrelevant girl is always near, her face aghast, frozen to the back of his mind. He can hear the shriek she sent up. Right in broad daylight, what was he thinking? And so out of character. He wonders if his father, his gentle dentist father, ever took a woman by such violent surprise. Surely, it's not something in his genes.

Gum grows nervous. Gum grows pale. He has trouble sleeping and trouble getting out of bed.

"Touch me," his wife says in the dark, running a hand along his thigh.

"I can't," Gum says. "Not with these hands."

His wife rolls over with an irritated sigh. "That's all you keep talking about," she says. "You and your hands."

Gum lies awake. He has to. He's not sure what he might do next. He has been wearing thick, wool gloves to work. In the morning, he sprinkles some Comet from the bathroom into each of the fingers so that his hands are gritty and grow raw. He shuffles papers, and when anyone asks, he tells them he is sensitive to photocopies.

When an attractive woman walks by, he imagines she is a zebra made up only of lines. He doesn't let his gaze rest anywhere too long. He doesn't want to suddenly do anything crazy or let a woman's visage stick around in his vision too long. It's bad. It's very, very bad. His wife tells him he needs to see someone. And he does. He does need to see someone.

"But I don't want to *see* anyone," he tells his wife. "I don't want to see period. I wish humans would evolve without eyes. I wish we all just looked like a bunch of shapes."

"Whatever do you mean?" his wife asks.

"I wish all people were triangles or squares. Maybe there would be some slight variation—along the hypotenuse. But then we would get into arguments over who was pointier. Forget it," says Gum, going back to his work.

"Are you having trouble seeing?" His wife bends low and looks at him through his glasses. She touches the edge of his frames with her thumb and forefinger. Then she squints and looks deeply into his eyes.

"Who's that?" she asks, craning her neck into his face.

Gum looks at her lips, which form a diamond, her triangular nose, her trapezoidal eyebrows.

"Mr. Gum," she says slowly. "There's a woman in your eyes."

Gum leans back in his chair and takes off his wire-rimmed glasses, rubbing his eyes with his knuckles. "It's your reflection," he says. "Any time you look into someone else's eyes, you're going to see your own face."

Mrs. Gum sits down on his lap in the dining-room chair and takes his chin in her hand. Gum struggles for a moment and then relinquishes his retinas to her gaze. Mrs. Gum has small gray eyes like a pelican that can detect fish underwater half a mile down.

"The woman in your eyes," she says, "is facing away."

In his ski goggles and wool gloves, Gum goes to his office every morning and meets with the few clients he has, mainly unsatisfied husbands and wives filing for divorces. It is fall. All the leaves are tinted black.

"Getting ready to go to Aspen, I see," one client comments. "Which resort do you and the missus prefer?"

"Are you trying to look like Roy Orbison?" someone jokes. "I hear he always wore those shades because he was cross-eyed."

An older woman comes in crying. "You've got the right idea," she says. "I could never do your job without having to wear shades. Sometimes I cannot bear looking at the world either." With that, she draws out a pair of Ray-Bans and puts them on for the rest of her visit.

Mrs. Gum never makes another reference to the girl in Gum's eyes. Gum himself has not looked in the mirror since. Even worse than being haunted by the girl is to be haunted by himself.

"I'm marked," he says to himself, sitting in his car one evening in an empty parking garage. "It's like having a yellow star or a pink triangle. It's like having stripes all over me in the midst of a lion's den." He rubs his gloved hands against the lightweight fabric of his pants. Then he weeps. He thinks of a line from a Leonard Cohen poem he memorized in law school: *They could only drone the prayer, They could not set it down.*

That's how it is, Gum thinks—like a prayer he could not set down.

Not only can he not set it down, he can't keep his memory from retrieving the same information over and over. Even when he closes his eyes, she is there with her small mouth open, her eyes almond-shaped and greenish brown, staring horrified at him, staring at him: Gum. At night, the incident plays on a dark reel at the base of his brain, like the famous Zapruder film. Where exactly had he grabbed her? He remembers the feeling of her breast, stiff like a stack of coffee filters in her bra. How long had it lasted? How soon had she turned? Had he grabbed her hips? Had he kissed her? Had he unsnapped her khaki pants?

The recollections don't stop in real time. They go on, becoming more elaborate and fantastic until he can no longer separate what might have happened from what really occurred. Where does memory bisect truth? Where does the bad dream intervene? He no longer knows.

Gum pushes his wool knuckles up under his ski goggles and wipes at his eyes. Then he leans over and opens the glove compartment where he keeps his Dictaphone. He rarely uses it. There is an empty tape in there, ready to go.

"This is to set the record straight," Gum rasps. "Here's what happened." The recorder is voice-activated, which is good. It allows Gum to lean his head back against the headrest, get comfortable, close his eyes.

"Let me preface by saying that I am an honest and well-meaning man," Gum begins, settling his shades on his nose. "I am the son of a dentist from Dayton, Ohio. I am not a religious man, except for Easter and Christmas, upon which I present myself before the United Methodist Church. I have a liberal arts education, graduated Phi Beta Kappa and magna cum laude." Gum clicks the stop button and rewinds the tape so he can begin again.

"Let me preface by saying that I am not a pervert. I will admit to having fantasies about older women all through college, to entering a sex booth in Munich whereupon I watched fifteen minutes of graphic intercourse between partners in latex suits for five marks. I will also admit to several one-night stands in my youth, which, for lack of better judgment, I consider to be my fault. I was breast-fed and sheltered, and as a child never witnessed any sexually aggressive behavior other than a bull mounting a heifer."

Gum tosses the Dictaphone onto the passenger seat. What is he doing? What does any of this matter? He isn't before a judge and jury. He is sitting in his Honda Accord.

"*I have no money, I murdered the pharmacist,*" Gum says aloud. That is from a Cohen poem called "I Have Two Bars of Soap," which Gum's college roommate had laminated to the tile in the shower. By the end of their senior year, the water had made its way under the plastic and turned the whole page pink with mold, but he could still read the words. Gum never thought they made much sense, but he liked the idea of poetry serving up a joke on perceptions.

Gum drives home to his wife. It is after dark. He feels he has a new attitude about life now, after his hour or so of meditation on the parking ramp. He is not going to let himself think about the girl. People allow stuff like this to take over their whole lives. A bad decision turns them sour on life. He has repented enough. He has been thinking about it for weeks now, atoning for it in small ways, like with the wool gloves and the Comet. He has rubbed his palms raw.

"Screw the girl," he says to himself, putting on his blinker. "Screw the girl. Just forget about her."

He nods to himself. "Yes!" he says. "The girl is over and done with. She's dead, done, down the drain. Ha!" Gum sends a fist up into the air.

Inside the house, Gum's wife is waiting for him at the door. She is wearing a dark red robe he has never seen her in before.

"Do you like it?" she asks, helping him with his jacket. From the kitchen, he can smell dinner—a roast in the oven. His wife hands him a glass of wine, and he takes it and sips it, walking over to the couch in his gloves and scarf and shades.

"Take off those glasses. I feel like I have an impostor in the house," his wife says, lighting a candle on the table.

Gum kicks up his feet and laughs. "That's why this is a special occasion," Gum says, turning to look at her. "I am the new Gum. I am the unabridged and uncut version. This is my new look."

His wife smiles at him from the kitchen doorway where she is stirring something in a pot. "What is your new name?"

Gum thinks for a second. "It is—Gum backward."

"Mug?" his wife asks.

Gum jerks his head back. "Is that what our last name spells?"

"Of course," his wife says. "Don't tell me you've never noticed."

"How long have you known?" Gum asks, sitting forward on the couch, as if she has just disclosed something terrible about her health.

"It's the first thing I thought of when you introduced yourself to me," his wife says, turning off the kitchen light and entering with the roast. "I thought, I am about to fall in love with a man whose name is both a noun and a verb, forward and backward."

His wife smooths her robe under her thighs as she sits down at the table. The lights are off, one candle burning, Mozart slipping from one reel to another on the old tape deck.

"I can't believe this," Gum says, joining her. "Backward, I am Mug."

"Take off your shades," his wife says, extending her monkeylike arm. She lifts them off for him and blows out the candle, so that the room is completely dark.

Gum puts his fingers to his temples. Mug—it's in his genes and in his name. He is destined to violate. Now it makes sense, though it makes no sense at all. At least it lends a farfetched explanation as to why he simply walked down the street one day and attacked an innocent woman: it had nothing to do with who he thought he was but who he was destined to be. He'd always thought of himself as a respectable and respectful human being, but clearly he was not. That was his forward self. His backward self, the deep region of Gum, had its own set of demands.

"I have no control," Gum announces.

"Should I turn on a light?" His wife's chair moves.

"No, not the light," Gum says. "I didn't mean what I just said. Everything is much better perceived in the dark."

His wife laughs her wine-filled laugh. "Would you like to perceive these carrots?" she says like a grackle.

Gum can feel the heat of the bowl. He takes it and begins to pile his plate full of warm food. It's dark. He wants to take his gloves off. He wants to eat with his hands, eat the little carrots one at a time and suck the butter from between his fingers. It's been weeks since he's taken off the gloves except in the shower. His hands feel alive when the air hits them, when he holds them over his steaming plate. He cleans them on the tablecloth, feeling like a sneaky rabbit, and plunges them into a mound of mashed potatoes.

"Great dinner," Gum says. "This was a terrific idea." He can hear his wife pouring wine as he pushes handfuls of food into his mouth, feeling gravy run down his chin and drip down his front. He delights in the mess he is making in the dark, where his wife cannot see. I am Mug, he thinks.

"I am going to turn the music up a little," his wife says. "I love this movement."

"Sure," Mug says, laying a thin slice of roast across his face like an all-beef mask. "Do anything you want to. I haven't enjoyed myself this much in weeks."

Then she is at his throat, not trying to strangle him, but to hug him, though later he is not sure. First he feels her fingernails, then her arms coming up from behind. The slab of roast on his face alarms her as she bends down to kiss him. She gasps and he tries to grab her so he can explain, but she pushes him away.

There is a short scuffle on the floor, then the lights go on. He is standing there with gravy spots all over his white shirt, dressing in his hair. There is meat on the floor. She is standing by the wall, her shoulders rising as she gulps for air. One arm is around her stomach. She stares at him across the room, and there is the aghast face. There is her disbelief. Her eyes are memorizing him, taping this vision.

"What is going on?" she whispers.

He can see her eyes moving quickly over the table with its white tablecloth, burgundy napkins, platters full of food, vase of pink carnations. She is memorizing, reviewing, remembering. This is how she will describe it to her friends.

She pulls her robe closed about her neck and glares at him, horrified. "Look at you. You've turned into a maniac. Just who do you think you are?"

Gum stands with his hands at his sides, surveying the supper from the other side of the room. He does not want to forget any of it. No, he wants to make sure he has it right this time. In his mind, he will go over and over this scene again and again, and he wants to keep everything straight, so it doesn't begin to take over, metamorphose in his mind.

Then she is gone. In her new red robe she is gone, leaving everything just so, the front door open in her wake, in her haste to escape. His car is out of the driveway before he can even get to a window. He sees the two rear lights cut down the street like eyes.

A man named Gum or Mug is walking down the street in a pair of jeans and a dark jacket. His hands are stuffed in the pockets of his jeans. The air is crisp and there is no one outside. He is a man whom cars pass, whom people glance at without taking notice. Who expects a single man walking down the street at night with his hands

in his pockets to be meditating on violence? Has he attacked someone before? Has he just tried to strangle his wife? We don't ask these
sorts of questions unless we have had some prior encounter with
fate, in which case we are a little leery of Gum—his potential to be
Mug. Is this man walking forward or backward? Are his perceptions
scrambled? Is he vile or evil, live and let live? Has he lived the devil?
A simple word like desire spells die, rise, seed, sired, and red sir.
Thread is death with an r, and pear spells reap and rape. Threat is
also tear, heart, and rat. Everyone knows about God.

At the steps of the relevant girl's house, Gum fumbles with his
hands, trying to decide how to make his entry. What if she answers
the door? She will (a) recognize him, or (b) not recognize him. If (b),
then she may (a) slam the door in his face, (b) lunge for his Adam's
apple, or (c) reproach him verbally. His only logical choice is to (a)
introduce himself and apologize right away unless she does (b). Hope-
fully, she will (d) do none of the above. She will (e) either not be
there, or (f) refuse to come to the door altogether. If she (c)'s him,
he will try to explain what he has not been able to explain to anyone
else, not even himself.

He will say, Miss, I don't know if you remember me or not, but
months ago now, I came up behind you and grabbed you as you
were walking home. After that, I don't remember what truthfully
happened. I hardly remember the moment it occurred or the moments before it occurred, but since that moment, I have lived with
your face in my face. I have not been able to lead a normal life. I
have not been able to sleep or eat normally, to touch my wife, to
fulfill the duties of my job, to exist as what I call myself: Gum. I can
assure you that what I did was not out of some malicious intent,
that it can only be explained by some unconscious ill-humor, some
fateful side of my personality that slid past me between blinks. I
have not come to your door to ask your forgiveness, only to acknowledge what happened, to get a second glimpse of your face as a
human being.

She is in every window behind the curtains. She is coming up behind him on the walk. She is lurking in the dark shrubbery and has been waiting all these months for him to come looking for her. The house is dark, but there is a glow behind the drapes upstairs as if someone might have lit a candle.

Gum shifts restlessly around on the porch after he has rung the bell. He looks around at the things on the porch: a couch, a child's rocker with the padding ripped out, a strand of Christmas lights, several coffee cups full of cigarette butts, a yellow towel, a bunch of plastic flowers branching from a single plastic stem, a bike lock, and some cardboard boxes folded and propped behind a chair. Gum goes over to a wooden support beam where there are two mailboxes. Under a piece of clear tape, written on a piece of white paper, are the last names of the inhabitants: Cormican, Daniels, Maurer, and Moll. He wonders which last name belongs to the relevant girl. He wonders why there are two mailboxes to begin with.

It takes a second ring to bring footsteps to the door. By this time, Gum has broken out in a cold sweat. In the next moment, Gum thinks, my whole life will change again. Maybe I will end up on the lawn with a broken nose, but at least I will be acknowledged for who I am.

It is not the relevant girl who answers the door, but another woman. She stands behind the screen with her hand on the latch. Gum can barely make out her short brown hair, her glasses behind the mesh. There is a pen behind her ear. One hand is in her pocket.

"I'm looking for someone," Gum says. "Is there a woman who lives here with waist-length, dark hair?" He indicates the length by touching his own hips with either hand.

"She doesn't live here anymore," the woman says. Gum notes a faint accent in her voice.

"Do you know where I could find her?"

"What's this about?" The woman comes a little closer to the door, still holding on to the handle from the inside. The screen is torn. He could reach right in. But he's not that kind of man. Still, the woman looks at him skeptically. He is not wearing his shades, and he wonders if the woman can see the relevant girl in his eyes.

Gum takes his hands out of his pockets and rubs them together to keep warm. He knows that if he doesn't say something convincing, the door will close. He will never find out where the girl has gone. He will never see her again. In person.

"This is about Leonard," Gum tells her, tilting his head to the side, squinting beneath the porch light.

"Leonard?"

"Yeah, that's right," Gum says, trying to give his voice the air of importance. "This is about a man named Leonard Cohen. Do you know where I might be able to reach the former tenant?"

It's obvious the woman in the doorway has never heard of Leonard Cohen. She is Irish, and even if she weren't, it isn't likely that even many Americans would recognize the name Leonard Cohen even though he is a celebrated songwriter, folksinger, novelist, and poet. One of those guys who has it all.

"Look, I'm a lawyer here in town," Gum says, holding up his palms like maps explaining everything.

The woman opens the door a little farther, more trusting now. "I wish I could help you out. All I know is that her family's from Iowa, but she didn't say where she was going."

"Thanks," Gum says. "Sorry to bother." The woman nods and Gum heads down the steps back into the darkness.

Two days later, Gum gets a call at his office. He is there cleaning out his desk, taking his name off the door: GUM. From the inside, the letters spell MUG. How could he have sat at his desk for so long and missed it? He has spent the past two nights alone, sitting at his wife's vanity, staring at himself in the mirror. The girl was still there, standing with her back to him, her backpack on, the umbrella and the brown coat in her right hand. He could even make out the gleaming bracelet on her arm, tiny though it was, this little dollhouse version of her. It was because of her. It was because of himself, his selves. He was starting to talk to himself about himself in third person: What has Gum done? How long must Gum remember in order to stop remembering?

A voice on the phone says, "Now you're done for. I found your tape."

"What tape?"

"The cassette tape in the car. What's this about the pharmacist?"

Gum is puzzled. "What pharmacist?"

"The one you murdered. And what's this about the girl, screwing the girl?" His wife's voice is icy, and she is overenunciating.

"I don't know what you're talking about," Gum says, dumping the contents of his pencil drawer into a box.

"It's a good thing you're a divorce lawyer, Gum, because that's what I want."

"Listen," Gum says, trying to keep himself from reeling.

"I can't believe this." His wife suddenly breaks into a sob. "And to think that night at dinner—I just don't understand how you could do this to me, to anyone."

Gum is at a loss. "It's not what you think." He tries to make his voice sound soft, but it is shaking.

"And that girl I saw in your eyes a few weeks ago—I suspected it, but I never would have imagined that you, of all people."

"Sweetheart," Gum says. "Darling, dearest."

"Just who do you think I am anyway?" she asks, angrily.

"You're you of course," Gum says.

"What about you?" his wife sniffs. "Who do you think you really are?"

The Zen master Shunryu Suzuki once said that "When we express our true nature, we are human beings. When we do not, we do not know what we are." Gum had read this from a book called *Zen Mind, Beginner's Mind*, which he had once found in his seat on a plane. He had memorized it. He had also memorized the seat number, which was 36B, because he considered the book to be a sign, and from time to time, when he requested that seat on other flights, he found other things—someone's bifocals in a leather case, a child's drawing of some horses.

Gum, when he had existed in his true Gum nature, not as Mug or modern Gum, had often believed in signs. He believed in stop signs and signs that warned him of avalanches. He also believed in omens. The girl was an omen, the girl was more than an omen. He has begun to believe that maybe she was sent to test him or maybe to save him somehow, if not to expose him: his true nature to himself. Does he have a will? He is not sure. And so when he finds himself on the road in his wife's Beretta, driving aimlessly with his backseat full of divorce files, he lets a higher force lead him.

The future has caved in on Gum. The past has caved in on the future. The past rewinds itself and plays itself back. Some events do that. They haunt us. They walk around us and around us with their striped flanks so that we can do nothing but trace a pattern of destiny, right or wrong.

Gum listens to the sound his wheels make, humming through the light layer of snow that is beginning to line the paved road. He is outside of town, winding through a maze of fields. Anything can happen. He has on his gloves and his shades. He's wearing his wife's hosiery under his slacks. He thinks about driving to the other side of the continent and going by the name of Blank. Right now, he is Numb. He is not sure of his destination, if there is one. Maybe he will keep searching for the girl. With one eye on the road and one eye on the mirror, he feels like he is driving both forward and backward. Maybe that's all he will ever do. Maybe that's all any of us are capable of after we realize we don't know who we are. We run over ourselves back and forth in the dark, trying to figure out if we've hit something or if what is dear has run off into the trees.

# A MORNING FOR MILK

SEAMUS BOSHELL

Twelve years old, I bolted up into the dark of a cold June morning, my sheets in my hands, dark lumps at the end of my bed—my feet! my feet! I realized just before I screamed. I was awake. I wanted to jump out of bed, a juvenile energy already at my heart, but I didn't know why, and it was cold enough that I wanted reasons. My brother, Michael, in his new bed beside me, was asleep, the dark shape of his head nudged in against the far wall. The curtains on our one window were up, but there was no light, only the endless infiltrations of more and more darkness. Our door was closed. What time was it? I suddenly had to know, just as suddenly as I remembered that it was Saturday morning, and that Da had already tried to wake me. Or had I been dreaming?

I checked on my brother—okay, okay, I pinched his nose. He didn't stir, so it must have been early. But we got up early, me and my Da—James and James Senior—to deliver milk. He worked for Premier Dairies, delivering milk, cream, butter, and lately yogurt. What was next? he would complain. Apple tarts! His round comprised three hundred houses, mostly semi detached, situated on the affluent side of East Finglas—good, well-bred customers who could be quite fussy about the timely arrival of their milk.

I creaked open the door. It required a bit of effort because Ma had painted it the previous day on one of her decorative tantrums. The paint, lathered rather than glossed, was her slapdash way of arguing with Da. He hated the smell, hated the garish white and in private moments, out on the milk round, liked to refer to it as "Mary's house of hard licks." Ma had painted two coats on both sides of the door, so it was fairly serious, whatever was going on. But it wasn't just Ma. Where she was active, Da was inactive, malingering into a recalcitrant inertia, refusing or forgetting to fix items around the house. In truth, both of them had the habit of letting their arguments slide into metaphor.

I left the door open and stepped outside, pausing, allowing my breath to accustom itself to the colder air, my eyes to the brighter shade of darkness. We had a small house, three bedrooms that looked inward to the smallest landing imaginable—a tiny square penned in by the banisters. Ma and Da had the front bedroom, the biggest of course, but also the noisiest as it looked onto our street, Westwood Road, the first street in a relatively new housing estate, pullulated with kids, dogs and cats. My sisters, all four of them, Deirdre, Michelle, Linda and Mary, had the next room, again quite big, quite pink, and quite helpless in the face of their decorating binges—every other week they had something new and fluffy swanning out of the ceiling.

My parents' door was open. Never a good sign. I stood to standing the collar of my blue-striped pajamas, cotton comfy, and listened for any movement downstairs. Da could be down there, drinking his tea, eating his two slices of toast, allowing me the reprieve of a last few winks of sleep. I really hoped so. I'd missed him the last two mornings, victim of a recursive drowsiness that really was a rare enough occurrence. I wasn't exactly a morning child, but when I woke I usually stayed awake.

I'd felt awful about missing him and hadn't been able to tolerate breakfast, neither the usual choppy cereal nor the more exotic temptations of Ma's egg and rasher sandwiches, and even the inducement of painting class at the Summer Project failed to cheer me. I refused all monies and all food, and retreated to my room for multiple afternoons of prayer. I prayed to Sister Mother Concepta, the rubicund and steatopygous head of our school, an icon more potent than Jesus or any scrum of saints. She would understand my guilt. It was shameful enough sleeping it out, but at that time Da was nursing a dodgy knee, or a banjaxed knee as he called it, the cynical and intentional legacy of a tackle one derby Sunday. He played center forward the old way—all body and as much brawn. For days afterward he had tried to mask his limp, before Ma forced him, at the point of a paintbrush, to go to Doctor Swaine.

I listened as ferociously as I could, but there wasn't a sound from downstairs, or any light when I leaned over the banisters and looked, and I did look, gawking through the gap of stairs and ceiling. Maybe Da was in the bathroom, reading, and I leaned further, looking backwards along the hall, hoping for a touch of light.

There was none. Maybe he was still in bed, indulging his own sleep-on. He had to be. Though maybe I had got up too early. The previous night, much to the ridicule of my TV addicted family, I had retired to bed early, forestalling their taunts with a reminder of my milk-delivering duties, a gesture strangely not seconded by Ma and Da, and, as a consequence, only effective for the ten minutes it took my brother to come roaring up, shouting that *Starsky & Hutch! Starsky & Hutch!* was on. I dismissed him. I had better and more adult things to do, like sleep. In an effort to muffle out their shouts and hithering calls, not to mention the blitzkrieg of Starsky needing Hutch, I resorted to an enumeration of sheep and bishops, and when that proved a flock too meek, a gaggle too uncaptivating, I added a bunch of leapfrogging nuns for fun and attention. It worked, it distracted me. I choreographed and they complied: a sheep beneath a bishop below a high hurdling nun. It took me half the night to sleep.

Cursing the darkness downstairs, I moved ahead, tip-toeing into my parents' bedroom, heading directly for the window, too nervous to turn any sort of investigatory glance toward their double bed. I stepped up onto the small ledge at the side of the window, a step-up into the closet where old toys, clothes and Granny's extra set of teeth were kept. I ducked under the curtain, eager, teeth on the edge of chatter, and looked down and down and down into our empty driveway. At first I saw nothing, then I saw there was nothing, no car, no waiting, just the breezy, open gates and the oil stain eyesored in the middle.

Da was gone.

I looked further up the bare avenue. Maybe warming the car? Like the way we had to warm the telly? Other cars were parked in other driveways, other gardens slept soft and mute, other windows stood curtained and closed. The tall poles of street light, four on each side of the street, waxed in their own spills of yellow, not quite connected, not quite touching, but strong enough to bestill the small houses in a flare of jaundice. At the end of the street, past a soccer-pocked grab of greenery, was a squat of buildings, hunkering low under the darkness. There didn't seem to be a sky yet. This was Patrician College, our local secondary school, waiting for me at the end of my summer. I looked at it for a while, cadging hopeful moments from its quiet roofs and sentried railings, trusting that when I looked back the car would be there, just a mistake, a fright, a look too early in earnest.

But there was only the oil stain, a black mark flattened and final, but that blurred, everything blurred, hit into haziness as my shoulders shook, as I laid my head on my arms and cried, the white lace curtain heavy and useless around my shoulders. Da was gone and I was crying, though it seemed more like coughing, as if I was trying to bring something up, my bony chest heaving, my throat ripping, my pajama collar folding itself back down. I checked the driveway again, but it only made me worse, only made me louder as I gulped back tears, my nose running, but I couldn't stop looking, my teeth chattering, my feet cold against the wall.

I may have been there for ages, glad that the window was mist-ing, glad of the cold against me, glad everyone was so happily asleep when I heard Ma telling me to go back to bed, a shush in her voice that meant to soothe but only scalded.

"James, it's okay, go on back to bed, love. It's too early."

There was a space beside her, prickled and rucked, a pillow at its peak, but empty, lengthily empty. On the wall over the bed hung the dark rectangle that in the day held the lot of us, Ma and Da and their football team of six, smiley and heat-beat on the beach in Portmarnock.

"Go on back to bed, love," she whispered.

I flipped back up my collar and walked out of that room, away from her, away from her slow, clumsy rising, irritated that she might follow and tuck me in, or something as awful. Tears cold on my cheeks, I vigorously opened and closed my sticky bedroom door, and when I listened, and when I heard Ma rustle back down into bed, I sneaked downstairs, nervous that if I went back into my room I might impart my commiserations to my brother. I held onto the banisters, and monkey-leaped over the fourth step, the creaky one Da still hadn't fixed.

Downstairs, I was still crying, but cursing too. Cursing myself. Slapping my chest, trying to flatten it, but it heaved and heaved, a childish turbulence I couldn't rid myself of. I hit my head too, trying to knock my Da out of it, trying to erase his limp around Finglas East, arms heaved with milk and butter and eggs, and that mongrel, Rex, at Willow Crescent, snapping at his leg. That dog was a bastard.

For once, I had the run of downstairs to myself and I hated it. The wide open doors, the neat nightfall order of things, the extinguished lights seemed to mock me, and the sitting room clock tick-tutted at my lateness. So I did the only thing that ever calmed me. I got on my bike. A Raleigh Grifter five speed, devil red, thick bumptious wheels, wide, padded handlebars and a clownish horn I was beginning to grow out of. It was kept in the hall under daily newspapers, and not out in the back shed where it might had proved too invidious for some of our busy light-fingered neighbors.

As soon as I was high on the saddle, feet deliciously bare on the pedals, I felt better, lighter, even a little warmer. My tears had stopped and I nearly smiled at a suggestion of morning flickering through our front door, the shy light warped by the beveled glass. It roused and just a little launched my mind. I imagined myself cycling—no hands!—around Finglas East, bristling in and out of gardens short and long, revved on by my Da who loaded and unloaded me, commanding like a ringmaster, flicking with centrifugal tenderness his better son out and back, and before we knew it, and before Rex could even think about it, we were finished, record-ramming speed. The men at the dairy would laud our achievement: James and little James were the fastest milkmen in Finglas, maybe in Dublin, though probably not Ireland, the country crowd were lightning.

All this good motion gave me an idea. But I needed to know what time it was. I unlocked the kitchen door, in my excitement forgetting the sitting room clock, staunch and accurate on the fireplace. Our kitchen was small, once you entered you were there, and everything was reachable.

It was only six o'clock, unless the battery was dead, and so I varoomed back into the sitting room, on the way tapping my bike for good luck. Yes! It was only six. Da would still be at the dairy, enduring the triplicate tympanies of Dessie the checker, the pedant who worked the butter room as if he were dispensing pounds of his own marginalized flesh. Though to be fair, he could spare a churn or two.

I had time, I had time. It would take Da twenty more minutes to reach the round, the exact pedal time for me. It would be a race: Da in his small electric truck, or float as it was called, and me eagled over the handlebars of my Grifter five speed. Da would be delighted, once he calmed down. Ma would pretend a bit longer, deducting some of my summer privileges—larking with my best friend, Bomber

Higgins, at the Phoenix Park, ducking and diving in the canal—but she couldn't really argue, always enjoining me, the eldest, to take matters into my own hands. And what better matter than my Da's banjaxed knee.

So, I, a working man again, went into the kitchen for a deserved breakfast. I discovered a heel of bread in the breadbox. Da usually took the heel, and ate it raw with butter, but I decided this fat specimen needed toasting. I wasn't in a hurry. I *was* going to help, but I hated the start of the round—Willow Crescent and Rex, that mad mongrel. I think Da actually appreciated the matadorial challenge. He'd stamp and feign a charge, frightening Rex back and over into an adjacent garden, but circling, always circling, the stupid mutt, chasing the truck, a snarl curdling out of his black, rabid mouth. And in the same crescent lived the Fitzgibbons, a whole family of bakers, including Mr. Fitzgibbon, who once answered the door in an apron, flour rouged on his cheeks. I think they were apple pie entrepreneurs, always busy, intent on spreading their sweet, flaky gospel through the shops and supermarkets, and so busy they wanted buttermilk everyday, and so bovinely busy that they never had time to wash their buttermilk bottles, or apply a simple rinse to the maggot white lumps stuck around the necks of the bottles; necks that I sometimes, already weighed down, had to stick my fingers into. But most mornings I was as scrupulous as the Gibbons, and wiped, under the likeness of birdshit, the white muck onto their black Toyota.

But it wasn't easy. I had a sensitive stomach. Da knew this, and maybe because of it he always insisted that I deliver to the Fitzgibbons. He could be tough like that. I didn't argue. I bought a pair of gloves from my own money and, at the point of pickup, kept my eyes closed.

I put the kettle on; bread without tea had all the wrong Protestant connotations, though, of course, I didn't know any Protestants. I listened to the kettle swagger its way into life, its watery ebullience, bubbling, building, a bird outside trilling, a rising dog barking, the electric light flickering, and presently the chortles of steam made me just a little bit happy, and just a little conscious of my cold, bare feet on the lino. I should have been dressed. Da always ate his breakfast dressed, and standing, holding down the newspaper with one arm and squinting at it. Close to six foot, he had brown, unmanageable hair, was well muscled if a little chubby, prodigiously freckled, and right in the middle of his face he grew this big brush of a mustache, ideal for street sweeping, according to Bomber Higgins. Other than the whiskers, I was my father's son, with my brown hair and twin cowlicks, my hazel-brown eyes, and a similar and ferocious thirst for a cold pint of milk at the end of a morning.

Happy with toast and tea, I sat down and listened. Ah, the silence. Everywhere. And everywhere miraculous. Once I was up I was happy. I felt old, I felt ancient, I felt wise. I felt the tea establish a warm center in my stomach and, with the smell of toast in my nose, I was ready for anything, though not just yet. I would relax a little. Sometimes Da opened the back door, letting the cold morning slip in, and we'd watch the fields beyond the back wall, pearled in mist, lit by the frail inundations of morning light. I wanted to do the same, the exact same, and then I heard Ma and the quiet snuffle of her snoring, but mellifluous, not elephantine like Granny, who, cave-mouthed on a Sunday afternoon, would, as Da said, wake the cremated. No, I liked to hear Ma snore, though the opportunity was rare. When I wasn't working with Da, she was first up, making breakfast, brewing tea, even ironing.

And that morning I could have opened the back door, and listened to her snore make its way out of the house to meet the first sparrows of morning, but I was too cold, too childishly cold.

I ran upstairs, got my clothes, but couldn't find my favorite cardigan. I loved that cardigan, an unsurpassable navy with a rainbow of hoops circumambulating its chest, but best of all, a full length zipper that made it zip-zip like a tracksuit top. I always wore it delivering. Always. I looked everywhere, even under my brother's pillow. Nowhere. I took a newer cardigan instead, the itchiness already washed out of it compliments of a half dozen or so preemptive washes. Ma always softened things up for my sensitive skin.

But I kept looking and finally found the cardigan balled and belligerent in the laundry basket in the bathroom. Inexplicable. Ma would never have done that, and right then, as if discharging her side of a responsorial psalm, she snorted in her sleep.

I dressed in the hall, giddy, half naked, and more than half tempted to lash around the estate on my bike, emperor style, before my friends, neighbors and thieves arose. But half dressed, half mature, I let the whim pass.

I liked this part of the morning, me and my Da, leaning against the wall, standing into our boots, putting our jackets on. I wore monkey boots, a sort of juvenile rendition of my Da's, not as big or steel tipped, but boot enough to chafe my feet for a few months. Surreptitiously, I had stuck socks between my heels and boots, a palliative I didn't like needing, but soon my heels hardened and the mangy socks disappeared into the Fitzgibbons' garden.

My Da had acquired a Premier Dairies smock for me, just like his, knee-length, green, smooth, multi-pocketed, and after a few days of work it exuded a lovely smell of stale milk, sometimes embellished with the waft of cracked egg and yogurt. It was great. It was the odor of work, almost as sweet as when the smock returned from the dairy's launderette, spring pressed and clean, lustrous after spending a sudsy hour with the smocks of all the other milkmen and helpers—we, sons and youths, were called helpers. It would have been great to visit the launderette and watch mine rollick round with the others, a big singsong of smocks, yodeling out their milkman stories, and Da always promised, but we never went.

In addition, Da handed me down one of his old donkey jackets—he got a new one every year—a heavy, black, woolen jacket with a reflective yellow patch on the back, stretched from shoulder to shoulder. It was brilliant; where the smock could look a little girly, a little shiny, this was the real industrial thing—builders and truck drivers wore them—and though it was a bit warm for it that June morning, I nevertheless put it on. It might be cold on the bike, and I wasn't one for the cold. In the winter I wore everything: cardigans, tracksuit, smock, hat, gloves, donkey jacket. Da never actually ridiculed me, but I think he would have preferred a hardier son.

I was all ready to go and took a slice of toast for the trip.

Ah, it was magic, opening the door that sparkled morning, wheeling out my bike, chomping on a piece of toast, my whole day ahead of me. Even the sun skipped past a cloud and peeked out. I wanted to run up and kiss my mother goodbye, but I knew better, so I just closed the door quietly, jumped on my bike and rode right over that oil stain.

I'd been working with Da nine months and was beginning to get the hang of it, beginning to pull the little bit of weight I had. But it wasn't an easy job. The products we delivered were bulk and needed brawn. There was the milk: skimmed, jersey, and original, all equally heavy, either in glass bottles or the lighter but more explodable plastic containers. There was the eggs: small, large and dinosaur, too bulky for pockets and too unbalanced for my head. There was butter: pounds and half pounds of it, cold and uncultured. There was cream: light, heavy and double delight. There was orange juice and apple juice and 'Fruice', a rebarbative mix of orange juice and cream, heavy on the stomach and ugly on the eye. There was yogurt, a cornucopia of flavors, even chocolate, that sat lightly in the pocket but nicer in the mouth. There was buttermilk, ugly crates of it that I humped up and down the Fitzgibbons' garden.

I wore monkey boots and double socks. I wore a cardigan, smock, donkey jacket, monkey hat, leg warmers, scarf, fingered and fingerless gloves, sunglasses, pencil, and pen. I carried elastic bands, paper clips, small change, disappearing ink, a catapult and fake vomit (Fitzgibbons).

I knew helpers who carried Walkmans, xylophones, shamrocks, whiskey, Batman comics, not to mention more blunt objects such as fishing rods, hurleys and the always popular hunting knife. But there were causalities, tragedies even. Milkman Murphy carried his sick mother around with him. Milkman Gallagher carried his dog with him, two years dead and badly stuffed.

I carried cold toast and a sensitive stomach, but I never carried my Da. He worked like a demon, everyone said so, and I blitzed around trying to keep pace with him. I'd take one side of the street, him the other, the open, square truck of milk between us. Whistling, always whistling—sadly a fading part of the profession—we'd tune our bilateral way up the avenues, down the streets and even quicker around the unilateral crescents. After a few months, I got to know my side of the round, and other than an infrequent update or admonishment, the only music between us was our cantata of boots, mine light, his heavy, weaving in and back from the truck, like the two ends of a violin bow. We were a morning duet and around his implacable rhythm I raced, like a skittish virtuoso. No matter where I was—at the truck, kneeling at a doorstep, side-saddling a wall with a swaddle of milk in my arms—I could always hear my Da, hear his clinks of glass, his chirpy whistle. And he mine.

Of course, I wasn't infallible. I made mistakes, and that very morning, and the two I had slept through, I had been hoping to curtail a recent bad run.

So weaving through the flat, narrow streets, I garnered up a bit of speed. Finglas East was a fast twenty minute ride away. Once I got up the hill and past our church—a behemoth thing, cathedrals away from anything as simple as a barn—it was a straight freewheel past the swimming pool—a sorrel-looking leper of a building—and on past Finglas Village, shuttered and shut-eyed, then a whiz round a couple of roundabouts (I did do a couple of extra laps, without hands, with a crust of toast in my mouth, but to be fair, there was very little traffic), and lastly a no-signal swerve into Pinewood Avenue, the start of the estate, the end of the round, the home of Nora Baresi.

I could blame my clumsy run on Nora, a gorgeous Irish-Italian girl whose family were prodigious in the fish 'n' chips trade, but that wouldn't be entirely fair. Every Friday we collected the milk money and every Friday she, as giddy and as young as myself, answered, paid and tipped me handsomely. So I was a bit embarrassed when one morning, about three weeks prior, a bottle slipped and smashed in her garden. Out she danced, barefoot in her lilac dressing gown, smiling, her brown eyes small from sleep, her skin pillow white, her black hair long and morning loose, and so I was even more embarrassed when the same thing happened the next morning, and might have happened a terrible third time if my Da hadn't forced me to switch sides. But Nora loved it all, tut-tutting and giggling at me on Fridays, and perhaps I did get a little swoony, a little distracted, because sadly her garden wasn't my only white out—other more prosaic households slipped under my butterfingers.

Da was gracious about most of them, even assisted me in the first few clean ups, and sometimes, when we were both on our knees, gathering the splinters and shooing the milk into the grass, I wanted to throw my arms around him, to tell him not to worry, that it was all minor and miniscule compared to the love bursting in my heart. But I couldn't. He might have considered it an excuse. He might have laughed, or wore, for a second, that fast, awkward smile while he smoothed out his smock, fussed with his mustache, and said we had to get on. He wasn't fond of breakages.

No, it wasn't all Nora's fault. I was a boy who had to do everything fast, except getting up, of course. I was ambitious, industrious—hadn't I bought a bike at the age of twelve. I was a boy with my own money and wit, and I never suffered fools easily. I'm certain Da was the same, that underneath those three decades of customer relations, he was as consubstantial as I was about Mrs. Gosset, the windbag at 48 Pinewood Drive, who, if she'd changed her clothes as much as her mind, we wouldn't have had to stay so far downwind.

Mrs. Gosset or the mere thought of her always interfered with my breath, so I dismounted from my bike, and by a lucky turn of geography, I was outside Nora's house, quite posh and pillared in its own Romanesque way. I set my bike carefully against her gate and, pretending to tie my laces, permitted my imagination to advance up and over her house and twirl, by fancy alone, into the back bedroom, where I supposed she was dreaming and drooling of me, but Mrs. Gosset wouldn't leave me be, carping on about her bill, her maligned deliveries and her implacable lack of health.

No wonder I had told her to shut up. Well, no, that's not true. I told her to shut her arse, but I made my request rhetorical and quiet, and if her hearing was as bad as she claimed, she could never have heard me. Not to be rude about it, but I was certain she was a filthy dug-up relic of some goblin civilization eradicated centuries ago. It was obvious she was a nut, her and her shovel-faced husband and their gnomed-out kids, but yet Da took their side, agreed with them that I had left skimmed instead of original (easy enough mistake to make, it all being white) and made reparations in the free forms of a couple pounds of butter. And gave me a stern word or two. I think he was impressed by Mr. Gosset, an accountant or something soporific on the stock market.

But I was intent on putting the whole imbroglio behind me. I blew a kiss to Nora and cycled my red Grifter five speed down Pinewood Drive, past the miniature immaculate lawns, the two car driveways and the empty milk carriers emblazoned with milkdials, "Today, can we have—" and there'd be a choice of one to six; any more than that and we needed a note from the mother.

I imagined Da would be thrilled with my initiative, my go-ahead gumption and would quite heartily exchange it for my recent peccadilloes. We'd be back in business: James Curran and Son, in a truck built strictly for two, and he was strict about this, but there was always room for a devil-red Grifter on the back.

I was right about his location. The little blue and white truck was parked at Willow Crescent, an inlet of some twenty big houses, foregrounded by a grin of greenery. Actually, I thought he would have been further on—perhaps his leg had worsened—but I was glad that he was past that mutt Rex, and even happier that he was close to the buttermilk bottles of Fitzgibbon's, so close in fact that I decided to park behind a deciduous tree and wait out their white-maggoted removal. I must have been a good hundred yards away, and at that distance, behind one of the seven leafy trees, I was well concealed. I felt a bit guilty about it, but Da, who never wore gloves, had a better constitution than me.

He was taking it slow, not limping so much as dragging his leg, his smock long and sleek, and his morning hair eking out its own mad horizon. Fitzgibbon's was the next house, a mucous jungle of trees, bushes and scorbutic ivy, and right out of it strode this tall boy, as tall as Da, buttermilk bottles on his fingers, heading for the truck. As if he knew, or maybe Da had alerted him, he clattered them into a crate at the back of the truck, exactly where we sequestered the filthier empties. The noisy fit of glass against crate, with nothing but silence to buffer it, went right through me. I sort of crumpled onto my knees—maybe I was startled, or maybe I was trying to get further behind the tree.

I imagined the boy was a long lost Fitzgibbon son, finally freed from the Foreign Legion bakery, already accustomed to early rising, but not yet inducted into his family's anti-milkman ways. But he didn't stop there. He took some more bottles and headed into the next house—Donnelly's, a skim and three pints of ordinary, and a pound of butter on Tuesdays. I didn't recognize the boy. Was he wearing a smock? I leaned forward. But to spite me, the sun, until then slumbering behind a bed of clouds, blazed up in an interfering way. I was shaking with curiosity. Maybe he was some local insomniac, but whoever he was he was helping, moving them up the crescent, away from me. Da jumped in now and then to advance the truck, its electric whine, its shudder of crates pushing me lower and lower into the ground until I was lying flat, grass at my chin, my arms around the tree. It could be just a neighborhood kid, maybe that autistic kid I sometimes saw. Da would let him help. But I couldn't see what he was wearing. I thought about getting on my bike and just as I decided to, the sun retreated and the boy strode out of Murtagh's—six bottles of ordinary and orange juice on Mon-

SEAMUS BOSHELL

days—and I saw it, a knee length something flap around his legs, a
smock, a Premier Dairies liver green smock, and whistling, they
were both whistling, fast, efficient, the boy running into the last
house on the crescent—Riordan's, two pints and a half pint of cream
on Sundays—and then he jumped back into the truck, Da waiting at
the steering wheel.

With an applause of crates, the truck jerked away and turned
back onto the main road, Pinewood Avenue, its red indicator winking. I watched Rex trot after them, the stupid mutt wagging his tail,
his brown coat looking more septic than ever. The truck headed off
in the direction that would eventually take them to Nora's house.

I pulled my collar up and laid my cheek on the grass, grateful
for its prickly caress, the tickle at my ear, the lump at my throat. I
felt stupid in the warmth of my layers, the superfluity of cardigan,
smock and donkey jacket, but I didn't have the heart to remove any
of them. I closed my eyes, now too heavy to hold. I wanted to cry; I
was going to cry, but there came to me then a moment's hesitation,
a reprieve of stillness, and into that stillness strode the boy, tall and
immense, laughing at me for crying like a little girl on the grass.
Laughing at me. Laughing. I bit the inside of my cheeks, bit them
hard, and out of them came not blood, not anger, but understanding. A hard understanding.

Da hadn't called me, not that morning or the previous two. I
hadn't slept it out. I just hadn't been called, that's all. It was as
simple as that. He had someone else, someone bigger, taller, not as
squeamish, not as clumsy. And Ma knew, she knew. She never would
have washed my favorite cardigan. Tears nearly came but I bit harder.
My knees curled up, my head tucked and I just lay there, small and
twelve, underneath a tree, my bike waiting, the doorsteps full with
milk. I hoped for anger and it came, profuse in a proliferation of
schemes I would now undertake: I would get another job, I would
forget about Nora, forget about Da, get all As at school, help Ma at
home, give her some of my wages, play more with Michael, my

brother, and even be nice to my sisters. That's what I would do. That's what I would do.

I jumped up, but too soon, too quickly for my stomach which emptied a porridge of tea and toast on the grass. Bits of it splashed on my bike. I spat out the remainder and cursed the whole fucking morning. Rex heard me and came over barking, but I was already on my bike and pedaling. I didn't want to go home but there was no other option—Bomber Higgins would be still out with his Da. But home would be fine if I got back to bed undetected. Then nobody would know, and I'd do exactly as they planned—lose interest in the milk round and "enjoy" my last summer before secondary school.

The only thing I remember about my cycle home was Ma standing at the door, her arms folded, wearing that long purple dressing gown of hers. I didn't say anything to her, just excused myself past her, her arms goosepimpled and paint still spotted on her hands. I didn't listen to her as I hung up my coats and threw my cardigan back into the laundry. But no matter where I went I was hounded by love and comfort—a breakfast of rashers and sausages on the cooker, the hot water on for a shower, the TV warmed up and the picture almost visible—but I didn't deserve any of it and went to my room. She followed me and said all the things Da said when he came home: that he had had no choice, that because of his banjaxed knee there were safety and insurance issues, that the dairy had insisted he take an official helper, and he even mentioned his name, Rory. He said he had wanted me to help too, but, as I well knew, the truck held only two.

But the terrible thing is I didn't believe him. I didn't believe my own father, or my mother when she said she had wanted to tell me. Even now, thirty years later, I can't talk to my Da about it. He's in a wheelchair now, his arthritic knees too painful for walking, and I never bring it up because I know he'll lie. What else can he do?

# PORK CHOPS

EILEEN FITZGERALD

Gina was standing right beside the boxes she'd piled in the break-fast nook, but neither she nor Phil mentioned them. She knew Phil was worried, but he needn't be. Yes, she was going to move out, but as Gina had said again and again, it was an experiment. It didn't have to be an ending.

She held the Styrofoam meat tray, the six, small premium pork chops, carefully arranged in two rows of three. Affixed to the clear plastic wrap was·a bright orange sticker that said Corn-fed. She pushed a finger into the plastic then studied the dent in the pink-ish, grayish flesh. "They're not ours," said Gina. "It's like stealing."

But Phil was already paging through his cookbooks, looking for recipes: pork roast, Chinese pork, pineapple pork. He explained again, patiently: "I went to the store. I picked out my groceries. I waited in line. I paid my money. It's not like I put the pork chops in my pocket or shoved them down the front of my pants, but some-how it happened—they got in my bag. My position"—he laid his hand on his chest for emphasis—"is that if the store screws up, the store should suffer." It was true that he'd noticed the package while he was still in the parking lot at the grocery store, but he was in a hurry then, with barely enough time to get to the dry cleaners before it closed. In any event, he wasn't sorry, and he didn't feel guilty either. He and Gina had come home from the supermarket plenty of times minus some item they'd paid for: dental floss, garlic, laundry soap. Gina was forgetting that, thought Phil. She was forgetting all those other times.

Looking at the pork chops, Gina remembered the foul-smelling petting zoo her parents had taken her to when she was a child, the goats balancing on the fence and bleating, the dank barn and the enormous pig she'd seen there, the ten or twelve snorting, squirming piglets attached to the big sow's nipples. "You like bacon?" her father had said. "That's bacon right there."

It had taken her a long time to decipher Phil's system of morality, and even that understanding was incomplete. If a cashier gave him too much change, he never mentioned the mistake, even if the person seemed very young or very dumb, even if Gina poked him and raised her eyebrows. "How will they learn if I do the math for them?" he reasoned. But at restaurants and stores, he always put spare change into the tins and jars soliciting donations for the Community Kitchen or the Lion's Club or for some kid in Martinsville who needed a kidney. Phil copied computer software but wouldn't tape off CDs, and he offered no convincing reasons as to why one practice was acceptable while the other was not. Was it because software was technology while music was art? Though Gina had spent more than two years with Phil, she still hadn't figured him out.

"We never eat pork chops," said Gina.

"I do," he said. "I eat them at lunch in the cafeteria. I eat them all the time when you're not around."

It was strange to think of, Phil eating pork chops when she wasn't around, one after another, nothing but pork chops. What would he do when she left? "I'm thinking of the people who bought them," she said. "It's not the store that suffers."

The most likely suspects, Phil thought, were the people in front of him in the checkout line, an old couple buying old people food—saltines and eggs and hard candy, red-and-white peppermints for the grandchildren, butterscotches for themselves. The woman wore a tailored coat, the man a suit and tie. They looked like they could get hold of more pork chops if they wanted to. If they really wanted pork chops, Phil decided, they could have them; they could go to a restaurant and order them with mashed potatoes on the side.

"They were old," said Phil, "but they seemed rich or at least comfortable. Anyway"—he held out the unwieldy mass of his keys—"if you feel that strongly, why don't you take them back?" He didn't push the keys in Gina's face or rattle them menacingly; they lay quietly in his opened palm. The relationship might be spiraling downward—it might even be over—but for now they shared a house, a bed, a refrigerator. If he walked on tiptoe and spoke in whispers, she might change her mind. She might decide to stay.

Gina frowned. "You take them back."

"I don't have a problem with them. If it's up to me, I'll keep them."

She stood with her hand on her hip, with boxes stacked up behind her. "I won't eat them."

"There's tuna," said Phil, flipping through the cookbook. "Turkey, yogurt, eggs. Eat whatever you want."

The pork chops landed on the table with a thud, and Gina left the kitchen. Never the satisfaction of a real fight, she thought. No matter how shrill she got, no matter how nasty, Phil was mild-mannered, a compromiser. He was annoying. "Fine, fine," he'd say. And meanwhile, he was making the pork chops; he was doing exactly what he wanted to do.

Of *course* she wouldn't take back the pork chops. They had nothing to do with her. She didn't buy them, she didn't want them, they weren't—were not—her problem. Lying on the couch, she picked up the newspaper, shook out the pages, read.

Phil cut slices of onion and laid the circles flat on a plate. He watched the blade as it sliced through one of the rounds, metal hitting porcelain with a ping. If Gina was in the kitchen now, she'd shake her head and sigh; she'd take the knife from his hand, and he'd have no choice but to stand stupidly by and watch her. She'd have some fast, efficient method—six quick whacks and then sweep the chopped onion into a bowl. Well, she wasn't here now, thought Phil. He could do as he liked.

He imagined the people who'd paid for the pork chops, the old people. Once they got home, they pulled out the heavy black skillet. They melted fat and then reached inside the grocery bag, reached, reached. . . .

Phil wondered if they were the kind of people to turn off the burners and drive back to the store, wave the receipt at the service desk, and demand restitution. Or would they simply resign themselves to the loss and find something else to fry? They'd sit at the table, two old people, eat fried eggs and talk about the pork chops. What could have happened? Had they just plain forgotten to pick them up? No, the receipt said clearly, said without a doubt, that they'd bought them. Oh, well, they thought. Such is life.

Phil wondered what their names might be: Trudy and Oscar or maybe Emily and Warren. No, he decided, they were Millie and Jack, and though they were old, they still enjoyed sex. Sometimes when the weather was mild, they closed all the blinds and went around the house without any clothes on, each at perfect ease with the other's saggy body. Who cared about flab and wrinkles? They loved each other! Sometimes Jack and Millie would stop puttering for an hour or so; they'd lie on the couch or right on the rug and make love. Their children had moved to different states and had good jobs, careers even. They were gynecologists and economics professors. In the summer the whole family convened at a lake in Michigan for canoeing and swimming, sun and trout.

What did they need pork chops for? They had afternoon sex

and a lake in Michigan. Phil, meanwhile, had nothing. He had five days a week of junior high math students. He had Gina bringing home more boxes every day. "I hope we'll still be friends," she said. "I hope we'll still do things."

He pushed his fingernail against the clear plastic that was wrapped around the pork chops. The film stretched, then sagged, then finally tore. Phil looked at the punctured plastic, the exposed pork chops. From the living room he heard Gina rattling the newspaper. If she was reading Ann Landers, she'd be in the kitchen in two minutes. "Who does Ann Landers think she is?" she'd say, shaking the paper in Phil's face.

"Don't read it," Phil would advise, and Gina would twist the newspaper into a tube then slap the table with the mangled pages.

"Everyone reads Ann Landers," she'd say. "How can I not read it?"

Phil would stand quietly and consider his possibilities. If he said, "You're irrational," she'd say, "I'm leaving." And if he said, "There, there," she'd leave him anyway. Every option seemed to have the same outcome: Phil in the kitchen, alone with his pork chops.

Onions, oil, lemon, garlic. Two hours to marinate, then sauté, then bake. There was plenty of time to venture out for bread. Phil put on his jacket and went to the garage for his bike. He thought of the first months after Gina had moved in. On Saturday mornings they used to bicycle to the bakery and buy a loaf of Amish dill. At home they boiled a dozen eggs and made a huge vat of egg salad, which they never came close to finishing. But Phil felt there was an appropriateness to a dozen eggs, the carton full, then empty, the eggs in a single layer at the bottom of the pan.

Gliding silently on his bike, Phil felt like some kind of nocturnal animal. He made out details in the darkness—a cat's yellow eyes and then the brownish remains of a pumpkin. Gina had vetoed the idea of Halloween candy when they passed the holiday aisle in the grocery store, and Phil had gone along with her then. But he liked

Halloween; he didn't want the holiday to just slip by, just another gray, chilly day. After work on the thirty-first, he stopped at Target and bought an orange plastic pumpkin and a bag of miniature candy bars. He put on the porch light, but as Gina had predicted, no trick-or-treaters came knocking. When the news came on at ten, Gina pointed to the heap of little candy bars. "Now what?"

"We eat them," Phil said, grinning and rubbing his hands together. "We divide them half and half." But Gina didn't want all that candy in the house, and Phil took the plastic pumpkin to school the next day and passed it around in homeroom, to seventh-graders who were already sick from too much candy.

They were going to get married, and now they weren't. They'd been engaged. They'd told people, they'd picked a tentative date, but now she was leaving, and there was nothing Phil could do. He assumed they weren't engaged anymore, but he wasn't sure. Neither of them had issued a statement. When friends asked Phil about the wedding, he said simply, evasively, that they'd hit some snags. He didn't know what Gina said; he wasn't even sure what snags they'd hit. He knew only that she wanted time and space, friends, direction. She'd joined a Masters swim team, and four days a week she went straight from work to the Y. She came home after nine, her hair in wet strings, her skin smelling of chlorine—though she claimed to have taken a shower. "With soap?" asked Phil, and Gina showed him her plastic soap dish, placed his fingers on the wet bar inside. Phil imagined the men she might be swimming with—barrel-chested, hairless men in Speedos—is that what she liked? He pedaled faster just thinking about it. Big-shouldered, slim-waisted men with hair that looked like metal. At first he tried to fill the swimming hours with tennis, but now it was too cold to coax anyone to play, and he mostly just watched TV or read the paper or planned the next day's classes.

"Isn't it boring to swim laps?" asked Phil. "Isn't it like walking back and forth in a little room?"

"I think about things," said Gina. "It's not like I leave my brain

[231]

in the locker room. On the other hand, it's great sometimes to think of nothing at all, to have water all around and quiet."

Phil would imagine floating on his back in a lagoon in the Caribbean, blue sky and water all around. But no matter how appealing Gina's descriptions and his own mental pictures, Phil didn't like to swim. He flailed, he sank, he got water up his nose, and all the next day he sniffled and sneezed.

At the bakery the racks were almost empty. Instead of French bread, Phil had to settle for a homely, lumpy loaf of German rye. He stood for a time in front of the cookie counter. Maybe he should get dessert. What went with pork chops? The cookies were enormous, almost as big as his outstretched hand. If Gina didn't want hers, it would be more than Phil could manage to eat two. He pictured Gina's cookie sitting in its bag on the kitchen counter, getting stale, grease spots showing through the paper. She wouldn't eat the cookie, and neither would Phil, but they wouldn't throw it away either, until it was beyond hard. Or the more likely scenario: she'd move out and leave the cookie, and Phil would be too depressed to ever throw it away. Did Gina even eat cookies now that she was so serious about swimming? Phil didn't know. He didn't know anything about her anymore.

He'd parked his bike in front of the store, and now as he loaded the bread into his backpack, he prayed he wouldn't see anyone he knew. He still loved Bloomington, but lately the town seemed so small and claustrophobic. He'd lived here since his freshman year in college, and he was thirty now. That was twelve years, long enough. He couldn't go anywhere without seeing someone he knew, friends from undergrad days or men he played softball with or fellow teachers at the junior high or even his students. Stop, chat, move along. When Phil and Gina went to their first appointment for couples' counseling, they saw a college friend of Phil's in the hallway of the medical complex. They had to pretend nothing was happening. "Hello!" they'd said. "And what's new with you?"

For months they had talked of being married; they had decided, had gone so far as to look for rings in the mall, but after no more than five minutes of viewing selections, Gina had fled the store. Phil excused himself and wandered the mall looking for her. He saw twenty or thirty women with straight brown hair and jean shorts, women who could have been Gina, but weren't. There she is, Phil would think, but then she wasn't. He found her finally on a bench outside Penney's, where she was sitting beside a large, yellow potted plant.

"All those names were driving me crazy," said Gina. "Everlasting. Sweetheart. I hated sitting in those purple chairs, and that man with his hair all puffed out, being so helpful and holding out the rings. He was driving me nuts."

Phil wondered how else such a transaction could be managed— he could pick something out and give it to her, the old traditional way, but he wanted Gina to get a ring she liked. Maybe they could look through a catalogue. Once he'd had a girlfriend who left jewelry catalogues lying around his apartment; she'd open the pages to a spread of diamond rings, with circles drawn around the ones she liked. Once she wrote, "Phil will buy me this ring."

But Phil, who was fast losing interest in the woman, wrote, "No, he won't."

"What do we need rings for anyway?" asked Gina. "If we love each other, shouldn't that be enough?"

"Whatever you want," said Phil. "If you don't want one, we won't get one." But gradually Phil realized: it wasn't just the rings.

A few weeks later—six months ago—Gina joined the swim team. She signed up for a Spanish class once a week. On days she didn't swim, she jogged, and sometimes Phil would join her. But more frequently, she left without him, and when he got home from work, she'd be sitting on the floor in the living room, stretching out.

"I would have gone with you," Phil would say, trying to hide his disappointment.

"Oh," Gina would say. "I just wanted to get it over with."

And now she was starting to go out with her new swimming friends. On Saturday mornings they all went out for pancakes, for carbo loading. One night after practice a group of people had drinks and dinner, and Gina didn't come home until eleven. Phil, meanwhile, had waited anxiously, picturing her car spun out of control and smashed against a tree, her spine severed and blood pouring out of her nose. "You're paranoid," she said when he met her on the porch that night.

"I'm not paranoid," said Phil, "but I do worry."

She mentioned names, but she really didn't describe any of her swimming friends, except the coach, Greg, who was spacey and knew Mark Spitz. "Greg says, don't come so much out of the water for butterfly. He says Mark Spitz just did that for pictures, to look cool in pictures.

"Greg said if I had started swimming when I was nine, I could have been a good college swimmer. He says I've got a good feel for the water.

"Should I be disappointed," she asked, "that I didn't swim in college? That I'm twenty-five now and didn't become what I could have become?"

Phil didn't know what amount of regret was appropriate. The only similar situation he could think of was when he was in eighth grade in the all-school spelling bee, and he missed a word on purpose, to avoid the embarrassment of winning. Then in high school he quit the tennis team, but that was because he realized he'd never make varsity. Regret had never seemed like a useful emotion; it just wasted time and made you miserable. If Gina took her boxes and left tomorrow, he'd miss her, but he wouldn't necessarily have regrets. If he got to be eighty years old, though, and never married anyone, if he was living in a trailer and eating beans out of the can, maybe then he'd have regrets. Maybe he'd wish he had spelled that word correctly so many years before: c-o-n-f-e-t-t-i.

Back home Phil parked his bike in the garage. Inside the house he could smell onions and garlic, good, strong smells. Gina was gone—out running, apparently—though he'd asked her many times not to go by herself after dark. He reasoned with her, pleaded with her, but to no avail. "You're crowding me," she said.

If she wanted privacy, Phil thought, if she wanted room to breathe, why couldn't she just move into the second bedroom; why couldn't they just be platonic for a while? She could have her own little space. They could buy groceries separately, maybe just share milk and toilet paper. But what would the parameters be then? If she got a new boyfriend, would she bring him home?

In the early days there hadn't been any problems with closeness, with crowding. Gina and Phil did everything together—jogging, shopping, laundry—everything. But now that Gina was so busy with work and exercise, Phil almost always did the shopping by himself. He changed the sheets on the bed; he cleaned the bathroom, hung up the wet towels. On Sundays while Gina was at church, he made cinnamon rolls with icing. He made them for Gina more than for himself, and usually she seemed pleased, though sometimes she didn't want them—she'd eaten doughnuts during the community hour after the service.

Gina almost never thanked him. She asked how much the groceries were and gave him half. Sometimes she asked him to buy tampons or deodorant for her, but that was the extent to which she acknowledged how much of the grunt work he'd taken on in recent months. To be honest, he liked the routine, but he would have appreciated a little gratitude nonetheless.

They almost never fought during the time they'd been together. Even now that relations had gotten strained, anger came out in brief spurts—a slammed door, a few sharp words. Most often they spoke calmly, reasonably, with Phil making great efforts to understand Gina's point of view. But as careful as he tried to be, he still said things he wished he hadn't: "If you're so unhappy," he'd said one night, "maybe you should move out."

"Maybe that's the answer," said Gina. "Maybe I will."

Phil cracked two eggs into a bowl and beat them with a fork. Why didn't she just get on with it, take her boxes and move in with one of her swimming friends, submerge herself completely in that world of wet hair?

Then he thought of himself bent over the toilet, wiping the porcelain with a sponge, and the question reversed itself: Why would she leave?

He filled another bowl with fine bread crumbs, added spices and parmesan cheese, then sifted the grains with his fingers. Why did it keep coming back to what Gina wanted? Why spend all his energy worrying over that question? Why didn't he wonder what he wanted himself?

He wanted to go to a country where parrots would fly past his window, or to a place that still had glaciers. He wanted to walk along the ocean and pick up sand dollars—with Gina if she'd go, and without her if she wouldn't.

He wanted Gina to stop swimming, to stay home, to get old with him.

Sometimes when they sat on the sofa watching TV, Gina would hold out her arm. "Feel my muscles."

He'd press his fingers against her bicep. "Amazing," he'd say.

During the day, Gina would run through the cemetery near their house, but at night the grounds were too isolated, too scary. Most of the nearby roads were busy, and the sidewalks were unreliable, leading into ditches or ending without warning. When she ran at night, Gina circled the block, around and around, past the same houses until she'd logged four miles. When she moved, she'd live in town, closer to the center of things, and she could run on the high school track. It would be the same thing, running around in circles, but she'd feel less silly somehow.

She'd found a place; she'd signed the lease. He must have guessed about the boxes. It was so strange to think about: they were going to get married—they had interviewed caterers and discussed rice pilaf—and now she was moving out. She hoped they would stay friends, maybe even date, spend Saturday nights watching TV, hanging out.

The air was chilly but comfortable, and her pace was steady, a bit slower than usual. She felt good, though; she felt strong. She was ready to move on. She had her futon, her answering machine, her dishes, her papasan chair. She'd be paying more for rent than she paid now, but financially she'd be okay. She worked as a secretary at a law firm, and though the job itself was rather grim, the pay was reasonable; the benefits were good.

Of course, Phil was the one who first suggested that she move. And once the idea was out on the table, he certainly hadn't made any efforts to convince her to stay. He hadn't done anything except turn into a neat freak overnight, bleaching out the kitchen sink every day and changing the sheets two times a week. She couldn't even use a glass in the kitchen without him washing it as soon as she was finished. And the pork chops—weren't they just another way to annoy her, another way for Phil to prove he was in the driver's seat?

And yet, how could any of this be Phil's doing? After all, he was the one who wanted them to try counseling. She was the one who couldn't find the time after the first two sessions, after the therapist said, "Some couples decide that they don't have enough common ground for a lasting relationship."

No matter how Gina sliced up the situation, no matter how she arranged the facts, she was the one who wanted to leave. She was the one who had panicked in the jewelry store. All that talk of pear cuts and facets, settings and carats and prongs, all the words that conveyed the same terrifying message: forever forever forever.

"We want good value," Phil had said, and that's when her insides seized up, when she ran away, had to run.

She thought of what the swim coach had said—she could have been a college swimmer. She was trying to decide whether she had regret. She wished she'd had the excitement, the camaraderie. But she wondered, can you regret something you never really had a chance at? It wasn't as if she'd been a swimmer and then gave it up because she was lazy or started smoking pot every day. It wasn't as if someone had given her a plane ticket to France, and she'd been afraid to use it, afraid that her French wasn't good enough. Would she regret not marrying Phil? She didn't think so, but it was hard to know for sure. Maybe they'd still get married. Maybe this was just what they needed, time to think and room to breathe.

Gina turned off Park onto Nancy Lane. Though it was just the first week in November, the house on the corner was blazing with Christmas lights. There was a green plastic sleigh in the yard with an illuminated Santa perched on the seat. The edges of both sleigh and Santa were blurry, as if obscured by a snowstorm, though the night was clear, not even foggy.

She couldn't explain what had happened to the relationship. It wasn't until the moment she said she'd marry Phil that she realized she didn't want to. Now she thought back to the day they'd met, a cold afternoon in February at the counter of Mr. Copy, where she'd gone to get resumes printed, and Phil was copying his tax return.

Over coffee she told him how she'd come to Bloomington to get a master's in English, how she'd dropped out of the program after one miserable semester. And Phil just listened; he let her talk. Unlike the rest of the world, he didn't bombard her with suggestions about careers she should consider: Have you thought of going to library school? What about nursing? That night they went to a movie, and on the weekend they went ice skating. Before a month had gone by, they moved in together, or, rather, Gina moved her things into Phil's house.

It was fun back then: Phil planned picnics to the quarries and long bike rides in the country; he made her a piñata; he bought her a cactus. One weekend they drove up to Chicago on a whim, ate Indian food and visited the aquarium. They'd walked down busy streets in the brisk air, and Gina remembered throwing her hat up, like Mary Tyler Moore, giddy and happy, and then catching it again.

He told her he'd become a teacher in part for the summers off, so he could travel, and Gina admired his foresight, his adventurousness. He liked to go to travel agencies and bring home booklets about cruises and safaris and wine tours of France, but Gina realized soon enough that he never advanced beyond reading. He never actually went anywhere, except occasionally to Evansville to visit his parents. Once or twice a year he went to the post office and got forms for a passport, but he never finished filling them out.

Of course, thought Gina, these were petty complaints, excuses that would sound foolish if she spoke them aloud. "I'm leaving you because you don't have a passport." "I'm leaving you because you change the sheets too often." She couldn't help it, though. She didn't want her life to be so ordered and so dull: groceries on Thursday, laundry on Friday, egg salad on Saturday.

She thought of the night a few months ago when she'd come home from swimming, still buzzing from the adrenaline of the final sprint, still replaying her flip turn, her push off the wall, her burst of speed. She found Phil slumped in an armchair that had been pulled close to the TV. His legs were stuck out straight in front of him; his hands were folded on his chest. He was watching a car race, absolutely motionless, a television zombie.

"Don't you have anything better to do?" asked Gina.

"I guess not," he said, and he still didn't move.

Back on the porch Gina cleaned the mud off her shoes on the dirty doormat. Phil was back, and the house smelled wonderful. He didn't say anything when she came in. Gina sat on the floor in the living room and stretched. It had been cool outside, so she wasn't too sweaty. She could get by without a shower.

This is how it would be when she lived alone. No one would call out to her from the kitchen when she came back from running. There wouldn't be this smell of cooking, but there would be quiet and calm. There would be room for her to stretch out; she could take half an hour if she wanted to. She'd go swimming and then eat pancakes. She'd study Spanish. She'd go to work. Every once in a while she'd call Phil and see how he was doing. That would be her life, and she would be happy. She stood and pressed her hands against the wall, stretching her calves then wandered into the kitchen, where Phil was snapping green beans. She inhaled deeply, with her eyes closed. "Yum," she said.

"I can set you a plate," said Phil.

"Look at this bread." Gina pulled off a chunk, smelled it, then ate it.

Phil decided he wouldn't push; he wouldn't ask her again, but he'd set her place at the table. He'd say "Dinner" like it was nothing, like he was saying "Phone's for you" or "You got a letter." And she would eat. And she would stay. He should have gotten ice cream—mint chocolate chip or coffee—but he hadn't thought of it until right now. He hadn't realized how important it might be.

"It smells really really good in here," said Gina.

"Just a few more minutes." Phil dropped the beans into the pan and put on the lid.

At the last minute he put candles on the table, turned off the overhead light in the dining room and switched on a smaller lamp. When she sat at the table, Phil passed her the platter of pork chops. He was nice enough not to tease her.

"These are great," said Gina, chewing. "I don't even like pork chops."

Phil described the recipe he'd followed: the marinade and the breading, then sauté and bake. "The green beans are just steamed, and, of course, I bought the bread."

"Delicious."

If she was going to make her announcement, he didn't have to make it easy for her. If he made it hard enough for her to say she was leaving, maybe she'd decide to stay. Phil could dream up some elaborate plot, like putting an engagement ring at the bottom of a bowl of chocolate pudding, and they could try again—they could fall in love again.

"You know," said Phil, "all the famous swimmers eat pork chops—Diana Nyad ate pork chops."

"Who's Diana Nyad?"

"You call yourself a swimmer? Didn't you watch that movie in school? She swam to Cuba. She ate a lot of food before she went. The object, I think, is to make yourself look like a dolphin so that you blend in with the rest of the ocean."

Gina laughed. She ripped off another chunk of bread, and watching her chew, Phil could see the future. After they ate they'd settle in on the couch. They'd kiss to try to taste the flavors on each other's lips—garlic, lemon, oil—and from kissing they'd drift seamlessly into sex.

"Did she make it to Cuba?" asked Gina.

"I don't think so. I think she ran into sharks."

"You know," said Gina, "I've been thinking. So what if I wasn't a college swimmer? I'm not a ballerina either. Or a chemist."

"That's true," said Phil. "I wouldn't worry about it."

"It's stupid, I guess, to spend so much time swimming." She stuck her finger to the plate to pick up bread crumbs that had fallen off. "What's it for? I'll still be twenty-five. I can't change that. I can't go back to college."

"It's not stupid if you like it."

"I do like it."

"Then why is it stupid?"

Gina held up her plate and looked sheepish. "Can I have another pork chop?"

After they ate they turned on the TV and sat on the sofa, and one thing followed another, just as Phil had imagined. They kissed first, savoring the taste of meat and garlic, and then they made love with the sounds of CNN in the background: Bosnia, Haiti, unemployment, housing starts. Phil was polite; he was careful. He ran his hand over Gina's back, but he waited for her to unhook her bra herself. He waited for her to move her hand to his pants. But once Phil was inside her, he felt fierce, not gentle. He pushed into her hard, pushed as far as he could go. Maybe he was trying to hurt her, but she wrapped her legs around him and moved with him. When Phil looked down at Gina, her eyes were closed, and she was smiling, and he loved her. He loved her.

Afterward, Gina stood in the shower humming "Sleigh Ride" as hot water ran over her body. She soaped herself once and rinsed off, then soaped herself again just so she could stay longer in the warmth of the water. She felt comfortable, happy, almost free.

Often in the past she'd moved from boyfriend to boyfriend, without leaving any gaps. But now there was no one on the horizon, no cowboy on a white horse. She saw a clear space out in front of her where she could be by herself. She could think about the things that needed to be thought about. She could quit her job and go to Spain, eat paella and sleep in monasteries. She could go to Aspen and work in a ski lodge.

As for Phil, it was just—was it wrong to feel this way?—she didn't need him anymore.

In the living room, Phil sat alone on the sofa. He felt as if his insides had been scraped out, even though she'd kissed him on the nose just before she stood up. He thought of how he'd been afraid that Gina would get shoulders like the East German women swimmers. But Gina, while she certainly got stronger, also got sleeker, sexier. It was steroids that made the East Germans looks so misshapen. Swimming alone didn't have such an effect. Swimming made her beautiful.

He knew this was just the moment she was waiting for. Some moment she could call an ending, a special evening to remind her why she'd loved him in the first place. She'd be gone next week, or she'd be gone in the morning. And as time passed she'd forget how they used to ride their bikes to the bakery and to the park; she'd forget her suggestion that they still be friends. She'd forget the head-spinning taste of the pork chops. She'd tell people that Phil had stolen them; she'd say he forced her to eat them, that she hated pork chops.

When Phil heard the bedroom door close, he went into the bathroom. Opening the door he released a cloud of steam. The floral fragrance was from Gina's shampoo, but he couldn't help thinking he was breathing in her essence. She'd hung her wet wash-cloth on the edge of the tub to dry, and he picked it up. He laid the cloth on his face and breathed in the smell of her soap, her skin. He was smelling soap and crying, sitting on the side of the tub in the steamy intimacy of the bathroom, his body heaving with the force of his sobs. There was nothing to be done. She was going. She was gone.

In bed Gina was asleep already, warm and washed and dreaming. She was moving steadily through the water, over waves and under waves, swimming out to sea.

# THE NINE IDEAS FOR A HAPPIER WHOLE

AMOS A. MAGLIOCCO

I come on these trips because Patty hates needles. She cannot, she claims, pierce her own skin with a syringe filled with thick, clear insulin.

Apparently it's not as easy as shoplifting. At home, her mother drives from across Dallas twice daily to give her the shots. With the syringe in her hand she removes the cap and examines the skin of Patty's upper arm or her ass, choosing new areas to avoid bruising the skin. When Patty and I go to Oklahoma, we're out well past dinner, and she needs insulin after she eats. I ask her where she's been taking her shots lately.

We're in her car, going ninety miles per hour.

She used to give me a mock laugh. Now, she looks away and lifts her sleeve. "My arm is fine," she says. It's not funny to her anymore, I can tell. That's my fault.

I give her the shot and dab her arm with a thin alcohol swab. An orange safety cap locks over the needle and I store the used syringe and insulin vial in the plastic tacklebox Patty uses for this stuff. The safety cap is narrow, and replacing it over the needle is tricky business in a moving car, a bad idea since I'm liable to jab myself. I pull my book out from the tan pouch under the door handle. I've just finished reading *The Nine Ideas for a Happier Whole* and I'm sitting in the passenger seat of Patty's '57 Chevy Bel Air, hoping nobody saw her swipe a six-pack at the Allsup's Pit Stop in Frederick.

On my agenda: making it through the year without being accused of sexual harassment at work. Patty doesn't set goals like that. She likes to steal Shiner Bock beer in Oklahoma and buy superunleaded in Texas. Her wide brown eyes flutter back and forth between the windshield and the rearview mirror. She's careful, watching her speed, changing lanes with the clunky old turnlamps: click-clack, click-clack. Patty Mullins is an engineer, crazy as a moonrock, and I wonder if I'll ever find a self-improvement program to let me keep her.

*The Eighth Idea: Find Your Hiding Place. Everyone has a place where they can think, laugh, or cry most easily. Find it right now. Get out of your car, climb down from the SUV—no road sign will point the way. Never tell another soul.*

"Want a beer?" she asks.

"No thanks. You pay for them?"

"Of course not." She laughs. "I don't have a cent on me."

"Beer throws off your blood sugar," I say. "You shouldn't drink beer." The road snakes around midget hills, and patches of green winter wheat interrupt faded pasture. We're a striking sight on the prairie, a bubbly old car, two-tone electric blue and white, defiant fins parading over the trunk. Then the stunning moon-faced driver with yellow curls. We're a cartoon against that drab, drought-dead background of cold yellows and flat orange, a tropical fish on wheels. The gas gauge, as always, reads well past "F," fuller than full.

The gauge is broken, but Patty never runs out of gas.

I think about the Nine Ideas, these simple suggestions to live by. I make a note to tell Samantha, my personal coach, to read the book and help me incorporate the lessons into my life. I've never actually seen Samantha. I only talk to her on the telephone.

"I have to pay more attention to what I consume," I say to Patty. "Not just what I eat, but everything: emotion, energy, even information." I raise my eyebrows at this last item. I want her to know that I'm watching the way she frames reality, Patty the myth-maker.

"Here," she says, holding a brown bottle in front of me. "Drink the evidence."

"You don't listen to me," I say.

She banks a curve at almost eighty. The tires whine. Her hair slides across her neck and shoulders. She has tiny ears—you have to brush back the curls to see them.

"I listen, Thomas." She checks the side mirrors. "Sometimes you say so much."

Know this about her: Patty is a brittle diabetic. When her blood sugar level drops from too much insulin, her brain starves for fuel. Sugar is brain food. Strange things happen then. Too much sugar and she can have a stroke. She makes it worse by eating and drinking whatever she likes, ignoring the prescribed diet, disregarding her own program. "It's hard to find a program that *doesn't* work," Samantha often tells me on the phone. "It's harder to find a person who does. You have to be a stickler." Samantha is a graduate of Coach U, an internet-based institution cranking out personal coaches by the bushel, energetic men and women to guide the lost and lonely for a nominal fee.

I feel good about the Nine Ideas. They're practical. They just might work.

Patty drives into a curtain of dark rain. Lightning flashes from the storm tower overhead and the wind sprays Patty's Bel Air head-on. If anyone saw Patty grab that beer and run out the door, they'd never forget this gorgeous blue and white car, the silver side mirrors like flashy chrome earrings. I can see Patty wearing them, taming them with her willful style. People might snicker, make space for her embarrassment, but she'd lean into them with that slapstick smile: "What, you don't like them?" Yeah, this thing is an *automobile*.

Patty said planning my financial and professional future with a stranger on the telephone was ridiculous. And it was my third session with Samantha when she said *Patty* had to go. I listen for a hitch in Samantha's voice after I detail what Patty and I are up to. The intolerance on the other end of the line is brittle and distorted like static.

It's all very thin, what Samantha tells me, reciting her generic advice from prepared scripts. She sits in a call center like the one I manage for a living, with hundreds of people around her wearing headsets and watching the clock. Rows and rows of cubicles with blue cloth sides. Like I say, it's all very tinny, but even crass commercialism can't blunt old-fashioned, objective wisdom. The species has gathered so much of it; all you have to do is call. Operators are standing by.

Samantha insists Patty is my "Failure Point." It's a psychological trick knee. A habit or substance or person can fill that space. Getting rid of the incarnation doesn't necessarily dismiss the flaw. The way Samantha explains it, Patty and I might have an entirely different and healthy relationship under a new and distant set of circumstances. Dismissing Patty will uncover the problem. I tell Samantha that I'll always want to get Patty in bed. She's a knockout. Samantha acts as if I'm not co-operating. I tell her she's not dealing with reality.

*The Second Idea: Dietary Discretion. Garbage in; garbage out. Lift your face from the trough, friend. If you're not ready to make this change, put the book back, please.*

"I wish you'd slow down." I drink the beer. "The roads are wet." Patty fixes her eyes on the windshield.

"You're right," she says with a smile. My knees draw as if to buckle.

"Let's stay in the rain as long as we can," I say, "or until the sun goes down." Patty leans over and looks up to the ragged gray base of the storm. Red needles wobble inside the silver-rimmed gauges of the instrument panel. Her eyes are quick, the calculating engineer, the sexiest damn thing I've ever seen.

"The storm may not follow the road," she says. "It doesn't have to, you know."

"This is farm country," I tell her. "There's all kinds of little roads." I reach in the back for *The Roads of Oklahoma*, a detailed map with an entire county on each two-page spread, and every U.S. interstate, state highway, county road, farm-to-market, gravel trail, and dirt path clearly marked. It's invaluable when we leave Texas in some unorthodox manner, which is nearly every time we come. We'll roll down the windows and howl like wolves when we cross back over the state line. The Red River is stone-shallow like a creek these days, as though the distant heart of the thing beats softer and softer. The rain will do us good.

The day I met Patty I saw her car first, then the pretty girl inside. She didn't smile, but she and the car glowed together, the combination more radiant than either element apart. Samantha, my coach, wasn't interested when I told her how Patty looked as if she'd been born in there, as though the car had grown around her like some neon metallic hairdo.

"Gotta watch the time," Samantha said. I was always surprised when we reached our limit of one hour per call—we always seemed just about to reach the heart of things and then it was over.

My friends told me it was just that old car, but I disagreed. Patty *likes* people, and you can tell. She's a good lover, strong but soft and obliging, and the first time she said she loved me she gave a bitter look, as if I'd forced it from her. Now I'm in that car with her and we're driving fast.

"How's work?" she asks. Patty thinks managing a room full of people is exciting. She's a mechanical engineer, and draws blueprints for gas pump parts. The debit card revolutionized the gas pump industry: every station needs new ones. People won't stop at the old ones anymore, Patty says. They want to use their debit cards. Patty designed a pump with little TV screens playing CNN while you fill the tank. Times are good, I tell her, when people can afford enough gas to watch the news while they pump.

I've got a smaller office than any department head in the building. Because the managers make do with offices the size of large closets, we have space for vending machines in a large break room, with fried apple pies and steaming coffee. On Sunday mornings, a few employees come early and cook bacon and scrambled eggs in the microwave, fill clear plastic cups with orange juice and make other breakfast sounds: warm, tired voices and small laughter. Hell, it sounds like someone's kitchen. Of course they say nasty things about me behind my back—that's human nature—but I know where they'd line up in a fistfight. You have those in big companies. No blood, just words and emails, poison memos and trips to the Human Resources Department. None of ours transfer out. I see a new request to transfer *in* every day from some brave soul in another area. Their bosses see it, too.

We have our own entrance and exit, and we lock the glass door to the rest of the building to keep them out. When my boss visits from the executive suite, security calls and I buzz him in. The rest of them stop at the door and stare through the glass. My people wave and smile.

"It's *good*," I tell Patty. "We're making it a good place for people to work."

Wind blows rain back and forth across the road. Clouds to our west glow green with hail, but I don't mention it since she's going plenty fast already. Still, it would be a shame to drive this old bird under the rocks.

*The Seventh Idea: Write Glowing Reviews of Yourself. Write about your goals, and what you did today to draw nearer to them.*

"A good place to work? Meaning the boss doesn't try to talk girls into storage closets with him?" Patty says things like that, like I'm some predator. The girl in question had felt comfortable enough to roll her eyes and say, "In your dreams." She quit a month later and sued the company for sexual harassment. It's hard to help myself. The women in our building are feisty.

"You should come work for us," I say. "You'd see for yourself."

"I'd cut your dick off and microwave it. You should read self-castration books to improve yourself." She laughs. She hadn't laughed when the lawsuit was filed though, mainly because there'd been a similar problem the year before, another case of poor judgement: the wrong quip to the wrong person. She did everything but laugh. She packed her clothes, rolling them tightly and lining her suitcase, removing photographs from frames I'd bought and sliding them carefully into a manila envelope, labeling each with a black felt marker. I joked about cataloging relics while she sorted pens from the desk, dropping a handful into the front pocket of her bookbag. You don't find me funny anymore, I said. It was the end for Patty and me, that second time. Now we were friends, co-conspirators, monitors sent to inspect the rebuilding process of one another's lives.

Patty called me a criminal, a sex fiend.

"My God, Patty," I say now, wondering how far she might be from considering some violent act. If we were married? One never knows another person completely.

A white pickup appears behind us, a red strobe light over the driver's side.

"What's the next east road?" Patty says.

"I don't know, let's ask this cop."

"Find the next east road. Please."

"East is a bad idea, Patty. There's hail moving this way."

I learned about Patty's diabetes while we were dating in college. Someone approached me in a topless bar and said I had an emergency phone call. A naïve stripper named Diamond was sitting with me. I'd seen Diamond come in wearing too-high heels, and watched her stumble around: her first day, and I was talking her out of the career choice when they said Patty was unconscious in the drunk tank. An hour later she was comatose, white as linen, like the blood had drained from every cell. I couldn't believe she wasn't dead.

---

*The First Idea: Exercise. Tap the natural spring. You don't require Siberian, Korean or any other communist ginseng. Your body has all the energy you need.*

We're out of Oklahoma's Arbuckle Mountains now, emerging onto the flatland like a circus tent in the desert. The storm swallows the reddening western sky, closing on us.

"The next east road is a gravel trail," I say. "We'll get stuck." Patty doesn't need me to explain traction. "Then we'll get hailed on. We need to get south of the storm or turn around and stay north of the hail. We're running out of options." The sheriff's truck follows at a distance, light flashing dimly in the rain, waiting for us to decide.

"I'm all for not stopping," she says. "Not until they send the helicopters." When her sugar drops, Patty's brain closes systems one by one, the gas-guzzlers first: higher functions like reason and delicate motor skills. Most diabetics grow tired and lie down until they can eat. Patty runs from the law, riding a 455-horsepower Chevy engine through the Red River Valley like a last, wild Apache before the clatter of infantry.

The best thing Patty could do now is drink a beer.

Because I know Patty's disease, I'm not surprised that she keeps driving and talks about helicopters. Stress chews up glucose fast, and we haven't eaten since breakfast. Her eyes are blank, the brain-drain unfolding like a play, and I imagine her floating out of the car, through the window maybe, head-first, snaking through the opening and up, up, up into the storm, leaving a serene pet Patty down here with me, the one she thinks I want, the one she thinks I'm looking for in books. Her perfume smells like the first fall day wet leaves clump together on the grass.

The sheriff's truck closes in, a few yards from our bumper. I lift the *Nine Ideas* from the door pouch. The cover is that slick, soft paper, cool to the touch.

I read aloud: *"The Sixth Idea: Eradicate all negative agents in your world. Celebrate their exile. Then never give them second thought."* Thunder rolls like we're in the crawl space beneath a bowling alley.

"Wow," she says. "I'm so glad you reminded me." She smiles and shakes her head. She's entertaining herself. "Thomas, Thomas. So much time learning how to live. Call me when you figure it out."

"I'm improving myself. It's possible, you know. You can roll up your sleeves and do it."

"Accept circumstances or waste time," Patty says. "Like you." She'll only talk to me about this when she's having an insulin reaction. It's how I know it's in there. "You waste time."

If I go to jail in Oklahoma, I probably miss work on Monday or arrive embarrassingly late. Sunlight approaches the storm's edge. Then we're out from under the cloud, and the brightness makes us squint. I turn to Patty. "Now they've got us."

"Optimist," she snarls, rolls her head around, goes downhill fast. The engine sputters once, and again, and Patty floors the accelerator and pounds the big brown steering wheel with both hands. When she exhausts herself and we're barely moving, I pull the wheel towards me to guide the car to the shoulder where we roll to a stop.

I'm amazed. She looks from the instruments to me to my book.

I turn in my seat as the deputy approaches. Patty rolls down the window before he gets to there.

"The gauge is broke!" she shouts. The deputy stops.

"How's that?" he says.

"The gauge is broke. You didn't catch me—I ran out of gas." He walks to the window now, peels off his silver sunglasses. "Shit," she says to him. Like he's cheated.

"People tell me everyday about broken *speedometers*," he says, looking at me. I nod to agree. Black letters on his silver nametag spell "Godwin." He's lamppost thin and acne-scarred, with a struggling red mustache and small eyes. He reminds me of the applicants we turn away out of some instinctual sense of malfeasance, though their resumes are filled with swaths of unaccounted time between jobs and provide us comfortable justification. Here was one with a gun, nearly larger than his hand. "You'd think not one of them came out of the factory working," he says, "so many broken out here." Now he looks at Patty. "Right here on this highway." He tugs his red moustache. "But nobody ever said they pulled over because they ran out of gas." He looks in the back seat. "Heard you forgot to pay for some beer."

"Yeah," Patty says. She taps the speedometer glass with a clear fingernail. "It's never worked right." She tries to start the car again.

"Whoa now," Godwin says and steps back. He lifts the leather strap on his holster. I pull the keys out of the ignition. Patty glares at me. I go into the routine.

"She's a diabetic, officer. She's having an insulin reaction right now."

"Is that right?" The outlines of hills press through the rain to our north. We're in the sunlight, and a broad, bright rainbow parades overhead. I feel like we should be drinking champagne. Godwin moves closer to the window. He's chewing gum.

"She needs a candy bar or some orange juice," I say.

"And a new gas gauge," Godwin adds.

"Right."

"Feeling faint there, little lady?" he asks. I clench my jaw.

"I'm not your lady," Patty says sweetly, as though he's mistaken her for his mother. She turns to face him. "I'm a real bitch." Deputy Godwin laughs from the belly and tells her to get out of the car. While he adjusts the silver handcuffs around her wrists, Patty says that he stinks like a milk cow, and that her uncle could use someone like him out at the Dairy. They count breedings every day, she explains, plenty of action for him. Godwin pours a gallon of gas into the empty tank and tells me to follow him back to Frederick. Patty is going to jail and we won't know bail until he finds the judge.

*The Ninth Idea: Occupy all the Universe. Bring the Ideas together, and honor the potential of every action. The power of all creation becomes yours.*

The Western Union office is closed, but the clerk arrives ten minutes after I pull in the parking lot. She's gray from head to toe and thin as a rail. She knows the whole story, no doubt.

"Got some trouble?" she asks. She walks to the door and fumbles through her keys.

"It's always something," I say.

"Don't I know it."

I write out the wire order and wait with her. We sit on stools and talk across the scratched wooden counter. A ceiling fan turns above us. I tell her about the Nine Ideas, and she shakes her head and waits patiently for me to finish. She tells me about the Bible, and the story of the Baby Jesus, who had so many ideas that guys wrote four versions of his story, each with different ideas than the others. A self-improvement extravaganza, I tell her. She nods and says she never thought of it that way, but she supposes that's exactly what it is. I tell her I'm a person who has to work on a few ideas at a time. Like Gerald Ford, I say, and she laughs a sweet, quiet laugh as we wait for Patty's bail money.

We'd run into the wrong cop. Back at the sheriff's office, Godwin fishes a few coins from his pocket and drops them into a vending machine. The bottles are stacked vertically and the glass door swings open like a refrigerator. Even the "Enjoy Coca-Cola" in flaking red paint is a classic design.

Patty's Chevy ran out of magic on us, as though there were a gauge for that sort of thing and it broke too. Godwin tosses a bottle to me with the key to her cell. Patty presses her face to the bars, singing badly.

"Make her drink that and don't let her take so much insulin," Godwin says. "Cook your brain that way, or crack up that shiny car. Wouldn't that be a crime?" I nod my head. There's no doubt that it would be.

"I don't think she'll drink it," I say. "She's belligerent." I'm off the script. Cops had always let us go, happy to do without the coma in their jail.

Deputy Godwin smiles. "Thomas, you let me know, and I'll call the medics to bring some glucagon. We'll give her a shot if she can't drink the pop. Fix her up good as new." Glucagon was the instant cure: pure glucose. Patty stops singing.

I bail her out and drive us back to Corsicana, Texas, in her Chevy. I tell her we shouldn't see each other for a while. I leave my book wedged in Patty's sun visor over the driver's side.

"I'm sick of your New Age crap anyway," she says. "I'm sure Samantha can find you somebody with the right number of ideas." Patty's not the type to cry. A week later, she won't return my calls, and I phone the County Attorney in Frederick for the trial date. I drive to Oklahoma alone.

*The Third Idea: Direct your Energy. Focus on one or two primary goals. Feel the power move through your hands; sculpt a new life for yourself.*

My silver Chrysler blows chilled air and has a first-class sound system. Stock ponds near the road are still and dark. Children fish from the knobby docks. I cross the Red River knowing Patty needs confrontation, someone to stand up in court and tell the truth. She needs me to show how much I love her that way.

She's somewhere on this same road, checking her rearview mirror for me, suspicious of that broken gauge now.

I'll sing like a canary. That's the right way to do it, the cleanest break. She'll know my intentions, but fold and go home anyway, I'm convinced. I imagine her dabbing cherry lipstick on her lips, the scent like ice cream.

I call Samantha on the cell phone and tell her my plan. She's quiet, and I hear the lightest clack of keys as she types a word into her database. Probably "confrontation."

"No, no," I say. "This is not about that at all. Not like confronting an alcoholic. This is revelation, public confession."

"Now let me think this over, Thomas." More typing, louder this time.

"Listen. Stop typing. I'll show her I love her and leave. My going away present." Samantha sighs. "I want to know what you think!" I say. I've never told Samantha about my problems at work. It didn't seem important, the past. Misunderstandings.

"I just think I think you need to do your own thing, Thomas. Stop following Patty around."

*The Fourth Idea: Love Yourself Most. You're the most important person in the world.*

I sit in the back row with my hands wrapped around a black umbrella. The place is packed with repeat traffic offenders and those accused of alcohol-inspired misdemeanors. One old gentleman in a green and yellow John Deere cap challenges the constitutionality of the seat belt law. Three rows of ceiling fans stretch across the high ceiling. All the chairs and benches are dark cedar. The benches are like pews, with wooden pockets on the back of each seat. A selection of magazines faces everyone through the long wait. There are no windows.

When Patty's trial begins, the county attorney introduces the owner of Allsup's Pit Stop. On the stand, he recounts how Patty took the beer and beat it out the door. He describes her car like a connoisseur, enjoying himself, as if the jury needs to know about the silver body striping and how you can't help but notice something gleaming like that in a gravel parking lot. The judge yawns, exposing her enormous teeth.

Against the advice of the bench, Patty represents herself. She's elegant in the courtroom, striding to the jury box like a powerful swimmer. Their faces are rapt at her approach, as if the document in her hand tells how all this will end. It's the doctor's letter describing her condition and erratic behavior. The medical explanation. Disgusting, Samantha had said when I told her that Patty kept the letter in the glove box for emergencies. Patty reads it to us. She slides it back into the envelope and faces the jury.

"I'm a mechanical engineer and I've worked hard to get where I am. There are not many women doing what I do," she says. "I make more than enough to pay for my beer. Normally I don't drink beer. Normally I don't take things without paying for them. I'm no shoplifter. I'm a good person." Her voice thins. She hates to cry. Hates it.

*The Fifth Idea: Love your Family and Friends. Don't expect love in return and see what happens.*

I stand fast and straighten my tie, ready to tell all. I'd known her for years, and I knew her diabetes better than anyone. I'd seen her insulin reactions from their first moment, a tilt of her head, the slowing smile as her thinking distorted like the pebble's first ripple on a still pond. The discomfort in losing control. Patty spins to face me, her eyes round as the bottom of a beer glass.

Before I can speak, the county attorney stands and expresses his sincere regret for the circumstances. "The State of Oklahoma drops all charges," he says with a broad smile, as if looking down a long table at his entire family.

The judge cracks the gavel on her desk. "You're free to go, Miss Mullins. But let me say something to you. Deputy Godwin is a diabetic himself. He tells me he doesn't believe you were suffering from, what is it?" She reads the word from a document: "Hypoglycemia . . . at the time of your arrest. The deputy is no doctor, certainly." She takes off her glasses. Patty folds her arms in front of her.

The court reporter taps his keys to catch up.

"We don't have engineers here," the judge says. "This is a farm town. The town supports farmers, Miss Mullins." I hang the curved handle of the umbrella from my front pocket. I hold my arms down by my side, palms outward, trying to embrace the weight of the words. "I don't want to see you here again," the judge says. "You're just a thief, and you're dismissed."

Patty walks alone down the aisle. She's wearing a handsome suit, and her white shoes tap a charming rhythm on the wooden floor. Deputy Godwin sits two rows ahead of me and turns to watch her leave, disappointment on his face like he'd have enjoyed her company a little longer, her grace a rarity. I step out of the row and follow her through the front door and down a flight of concrete steps. She crosses the street. The wind blows her hair back and I can see her small ears. Then she climbs in the old Chevy and starts the engine. The electric blue bleeds through the sunlight and we're a cartoon again. I want animated lips so I can stretch them fifty feet and kiss her on the forehead. I jog across the road.

She rolls down the window. "What a loser," she says. "Not you." She jabs her index finger toward the courthouse. "Him. The fat-ass *prosecutor*. He didn't even try to fight it out, that chickenshit."

"Jesus, Patty. He cut you a break." She leans back to see past me, watching people coming down the steps.

"Coach Samantha should have kept you away from here," she says. "You should fire her ass." Her eyes are on the courthouse. I smell potato soup and fresh bread from the diner behind us. There's a line forming at the door. "But then you haven't seen *her* ass yet, have you? Maybe you should ask her office hours." She looks up when I don't reply. "You were going to tell them it was a lie, that I wasn't having a reaction when you *knew* that I was. You knew I really was this time. That's why you stood up. I would have *never* spoken to you again."

She spots the county attorney. "Hey!" she yells.

"That," I say, "might be the best thing for both of us." She glances up to me, shakes her head and looks back at him.

She cups her hands around her mouth, a makeshift megaphone. "Fatboy chickenshit!" I back away from the car. "You fat ass!" she says.

The county attorney puts his briefcase down and points to us. "Now you look here," he shouts. He looks at Godwin and points to us again. Godwin jogs down the steps, his arms bent at his side like a sneaking ghost.

Her tires spin, whitewalls clean enough to disguise rotation un-til they conjure white smoke—the scent burns my nostrils. A streak of electric blue and white, with a dash of red in back, those tall tail-lights pointed like a church steeple. The yellow curls are in there, too, and I imagine the front half of the car leaping forward like a Slinky, nearly across the state line while the back tires still spin in place, dusting my black shoes like the Road Runner revving up un-til the last second and screeching away when Wile E. Coyote ap-pears. Godwin stops in the road and watches her leave.

"What is the matter with that woman?" he says to me. He wipes his hands on his trousers.

"She's a diabetic," I say. "She's sick."

The Chevy stops with a screech. A book flies out her window, the white pages flapping like the wings of a doomed bird.

"Son of a bitch," Godwin says and runs for his truck. He'll arrest her for littering. He has no choice after such a flagrant violation in front of everyone crossing the square for lunch.

She'll laugh about it later, how my book slid out from above the visor when she floored it and smacked her somewhere, in the head probably, scaring the shit out of her. She'll yell and scream and laugh until those tiny ears are bright red. If I'm there, that is. I want to be there for that. These days, that's a thing I want to see.

I run for my Chrysler. I wait for Godwin to pull away and I fall in behind him, heading north towards Lawton, all of us driving *away* from Texas and the river. Patty doesn't even know she's going the wrong direction.

# STEPPING IN
# MS. CENT-JEAN'S SHOES

CRYSTAL S. THOMAS

My aunt always says ain't nothing new under the sun, but when we found out Ms. Cynthia Jean's husband was cheating on her for another woman at the salon, it was *news*; not like you couldn't imagine it, but surprising, you know, like if Michael Jackson were to go back to the afro. The night two and two came together was a Wednesday, and the shop was kind of slow, but everyone had a customer so the air was filled with all the smells I had come to tell apart: peppermint from the shampoo Aunt Bennie ordered each month, the raw egg smell of neutralizer, fried hair, oil sheen, and the stink of nail polish remover.

I was leaning on the counter of Aunt Bennie's station, flicking through the latest *Ebony* and trying to keep a watch over the pickle in my hand as it steadily soaked through its wrapper. Duke, the barber that rented a booth from my aunt, was doing his laugh-because-I'm-cute routine, and telling some joke we'd heard a thousand times. It was the one about a head being so ugly the razor ran, which was not even the funniest joke, but for some reason whenever Duke said anything and those dimples jumped out like flashers everybody wound up laughing, even my aunt who tried hard not to.

Maybe it was because the radio station had been playing all the good jams—you know, "Rock With You Tonight" and "Let's Get it On" and "Caught Up in the Rapture of You"—or maybe it was because finally a cool breeze had started to push up on the Florida heat, but the shop seemed in such a light mood that nobody noticed when *the other woman* slid out and into Ms. Cynthia Jean's husband's car.

Now when she had first come in about a month earlier, Duke had said, "Dang, look at that ice cream cone—," stuck, of course, on her big chest and long legs, but I remember looking at her skin. Like honey being squeezed into tea, or maybe copper melting.

She said her name was *D-e-e-n-a* when I penciled her in, smiling, all lips and teeth. Yvette, the other hairdresser in my aunt's salon, never liked her from the get go, but I think that was because when Deena started coming, she gave Yvette fashion competition. Even on long days, Yvette would wear nice Guess clothes and sometimes black stiletto boots, but Deena's style was straight off the runway. Outside of liking her outfits though, I never thought much else of her until Ms. Geraldine—who I promise used lipstick for blush—rushed in that Wednesday like she'd just discovered Christmas.

"Ooh, now Bennie," she moaned, all wound up. "Now, you know I don't like to stir up no stuff, but I'd be lying if I didn't just see Rufus Henderson pull off from your parking lot with another woman in his car."

My Aunt Bennie didn't even look up. She's like my mama when it comes to busybodies, except a little less nice about it. "Geraldine, don't be bringing no gossip in my shop," she warned, and just kept twisting and tucking her client's hair, stacking the rollers like bones.

But Ms. Geraldine can be hard of hearing when she feels like it.

"Bennie, I'm telling the truth. A light-skinned woman got into his car, and Cent-Jean is over at Bible study!"

"Hmm, mm. Didn't I tell you that woman looked like trouble?" Yvette said, pointing the end of a comb in Aunt Bennie's direction. I sucked on my pickle, just watching.

"Well, I just wonder where she comes from," Ms. Geraldine said, putting a hand to her chest like she was *so* concerned. "She doesn't look like anyone *I've* ever seen."

I wanted to suck my teeth at this. Like she personally had seen every known body that drove and lived in Mulberry. With that brown hat and green sweat suit. What she needed to see was a fashion magazine.

"Men are such dogs," Yvette snapped, and pursed her lips like, "yeah, you," at Duke.

"Y'all are jumping to conclusions," Aunt Bennie said. "Maybe the woman's a *friend* of Rufus *and* Cent-Jean," she pointed out, but I couldn't tell if she really believed it.

"And maybe they're just off to have a little priiivate Bible study," Duke joked back, flashing those killer dimples.

"Oh my Lord. Hmgh, mgh, mgh," Ms. Geraldine said, like that wasn't what she had been implying.

"You really think that woman could be a friend of Cynthia Jean's?" Yvette asked.

I thought about it, and it *was* hard to picture. Ms. Cynthia Jean was pretty, but in a church choir way, and she never wore move-something dresses like we'd seen Deena in the past few weeks.

"I'm just telling you we need to stay out of other folks' business," my aunt said and nudged her client over to the dryer. "Geraldine, I reckon I can take you tomorrow if you want to. Rashawn, go ahead and sweep up."

That was my cue to move and quit listening, and for everybody else to be quiet. Aunt Bennie wore religion as sanctified and serious as a lace communion cap, and anybody who came to her shop had to respect the rules laminated and posted above the door: *NO Cussing, NO Fussing, and NO Gossip . . . This is a Christian Environment.* Because they knew about her strictness, my parents let me help out around the shop, sweeping up after cuts and keeping the candy jars full in exchange for twenty dollars a week.

I liked working in my aunt's salon. It was a gutted-out, two-bedroom house with hardwood floors and silk flowers in all the corners. In addition to sweeping and mopping, I also straightened magazines on the fireplace and cleaned out the black pearl sinks. It was from the sink area—in what used to be the first bedroom—that you could see the parking lot, and picking up that night I glanced out the window, wondering if the *femme fatale* Deena had slid into Mr. Henderson's car all slow like it was a stretch limousine, or if they had kicked up gravel while driving away like Kitt in the TV show *Knight Rider*.

The next day Ms. Geraldine and Yvette aired the matter whenever my aunt walked out of earshot. They spent half an hour guessing whose people Deena came from, or whether she was completely new to Mulberry. "I wonder where she works," Ms. Geraldine said.

"Some sit on your tail job, or he's probably putting her up," Yvette declared.

She was always going on about too fast women and no good men, especially women who stole other people's boyfriends, and her son's father Clay. "That's how Clay had me: strung out, put up, sitting around thinking we were getting married one day, and he would cut out all his bull."

"You think she knows about Cent-Jean?" Ms. Geraldine asked.

"You think Cent-Jean knows about her?" Duke piped in, and everybody paused.

"I know y'all not still talking about that," Aunt Bennie warned again, bringing a client over from the sink.

I didn't feel like hearing the gossip that day either. My mind was on the Winter Dance and Peanut, the junior who'd asked me.

It was all we girls at Mulberry High could talk about: would it be too cold for sheer shirts? Should we go casual or dressy? And if we danced with somebody, would they sweat us the whole time?

I had heard last year's dance was fun but that there was a fight. My friend Tanika, a sophomore, said that one girl ripped the other girl's shirt, and both of them lost their earrings. "Girl, they looked like two seals slapping each other," she said, but as fights go it wasn't that serious. Anyway, the drama helped to loosen things up because before that Tanika said people were acting too scared to dance.

Since I had just started the ninth grade, it would be my first year going to the Winter Dance, and I had saved up money for a new outfit. In eighth grade all I thought about were the parties in the old Mulberry gym, and even though I lived a couple of neighborhoods away when I lay really still in bed on Saturday nights I could hear the bass from all the music. Crooking my ear to the window with my eyes closed, I would imagine the walls of the gym shaking and dream about high school. The trouble was that this year all my friends were going in a group, and I secretly wanted to go with Peanut.

Peanut was a guy that I kind of had a crush on. He wasn't in any of my classes, but we both had first lunch, and he and his friends sat across from mine. Big dark eyes and a little taller than me, Peanut shuffled more than walked around the lunchroom, you know, like a baseball player who's too cool to run home. He wasn't the finest guy in school, but he was in the same crowd, and one smile set off a band in my heart. The first day we spoke, I was carrying my lunch tray alongside Tanika, and Peanut passed by, then looped back, checking me out like he was reading a new label.

"How you doing?" he had asked.

"Fine," I said. Lunch had just started and everyone was walking up and down, making a parade line in the blue cafeteria. I wanted to look at Tanika, but didn't. Instead I shifted my lunch tray to the side of my hip so my matching jean jacket and skirt showed.

"You must be new. I'm Charles."

"Peanut!" Tanika corrected.

"Like I said, my name is Charles, but you can call me whatever you like. Where y'all sitting?" he asked, looking at me. We told him, and from then on our table had permanent company. Boys pulled up chairs, stole our fries, threw cards over our shoulders, and made us their allies and butts of their jokes. They were grasshoppers chomping down on a new plant, but of course we didn't complain. Peanut asked me for my phone number after a while and then started calling me every night. Holding my breath, I would lie in the dark with just the closet light on and watch my toes scrunch in my white crew socks whenever he told me I was cute. I liked Peanut because he made me laugh and because he wasn't mannish like the boys in middle school. When he asked me to the dance a trumpet hooted in my heart—actually I put him on hold and did the wop—but then I got nervous and asked if I could think about it.

If Peanut and I went to the dance together people would assume we were a "thing" and while the idea made my toes scrunch even more I wanted to know how things would end up. Would we be like the senior class president and his girl that had been together all four years? Or would Peanut do like a lot of guys did and have a different girlfriend every lunch period?

I was so stuck in these thoughts I didn't even notice that Thursday afternoon had become Thursday evening. I tuned in just in time to hear Yvette and Duke asking what Aunt Bennie planned to do since Ms. Cynthia Jean was *her* client *and* scheduled for this Friday.

"Hmm, mm," Ms. Geraldine chimed in. "You know the Bible talk about being your brother's keeper."

"The Bible also talks about not being meddlesome, and y'all expect me to confront Cent-Jean without any facts?" Aunt Bennie rolled her eyes at them and wiped a towel across her station.

"Looks like a simple case of two-timing to me," Duke said.

"I know, Bennie, my god! Don't you think we should drop a hint or something?" Yvette had turned from her client and was primping her own hair in the mirror. She sounded irritated, but over her shoulder I could see that she didn't look any sourer than when she chipped a nail.

"The acts of the sinful nature are obvious," Aunt Bennie certified. "If Rufus is messing around, it'll come to the light. Besides, ain't no man into something and his wife don't know it. Rashawn, run and put these in the machine." She waved a handful of towels at me, and that was the end of the conversation.

I could see as I passed the dryers that Ms. Geraldine was appeased. Her eyebrows stayed raised (they were penciled on), but she smiled as she flipped through the magazine on her knee, and muttered, "A widow ain't got such trouble." I recognized her smile as the same one that stretched my friends' lips when we discussed dirt going down at school. So and So's pregnant and the father just dumped her. Such and Such got beat up after the football game last night. The Ed teacher told a boy that he was never going to college. It was like that—people dissed each other, dropped out, were kicked out, got in fights, cheated on each other. Life was as crazy as the soaps.

I guess things happened so you had something to talk about, road accidents to look at but go around. If Ms. Cynthia didn't know the truth she probably suspected it. In Mulberry gossip ran on the track team and sooner or later caught up to everybody, whether at church, the grocery store, or the salon.

Although I had grown up watching women and their daughters get their hair done, I never got tired of the daily miracle. It amazed me when a woman eased into the salon chair like a broken automobile, got pumped up, spun around, and stood up a new person. Women came to Aunt Bennie's shop with short hair, bald spots, naps like popcorn kernels, ponytails thin as pillow feathers, split ends, afros, and curls drier than Spanish moss, showing up in scarves, hats, wigs, and skinny rubber bands a little embarrassed, or sometimes dragging in with hair looking wild, falling back against the chair and saying "do me." The hair station was a cross between a mechanic's garage and an operating room. Spray bottles, pins, and clips took up one side of the counter and tong-like hot irons took up the rest.

Of all the different ways women got their hair done, I was most suspicious of and impressed by "straightening" or "the hot comb and press." How anyone sat still while a comb on fire like a cattle brand was dragged through her roots and kitchen was beyond me, especially since I knew how the heat from the comb caused your scalp to sweat and how those water beads combined with grease popped and sizzled. Up until I was ten, my mama or Aunt Bennie would wrestle me next to the stove and hold me there until the hot comb heated up. Now I sat watching Ms. Cynthia Jean get her hair pressed and was shocked that she could sleep like a baby.

"Out, ain't she?" Yvette said, looking over.

"She probably had a long day at school."

Ms. Cynthia Jean was the speech therapist at Mulberry Elementary. She worked with first through fifth graders and taught them not to speak slang. Elementary school teachers could wear shorts and T-shirts, but Ms. Cynthia Jean always dressed nice. Today she had on a long denim skirt and a long sleeved sweater, even though the weather hadn't turned cold yet. Ms. Cynthia's skin was actually lighter than Deena's and always made me think of Ritz crackers. I knew she and Mr. Henderson had two little boys, but she only brought them to the shop once in a while. There was nothing you could really point out that would lead someone to cheat on her. She was pretty, always smiled and spoke to everybody, and didn't even snore.

We all kind of whispered as she slept in Aunt Bennie's chair—legs crossed, chin on her chest, and lips partway open. She looked like a black Snow White.

After her hair was straightened and curled, and she left, Duke said, "That's a shame. It's almost Christmas."

"Yeah?" Yvette answered. "Well, ho, ho, ho."

"You're so wrong. Crazy self," he said, grinning.

Aunt Bennie just frowned and said she was going to pray.

"Do you think the woman always knows?" I asked my mother

at dinner that night. She was scraping the last potatoes onto her plate.

"Knows what?" she asked, chewing.

"You know, if her husband is cheating."

"Ahem," my father coughed. "What brings this on?"

"Everybody thinks Ms. Cynthia Jean's husband is playing her for another woman, and Aunt Bennie said she probably knows."

"Is that why we got you working at the shop, to be in grown folks' business?"

"I'm not in anybody's business. That's just what's going on."

"You know we don't want you gossiping," my mother said and looked down her nose at the mashed potatoes. Like even they knew she had taught me better.

"I'm just asking a question."

"When two people love each other, they don't have to worry about cheating, especially if they get a lot of *loving*," my father said, and then he winked at my mama.

"Ew, gross, Daddy!" To hear my father make a crack like that was way too much. In my eye my parents were just roommates that went to church together, split bills, and each had their own end of the couch. I didn't think about them cheating because I never thought about them doing it.

My disgust, however, didn't faze my father, and he left the table chuckling. I wanted to repeat my question, but then my mother said, "Somebody named Charles called for you. Wanted to know if you had made up your mind about the dance."

"He did? He did?"

I kissed my mother on the forehead, and asked to do the dishes later. If Peanut had mentioned the dance to my mama, that meant he must really like me. My mind was made up. Who cared what my friends thought or did, I was going to my first dance with a junior!

I was almost to the hallway and heading to my room when my mama called me back and said, "It's true, Rashawn. About women. We can always tell."

Christmas came closer, and the palm trees shook like pony-tailed girls in the cold. It was the week of the Winter Dance. Two weeks had passed since Mr. Rufus had snuck by and scooped up the lady-in-whatever-color Deena. She and Ms. Cynthia Jean still kept their regular appointments, and whether Ms. Cynthia knew it or not the shop was mad on her behalf. We had discovered that Deena wasn't the sharpest knife in the drawer so now *everybody* cut their eyes when she came in, but since Yvette was her beautician she snubbed her most. One time I tried to pencil her in wrong just to do it, but "D-e-e-n-a" was looking over my shoulder and caught me.

By Wednesday before the dance I was used to taking sides, but like Aunt Bennie said, everything comes to the light.

At five o' clock as usual, Deena strolled in wearing an outfit that made us all jealous. She wore a turquoise-colored cat suit under a brown leather jacket, and I tried not to notice her matching heels. Duke went into this coughing seizure, but other than that, she sat down in silence.

Then at five-fifteen, guess who walked in after her? *Ms. Cynthia Jean*, fresh from school. Bible study had been cancelled.

"What you doing here today?" Aunt Bennie asked her, panicking.

"Come on back to the sink," Yvette told Deena fast.

"Well, I thought I'd come in early, since church was cancelled. Rufus and I are going to dinner on Friday night."

"I got too many," Aunt Bennie said. "You're going to have to come back." It was an obvious lie because her chair was empty and Ms. Cynthia Jean looked confused.

"You don't think you can squeeze me in?"

"Yeah, Bennie. I think your six o' clock cancelled," Duke said.

And as if the fire needed one more stick, Ms. Geraldine clip-clopped in.

"Cent-Jean," she cried. "You're here on a Wednesday." Then, in a deeper voice: "Are you the only one here this Wednesday?"

Poor Ms. Cynthia Jean. She patted Ms. Geraldine's hand, not

understanding, and said, "No, Ms. Geraldine. There are lots of people here with us."

"Oh, just come on. I'll take you," Aunt Bennie snapped, and Ms. Cynthia Jean scooted over to her chair.

The next hour was crazy, moving them back and forth. It was like a terrible, slow game of foosball. I was supposed to fill the candy jar but kept dropping Now-A-Laters. Yvette and Aunt Bennie made eyes at each other, and Ms. Geraldine made loud conversation. I guess Ms. Cynthia and Deena were in their own worlds though because neither one of them paid the other any attention.

At six-twenty, we almost had them out when some kid yanked the door open and yelled death. "Anybody here know a blue Lincoln?"

Ms. Cynthia Jean was holding still for the comb, and Deena was under the dryer, but Yvette, Duke, Aunt Bennie, and I froze. None of us had to look to know the blue, two-timing Continental.

Still, forever meddlesome—the big mother hen—Ms. Geraldine asked, "What kind is it?"

"It got a dent on the side."

So Ms. Cynthia Jean said, "That's Rufus. He got side swiped last week by the garbage man. Tell him to come in." I moved from a chair near the door to the corner, which gave me a better view in case something broke out. "Tell him to come in."

It was five long minutes before Mr. Rufus appeared, and when he did the salon jerked into slow motion.

Mr. Rufus stepped in the door. Deena raised her dryer. Ms. Cynthia lifted her eyes. She called to him. He looked at her. Deena stood up. Ms. Geraldine coughed. Mr. Rufus turned around. Deena opened her arms. Ms. Cynthia noticed Deena. Deena smiled, all teeth, and said, "Rue?"

I had seen a nature show one time where some tourists were taking turns having a snake dropped around their neck. Everybody laughed like they were having the most fun of their life, except for one woman who, when that snake touched her skin, jerked loose so fast the snake's body snapped in the air before dropping to the ground. That's how fast Mr. Rufus pushed Deena away, so hard he made her bump into a dryer.

Ms. Geraldine's eyes were big now, and her legs kept slapping together like they wanted to leave without her and go tell somebody. Yvette stood with a hand on her hip and just looked mad, and Duke started to laugh but caught himself.

By this time, Ms. Cynthia had pulled away from the hot comb and stood up, the top of her hair all fanned out. "What is going on?" she said.

"Cent—" Mr. Rufus answered, pulling on his sleeves. "I thought you had Bible study tonight."

"It was cancelled. Who is this?"

But then she figured it out.

If I traded away my eyes, I still wouldn't forget the expression on Ms. Cynthia Jean's face when she realized her husband had a girlfriend. She looked like someone who had been cut and was going through the shock before the pain burned and ached, when you either bit down on your lip or leaned back and cursed. She looked like kids do when someone mean tells them Santa Claus isn't real. Like you would if your house burned down. Hurt. Shaky. Alone. I never wanted to be in her shoes.

That Thursday I was so depressed I decided I didn't want to go to the dance. I couldn't stop wondering 'what if it had been me.' What if someday I walked down the hall and saw Peanut with another girl, hugging and kissing her by his locker? What if I found out that everybody knew and was watching, just waiting for a hamper to fall over with my dirty laundry?

I felt bad. I had never stopped to think how Ms. Cynthia Jean might feel if she ever really found out. I had been so caught up in talking about it, toeing around her, that I forgot that it might just happen. All those sly comments I had laughed at. The way I deep down expected a fight. I even felt bad for penciling in appointments.

Every time I wrote down a Wednesday or a Friday was another time I went along with the charade.

I was also angry with everyone for casting stones at Deena because it turned out she was just as surprised as Ms. Cent-Jean. I was even angry with Aunt Bennie because she stepped in too late, waiting until Deena took a swing at Mr. Rufus before clapping her hands and saying, "No, no, not in here. Rufus, you follow Cent-Jean on home."

I was this close to canceling my date with Peanut, but when I called Tanika she talked me out of it.

Friday of the dance, Yvette and Duke rehashed the scene from the day before, not content unless they were blowing on cold ashes.

"I mean, that was just plain dumb—bringing both your women to the same shop."

"Chile, men don't know how to be slick," Yvette said. "Men leave the peanut butter and jelly on the counter and then ask how you know they made a sandwich."

I suddenly got so tired of their all-wise, too cool, hands in the business, but out of the pot commentary, that I blew. "Can we PUHLEASE talk about something else?"

Aunt Bennie looked proud of me as I walked back to the sinks, but I was hoping she would be quiet too.

Under the water I felt duped, like I had been set up to believe a lie. People did what they shouldn't do and didn't know what you thought they should. Everybody said Ms. Cynthia had to know, and nobody figured that foxy Deena didn't. So what did Aunt Bennie and my mama know then? What could anyone know about anyone else? While Aunt Bennie massaged my scalp, trying to soothe away my feelings, something else that had bugged me foamed to the surface.

I had always thought that cheating men had a nasty twinkle in their eye. They walked guilty, either real proud or embarrassed, and I thought women could spot them as easy as Payless Shoes. But when Mr. Rufus came in the shop, he didn't fit with my description. He looked . . . *nice*. Hardworking. Honest. He looked like someone who would marry Ms. Cynthia Jean. And then another thing I saw which scared me more than that was that every other woman in the beauty salon thought the very same thing. For a moment, just a second, Yvette, Aunt Bennie, and two other women who had overheard the scandal all seemed to question, "Could that be my man too?" And then I wondered if my mama knew how wrong she was when she had answered my earlier question, and I thought of my daddy winking, and I started to cry.

"What's wrong? What's wrong, baby?" Aunt Bennie asked, cutting off the water.

I curled up in the chair, my body heavy. "You just c-can't trust nobody," I moaned, and all my tears ran to one side.

"Ohh," Aunt Bennie said, shushing me. "Sure you can. Trust God."

We walked back out to the salon chair holding hands and with me blowing my nose on a towel.

"What do you want?" she asked, pumping the chair up.

"Crimps," I said, and sat back to wait until she was done. When she turned me around, everybody oohed and aahed, which made me a feel a tiny bit better.

So there I was, walking into the huge Mulberry gym, holding hands with a cute eleventh grader. The blast of cool air surprised me, coming in. I had always imagined the dances as hot and sweaty. The rickety bleachers were pushed back into the wall, and red and green bells made out of crepe paper hung above all the entrances. We got there late on purpose so most people would already be dancing, and I could see Tanika and my other friends skipping around. I felt nervous holding Peanut's hand and started to wonder how many people there might know something about him that I didn't. But then Bobbi Brown's "Tenderoni" came on, and Peanut pulled my arm, smiling, "Girl, you know this is our song."

We walked together to the center of the floor and then slowly put our arms around each other. Anybody looking would have seen the perfect couple: me, in my long crochet vest, tight black shirt and purple jeans, and Peanut in his leather jacket and Kangol. I leaned against his shoulder but didn't close my eyes, inhaling his cologne and the gym's funk. Other couples moved to our same rhythm, but a lot of people stood on the side and watched. This was life around me, and I couldn't know what would come my way, but in my heart I still hoped for love.

# DREAM HOUSE

BARBARA BEAN

Tony was a friend of Hank's. He ran Tony's Foreign Auto down on
Walnut Street where Hank had taken the BMW practically every
Friday like a ritual, five hundred more dollars down the drain. Now
Julia was left with that car, with its sheepskin seat covers and its
smell like crackers laced with sheep and some faint motor smell,
more delicate than gasoline. The car was running pretty well now,
but when Friday came she took it in to have Tony check the oil and
the transmission fluid. Tony was wearing old khakis, grease-stained
and baggy, and an unbuttoned cotton shirt. He was sitting in the
swivel chair in his office, surrounded by papers and small parts,
drinking out of a coffee mug that said "Good morning, sweetheart."
He brought it to his lips just as she came in. Now that Hank was
gone, Tony seemed like a good person to call in an emergency. She
was running out of money.

"Listen, could you by any chance use an assistant? Someone to
answer the phone, do the paperwork?" A small wind could have
knocked her down.

Tony looked at the mess in front of him. "An assistant is exactly what I need," he said. "Start on Monday."

Julia got back in the car and drove home, out to the fanciest subdivision in this small university town, where she and Hank lived. All the houses on their street had security systems. After Hank left, she had disconnected theirs. It made her nervous. When she pulled into the driveway, there was a young black man in khaki shorts standing on the front porch of the house, ringing the doorbell. Julia felt a wave of embarrassment. It was a huge house with a sun porch, a tower, a music room. "I don't really live here," she said, stepping out of Hank's car. And then she laughed. "Well, I do. But we're not rich."

"I know what you mean." He held out his hand and she took it. "I'm Emmett. Collecting for the Citizens' Action Coalition."

She opened the front door and invited him in for a glass of ice water. "My husband inherited some money and spent it all to build this house. And then some." Hank was bad with money, and she was worse. She believed all the adages about money. Can't buy love. Root of all evil. Still, she liked the refrigerator with its ice machine on the door. She fixed herself and Emmett a glass of cold water. The sunny kitchen stretched on forever with its acres of Saltillo tile bearing the paw prints of coyotes who had walked across it while it dried in the Mexican sun.

Emmett drained his glass and looked around. "Amazing house," he said.

"I know," Julia said. "He thought of everything." Skylights and windows from floor to ceiling in every room. Surround sound. Outlets, phone jacks, stereo wires everywhere. He had hovered over the framers, worrying about light and symmetry. Julia had shivered when he called it his dream house. "Never say that," she said. "You can't build a dream house. A dream house is only a dream. It can never be real." He tried to build a house so perfect that no one would ever want to leave it. But their son Josh left for college. And then Hank left.

Julia got out her checkbook. Emmett waved it away. "I understand if you can't afford it."

"It's OK," she said. "I got a job today."

Julia was sitting at the kitchen table. She could see the morning glory vines strangling the bee balm and cone flowers in Hank's garden. At the edge of the yard where the trees were thick, a brown dog sniffed the grass. The remains of dinner lay sprawled across the table.

"What are you looking at?" Luke said, standing up.

"Weeds. A brown dog."

"Looks like a chow.'"

Luke was living in the basement. He was a friend of Josh's who had grown up with him in their old neighborhood of small houses and no sidewalks. He needed a place to stay for the summer and she had plenty of space.

On the other side of the yard was the vegetable garden. It seemed important to make sure the gardens thrived in Hank's absence.

"I'll help you weed," Luke said. He had been borrowing books from her since he was ten. She'd told him that Hank was away on business.

"Thanks," Julia smiled.

Luke sat back down. He was wearing a faded purple T-shirt and his hair almost covered his eye on the right side. "Do you believe in true love?" They had been talking about Erika, his girlfriend.

"Depends on your definition of true love," Julia said.

"Erika's favorite movie is *Romeo and Juliet*."

Julia laughed. "My own son doesn't see why polygamy is illegal." Before Josh left to go up to Ann Arbor to his summer job, the three of them sat up late, talking. "But what is *inherently* wrong with it? I mean if all the people involved agree. It's not bad for your health, like smoking. Who decided to make it illegal in the first place?"

"Yeah, but Josh is weird," Luke said. "What's your definition?" His eyes were unwavering.

"Man. Ask me something hard." She was thinking that all her life she had been unfaithful. She had gone to graduate school in classical studies, never finished her thesis, never kept a job for over a year. She had gone to four different schools in college—each time transferring when she fell in love, packing her bags, cleaning out her desk, listening to a new story, about mountain climbing or mysticism or the beach between Jacksonville and St. Augustine. She wished she could be more like Hank, steady and faithful. She wanted to tell him that, but he had given her no phone number, no address where she could reach him.

*I'm up here in Wisconsin,* his first postcard said. *Saw an old friend from college. I'm fine. I'll let you know when I'm coming home. Love, Henry.* She'd never gotten a postcard from him before—they'd never been apart long enough. The handwriting looked unfamiliar. On the front of the postcard were some men from the fifties at a food convention. *Henry?* she thought.

On Monday she drove the BMW, a 1979 Bavaria, to work. It was wide and difficult to steer, like a room going down the street. Hank's things were still in the glove compartment. Tools, geodes, garden seeds. When he left, he took the new Toyota, a much more reliable car. The Bavaria might not have gotten him past the city limits. Hank liked things to be reliable. When he was young he'd had a BMW motorcycle—BMWs, he told her, were the motorcycles people drove across China when there were no hand tools or repair shops available in the whole country. *Not this car,* she thought.

Tony kept no pictures of his wife Nancy in the garage, Julia noticed. "I want to keep her out of this place," Tony said. Julia loved the garage, its chaos and complexity. Above his desk was an Egon Sheile calendar. Tony had studied art in graduate school, he told her. The garage had been his father's. He lit a cigarette and hunched over his coffee in the office where only a little light came through the dirty window. "Nancy," Tony said, "is a nomad. She camps out in airports, travels all over the world. She's a photographer. She's gone a lot."

"That must be hard."

"Not for Nancy. She loves it."

At lunch time, Tony said he was going to the bowling alley to eat. Julia hinted that she would like to go along. She took in the smell of the bowling balls, the shoes, the alleys, the smoke. "What would you like, hon?" the waitress asked. Tony ordered a beer and a cheeseburger. Julia ordered a BLT. Next to her he smelled of smoke, of grease, of clean clothes, his dark-skinned hand wrapped around his beer. She could see Tony's intelligence in his hands, the well-trimmed nails like clean, sweet faces rimmed with black. Swift mechanic's hands. She put her hand up to her chest, over her heart. Tonight she would try to locate Hank, call her mother, cook dinner for Luke, although Luke was a good cook—better than she was—he would make pancakes for dinner tonight, or mushroom fettucine with fresh tomatoes from Hank's garden, she could almost guarantee it.

"You OK?" Tony asked.

"I'm fine," she said, trying not to let panic rise. Where was Hank?

The Citizens' Action Coalition man came back that night when she and Luke were sitting in the empty house eating pizza from Mother Bear's.

"Hey," Julia said. "You're back. What's up?" He had a blunt, kind face. "Want some more water?" He followed her into the kitchen and Luke convinced him to eat a slice of pizza.

"I hardly know you," he said, "but I'm going to ask you a big favor." He needed a place to stay, he said, until he could earn a little money at his job at the movie theater, get back on his feet. After they ate, she took him up to the music room; he could put his sleeping bag beside the piano. It was Hank's favorite room, the room he had spent the most money on with its banks of windows and tall green plants and Oriental rugs. Hank meant to play again; he had once been a jazz pianist, gotten several gigs in high school and college and then let it go. She wondered what the neighbors would think if she knew she was living with Luke and now Emmett—this was a neighborhood of doctors and businessmen and their wives who had eyed them suspiciously when they began to build the house.

It was Emmett who got the dog to come inside with some hamburger. It had a shaggy thick coat, wolf-head—exactly the dog Hank always wanted. It didn't look hungry. It looked rich. As if it were just out for an evening stroll. But she knew it didn't belong to anyone in this neighborhood; it had no collar. Luke named him Chewbacca. She was relieved they'd gotten the dog inside. She wanted the dog to be there when Hank came home, a present for him.

After dinner she called her mother. Emma still lived in the farmhouse she was born in. Julia's father had been born a mile down the road. She told her mother Hank had been gone for almost two weeks and she wasn't sure when he was coming back.

There was a long pause. "It's dangerous to let a man go too far away for too long," she said. *Or a woman,* Julia thought. He was the one who had left her alone in his big perfect house.

"It's not like I have a choice, Mother."

"Better find out what he's up to."

"Remember all those trips Daddy took?" Her father had sold corn syrup. As soon as he left town on the train, her mother took her to the carnival, where she won prize after prize for Julia shooting down ducks and paper targets, hitting the bull's eye time after time. She and her mother and sister would clean house, have the great aunts over for pears and dumplings, eat watermelon on the front porch. Her father always brought back gifts, champagne, danced with her mother around the living room, singing "Let me call you sweetheart."

"We had fun, didn't we?" Emma said. "But Hank doesn't travel for a living."

"He's just visiting old college friends, Mother," Julia reassured her.

Julia looked forward to going to work every morning, getting out of the house, driving Hank's car. He had left a tape of the Talking Heads in the tape player and she played it over and over, bringing a sachet of lavender that dangled from the rear view mirror to her nose while she waited at the stoplight. *Where had it come from?* In the office she answered the phone and talked to customers while they waited. She knew nothing about cars, but she was discovering that there was sometimes no logic involved when things went wrong. One woman's car was making a mysterious whirring noise that disappeared as soon as she brought it into the shop. "Try resting it for a week," Julia suggested. "Sometimes I think cars just need rest." Tony and the other mechanics were all busy in the back. The woman agreed to try it.

On Friday about 4:30 it began to rain, a hard steady rain at first. By closing time, there were cracks of thunder and lightning strong enough to split tree trunks right down the middle. Rain drenched the cars parked outside. Tony came out of the back room, wiping his hands on a rag. "Any chance you could give me a ride home? I don't have my car."

"Sure," she said.

Tony's house was so old it still had radiators. There was no real trace of Nancy here either, except she did find a picture on the sideboard in the dining room of a woman who looked nothing like the Nancy she had imagined. This woman looked rather fragile, even delicate, possibly blond. The picture was blurry. Maybe it wasn't her. She put it down quickly. "Where's Nancy?" she asked when he came up behind her.

"She's on a job. Out in Arizona. Photographing buttes."

"I was hoping to meet her."

"You will, you will. One of these days."

He swallowed something he was holding cupped in his hand. "Back's been bothering me," he said.

Tony had gall bladder attacks, shin splints, prostate infections. Once when she came into the garage, before Hank left, his arm was in a sling. "Car accident," he said. "Somebody ran a red light." Chain smoked. He was always falling apart, breaking down, openly, without pretense.

There was a thunderclap so loud it seemed to be right inside the kitchen. Rain blew against the windows.

"Maybe you better stay for dinner," Tony said. "Toasted cheese sandwiches?" He stood in front of the refrigerator, holding the door open. "And strawberries. Where's Hank keeping himself these days? I haven't seen him in a while."

"Gone. He left," she managed to get out.

Tony didn't seem all that surprised. He poured the strawberries into a blue bowl. "Can you cut up some melon, too?" he said. "Why? Where did he go?"

"All I know is that he's in Wisconsin somewhere." She sat down. "I was hoping you might know."

"I didn't really know Hank that well. We talked cars." Tony opened two bottles of Corona and set them on the table. "Why do you think he left?"

"I'm unfaithful," she surprised herself by saying.

"Really?" he said, looking up.

"It's the one sin people can't forgive you for. "

"I don't know about *that*." He slid one of the golden sandwiches into the skillet.

"No, it's true. Ask anyone. Divorce, shoplifting, losing all your money, *anything* except that."

Tony wiped his hands on his jeans. "Did Hank know?"

"No. I don't think he knew anything about me, really. I don't know why he left. He took me totally by surprise." She sat up straight.

"This is your punishment?" Tony said. He set the sandwiches and the fruit on the table.

"Right." He accepted her logic like a gift, didn't shift his glance. "Have you ever been unfaithful?"

"No." He took a sip of beer. "You gotta have at least one person who believes in you."

Tears filled Julia's eyes. "I've always wanted to be that way," she said. "Devoted. Selfless."

Thunder rattled the windows; they could hear the wind tossing the trees outside. The lights in the kitchen flickered and died. All the appliances gave a last sigh and were quiet.

"Hang on," Tony said. "I'll get candles." She could see the glow of his cigarette as he felt his way into the dining room. There was a small crash.

"Here we go," he said. He set two large candles in the middle of the table, turned on a portable radio on the window sill above the sink. The local station warned people to stay indoors; the storm had knocked down several large trees, there was flash flooding.

"You better stay," Tony said.

She called Luke and Emmett to see if they were all right. She could hear the bass notes of "Lady Madonna" rumbling in the background. Luke said that was Emmett playing the piano. They had found the flashlight and candles. "Somebody saw a tornado touchdown in Whitehall," he said. "So stay where you are."

She and Tony sat at the kitchen table drinking more Coronas with limes, telling stories, almost until morning, until the candle burned out.

"You remind me of a teacher I had in college," Tony said. "She used to sneak into my dorm room at night disguised in a man's overcoat and fedora."

"Why?"

"She was lonely. My grandmother sent me cake, dried figs, walnuts—she used to devour it after we made love. My grandparents were extremely religious—Jews, mystics, charismatics. She wanted to know all about my grandmother's marriage. She wanted to know if it had been all devotion and baking cakes and spirituality, or if there had been other things. One night she left in a bad thunderstorm like this. I gave her my umbrella. There was so little I could do for her once she left my room. She was much older than I was, but all that disappeared in bed. We were like children in a way then." Tony sat hunched over the table, his thick, black hair curling behind his ears. He had on a soft white cotton shirt that looked billowy and luminous against his dark skin. "Mind if I have another cigarette?" he said.

"Of course not. I like the smell of smoke."

"Tell me about your unfaithfulness," he said.

"OK." Julia took a deep breath. "There was a man much, much older than I was, sixty years old, a man I met when we lived in Milwaukee."

"Um-hmm," Tony murmured. "And?"

"A long time ago, there was a neighbor across the street, a friend of ours who played the saxophone."

"OK. And?"

"Josh's sixth-grade teacher."

"That's it?"

"More or less." Julia turned her fork over. She didn't tell him about the awkward hug Luke had given her in the hallway late at night after one of their talks, or the way she crept into the music room to watch Emmett play the piano, the way the music he played moved her. Those things were nothing. "What happened to your college teacher?"

"She got tenure. She was actually a very good teacher." He was playing with the candle wax, making a little ball with his fingers. "No one ever found out about us. I think even if someone had recognized her they wouldn't have believed she was sneaking in to be with a skinny kid like me."

"Did she get married?"

"After me, she lived the life of a sad recluse."

"Yeah, right." Julia smiled.

"I don't really know. I used to make this grog for her on cold winter nights that she said tasted like apple pie. She wanted things I couldn't give her, I think."

"What?

"Complete, steadfast love. Loyalty."

"Yes. Of course. That's what she wanted."

Julia lay upstairs in Tony's spare bedroom. He was just down the hall, behind his closed door. She felt like she was sleeping in an abandoned railroad hotel, or a guest room in a recurring dream. She loved everything in the room—an old table with a silver-backed mirror and a hazy landscape on the wall above it in a gold frame, the clean quilt on the bed. *I belong in this room*, she thought. Outside in the dark she heard a train whistle moan. On the bookshelf were Meister Eckhart, *The Thirteen Petalled Rose*, *The Cloud of Unknowing*.

She had found an old T-shirt in a drawer and undressed in the dark, pulling the T-shirt over her head, taking her clothes off underneath it, afraid to look at her body. She slid between the cool sheets. She felt defenseless in the huge T-shirt, much too small, and as if she had never had sex before in her life. She would not even know how to begin. When she closed her eyes she could smell the dark fabric of Tony's overcoat that she had found hanging in the closet. Lightning lit the room every few minutes. It seemed like her old life was crashing apart in the storm. She didn't know if Tony came in through the closet door or the door in the hall. She didn't know if she was asleep or awake, dreaming or remembering something that happened a long time ago. But the door gave easily and the T-shirt provided no protection, no cover at all.

"What are you wearing?" he said, as if it filled him with pain.

He ran his hands up under the T-shirt swiftly.

"I can't stay," he said.

"I know," she said.

"Good night," he said and kissed her with his tongue.

He ran his small hand over her stomach. "I have to go," he said.

"Go," she said.

In the morning, Julia looked around the kitchen for some sign of Nancy—a pair of running shoes left behind or jewelry on the windowsill, but there was nothing. She imagined her sitting across from Tony like this in the morning, eating strawberries. She knew what she looked like now—hair short so it would dry fast, nothing extra to weigh her down, no earrings or make-up. Cotton underwear. Speedo. Everything she needed could be packed into a tiny bag. No rings on her fingers.

"What are you looking for?" Tony asked her.

"Nancy."

Tony laughed. "I'll tell you something. I have this skin disease. There's no cure for it, really. It's OK now but a couple of years ago it flared up. Touch was painful. Sex was impossible. I had to take long baths. Wear shirts buttoned up to my neck."

"But you have beautiful skin," she said.

"Nancy stayed home then." *Bathed him,* Julia thought, *dried his skin with a soft white towel, not afraid to look, brought him food and books he loved, read to him when the pain was bad. Sitting across from this man every morning, you could never think of being unfaithful. You would lie awake at night dreaming of gifts to bring him, surprises, comforts. It wouldn't be limiting as you had once feared. You would give up everything for this.* Julia could feel it as clearly as she felt the strawberry on her tongue. She could picture Nancy sitting in the third chair at the table with them, businesslike, eating swiftly. *How did you give it up? The risk, the unknown?* Julia asked her. In Julia's mind, Nancy daintily patted her mouth with a corner of her snow-white napkin. *It's nothing compared to the risk of loving completely. That's more mysterious than anything you've done, and better.*

Julia knew she was right. She imagined the blue and red shadows of Tony's naked back, his sharp hipbones, his legs, the tenderness in his fingers—what sex, what touch, what *breathing* itself would be like then, like drinking from a cup again and again, a cup of delicious wine, dark and engulfing, with no bottom.

In the morning when she got back to the big house, Chewbacca growled at her before he realized it was her. On the desk by the phone was another post card with a picture of dairy cows grazing on the back. *Julia*, it said, *I found a diner I like where I go to read the paper everyday. Everyone is surprised when I know the names of their flowers. Love, Henry.* Diners? Hank liked to hang out in diners?

Julia opened the refrigerator and took out the silver pitcher Hank insisted on using for orange juice and which took up half the top shelf of the refrigerator. She poured herself a glass of orange juice. It had belonged to his mother and Julia had always hated it.

Emmett wandered into the kitchen. He had obviously spent some time getting dressed—his shirt and T-shirt were two interesting shades of red and he smelled clean, sweet.

"Emmett," she said, "I think I'm going to get rid of some things."

"Like what?"

"This pitcher. Look at it. What kind of person would use a silver pitcher for orange juice?"

"I'm not sure that's the way to get Hank back, though, giving away his stuff. Don't you want him to come home?"

"More than anything."

When she first met Hank, she had no idea he'd be a good father. She met him on the beach in Florida during spring break her junior year of college. He stood down by the waves in a pair of cut-offs, smoking. He looked like a skinny farm boy with a sunburn. He looked like he swam in watering holes with ropes, like he'd never seen the ocean before, but it turned out his parents were wealthy and he'd traveled around the world. He looked like all he wanted was whiskey and women and a good time. He had bedroom eyes. He looked like nothing but trouble, too good looking to ever be reliable. They drank in the Florida bars until four in the morning, until Hank passed out on her motel room floor. Her roommates stepped over him politely.

But when Josh was born, he stopped drinking and smoking. They went back to the beach in Florida, and Hank carried Josh to the ocean, covered his chubby body with suntan lotion, made sure he wore his little hat. He stood patiently in the ocean with Josh on his hip, letting the waves lap the baby's toes until he was not afraid of the water, until he was slowly immersed in the ocean. He did the laundry in emergencies, packed their lunches, both hers and Josh's, for she too was always going off to school. When she or Josh was sick he sat by their beds with wet washcloths, brought them juice to drink, held their foreheads while they vomited, a devoted husband and father.

Julia began marking things for a yard sale. What didn't sell, she would give away. Hand-embroidered linens that had belonged to Hank's grandmother, the set of luncheon silver that his Aunt Clara had given them for a wedding present, his father's books, Aunt Evelyn's music box, his mother's silver candlesticks. Hulking pieces of furniture—sideboards and dressers and china cupboards and sofas. Hank's old shirts and pants, some of which he still wore. Emmett and Luke agreed to help her carry things outside, though Emmett looked worried. She moved out things that Hank had been saving for the future, pieces of cherry he meant to build things with, and whole stacks of magazines he meant to get around to reading— *Scientific American* and *Downbeat* and *BMW News*. He didn't need any of it. You could live in a place as small as a shell or a nest or a drawer, she would tell him, nestle in deeper and deeper.

The next thing she got from Hank was a letter, not a postcard.
*Sometimes my old life comes back to me in a picture, just one picture from one day*, he wrote. *I see Josh going through my closet looking for that shirt of mine he liked to wear, getting ready for school. Meg told me a story about how at work one of her patients told her she saw ghosts and Meg said, 'I have a friend who sees ghosts,' and she was reprimanded by the staff for reinforcing her hallucinations. But in the sane world, isn't that all we do, reinforce each other's hallucinations?*
Julia sank down beside the bed, all her strength gone. His old life? Meg. Who was Meg? Julia didn't have to be told. On her dresser

she kept a picture of Hank at nineteen in Italy on a college trip, leather jacket, head down, one leg forward. Meg was on that trip, a tall girl in a jumper. She was a doctor now? A therapist? She couldn't imagine Hank apart from her and Josh. He had never been like other men. Always cautious, sticking close to home, to safety. Like a mother. She closed her eyes. Outside the bedroom window she could hear the thudding of a basketball, children shouting to each other. She let the reality of it wash over her like a cold black sea.

Tony invited her to play cards with his regular Friday night poker group at his house, since one of the regulars couldn't make it. Nancy was once again away on a shoot. The other men seemed a bit uncomfortable with Julia being there, but Tony was so matter of fact about it, so easy with it, that as it got later the other men relaxed, too. They passed around a bottle of malt liquor and when she a took drink from the bottle, they relaxed. She was glad to be there. Tony was letting her farther into his world. From Tony she would get no false promises, no imaginary world of permanence, like the one Hank had always promised. Just this, cards. King Cobra malt liquor. He was smoking a cigar and wearing a brown vest. "Look," he said when she came in and pointed to the top of his head. "Stitches." He had scraped his head on the underside of a car after she'd gone home, had to go to the emergency room. The rest of the men, George and Bill from work, others she didn't know were joking about it, teasing him.

"I'm sorry, Tony," she said gathering up her cards. She wanted to kiss him through his thick hair, hold him, but this was poker. She barely knew the rules. It was like white-water rafting, hanging on for dear life, trying to keep up, to not be a nuisance. Dealer's Choice. Between the Sheets. Five Card Draw, Hi-Low. She played blindly, on raw instinct. Texas Hold-em. Once the phone rang. "Hi, baby," she heard Tony say in the other room. Not for anything would she be on the other end of that phone, trade places with Nancy. She liked being here in this room with Tony. She won the last pot, all the money.

As she was going out the door, he said, "Any word from Hank?"

"Just a letter." She hitched up her purse, weighed down with her winnings.

"Don't worry, Julia." He gave her a long, close hug before he released her into the dark.

Hank's next letter said, *I don't tell anyone my story here, I don't let anyone know who I am. I found a diner I like where I go to read the paper everyday. Have I mentioned that?*

*There's a sound like pigeons cooing in my ears when I wake up in the morning, not an unpleasant sound, but it blocks out everything else. By midday I can start to hear again. People's voices sound odd to me, perhaps because I'm a stranger here. I can hear how the inflections have developed as a truce with their pain.*

*Everyone I've met here smokes. I wandered into the kitchen in the middle of the night and there was a tall man standing by the dishwasher, tall and rangy like a retired pitcher or outfielder. 'Have you seen Annie?' he said in a hoarse, soft voice. Annie is Meg's sister. 'No,' I said, 'Isn't she in her room?' Then he wandered out of the kitchen again.*

*'He's my boyfriend,' Annie told me later. 'He has lung cancer.' You should see them together, him in his bathrobe, she running home after work to be with him every minute, the way they are together. So kind and in love. I bought a pack of Camels. I'm keeping it in my desk drawer. Henry*

"Sometimes I think Hank has gone mad," Julia told Tony. It was afternoon. George and Bill were working on the cars. Hank's BMW was up on blocks. The transmission was acting up again, but it would be ready in time for her to drive home. She and Tony were playing a game of gin in the office with a deck of cards missing the jack of diamonds, bending the rules to fit. Tony took a sip of his coffee. When the light hit his eyes from the side she could see the green in them, she could see through them. "Mad, huh?" Tony bent over his cards, arranged his hand.

"He hates people who smoke. Weakness of any kind for that matter. Infidelity, betrayal." She discarded. "But now he's—seeing this woman." Julia swallowed, fought back tears. "She smokes—her whole family smokes. He even bought cigarettes."

Tony paused, looked at his cards, took Julia's free hand in his. "I'll tell you a true story. There was a man who had been married for fifty years to a woman he deeply loved. But they had never been able to have any children. It was the only real sadness in their lives. One day this man saw a young woman. She looked at him and caught his eye and they fell in love and began seeing each other." He picked up his cigarette and blew smoke above her head. "His love for her was like madness. He couldn't resist it or hide it. He had to tell his beloved wife and friend. He left her and married the young woman and they had two children together." He looked at Julia. "That man was my grandfather."

Julia stared at him. "Then which one was the devout grand-mother?"

"The first one, my first grandmother. They were both my grand-mothers."

*I left because you didn't know who I was*, Hank's last letter said. *You thought I was a loving, faithful husband, but really I was scared of screwing up. I was doing everything according to some manual in my head of how to have the perfect marriage, be the perfect father, the perfect hus-band. Now the unthinkable has happened. I find myself living with Meg. All I want now is to come home.*

Finally, Hank called one night when she was baking bread for dinner. "Julia," he said first, "I've let you down."

"Things break down," she said. "I understand that. Cars. I'm working for Tony now. The BMW is still running, but you can't believe how many things go wrong. Bodies. Tony cut his head open, had to get stitches. The house." She was talking fast but she knew she was going to have to tell him. She thought of how he loved reliability, safety, loyalty, of how hard she had tried to provide him with the illusion of that all these years. "Hank, remember Miles Palmer, that painter we knew in Milwaukee? I slept with him."

When Hank came back it was on a Friday after work and everyone was there. Nancy was out of town again so Tony had come over for dinner. Later, she would imagine how the house must have looked to him when he came in the front door: the security system disconnected, the great gaping dark downstairs rooms, empty and hollow except for Emmett's and Luke's bicycles which they had been keeping in the living room, a three-dimensional puzzle of the Empire State Building Luke was putting together, a bird's nest on the kitchen window sill, a red velvet chaise lounge. He would have had to walk through those strange rooms to find them. They were upstairs in the music room, finishing dinner and drinking beer, listening to Emmett play Gershwin on the piano. Hank stood in the doorway of the music room and put down a small suitcase. He was wearing a blue shirt she had never seen before, old jeans with holes in the knees, boots.

"How are you?" he said.

She wasn't ready. The gardens needed weeding. The entire crop of carrots was lost. Bugs were eating the tomatoes. Chewbacca, who didn't take well to strangers, growled. Emmett and Luke were no longer really looking for another place to stay; they were comfortable here. She had taken the Bavaria's slip covers in to be cleaned, there was some trouble with the starter motor. Tony and Luke were playing a game of chess and they barely looked up when Hank came in.

"Hank," she said.

"Henry." He smiled.

"Henry," she corrected herself.

Luke stood up. "You remember Luke?" she said. Emmett nodded in Hank's direction from the piano bench. "This is Emmett form the Citizen's Action Coalition," she said stupidly. "And Tony of course."

Tony smiled and waved, one hand poised over his knight.

"I'm sorry about the house—" she began. "I made some changes."

Henry took out a cigarette, tapped it against his wrist. He lit it, shook out the match. She could see his hands shaking. Now she could really see him, see where he'd been. He seemed to be standing in a cone of light. He smoked! He had fallen in love. Lost all the money he'd inherited. His car was falling apart. He was trembling with fear and uncertainty. He had left without telling her where he was going. His dreams had crumbled all around him. And he had come back. The man she loved.

# HOME COURSE ADVANTAGE

CLINT McCOWN

Even while he was gluing the new set of grips on Mrs. Davies' old *Patty Berg* irons, Rod couldn't stop thinking about the carcass of the dog. The dewfall would have settled over it by now, which he hoped might dampen the smell. In the three days since he'd cut too sharply into the parking lot and caught the mangy stray unawares, the temperature had seldom dipped below ninety. This morning a couple of the club members had complained. The odor, they said, had been sucked in through their car air conditioners. They wanted it taken care of. The Member-Guest tournament was just a few days away, and a lot of out-of-towners would be coming in for practice rounds. It didn't speak well of the Club to leave a dead dog at the entrance to the parking lot.

So Rod had called the Highway Department to see if they'd come out and get the thing. They said they would, but it might take a couple of weeks—most of their trucks were tied up in the Route 15 bypass project, and roadkills had become a low priority. He told them he'd take care of it himself and as he hung up the phone he made a mental note to pass the chore on to the Wickerham kid, who was running the grounds crew this summer.

But then the special shipment of Izods arrived, the one he'd ordered to beef up his sweater stock before the Member-Guest weekend, and he had to check the merchandise for damage. When he'd finally logged in all the stock numbers, he set to work assembling the eight-foot cardboard alligator they'd sent as a new promotional display. He was still trying to insert tab M into slot Q when Bev came in from the snack shop to tell him the freezer unit was making clacking noises and defrosting itself again. It took him half the afternoon to track down Ed Betzger, who held the service contract on all the Club's appliances, and by the time Ed had the unit working again, the ice-cream bars were showing clear signs of strain. So Rod had to call Teddy Mumford, the Club's insurance agent, to find out how far the meltdown had to go before the bars could be claimed as a loss. Here there was a point of contention. Teddy said a partial melting didn't constitute spoilage, and as long as the ice cream was uncontaminated it could still be sold. Rod explained that the bars didn't even look like bars anymore, but Teddy said the snack shop could feature them on the menu, as a novelty item. Refrozen ice cream sounded exotic, Teddy told him, like refried beans. Rod said maybe it was time the Club got a new insurance agent.

Of course, that would never happen. Rod ran the day-to-day operations of the Club, but the Board of Directors made all the financial decisions; and Teddy Mumford was a member of the Board.

The injustice galled him, and as soon as he got off the phone with Mumford he stormed into the men's locker room to air a few complaints. But it was too late in the day, and there was no one there but Glen L. Hanshaw, himself one of the oldest Board members, sitting naked on the bench in front of his locker. It was a disconcerting sight, and Rod lost his momentum.

"Look at this crap!" Glen said, and he held up a pair of boxer shorts. "I haven't had these a goddamn month, and just look at them—the elastic's all shot to hell!" He threw them into the bottom of his locker and kicked the door closed with his foot. "I swear to Christ!"

Rod didn't know what to say, so he looked at his watch and hurried on down the row of lockers.

"Hey, wait a minute!" Glen pushed himself up from the bench and followed Rod to the side door. In the diffuse light of the windows, his skin took on a bluish pallor, like a body washed up from the sea. "I had a complaint about you today," he said. "Did I tell you?"

"What's the problem?"

"Shirley Davies says you were supposed to get her clubs back to her two weeks ago."

"The new grips haven't come in yet," he lied.

"Well, she was all over my ass about it." He ran a bony hand over his scalp. "I hear she's having a little trouble at home. Probably just needs to take it out on somebody. Anyway, I told her you'd take care of it. Right?"

Rod shrugged. "I'll see what I can do. If it's a holdup at the company, I know who to call. But if it's a problem with the shipping, we might have to reorder."

"Good man." Glen slapped him on the shoulder and padded off toward the showers. He moved unnaturally, Rod thought, as if he were picking his way across hot gravel. Strange what nakedness could do to some people. In his loud shirts and double-knit pants, Glen was the tyrant of his Cadillac dealership; here at the Club, all the kids who worked in the pro shop were afraid of him. But now he seemed just one more small animal caught outside its territory. Rod didn't know why, but the thought depressed him.

He climbed the stairs to his workroom and set about re-gripping Mrs. Davies' old irons. He got out the new grips and settled in on his bench by the window to start stripping the shafts. Only then did he remember that he'd never spoken to Jimmy Wickerham about getting rid of the dog. Now it was too late—the last few twilight stragglers were just coming in off the course. The grounds crew would have left hours ago. If Rod wanted the carcass disposed of before tomorrow, he'd have to do it himself.

It took him longer than usual to do the re-gripping. Somehow he mispositioned two of the new grips and had to strip both shafts and start again. The seven iron gave him particular trouble. The glue had hardened in a lump where the left thumb gripped the shaft, and though he knew Mrs. Davies would never know the difference, he couldn't let the imperfection pass. The seven iron was his favorite club, his luckiest club. He'd once holed out a hundred-and-seventy-yard approach shot with a seven iron on the final hole of the Doral Open. The eagle jumped him to eighth place, his best professional finish.

By the time he was satisfied with the positioning of all ten grips, it was after ten o'clock. He turned out the workshop light and stood for a minute by the window facing the highway. It was a moonless night, but the mercury-vapor lamp above the machine shed cast a yellow haze across the deserted parking lot. The dog lay just inside the edges of the light, and Rod could see clearly the dark lump waiting for him on the carpet of manicured grass.

But what exactly was he supposed to do with it?

He couldn't just sling it into the clubhouse Dumpster. The container wouldn't be emptied until next Tuesday morning, and six days of Dumpster heat was the last thing this dog needed.

He couldn't dump it anywhere on the course because the grounds were so immaculately trimmed it was impossible to hide anything larger than a golf ball. The only exception was the bramble thicket that ran along the out-of-bounds to the left of the third hole, but that entire stretch was usually upwind from most of the course and there was too much stink left in the animal to risk it.

He sure as hell wasn't about to load the remains into the back of his new Audi and go cruising around the countryside looking for a safe drop zone. He'd bought the car because he thought it might foster an image of stability and class—two things his ex-wife had often said he lacked—and he was certain that a lingering bad-meat smell would undercut his efforts. Besides, his trunk was full of all the unfinished paperwork he was supposed to be handling for the Club.

Of course, he could always take the Teddy Mumford approach of cheapskate practicality—run the carcass through the tree mulcher and spray the remains along the fairway for fertilizer. Even as he laughed at the thought, he felt a twinge of guilt. Mumford wasn't such a bad guy, really; he was just trying to keep the Club's premiums low. It had been a heavy year for claims against their current policy—there'd been some major plumbing and electrical problems, a fire in the women's locker room, vandalism on two of the greens, and a lot of theft. In the last two weeks alone they'd lost over eighteen thousand dollars' worth of equipment: three electric Cushman golf carts and a small tractor-mower. The insurance rates were bound to go up. Teddy had even told the Board that unless the Club could find a way to hire a night watchman, the home office might not let him renew their policy at all.

Rod hoped they would hire a watchman. He also hoped they'd hire a Club manager, an accountant, a full-time assistant for the pro shop, and a couple of bag boys to help clean the members' clubs. Then maybe he'd have some time to work on his game. The way things stood now, he almost never got out on the course, and in the four years he'd been Club pro, he'd lost a lot of ground. His putting was pretty much the same as ever—it came in streaks, and he rarely missed anything under five feet. But he'd lost some of his touch on pitch-and-run shots, and even with his wedge he couldn't seem to make the ball bite the way it used to. His overall game was about four shots worse than when he'd started here. At that rate he'd be a duffer long before retirement age.

He knew it was his own fault. Nobody had forced him to take this job. In fact, he'd been happy to get it. The course had a good layout, and even though the Club ran on a pretty tight budget, enough money went into maintenance to keep it one of the finest nine-hole operations in the state. He didn't have to be ashamed of working here. Besides, he'd gotten tired of running with the rabbits, of driving from tournament to tournament all season long, scrambling for some share in the winnings. In three years he'd only

CLINT McCOWN

made the cut nine times, and his career earnings wouldn't even cover his gas money. He quit the tour the week after the Doral Open, when his visibility was high enough to land him this steadier job. He didn't regret it. Even rookies had been finishing higher than Rod in the tournament standings, and the truth that sank into him after Doral was that eighth place was as high as he would ever go.

It was just as well, he told himself. He loved the game, but he wasn't cut out for business, and success made a business out of any game. Suppose he'd won the U.S. Open, or the Masters, or the PGA Championship: corporations would've come beating down his door for product endorsements. They'd have turned him into a "personality" and designed some ridiculous logo for his autographed line of leisurewear.

He did wonder what the logo might have been. Some animal, certainly—they were all animals. Alligators were already spoken for. So were penguins, seagulls, bears, jaguars, sharks, pandas, bulls, mustangs, dolphins, zebras, kangaroos, hawks, elephants, and flamingos.

No dogs, though—or at least none that he'd ever noticed. Certainly no dead stray dogs. No bloody, bashed-in half-breed German shepherds embroidered with infinite care into the tight weave of cotton-Orlon-Dacron-acrylic. If he ever did hit the big time maybe that could be his logo. He might even insist on it.

He picked up Mrs. Davies' seven iron to double-check the feel of it, and made his way downstairs and out the rear of the clubhouse. The night air was cool, and from the way the wind was gusting through the trees, he guessed a storm front might be moving in. Long rolls of heat lightning shimmered across the southern sky.

The window of the machine shed was unlocked, as usual, and Rod had no trouble reaching in for the shovel he knew would be hanging on the inside wall. As he walked across the lot toward the dead dog, a feeling of lightness came over him. Once he got the creature in the ground, the whole affair would be over. He'd never have to think about it again.

The night, he soon discovered, was the best possible time for the work. He'd been right about the smell: without the constant prodding of the sun, the flesh had sunk back into a more passive state of decay, and the dew seemed to keep the odor from rising. Only occasionally did little stabs of corruption dart up on the breeze, and by keeping the wind at his back and breathing carefully he was able to avoid most of the stench. The flies seemed to have settled down for the night—or maybe the wind was now keeping them at bay—and while there were probably slugs and other night workers swarming the rotten underside, they were all invisible, hidden by dog or darkness, so Rod could work easily, with his eyes open, in a way that would have been difficult for him in the full light of day.

The one thing that did bother him was the collar.

From the moment the animal had sprawled with a single yelp under the left front tire, Rod had avoided looking at it closely. He'd glimpsed enough to know the dog was a mixed breed, and from its general scruffiness he'd assumed it to be a stray. Now a queasy fear came over him that he'd open the morning paper and find some pathetic plea for the return of a family pet: Lost, in the vicinity of Route 30 west of town, a brown-and-black dog, part shepherd, answers to the name of. . . .

A silver tag gleamed in the pale light. On it, Rod knew, there would be some identification, but he couldn't bring himself to bend his face down close enough to read what the inscription might say. Instead, he carefully hooked the head of Mrs. Davies' seven iron underneath the collar and began to drag the dead dog toward the putting green. The body stayed perfectly curled, firm now as a piece of sculpture as it scraped along the gravel lot. The weight of the thing surprised him. Until now he'd thought of the carcass as just a husk, and it amazed him to realize that the dog was no less substantial for the fact of having died.

He circled below the putting green and drew the dog alongside the practice bunker. The raised lip between the bunker and the green spread a less diluted night across the sand so that at first the trap seemed bottomless, a sinkhole yawning in the grassy slope. But soon his eyes adjusted, and the shadow gave way to the dingy sparkle of the sand itself. It was a perfect spot. The digging would be easy here, and when he was through there would be no broken turf to give the grave away.

He stepped down into the bunker and began shoveling the whiter top sand into a far corner to keep it separate from the brown foundation grit and the reddish dirt that lay below. It took him only six or seven minutes to work his way down through the natural layer of topsoil, and though his progress then slowed from the increasing density and rockiness of the ground, he continued to make headway.

It felt good to work the shovel in the earth, so good he started humming as he dug, improvising variations on a single jazzy theme for nearly half an hour, until suddenly, as he strained to pry loose a stubborn, buried stone, it came to him what song it was, and with that thought the sound of it died away in his throat. It was a song that had haunted him for weeks now.

He didn't even know its name, but he took it to be an old blues number, maybe from the Billie Holiday era. The lyrics were hazy to him—some usual fare about love gone wrong—but what still burned in his mind was the one time he'd heard it, sitting in Herr's tavern drinking his fourth double Scotch, alone at a corner table in the otherwise crowded bar. A woman, heavily made-up but still somehow breathtaking, swayed on a low platform by the far wall and sang, with her eyes closed, in the voice of a grieving angel. Even through the smoke and the room's dim amber glow, he could see that her hair was red, deep red, and it clung in damp curls to her cheek and forehead. Her pale skin seemed unearthly, perfect, fragile as glass. Rod could have believed she was all the beauty left in the world; and that she was dying, now, in front of him. He envied her the grandeur of such public despair.

When her song was over, she opened her dry eyes and smiled warmly at the crowd, nodding to specific groups for their whistles and applause. Then her whole face brightened—she'd spotted some-one at Rod's end of the room—and without hesitation she climbed down from the makeshift stage, her bent leg spilling through the slit in her gown. She wove her way between the tables toward him, and he watched her intently as she moved, fascinated by the ease with which she'd left the song behind, like a snake shedding skin, or a butterfly, maybe, abandoning an outworn cocoon. It wasn't until she reached his chair that he realized he was the person she was crossing to meet, and before he could offer up any question she flung an arm around his neck and kissed him earnestly on the mouth. He was as stunned as if he'd been hit by a truck.

As she drew her face away from his, he opened his mouth to fumble toward some trite compliment about her singing, but before he could manage even a syllable a dark change came into her eyes, and she pulled herself up straight.

"My God," she said, her right hand fluttering to her cleavage. "You're not Randy!" A bubble of embarrassed laughter broke from her throat, then she turned abruptly toward the stage. "Hey, Marcie," she called, "look at this guy!" Half the heads in the room turned in Rod's direction. "Doesn't he look just like Randy?"

A woman from a table near the bar seemed to struggle for a moment with the task of bringing Rod into focus, then sank back into a confused frown. "You mean that's not him?"

"Hell, no! Can you believe this? And Christ, I just gave him a big wet one." Several people laughed, and she turned again to Rod. "Sorry, sugar. Thought you were somebody else." She patted him on the cheek and threaded her way casually to the bar.

Rod felt like she took his whole identity with her. It was as if for a few accidental seconds, he'd seen himself through her eyes and found that he was utterly invisible, a man so bland he could enter a look-alike contest for himself and still come away the loser. A shudder ran through him, and a spinning rose in his head that nearly tipped him over. He left the tavern without finishing his drink.

By now he'd achieved a pit nearly three feet deep, which he judged sufficient. He tossed the shovel into the hole and sat heavily on the upper rim of the trap. He was more than winded: the work had turned nasty toward the end and now ropes of undeveloped muscle began to knot along his back. He probably wouldn't be able to swing a club for a week. Still, he felt a sense of accomplishment, and in his sudden stupor of exhaustion he felt less finicky toward the condition of the dog—though he resisted the impulse to pat its mangled head.

The wind was stronger now and felt good against the side of his face, but the change in weather worried him. Clouds were swirling in thick and low, and if he didn't get the dog below ground in a hurry, he might end up soaked when the bottom dropped out. He pushed himself up from the bank and grabbed Mrs. Davies' seven iron, which was still hooked under the collar. The dog slid easily down the slope to the edge of the grave.

"Roll over!" Rod said, and with a twist of the iron the carcass disappeared into the hole. "Now, stay!" With some difficulty he retrieved the club, then tamped down the body with the shovel. The snug fit pleased him, though he felt somehow disconcerted that in the underground darkness he couldn't tell whether the dog had landed on its back or on its stomach. He even thought about getting a flashlight from the clubhouse to find out, but in the end fatigue convinced him to let it go. The dog wouldn't care, so why should he?

He was just pouring in the first shovelful of dirt when a pair of headlights swept across him from the highway. He froze like a startled animal and watched a large flatbed truck wheel into the lot. It pulled up by the machine shed fifty yards away, and a burly man in overalls climbed down from the cab. Rod saw at once that the man was ill at ease. Body movement, after all, was his specialty: he knew how to read imperfections in a stance, a turn, a swivel, a follow-through; and he watched this trespasser now with a coldly professional eye.

Whatever the guy was up to, it seemed to Rod that he needed

lessons. There was a tightness in the man's shoulders, and he moved his head with a birdlike jerkiness as he scanned the dark outer reaches of the lot. Rod knew he was too far away to be seen, particularly by anyone standing so near the security light, so he kept still and let the blind stare pass through him. There was something appealing in this—in seeing without being seen, as if he were no more than a ghost—but the interest Rod had in that aspect of the situation was offset by the column of stench now rising from the pit at his feet. He set the shovel down gently in the sand and eased his way upwind to the cleaner, whiter corner of the trap. He was just crouching below the smooth cut of the lip when the man in the lot let out a loud, shrill whistle. Rod thought at first he'd been spotted, but then he realized that the man wasn't looking his way. He was turned toward the machine shed with his head cocked to the side as if he were listening for something.

Rod listened, too. Except for the wind rustling the trees, everything was quiet. Even the crickets and frogs from the drainage ditch behind the first tee had grown still under the expectation of rain.

Then the man whistled again, but instead of waiting for a response he reached in through the window of the truck and took out what appeared to be a small tackle box. The next few steps were all too predictable. After so many years of golf, Rod knew how to trace a trajectory, and had only to watch the swing to know where the ball would land. When the man walked to the rear window of the machine shed and climbed inside, Rod could only shake his head. God, how he hated amateurs.

He climbed out of the trap and walked across the parking lot to the truck, Mrs. Davies' seven iron in hand. For a moment he considered bashing in the windshield, but gestures like that were more dramatic than effective; and anyway it might hurt the club. Instead, he just took the keys from the ignition and walked calmly back to his bunker. It was a good first move, he told himself. Every match hinged on psyching out the opponent.

A minute later the front door of the shed swung open and one of the new Cushman gas-powered carts came nosing silently out. Apparently the man had been unable to hotwire it, in spite of his tool kit, and he now trotted alongside the cart, pushing and steering at the same time. He maneuvered the Cushman into position behind the truck, then pulled out a pair of long planks from the flatbed and propped them in place as a ramp. After lining up the steering for a straight shot at the boards, he got behind the cart and heaved it forward. Rod thought this a foolish technique—the wheels could easily miss one of the rails or skid over the side halfway up to the truck. But the man seemed unconcerned, and when the front left wheel did slip from its plank, he was able to hold the four-hundred-pound cart level as he walked it forward into the bed of the truck. Rod was glad he hadn't smashed this guy's windshield.

As he watched the thief slide the planks back onto the truck, Rod wondered why he hadn't just slipped into the clubhouse and called the police. What made him think he had to handle this himself? He'd always been a smart money player, always staying with the high-percentage shot; and he knew better than to try to clear a hazard when the odds told him to play up short. Still, it was too late to worry about it now. The time to think was before the shot; never in mid-swing.

He took a golf ball from his pocket and dropped it into the spongy grass just off the apron of the practice green. Then he took a narrow stance almost directly behind the ball and opened the face of the seven iron. It was a trick he'd learned for putting more loft into a club, and though he'd never used the shot in competition because it was too difficult to control, he'd always known it was there if he needed it. He took a full swing across the ball, playing it more or less like a bunker shot, and with a sharp *click!* it vanished upward into the night.

The man across the lot was just lashing the cart to the flatbed when the clean sound of contact froze him in place, still as a photograph. For a full five seconds he held his pose, listening into the darkness. Then with a loud metallic *thunk,* the ball came down on the hood of the truck. It broke the stillness like a starter's gun, and the man bounded into the cab of the truck, slamming the door behind him.

Rod walked forward into the light and crossed the parking lot in long, brisk strides, like a tournament leader approaching the eighteenth green. He paused by the rear of the truck and for a long moment the two men stared at each other's reflections in the side-view mirror. At last the door swung open, and the cart thief climbed slowly out.

He was bigger than he'd seemed from across the lot—maybe six foot five—and old enough that middle age had parceled his bulk evenly between muscle and flab. His face was round, almost child-like, with a dark, sparse beard that sprouted in random patches over his cheeks. As he faced Rod in the gravel, he tucked his hands in his overalls with an air of defiant calm. His mouth hung slightly open, and his dull eyes looked haggard even in the dim light. Rod felt certain the man was not a golfer.

"Evening," he said. The man nodded and coughed, but didn't speak. "I notice you've got one of our carts here."

The man glanced briefly to the cart, then took a studied look around him, as if he'd only that moment realized where he was. "Yeah, well, we got a call to pick it up for some repairs. The transmission's gone bad."

"You work odd hours."

The man shrugged. "Some days are like that."

Rod reached up and touched the fiberglass body of the new cart. "You know, I hate these bastards. They're an insult to the game."

"That so?" the man asked, nudging the gravel with the toe of his work boot.

"Yeah. They kill the grass. Most of the really good courses don't even allow them on the grounds." He shook his head at the cart, which gleamed in the glow of the vapor lamp. "But we're not exactly the Augusta National here, so I've got to put up with them. I even have to fix them when they break down. So I know you didn't get a call from anybody."

The man's slack-jawed pose fused into a more natural scowl. "Then you must have my keys," he said, and started toward Rod, who shifted into a bunker stance and drew the seven iron to the top of his backswing.

"Buddy, I know how to use a golf club," he said. It was one of the few positive statements he could make about his life, and he was amazed at how little impact it had. The man hesitated for a moment—only for a moment—then, with his eyes fixed on the thin shaft of the iron, he gave a skeptical snort and lumbered into range.

The swing Rod used was smooth and relaxed—so much so that even the cart thief himself might have thought it was a halfhearted effort. But the timing was there, and that's where the power lay in golf. There was a trick to it, like ringing the bell with a sledgehammer at the county fair. Rod rang the bell now. With a good body turn and a snap of his wrists, he transferred the entire momentum of his arc into the club face. This was no stubby punch shot for getting out of tree trouble, but a full swing and follow-through, the kind that cuts down hard behind the ball and takes a deep, long divot. It did so now: the heavy blade caught the lower edge of the man's right kneecap and moved on through the shot for a clean, high finish.

With a startled gulp, the man tottered slowly sideways and crumpled to the rough pavement, too stunned at first to utter a sound. But that moment passed, and he launched into a shrill whine as he squirmed frantically on his crippled leg.

Rod stepped back to gauge the damage: the club was okay; the guy would be on crutches for a while. "I'm really sorry about this," he said.

The man glared up at him and spoke through clenched teeth. "I oughta kill you, you son of a bitch!" He looked as if he had more to say, but a fresh pain twisted through his leg and kept any words from forming. He turned his face away with a groan and began to rock back and forth in the gravel.

"I could call a doctor," Rod offered, but the man ignored him. He rolled onto his left side and whistled once more like he had when he'd first climbed down from the truck. The effort hurt him, and he groaned again. A queasiness rose up from the pit of Rod's stomach. "What are you whistling for?" he asked, though he thought he knew.

A strained smile broke across the man's face. "Somebody to tear your goddamn arm off," he said, and fell into a giddy laugh.

"It's a dog, isn't it?" Rod asked.

"It's a bitch," the man answered, and began to giggle uncontrollably. He leaned his weight back on his elbows and tried to straighten his leg in front of him, but the knee wouldn't unbend. "Christ," he said, still giggling, "what the hell have you done to me?"

"I think you've gone into shock," Rod told him.

The man lowered his head to the gravel and lay as still as he could through the small spasms of laughter, taking slow, deep breaths until he finally brought the pain under control. At last he raised himself up and leaned heavily against the grimy rear wheel.

"What about the dog?" Rod asked.

The man sighed and stared down at his crooked leg. "She got away from me last week," he said.

"What the hell do you mean she got away from you?" The sharpness in Rod's tone surprised them both.

"I mean she jumped out of the truck to run down a rabbit," the man said, now keeping a wary eye on Rod's seven iron. "I couldn't wait around."

Rod hacked the club hard into the pavement, sending up sparks and a small spray of stones. The man flinched and huddled closer to the wheel.

"You asshole," Rod shouted. "Don't you know better than to leave a dog to run loose by a highway?"

The man shrugged. "I came back," he said.

[309]

Rod hated simple answers. They weren't enough. Besides, they always seemed to back him into corners. For as long as he'd been a part of the game, he could remember only two times when he'd given in to simple answers, and both times he'd felt cheated.

The first was when he was a boy, playing with his father's clubs. His father had been a left-hander, so for his first two years in the sport, Rod had been a left-hander, too. Then when he was twelve his father bought him a right-handed set. He was furious about having to start learning all over again, and he demanded a reason for his father's forcing him to give up so much ground. "You're not left-handed," his father told him.

The second time was when he decided to quit the tour. He felt the same frustrations building up in him now, as if he were still somehow playing on the wrong side of the ball. "You can keep the cart," he said.

The man narrowed his eyes. "What?"

"I said you can keep the cart. We've got insurance."

The man slowly pulled himself up on his good leg and steadied his weight against the side of the flatbed. "That doesn't sound right. What's the catch?"

"I want you to give me your dog."

"What?"

"I want your dog."

The man looked around uneasily. "I told you, I already lost her."

"Then there shouldn't be any problem. From now on we can just say she belongs to me."

"And that's it?"

"That's all."

The man chewed on the inside of his cheek for a moment, and nodded. "Yeah, okay. Sure." Then he frowned. "What about my keys?"

Rod pointed to the darkness at the lower end of the lot. "There's a sand bunker just below that ridge," he said. "You might start looking down there."

The man eyed him suspiciously. "How am I supposed to do that? I can't even walk."

Rod extended the club head toward him. "You can have this."

The man reached carefully forward and took the iron from Rod's hand. "Okay," he said, then shifted his weight onto the shaft of the club and limped away from the truck. He circled wide around Rod and made his way cautiously toward the edge of the dark. Rod watched him until he'd reached the bunker, then took the keys from his pocket and tossed them through the open window of the cab.

He'd have to order Mrs. Davies a new seven iron. She'd be mad as hell when he told her he'd lost this one. She'd probably try to get him fired. But that was okay. Sometimes you just had to give up what you were used to, or you might never get anything right.

For now, though, the only thing he wanted to think about was hitting a bucket of range balls. He'd lost a little control lately, he knew that; and if he didn't work on it, his problems would only multiply. Golf was an unforgiving game, with no use for shortcuts or excuses. A good swing was built on fundamentals. The grip, the stance, the take-away, the body turn, the follow-through—all had to be kept in balance. If one went wrong, the rest collapsed like a house of cards.

He would start with his wedge to see how his short game was holding up. Then he'd work his way right up through the driver.

But he'd have to hurry. The wind was rising stronger now, and it swept in from the course with the clean smell of the coming storm. To the south he could see the glow of the town lights against the low-hanging clouds. The rain hadn't hit quite yet, but it would before long.

He knew it was bound to.

# ALL SAINTS DAY

ANGELA PNEUMAN

Word was that the missionary kid had a demon, though no one was supposed to know. The Boyd family was visiting East Winder only for the weekend, and already eight-year-old Prudence had heard it from her younger sister, Grace, who heard it from her new friend, Anna, whose father was going to cast it out. Prudence figured that a cast-out demon would look like a puddle of split pea soup the size of a welcome mat, and that it would move around the room, blob-like, trying to absorb its way into people. Her own father, the Reverend Yancey Boyd, didn't believe in demons or in talking about demons except to say he didn't believe in them, end of discussion.

"The demon made Ryan Kitter paint himself purple all over," Grace said.

"*All* over?" Prudence asked, "even his privates?"

"That's how they found him," Grace said. She was six. "The paint dried up and he was crying because it hurt him to pee."

The girls stood in front of the mirror in the spare room at the Moberly's house. It was the afternoon of November first, and that night there was an All Saints Day party for kids at the First United Methodist, where the Reverend Yancey Boyd might be the new minister. Prudence was busy cutting a slit for Grace's head in a piece of old brown sheet. Everyone had to go as someone from the Bible, so she was turning Grace into John the Baptist with his head on a platter.

"There's no such thing as demons," Prudence said, only because she hadn't been the one to hear the story first. She hacked at the sheet with scissors, the blades dull as butter knives. When she managed a hole, she threw the sheet over Grace's head.

Ryan Kitter's whole family were missionaries. They had returned from Africa ahead of schedule, due to the demon, and were camping in the church basement until they found a house. They got to cook on hot plates and take sponge baths. Prudence thought that if anyone deserved to camp in the church basement it was her own family, since her father was the one who might be the minister. He'd been ordained in three states. At the Moberly's house, the girls were stuck in a dark, damp room that smelled like motor oil. Before the Moberlys had done it over for their daughter, who was grown, it had been a garage, and twice already Prudence had seen centipedes, one rippling into a crack between cement blocks, one behind the framed picture of Jesus over the bed.

"Ryan likes to be in a dark room," Grace said, pushing her head through the hole in the sheet. "And he doesn't talk to anyone except his mother."

"Well, maybe he doesn't have anything to say," said Prudence, regarding her with a frown. Grace still looked like herself, only in a brown sheet, now, blond hair coming out of her braid, and nothing like John the Baptist.

In the picture over the bed Jesus wore a robe with billowing sleeves and a rope belt, and Prudence needed something to tie around Grace's waist. She rummaged through the cardboard box of odds and ends that Mrs. Moberly had provided. At home in North Carolina, their mother kept old towels and drapes in a trunk, and a drapery cord would have done the trick. But at home they would not be dressing like Bible characters for a party; instead they would have already gone trick-or-treating the night before. They would have worn last year's outfits switched around—Prudence as a floor lamp, Grace as a blue crayon—since their mother wasn't in any kind of shape to make new ones. Here in East Winder, Kentucky, no one was of a mind to trick-or-treat, because Halloween was pagan.

"Ryan's father thinks he has a demon and his mother isn't sure," Grace said. "They took him to doctors, but a doctor can't do anything against a demon. Anna saw a man with a demon swallow a sword in Tennessee. She saw another demon bend a man in half when her dad tried to cast it out."

Prudence made it a point not to be interested. She said, "Really?" and "Hmmm," as she unearthed a scarf and tied it around Grace's waist, so that the ends hung down, then pulled and tucked at the sheet. She put her hands on her hips and stepped back to look. "Not bad," she said. "We'll draw you a beard with eye pencil, but you've got to have a knife or a hatchet or something to make it look real. And a platter."

Mrs. Moberly stood barefoot in front of the kitchen sink, peeling apples for a pie. Her feet were puffy, and they smooched against the linoleum. It looked like she'd picked her baby toenails clean away. Prudence's mother, who was still sleeping upstairs in the Moberly's bedroom, had always told Prudence to keep her shoes on; if anyone wanted to see her bare feet, they would ask.

"How're the costumes coming?" asked Mrs. Moberly through a mouthful of apple peel. She wore a blue and white checked apron and had made covers of the same material for the toaster, coffee maker and some other small appliance that Prudence couldn't make out by its shape.

"Fine," Prudence said. "Could we please borrow a meat cleaver?"

"A meat cleaver?" Mrs. Moberly's hands stopped, knife poised over a peeled, cored apple. It looked naked and cold. "What Biblical character used a meat cleaver?"

"It's a secret," Prudence said, before Grace could open her mouth.

"A meat cleaver in church? I don't think so," said Mrs. Moberly. "Someone could get hurt. How about another idea? How about you go as a shepherd? Mr. Moberly has an old cane somewhere. Or Mary? Mary never used a meat cleaver."

"No one's *using* it," Prudence said.

"Meat cleavers are sharp," said Mrs. Moberly. "Meat cleavers are not toys. I don't think your mother would be happy if I allowed you to go to church with a meat cleaver. She's not feeling very well as it is." Mrs. Moberly sliced the apple into eighths in four deft strokes. "Your father tells me she likes apple pie."

"She's feeling fine," Prudence said. "She's just tired."

Mrs. Moberly looked at Prudence and smiled in the way adults sometimes smiled at Prudence, lips peeling back from patiently clenched teeth. Then Mrs. Moberly smiled at Grace, who looked at her feet. "What's that you're wearing, Grace?" Mrs. Moberly said. "Let me guess. You're Mary Magdalene, or Ruth."

Grace shook her head.

"Esther?"

"A man," Grace said.

"Moses?"

"It's a surprise," Prudence said again. "How about some tin foil? We could save it and you could use it again to cover something."

"Tin foil I can do," said Mrs. Moberly, and handed her the box. "Listen, girls," she said, smiling again. "What do you think of your visit so far? Think you might like to live here?"

"We won't live *here*," Prudence said. "We'll have a parsonage like at home."

"Well, yes," said Mrs. Moberly. "That's what I meant. East Winder's quite a town. I think living here would do your mother a world of good."

Prudence stared at Mrs. Moberly and raised her left eyebrow, something she'd taught herself how to do. Mrs. Moberly's eyes did not seem to be any real color. Under one eye, Prudence could see a tiny length of blue vein beneath Mrs. Moberly's skin, like a fading pen mark.

Mrs. Moberly blinked at her once and turned to Grace. "How about you, dear? Wouldn't you like to live here?"

Prudence answered for Grace as she pulled her towards the kitchen door. "We don't care," she said in her boredest voice.

*I don't care* was what their mother had to say about moving. Her name was Joyce, and *I don't care* was what she said about many things, usually at the end of a long, tired sigh. Then she'd talk on the phone to her sister, Char—who wasn't saved—and go to bed in the middle of the day, sometimes for days in a row, and when Prudence went in to kiss her goodnight she'd already be asleep and smelling like damp books. Yancey said it had to do with the baby who died before he was born in August, but when Aunt Char came to stay for a week she said no. She said this was Joyce in college all over again, or just Joyce waking up, finally, and coming apart, which he should have expected. Yancey said what's that supposed to mean, and Aunt Char said it means nothing, nothing at all, and that Joyce had made her bed. (Joyce used to testify, proudly, that her family in Greenville thought she was crazy for loving the Lord. She'd been raised twice-a-year churchgoing Methodist, not evangelical. Yancey's preaching had been what saved her before they got married, and Prudence could tell that Aunt Char didn't like that fact one bit.)

Back in the spare room Prudence emptied out the cardboard box of odds and ends. She cut the box apart at the folds, traced the top of Grace's head in the center of one of the long sides, cut out the circle and finally taped on sheets of tin foil. Then she fitted the whole platter over Grace's head and bunched part of the sheet into the hole at her neck to hold it steady.

Grace squinted at herself in the mirror.

"Do your head this way," Prudence said, leaning her head to the side and fluttering her eyelids. "Try to look like you just got your head cut off."

Grace stuck out her tongue and said, "Blllhh." Her head lolled to the side. Then she shrugged her head out of the platter and began cutting out a long, curved knife shape Prudence had drawn on another piece of cardboard. "They tried sending Ryan Kitter to regular school last week," Grace said. "He went to first grade with Anna King."

"Hmmm," said Prudence. She peered into the Moberly's closet where she'd already found her own costume. Behind the coats and jackets and Mr. Moberly's old suits hung several leotards clipped to hangers with clothespins, and one pink tutu, the tulle gone flat and limp as a newspaper, all from when their daughter had taken ballet. Inside a box underneath the pink tutu, Prudence had found a spangly halter top with matching tights and a long, gauzy skirt, store tags still attached.

Now Prudence took out the costume and laid it on the bed. The halter was red with long sleeves and tiny round mirrors sewn on and yellow embroidery everywhere. The neck and sleeves had silky yellow fringe, and at the bottom edge, just above where her belly button would show, the fringe ended in tiny wooden beads that clacked softly against each other.

"In the lunchroom he stood at the trash can and ate all the bread pudding and creamed spinach that nobody wanted, and when the teacher caught him and made him stop, he cried. Then he threw up, then he threw a fit and they took him right out of school." Grace stopped cutting, her scissors wedged deep in the cardboard, and eyed the costume. "Ooooh. Who are you again?"

"Salome," Prudence said. "The one who asked for your head on a platter."

Prudence slipped off her pants and pulled on the tights and skirt. She did a practice kick out to the side, and the gauzy material traveled up into the air with her leg then floated down. It was see-through. In the picture Prudence had seen in a book in her father's study, Salome was a dark-skinned, smiling, barefoot girl with her hair pulled back, wearing an outfit a lot like this one. Her arms had been raised high above her head, her body in mid-sway, a gentle version of the bump-and-grind Prudence had perfected from a dance show on television, before her father found out she was watching.

No wonder the king had wanted to give Salome anything she wanted. Prudence had curly dark hair, too—almost black—and now she pulled it into a ponytail so tight it made her eyes slanty. She moved her hips in a little circle and waved her arms, first out in front of her, then to her sides, then over her head.

"Does Mrs. Moberly know you're wearing that?" Grace said.

"Mrs. Moberly is a pain."

"I want to be someone who dances."

"You can't dance if your head's cut off."

"*You're* not even supposed to dance," said Grace, and it was true, though the Reverend Yancey Boyd said it wasn't because of dancing itself, but what dancing led to.

"This is different," said Prudence. "It's pretend."

Grace crimped tin foil onto the blade of the cardboard knife and began coloring the handle black with a magic marker. "Once a demon gets in, you act different," she said. "They get in when you get cut open and bleed. Anna's not allowed to have her ears pierced. In Africa, Ryan was crossing the street with their house woman and they got hit by heathens in a truck. They were holding hands and she died and he broke his arm. The bone was sticking out through his skin, and that's when it happened. Demons sneak in wherever they can, and someone has to get them out so you can go back to the way you were. Tonight Anna's dad is going to get the demon out of Ryan. It's a secret, because it's not that kind of church, but Anna's dad says it should be."

Prudence had the halter on over her shirt, and she was stuffing the bosom with Grace's dirty undershirt from the day before. "Stop talking about that," she said. "At the party they'll have to guess who we are, so I'll go first and do my dance, then I'll stop and say, 'Cut off the head of John the Baptist, voice crying in the wilderness, who

eats locusts and honey, and give it to me on a silver platter.' Then
you come on up and stand beside me."

"What do I say?"

"You don't say anything. We'll have the knife on the platter
and ketchup for blood and you just walk like this." Prudence staggered around the bed. "You could collapse, maybe, or just follow
me away. Wait and see. Everyone else will be Mary and Joseph and
Noah or some other dumb thing."

"A demon could have gotten into Mom when the baby came
out," Grace said.

Prudence stopped staggering. "No," she said. "She is just very
tired. She just needs her rest." Prudence kept looking at Grace until
Grace nodded. Then Prudence pulled up her shirt to see what the
halter would look like against her stomach.

"Ryan has a demon of shock," Grace said.

Prudence sucked in her stomach until it looked hollow. Sexy.
She turned her back to the mirror and looked over her shoulder for
the rear view.

"Mom could have a demon of tiredness," Grace said.

Prudence kept sucking in her stomach until it hurt. "Don't say
that anymore," she said, gritting her teeth. "That's the stupidest
thing I've ever heard."

The Reverend Yancey Boyd had eyes so light they almost weren't
blue at all, and wavy hair close to his head, and when he talked he
sounded wise. Aunt Char said that Joyce married him because he
looked like Paul Newman, and because he was sincere, though she
said it was no excuse. Prudence was used to women going weepy
around him, so it was no surprise when at dinner Mrs. Moberly
started sharing the heartache of their daughter.

Belinda Moberly had grown up and gone to college, began Mr.
Moberly (a good, evangelical college, put in Mrs. Moberly), and under the influence of a philosophy professor, said Mr. Moberly (who

was later fired, said Mrs. Moberly), she'd first become a Unitarian, and then an atheist. And she was living in sin, out of wedlock, with a firefighter.

"We did our best," said Mrs. Moberly. "I don't know what else we could have done."

Over the table hung a low, stained-glass chandelier that Mrs. Moberly had made in a class, which cast a ring of tiny yellow crosses around the walls of the wood-paneled dining room.

"She has a good foundation," the Reverend Yancey Boyd said to Mrs. Moberly, and he patted her hand. The patting of hands was usually Joyce's department. She took care of the comforting while Yancey did the talking. It wasn't a good idea for him to touch too many women. He was that handsome. "When children have been brought up in the Lord, He marks them for life. Children"— Yancey passed a hand over Grace's blond head—"have their own kind of openness to the Lord. They may grow up and try other roads, but something inside them always knows better. I believe your daughter has a great advantage."

The Reverend Yancey Boyd sounded encouraging, but he looked sad. Before supper Prudence had found him sitting on the bed beside Joyce, trying to make her eat some crackers from the tray Mrs. Moberly had fixed. Prudence couldn't see her mother's face, but she could hear her whispering how she shouldn't have tried to come, and Prudence had seen how the curl she'd put in her hair the day before, for the trip, had flattened out against her head.

"I don't understand it," Mr. Moberly was saying about his daughter. He was a plumber with shoulders so wide that Prudence didn't see how he could crawl under any sink. He split a biscuit in half and buttered it, and when he finished he put the whole bottom of the biscuit into his mouth.

"I tell her we want her to be happy," Mrs. Moberly said, "and she tells me happiness is overrated. She says she's as happy as she can be and live with herself. I ask her, but do you know Jesus as a *personal savior*, Belinda, that's real happiness—you know, Reverend—

and she tells me she would believe if she could, but she can't. I don't know what to do with her." When Mrs. Moberly paused to drink her water, her hand shook a little. "I guess we're not promised we'll always understand, are we, Reverend?"

The Reverend Yancey Boyd smiled in a way that made him look even sadder. "No," he said, "we are not."

Grace picked at her food. She had the nervous hiccups, which didn't sound like regular hiccups at all, but like breathing with little coughs. And she was chewing at the inside of her mouth, which she wasn't supposed to do. Once she'd made herself bleed. Prudence nudged Grace with her elbow, and Grace stopped.

By the time they reached the church parking lot that evening, it was dark and cold. The leaves smelled like fall turning into winter. Prudence had stuffed the platter down the front of Grace's long pink parka like a shield, to hide it, and she'd hidden eye pencil and lipstick and ketchup packets from Burger King in the pockets of her own coat. She'd put pants on over her tights and rolled up the gauzy skirt, too, because she thought Mrs. Moberly might recognize it before their turn.

"Where are the Kitters staying?" Prudence asked, as they walked through the parking lot towards the back entrance.

"Who?" asked Mrs. Moberly.

"The boy with the demon," said Grace, stomping up the cement steps to the door.

"What?" Mrs. Moberly said. She shifted a Tupperware container of cookies to her other hand and held open the church door. Inside she squatted down beside Grace and peered into her face. "What demon?"

"Never mind," Prudence said. "What do the Kitters sleep on? Do they have a bed or just nap mats? Do they have a sofa and chair and television or just Sunday school furniture?"

"I wouldn't know," Mrs. Moberly said. "I haven't seen it. It's their home, you know, for now, until they find a house. You can't just go charging into people's homes unannounced, even if they do live in the church."

"I wouldn't go charging in," Prudence said.

"You're going to have a great time at the party," said Mrs. Moberly, steering them down the basement steps. "Just think of all the new friends you'll make here." Mrs. Moberly spoke in a bright voice and smiled so forcefully her jaw muscles bulged.

They moved down a wide, dim hall towards the fellowship room at the far end, an open door full of light and spilling out muted voices. Three narrow halls branched off on either side of this wide hall, and at these dark openings the air came cool and quiet. Prudence lagged behind and slipped down the last hall before the fellowship room. She tried two doors, but they were locked. She peered through the long narrow windows over the doorknobs, but it was too dark to see anything.

Mrs. Moberly appeared silhouetted at the mouth of the hall. "Did we lose you?"

"No," said Prudence.

The fellowship room was full of kids and parents. A girl wearing a dingy white sheep hood with ears, her straight hair sticking stiffly out around her face, came right up to Grace and hugged her.

"Hi, Anna," Grace said. Prudence disliked hugging. She ignored Anna and checked the back of the room where tables had been set up with punch and treats, and the front of the room where kids were jumping off a foot-high wooden collapsible stage.

Mrs. Moberly hovered. "Why don't you take off your coat now," she said to Prudence. "It's warm in here, and look, Anna's in her costume."

"I'm cold," Prudence said. "We both are." She shivered, for good measure, and so did Grace.

Mrs. Moberly smiled the hard smile.

"It's very cold in here," Prudence said. "Someone should probably do something about it."

If the Reverend Yancey Boyd had been there he would have

made her mind Mrs. Moberly, and then he would have marched her back to the house and made her change. He didn't even want her wearing a two-piece bathing suit that showed her belly in the summertime, much less a skimpy dance costume. But tonight he was the guest speaker at a youth lock-in across town, at the high school gym. Their mother had been the one who'd planned to come to the All Saints Day party.

"I'd be happy to carry those cookies into the kitchen for you," Prudence said, taking the Tupperware container from Mrs. Moberly.

"Well, sure," said Mrs. Moberly. "But don't go running off. You'll want to meet some girls your age."

In the kitchen across the hall, a tall, thin woman with red hair was slicing through pans of Rice Crispy treats. "Are you Al and Debbie's youngest?" she asked Prudence.

"No," said Prudence. "I'm Yancey and Joyce's oldest."

"Oh yes," said the woman, "the new pastor's daughter. I'm Mrs. Spode."

"He *might* be the new pastor," Prudence said, but she said it in a nice way.

"He will be if my husband and I have anything to say about it," said Mrs. Spode. She lifted out sticky squares with a spatula and stacked them on a plate. "This church needs someone to get it back on track. People get some strange ideas."

"What ideas?" Prudence asked.

"Oh, nothing for you to worry about," said Mrs. Spode. "Is there a costume somewhere under that pretty coat?"

"Yes," Prudence said, but just then a small Mary entered, holding a blue hand towel that was a Mary-headpiece for Mrs. Spode to pin back on. Then another woman led more children into the kitchen because it was almost time to line them up for the costume show. There were two Marys, a Joseph, a Moses with swimming pool kickboards for tablets, a donkey, a sheep, a shepherd, a Noah, and a King David with a paper crown. Mostly they looked like children wearing pajamas.

Prudence found Grace and herded her into the corner. She unzipped Grace's coat and extracted the foil-covered platter. With eye pencil she sketched on a mustache and was working on the beard when she felt a poke at her shoulder.

"Well, now," said Mrs. Spode. She reached down beside them and touched the platter. "What's the story, here?"

"I'm doing her beard," Prudence said. "She's John the Baptist."

"Oh, terrific," said Mrs. Spode, clapping once. "We don't have a John the Baptist yet."

Prudence smudged the pencil marks into Grace's skin with her fingertips. Grace said, "That's my platter," trying not to move her lips.

Mrs. Spode picked up the platter and carefully turned it over in her hands. "I see," she said. "It does look like a platter. Your head goes into this hole, right here?"

Prudence took the platter from Mrs. Spode, who was frowning, and fitted it over Grace's head, securing it by tucking in the sheet. Prudence withdrew the curved cardboard knife from her coat pocket and wedged it tightly into the space between the platter and Grace's neck, at an angle so that it looked stabbing. She was just tearing open a ketchup packet when Mrs. Spode said, "Hold on a sec."

The other children had begun to gather around Grace. "Who is she?" asked Anna King.

Grace jerked her head to the side and showed them the whites of her eyes. She staggered a few steps the way Prudence had shown her.

"Listen here," said Mrs. Spode. "This is very clever—"

"Thank you," said Prudence.

"—but maybe we could do without the blood and the platter and the knife."

"It's not real blood," Prudence said. She turned around to the children staring at them. "It's not real," she said. "It's pretend."

"Maybe I'd better see your costume, too," said Mrs. Spode.

"I'm not ready yet," Prudence said. "I have to do my hair. I have to put on my earrings."

"Now is a very good time," said Mrs. Spode.

"Not yet." Prudence raised her left eyebrow, but Mrs. Spode only raised her own eyebrows and said, "Go ahead and take off your coat, please, miss."

Prudence slowly unzipped her coat. She kept it closed until Mrs. Spode took it off her shoulders for her. When Prudence looked down she couldn't see past the halter bosom to her feet.

Mrs. Spode was silent, regarding her. She sucked her lips in against her teeth thoughtfully. Behind Mrs. Spode, the children stared.

Prudence unrolled the waistband of the gauzy skirt until the hem reached her ankles.

"You must be what's-her-name," Mrs. Spode said. She closed her eyes, then opened them.

"Salome," Prudence said. Even though her coat was off and her stomach was bare, she was growing hot. She thought about taking off her pants under the skirt, and decided against it.

"Well," said Mrs. Spode. She seemed about to say more, but instead she turned to the other children and led them out of the kitchen and into the fellowship room, where the parents had set up folding chairs. She told the Biblical characters to go to the stage one at a time and let people guess, then she returned to the kitchen. She shut the door behind her, but Prudence could still make out the first clapping and laughing.

"Listen," Mrs. Spode said, squatting down. "These costumes are very creative."

"I know," Prudence said.

"The problem is," Mrs. Spode said, "is that some people might get the wrong idea."

"It's in the Bible," Prudence said. "Everyone knows how John the Baptist died."

"Not everyone will appreciate the details before them," said Mrs. Spode. "You've just got to trust me on this one." Mrs. Spode twisted her mouth at Prudence as though she was sorry she had to do what she had to do.

"It's not fair," Prudence said.

Against the wall, Grace was chewing the inside of her cheek.

Prudence remembered what she'd heard Aunt Char saying to her mother. "Don't you ever just want to cut loose?" she said to Mrs. Spode. "Don't you ever just want to live a little?"

"Oh, baby," said Mrs. Spode. "You're something else. You've got a row to hoe, I tell you." Mrs. Spode pressed her hand to her forehead. "Listen," she said. "How about I go get you a couple choir robes. They're gold and heavy, and you can be two angels."

"I don't want to be an angel," Grace said. She had a packet of ketchup between her teeth, trying to open it.

Prudence heard Mrs. Moberly before she saw her. She entered the kitchen with a quick, sharp breath that had some voice in it. "Where did you find that?" Mrs. Moberly said, staring at Prudence's chest, then at the long skirt.

"You said we could use anything," Prudence said. "You said 'help yourself.'"

"Belinda never wore that," Mrs. Moberly said, shaking her head. "We put our foot down on that one."

"We're Biblical characters," Prudence said. "You said to come as a Biblical character."

"I had a bad feeling about this," said Mrs. Moberly. She turned to Mrs. Spode. "I knew I should have checked to see what they came up with. Reverend Boyd's preoccupied with his wife sick."

"She's not sick," Prudence said.

Mrs. Moberly opened her mouth, then looked at Mrs. Spode, then closed it again.

"She's not," Prudence explained to Mrs. Spode. "She's very tired and needs her rest."

"She's got a little bug," Mrs. Moberly explained.

"Well, there's something going around," said Mrs. Spode.

"She's not sick," Prudence said again. "She's not sick, she's not sick." She heard herself speaking over and over, but she couldn't stop, and she couldn't seem to say anything else. She clamped her mouth tightly closed, because she thought her voice might be starting to sound like tears.

Mrs. Spode squeezed Prudence's shoulder. "Look, Mary Anne, I was telling Prudence here that they could put on choir robes—you know those pretty gold ones?—and go as angels. We could even tape on some paper wings, or make halos or something."

"I think it's a little late to construct anything fancy," Mrs. Moberly said.

Grace's ketchup packet came open and she held it between her teeth, squeezing with her lips so that the ketchup dribbled down her chin and collected in a soft gob on the platter in front of her face. From there it began a slow, red slide towards the edge.

Mrs. Spode opened the kitchen door to check on the show. The children were restless. Noah kicked the donkey, and one of the Marys had stuck the head of a baby Jesus under her robe to nurse. "Looks like I'm needed in there," she said to Mrs. Moberly. "Those gold robes are in the closet of the upstairs practice room."

When Mrs. Spode had gone, Mrs. Moberly turned to Prudence and didn't even try to smile. "You two shed these get-ups right now," she said, "and then you stay put and be ready when I come back, hear? I don't want to have to go back and tell your parents you didn't get to be in the show. I don't want to have to explain why."

Prudence kept her mouth tightly closed. She stared into the air just over Mrs. Moberly's head, and soon Mrs. Moberly was gone. As her footsteps faded up the back stairs off the kitchen, Prudence and Grace were sneaking past the fellowship room, headed down the hall the way they'd come in.

Prudence quickly turned off the wide main hall straight into one of the narrow dark halls of Sunday school rooms. They made two more turns until it was so dark that Prudence couldn't even see her hand in front of her. The basement went on and on. She remembered a story she heard once, about a maze so confusing that once inside you could turn down every single path you could find and never get it right. You could just keep trying out different turns until you died of hunger, or until whatever kind of animal or monster it was they'd put in the maze to go after you got to you.

The wooden beads on her halter made their small noises against each other, and Prudence wrapped her arms around her middle to still them. She was having a hard time breathing in her regular way.

"Prudence," Grace whispered. "Where are you?" Grace's platter bumped against the wall with a dull scraping.

"Here." Prudence stopped and Grace ran into her; Prudence felt ketchup, wet and sticky on her bare back.

Then Prudence could see her hand again, just barely, because down one of the hallways a light glowed through the long window above a doorknob. Prudence moved towards the light.

"I hear singing," Grace said.

"Shhhh," said Prudence, but she could hear it, too. It sounded like five or six people, and Prudence crept towards the door and peered through the bottom of the narrow window.

A small, thin boy with his arm in a cast sat in a Sunday school chair, his eyes closed. Two men and one woman had their hands on the boy's neck and head. The woman was crying and trying to sing at the same time. They were singing that song about the lovely feet of the mountains that bring good news, which had never made any real sense to Prudence. On the floor were two mattresses made up with sheets and blankets.

"Let *me* see," Grace said, but Prudence ignored her. She pressed her forehead against the glass.

"It's no big deal," she whispered after a time. "It's just people standing around a boy. They're laying hands." She knew all about laying hands—sometimes her parents touched people while praying for them so the Holy Spirit could move.

Another man and woman had placed their hands on the backs

of the people touching the boy's neck. They all closed their eyes and sang the first verse of "Holy, Holy, Holy," swaying to the words. The man standing behind the boy began speaking over the singing, but it was hard to make out the words through the door. The boy had opened his eyes and was blinking quickly. The fingers of his good arm fretted at the soft, worn edge of his cast.

"Who are you?" the man said now, loud and deep, clear enough for Prudence to hear. She could feel his voice on the door.

"Help him, Lord," said another man.

"Yes, Lord," said a woman.

The first man gripped the boy's shoulder. "Who are you?" he asked again, and the boy moved his mouth, but Prudence couldn't hear.

"That's Anna's dad talking," Grace whispered, wedging her face beside Prudence's.

"No," said the man. The singing was over and his voice was clear as day. "No. I am not speaking to Ryan, but to the evil within."

Prudence thought the group looked too ordinary to be casting out a demon. The men were in plain old slacks and jeans, and one of the women wore sneakers with her skirt. Under the fluorescent lights their faces loomed pale and big. Even with their eyes closed they squinted, as if they were all trying very hard to remember something.

"It's no big deal," Prudence said again, but she couldn't stop watching.

Anna's dad looked up to the ceiling and started to pray. He said how Ryan was not in control of his body. He said the forces of darkness had taken advantage of this little boy's weakness, and an evil spirit had manifested itself in Ryan's behavior. He said it was a cowardly thing to use a little boy, but that was the kind of method Satan stooped to. He might look like this little boy and sound like this little boy, but indeed he was something very different, something that really wanted only to destroy Ryan. *Impostor*, Anna's dad said, and Prudence felt the word in her stomach.

[329]

Prudence pushed Grace away and covered the whole bottom of the window with her face and arms, filling up the glass so her sister couldn't see. She didn't know what was going to happen, and Grace sometimes scared easily.

One of the men began to raise his hand over his head, the movement so slow that the hand looked as if it were floating. He turned his face to the ceiling. "Ruler of all," he said when Anna's dad paused. "You triumph over evil."

Ryan began shaking all over. The woman in sneakers opened her eyes.

"The New Testament tells us we have been given the power," Anna's dad began again, and Ryan started to cry. He scrunched his face up tiny, whimpering. With his free arm he brought his hand to his shoulder and tried to pick off the fingers that clutched him.

"Please," said the woman in sneakers. "He's upset." She moved her thumb back and forth in the boy's hair.

"It's not him," Anna's dad said. From above and behind Ryan, he placed his palms on the boy's cheek. Ryan jerked his head from side to side, but the hands were firm. "What's being upset are the forces of darkness. Just hold him steady."

The woman in sneakers sniffled and shook her head. Prudence kept her eyes on Ryan Kitter.

"In the name of Jesus Christ," said Anna's dad, "I command you to exit this earthly vessel." The sound of his voice resounded off the cement block walls even after he closed his mouth.

Prudence held her breath, watching for something to leave Ryan's body. He went so still she thought maybe he'd fainted. Anna's dad loosened his grip on the boy's face. Suddenly Ryan lurched to his feet, yanking his shoulders back and forth to shake off the hands and upending his chair, which skidded across the room on its side. The woman in sneakers cried out, "Ryan," and a man said, "Oh," in a soft, surprised way, but nobody moved. They seemed frozen, their hands still outstretched, now hovering over nothing, while the boy made for the door.

Prudence grabbed Grace and pulled her into the back hall and around a corner. The first room they came to was locked, but the door to the second one opened, and they crouched just inside, listening hard. A moment later Ryan pushed through and slammed the door shut, darting into the far corner of the room. The windows near the ceiling gave off a faint glow from the lights of the parking lot, and Prudence could just make out his dark shape against the wall. She listened to him breathing heavy through his nose, and when she heard more footsteps in the hall, she reached up and locked the door.

Then the boy was crying again, moaning softly.

Grace leaned in close to Prudence and clutched her arm as Prudence rose and made her way across the room through the dark, past tables and chairs and an upright piano. She reached out and touched the boy's head, and he scooted away. It sounded like he was saying "Oh no, oh no, oh no," over and over. Prudence had heard plenty of kids cry, but this seemed older, like the time she'd been dropped home early from school and found her mother sitting with her forehead on the kitchen table, sobbing, her arms dangling down by her chair.

"Don't be scared," Prudence said. "It's just me and my sister."

Someone jiggled the doorknob, then knocked on the narrow glass window. Prudence didn't turn around. A woman called Ryan's name, her voice muffled.

Ryan kept crying. Prudence's eyes adjusted, and she could see him huddled against the wall, hunched in on himself.

"Don't cry," Prudence said. "You shouldn't cry like that. You'll cry your eyes out." She was watching him very carefully. If there was such thing as demons, and they looked and sounded just like people, she wondered how you were supposed to know when one was gone.

"Ryan?" called the woman at the door, then her footsteps hurried away.

"Do you have a demon?" Grace asked. Her tin foil platter glinted in the streetlight. The edge of it had bent over her shoulder on one side, and her face and neck were smeared with ketchup. The knife jutted out from her neck at a forty-five degree angle.

Ryan looked up at her and sucked in a great, moaning sob.

Prudence knelt down beside him. "It's ketchup," she said. Then she thought that maybe they didn't have ketchup in Africa. "She's just dressed up," Prudence said. "She's John the Baptist." She told him all about John the Baptist and Salome, how the king liked Salome's dance so much that he promised her anything, and how Salome's mother, a spurned woman, had told her just what to ask for. When Prudence finished, she rose and stood in the light from the high window so the boy could see. He'd grown quieter, but when she stopped talking he started to cry again.

"Hey," Prudence said. "You just watch me. I didn't get to do my dance before. When Salome dances she gets whatever she wants, and I want you to stop crying." Prudence began humming a little tune. She started with just her hands and let the movement travel up her arms and into her shoulders, then down her whole body. The wooden beads slapped her stomach.

Ryan's mouth was open. He looked like a sad boy, sad in a part of him no one could touch. Prudence was thinking that it would be better if there *was* a demon than if there *wasn't*. That way something would be in him and then it would be gone, and he would be all right. She danced in and out of the light, and Ryan's crying grew softer. She hummed a little louder and danced some more, and soon she didn't hear him crying at all.

"It's working," Grace whispered.

There were footsteps again in the hall, and the faint jingle of keys. In a moment or two the lights would come on and Prudence knew she would be in *some kind* of trouble. They would be taken back to the Moberlys' where she would most likely be disciplined, and where her mother lay in the upstairs bedroom, her face to the wall, and there wasn't anything Prudence could do about it. But as Prudence did a little boogie with her hips, she thought she heard

Ryan giggle. Aunt Char had shown her some old-timey dances, and she did what she could remember of the twist, then she started in on the chicken, Ryan and Grace now laughing, laughing hard, gulping in air, their voices high and silly, and when the door opened and the lights came on Prudence closed her eyes and kept on dancing.

# CREDITS

"Casualidades," by Carolyn Alessio, originally appeared in *TriQuarterly*. Reprinted by permission of the author.

"Dream House," by Barbara Bean, originally appeared in *The Colorado Review* and was republished in *Dream House*. Reprinted by permission of the author.

"Who's Your Daddy?" by Bob Bledsoe, originally appeared in *Ploughshares*. Reprinted by permission of the author.

"In the Doorway of Rhee's Jazz Joint," by D. Winston Brown, originally appeared in *Yamasee*. Reprinted by permission of the author.

"Selling the Apartment," by Danit Brown, originally appeared in *One Story*. Reprinted by permission of the author.

"Relevant Girl," by Tenaya Darlington, originally appeared in *Scribner's Best of the Fiction Workshops 1998*. Reprinted by permission of the author.

"Pork Chops," by Eileen FitzGerald, originally appeared in *You're So Beautiful*. Reprinted by permission of the author.

"Surrogates," by Rachel Hall, originally appeared in *New Letters*. Reprinted by permission of the author.

"Three Parting Shots and a Forecast," by Christie Hodgen, originally appeared in *Scribner's Best of the Fiction Workshops 1999* and was republished in *A Jeweler's Eye for Flaw*. Reprinted by permission of the author.

"Mouthful of Sorrow," by Dana Johnson, originally appeared in *American Literary Review* and was republished in *Break Any Woman Down*. Reprinted by permission of the author.

"Six Ways to Jump Off a Bridge," by Brian Leung, originally appeared in *Story* and was republished in *World Famous Love Acts*. Reprinted by permission of the author.

"The Nine Ideas for a Happier Whole," by Amos A. Magliocco, originally appeared in *Southwestern American Literature*. Reprinted by permission of the author.

CREDITS

"Bocce," by Renée Manfredi, originally appeared in *The Iowa Review* and was republished in *Where Love Leaves Us*. Reprinted by permission of the author.

"Home Course Advantage," by Clint McCown, originally appeared in *American Fiction* and was republished in *The Member-Guest*. Reprinted by permission of the author.

"The Penance Practicum," by Erin McGraw, originally appeared in *The Kenyon Review* and was republished in *The Good Life*. Reprinted by permission of Houghton Mifflin Company. All rights reserved.

"Ways to Kill a Snapper," by Gregory Miller, originally appeared in *The Greensboro Review*. Reprinted by permission of the author.

"All Saints Day," by Angela Pneuman, originally appeared in *Virginia Quarterly Review*. Reprinted by permission of the author.

"Scarlet," by Mandy Sayer, originally appeared in *15 Kinds of Desire*. Reprinted by permission of the author.

"Ramone," by Judy Troy, originally appeared in *The New Yorker*, November 25, 1996. Reprinted by permission of Georges Borchardt, Inc., for the author.

# CONTRIBUTORS

CAROLYN ALESSIO is the editor and translator of *The Voices of Hope/Las Voces de la Esperanza* (2003), a bilingual anthology of poems, short stories, and memories written and illustrated by the children of La Esperanza, Guatemala. The former Deputy Editor of the Books section of the *Chicago Tribune* and the recipient of a fellowship in fiction from the Illinois Arts Council, Alessio is currently the prose editor of *Crab Orchard Review* and a teacher at Cristo Rey High School in Chicago. "Casualidades" first appeared in *TriQuarterly* and was the recipient of a 2003 Pushcart Prize and reprinted in *Pushcart Prize XXVII: Best of the Small Presses*.

BARBARA BEAN teaches creative writing and English at DePauw University in Greencastle, Indiana. Her stories have appeared in *Beloit Fiction Journal, North American Review, Laurel Review, Northwest Review,* and elsewhere. "Dream House" was first published in *Colorado Review* and later reprinted in her collection of short stories, *Dream House* (2003).

BOB BLEDSOE is a native of California and a recent graduate of the Indiana University M.F.A. in Creative Writing Program. "Who's Your Daddy?" first appeared in *Ploughshares*, in an issue guest-edited by Amy Bloom.

SEAMUS BOSHELL was born and blessed on the North side of Dublin, Ireland, where he grew to love soccer and where he ultimately earned both a B.A. and M.A. from Trinity College. After working as an accountant at Harvard University, he joined Indiana

University's M.F.A. in Creative Writing Program. He currently lives in Santa Monica, California. "A Morning for Milk" is his first publication.

D. WINSTON BROWN is a Visiting Professor of creative writing and English at the University of Alabama, Birmingham, and the recipient of the Marion Anderson/Alvin Ailey Award for the Creative Arts as well as the Russell MacDonald Creative Writing Award in Fiction. His novel, *Blue Sugar*, was a finalist for the Bakeless Literary Award for Fiction. "In the Doorway of Rhee's Jazz Joint" was published in *Yemassee* and reprinted in *New Stories from the South: the Year's Best 2000*.

DANIT BROWN'S short stories have been published by *Glimmer Train* (twice), *Denver Quarterly*, *Story*, *Massachusetts Review*, *Seattle Review*, and elsewhere, and awarded the 2003 *American Literary Review* Fiction Award. "Selling the Apartment" first appeared in *One Story* and is part of a collection of interconnected short stories about leaving Israel.

TENAYA DARLINGTON is the author of the novel, *Maybe Baby* (2004), as well as a collection of poems, *Madame Deluxe* (2000), which was selected by the National Poetry Series and was the recipient of the 2001 Great Lakes Colleges Association New Writers Award in Poetry. "Relevant Girl" was first published in *Scribner's Best of the Fiction Workshops 1998*. Darlington lives in Madison, Wisconsin, where she is a columnist for *Isthmus* newspaper.

EILEEN FITZGERALD lives in Salem, Massachusetts, with her husband, poet and essayist J. D. Scrimgeour, and their two sons. She was the recipient of a fiction fellowship from the Wisconsin Institute of Writing, and her stories have appeared in *Prairie Schooner*, *The Iowa Review*, *Puerto del Sol*, *Other Voices*, and elsewhere. "Pork

Chops" first appeared in her collection of short stories, *You're So Beautiful* (1996), which was selected as a *New York Times* Notable Book of the Year 1996.

RACHEL HALL is an Associate Professor of creative writing and English at the State University of New York at Geneseo. Her short stories and essays have appeared in *The Gettysburg Review, New Virginia Review, Black Warrior Review, Beloit Fiction Journal,* and several anthologies, and awarded First Place in *Lilith* Magazine's 2001 fiction competition. "Surrogates" was published by *New Letters* and was the recipient of the 2003 *New Letters* Award for Fiction.

CHRISTIE HODGEN was the winner of the 2001 Associated Writing Programs Award in Short Fiction for her collection, *A Jeweler's Eye for Flaw* (2002), which was also named one of three finalists for the 2003 Hemingway Foundation/PEN Award, given to the most outstanding first work of fiction published during the previous year. Hodgen's fiction has also been awarded a National Endowment for the Arts Fellowship, the Pirate's Alley Faulkner Society Award for the Novella, the *Quarterly West* Novella Award, the Tobias Wolff Award in Fiction, and First Prize in the Ernest Hemingway Days Festival Short Story Contest. "Three Parting Shots and a Forecast" was first published in *Scribner's Best of the Fiction Workshops 1999* and later reprinted in *A Jeweler's Eye for Flaw.* Her first novel, *Hello, I Must Be Going,* will be published by W.W. Norton in 2005.

DANA JOHNSON is a native of Los Angeles and the author of *Break Any Woman Down* (2001), which was the recipient of the Flannery O'Connor Award for Short Fiction and also named a finalist for the Hurston/Wright Legacy Award and the Patterson Fiction Prize. "Mouthful of Sorrow" was first published in *American Literary Review* and was reprinted in *Break Any Woman Down.* Johnson teaches in the creative writing program at the University of California, Riverside.

BRIAN LEUNG lives and writes in Los Angeles, where he is an Assistant Professor at California State University, Northridge. His fiction and poetry have appeared in *Crazyhorse, Gulf Coast, Kinesis, Mid-American Review, Salt Hill, Gulf Stream, River City, Runes, The Bellingham Review, The Connecticut Review,* and elsewhere. His collection of short stories, *World Famous Love Acts* (2004), was the recipient of the Mary McCarthy Award in Short Fiction. "Six Ways to Jump Off a Bridge" first appeared in *Story* and was reprinted in *World Famous Love Acts.*

AMOS A. MAGLIOCCO is a native of upstate New York and a recent graduate of the Indiana University M.F.A. in Creative Writing Program. "The Nine Ideas for a Happier Whole" was first published in *Southwestern American Literature.* His stories have also appeared in *Oxford Magazine* and *Iron Horse Review.* He currently lives in Bloomington, Indiana, and is completing work on his first novel. Each spring he chases tornadoes across the Great Plains and writes for The Weather Channel.

RENÉE MANFREDI'S first book, *Where Love Leaves Us* (1994), was the winner of the Iowa Short Fiction Award. She has been awarded a National Endowment for the Arts Fellowship and was named by *Granta* Magazine to its *"Granta's* Fabulous 52" list of the best young fiction writers in North America. "Bocce" was first published by *The Iowa Review* and later awarded a Pushcart Prize and reprinted in *Pushcart Prize XVI: Best of the Small Presses* as well as in *Where Love Leaves Us.* Manfredi's first novel, *Above the Thunder,* was published by MacAdam Cage in 2004.

CLINT McCOWN teaches at Virginia Commonwealth University and in the Stone Coast low-residency M.F.A. Program at the University of Southern Maine. His books include two collections of poetry as well as the novel-in-stories *The Member-Guest* (1995), winner of the Society of Midland Authors Award, and the novels *War Memorials* (2001), recipient of an Achievement in Literature designation from the Wisconsin Library Association, and *The Weatherman* (2004), winner of the S. Mariella Gable Prize. His short fiction has been published widely. "Home Course Advantage" first appeared in *American Fiction* and was awarded the 1991 *American Fiction* Prize by finalist judge Louise Erdrich and later reprinted in *The Member-Guest*.

ERIN McGRAW teaches creative writing and English at Ohio State University. She is the author of four collections of short stories: *Bodies at Sea* (1989); *Lies of the Saints* (1996), selected as a *New York Times* Notable Book of the Year 1996, and winner of the Ohioana Library Society Award for Fiction; *The Baby Tree* (2002); and *The Good Life* (2004). Her stories and essays have appeared in *The Atlantic Monthly*, *Story*, *The Georgia Review*, *The Gettysburg Review*, *Missouri Review*, and several other magazines. "The Penance Practicum" was first published by *The Kenyon Review* and later reprinted in *The Good Life*.

GREGORY MILLER lives in Apple Valley, Minnesota, where, every morning at the crack of dawn he crawls out of bed to write short stories, then, bleary-eyed and full of coffee, sets off for work after putting on his best Willie Loman suit and tie. "Ways to Kill a Snapper" first appeared in *The Greensboro Review*.

ANGELA PNEUMAN is a former Stegner Fellow in Fiction and Marsh McCall Lecturer at Stanford University. Her short stories have appeared in *Ploughshares*, *Glimmer Train*, *New England Review*, *The Iowa Review*, *Puerto del Sol*, and other literary magazines. "All Saints Day" was first published in *Virginia Quarterly Review* and later reprinted in *Best American Short Stories 2004*. Pneuman is currently finishing a collection of short stories entitled *Home Remedies*, and is also at work on a novel. She lives in Albany, New York.

MANDY SAYER is the author of three novels, Mood Indigo (1989), which won the 1989 Australian/Vogel Literary Award; Blind Luck (1993), and The Cross (1995). Her memoir, Dreamtime Alice (1998) was the winner of the Australian National Biography Award, the New England Booksellers' Award in the United States, and was named the Australian Audio Book of the year. Sayer also co-edited, with Louis Nowra, an anthology on the literary history of Sydney's red-light district, Kings Cross, entitled In the Gutter . . . Looking at the Stars (2000). Her collection of linked short stories, 15 Kinds of Desire, in which "Scarlet" first appeared, was published in 2001 by Random House Australia and is currently being adapted to a feature film. Sayer is also the author of a second, forthcoming, memoir, Velocity.

CRYSTAL S. THOMAS has received awards for her fiction from the Hurston/Wright Foundation and the Ledig House International Writers' Colony. "Stepping in Ms. Cent-Jean's Shoes" is her first publication. She currently lives in Orlando, Florida, where she is at work on her first novel.

JUDY TROY grew up in northwest Indiana. Before becoming a professor she sold pantyhose at a department store, owned a bar, was a waitress, sold fruits and vegetables on the side of a highway, and taught creative writing at an alternative high school. Her books include the story collection Mourning Doves (1993), which was a finalist for the Los Angeles Times Book Award, and the novels West of Venus (1997), which was selected as a New York Times Notable Book of the Year 1997, and From the Black Hills (Random House, 1999). Troy is the recipient of a Whiting Foundation Award and is currently a professor and the Alumni-Writer-in-Residence at Auburn University. "Ramone" first appeared in The New Yorker and was reprinted in New Stories from the South: the Year's Best 1999.

TONY ARDIZZONE is the author of seven books of fiction, including *In the Garden of Papa Santuzzu* (1999), *Taking It Home: Stories from the Neighborhood* (1996), and *Larabi's Ox: Stories of Morocco* (1992). His writing has received the Chicago Foundation for Literature Award for Fiction, the Milkweed National Fiction Prize, the Flannery O'Connor Award for Short Fiction, the Virginia Prize for Fiction, the Lawrence Foundation Award, the Bruno Arcudi Literature Prize, two individual artist fellowships in fiction from the National Endowment for the Arts, and other honors. Since 1987 he has taught creative writing, ethnic American literature, and twentieth-century American fiction at Indiana University, where he has twice served terms as Director of Creative Writing. In 2005 he was the recipient of Indiana University's Tracy M. Sonneborn Award for distinguished teaching, scholarship and creative activity.